MIXED
Signals

B.K. BORISON

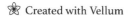

For everyone who has settled for crumbs.
You deserve the whole damn cake.

And for Eliza.

ONE

LAYLA

"YOU'RE NOT WHAT I EXPECTED."

That's a bold statement coming from the man slouched in the seat across from me. He picked me up forty-five minutes late, berated the waitstaff as soon as we got here, took two shots of—and I quote, *the cheapest bourbon available*—and then promptly ordered a steak without bothering to ask what I would like.

"Oh?" I indulge his attempt at conversation. It's possible that he's not as bad as he seems. I'm not sure how, but I've seen stranger things happen. Like the guy who picked me up for dinner in a horse and buggy. "How so?"

I cut my dessert into four perfectly portioned bites and try to make my face do something that resembles vague interest. He burps into his closed fist and I abandon the effort.

"Prettier," he tells me. His eyes dip down to my neckline and hold. "I had no idea you were hiding all that." He twirls his fork in my general direction. "Your profile picture doesn't do you justice."

Gross. I shovel another bite of passion fruit and coconut in my mouth.

"Probably all the baking you do, right? Those sweet treats make you thick in all the right places."

I don't even know where to start. "Yes, I own a bakery."

I own a little bakeshop tucked in the middle of a Christmas tree farm about forty miles west of here. I'm also part owner of the farm. I spend my days mixing and plating and rolling and wrapping inside of an old tractor shed that my business partner, Stella, and I converted into a bakery as soon as she bought the place. Big, floor-to-ceiling glass windows. Old oak wood floors. Walls lined in cozy booths with throw pillows and blankets. It's my very favorite place in the world.

Every day I flick on the lights and set out the tables and feel like I'm living inside a snow globe. Even in the middle of the summer when the humidity is so thick it feels like I'm walking through Jell-O, the sticky heat making my hair curl. I love it. Working at Lovelight Farms is the best part of my day, and being able to go to work with my two best friends is icing on the proverbial cake.

Stella manages business operations and Beckett keeps everything growing and thriving as head of farming. They're the kindest, loveliest people—in relationships with equally kind, lovely, beautiful people. I'm so happy they're happy, even if their so-cute-I-want-to-die relationships make me want to tip over an entire row of mini cakes in a fit of jealousy.

They have the sort of romances that dreams are made of. While I'm here with ... Bryce.

I didn't even recognize him when he pulled up in front of my house. Our tiny, tucked away town is hard to find on a good day, and most people bypass Inglewild completely on the way to the shore. When the car pulled up in my driveway, I thought Bryce sent a Lyft driver to pick me up for the evening. But then he rolled down the window, yelled *HEY LAYLA*, and I stupidly got in the passenger seat.

I should have ended it right there. I know better. He had a hamster bobblehead on his dash, for god's sake. I'm lucky I wasn't murdered.

The entire drive to the coast, I stared hard at his face. I could have sworn his profile picture was a tall brunette, and yet ...

He drags his hand through his bottle-dyed blonde hair. And yet.

He probably thinks he looks charming sitting there like that, all lazy and loose in his seat, his knuckles beneath his chin. Unlucky for him, I'm more sexually attracted to the warm rum butter sauce on my cake at this point.

I sigh and glance over his shoulder at the bar, trying to catch the eye of our beleaguered waitress. We'd shared a commiserate look earlier when he stared too long at the hem of her skirt. I'm pretty sure it's why she brought me this slice of boozy passion fruit cake that I did not order.

I grasp for a subject change. "You said you work in Ellicott City?"

He nods, shoveling another bite of steak into his pinched mouth. He chews with his mouth open and doesn't bother finishing before he replies, bits of food flying out with his answer. I want plexiglass between us. A ten-foot wall. "Yeah. That's where my dad's law offices are."

"And you work with him?"

"I just said that, didn't I?"

Alright then. We lapse into another uncomfortable silence. He stabs at his steak and I drag the tip of my fork against a thick layer of whipped cream. He told me he owned the law firm, organizing pro bono work across the Mid-Atlantic region. Po-tay-to, po-tah-to, I guess. I sigh and cut another corner off my slice of cake.

"Where are you from?" he asks.

The depths of hell. Sent to destroy men who lie on the internet and are mean to those in the service industry.

"Annapolis," I say instead. I am so tempted to get up from my seat, walk through the tables, and step into the ocean. It sounds infinitely more appealing than another moment with Bryce.

This is the third first date I've been on this month and I am tired. Tired of men who are entitled, small-minded, and generally disappointing. What spirit did I disrespect to curse myself with bad date after bad date? I pay my taxes. I don't leave my popcorn bucket stuffed under the seat at the movie theater. I obey traffic laws and donate to that one charity for three-legged goats that Beckett quite literally never shuts up about.

Why can't I find a single human being that I connect with? My standards are not impossible. I want someone who makes me laugh. Who cares about what I do and what I say and what I think. I want to sit on the couch with someone in blissful, perfect, comfortable silence—pizza on the coffee table and my feet tucked under their thigh. I want someone to hand me the recipe section of the local paper while they read the headlines. I want to share all of my small, silly, silent moments.

I want someone to give me butterflies.

I stare at Bryce-who-lied-about-everything-but-his-name and watch as he picks at something in his teeth with his thumbnail.

Maybe that someone doesn't exist.

"Did you go to college?"

There is no curiosity in his question, just a smug satisfaction and a callous condescension. A familiar insecurity pricks at the back of my mind, a twist in my stomach that pulls tight.

"I went to Salisbury."

He laughs like I've made a joke and then reaches across the table with his fork for a bite of my cake. I don't slap his hand away, but it's a near thing. To me, dessert is *sacred.* "Ah, the party school. That makes sense."

I clench my teeth so hard I'm surprised my molars don't crack right in half. "What does?"

"Bakers don't need to go to serious schools, do they? It doesn't matter where you went or what you did. You probably could have gotten a degree from circus school and been just fine baking your little treats all day."

Circus school.

Little treats.

Oh, my god.

It takes me a second to collect my bearings. When I do reply, my voice is quiet fury laced with exhaustion. I am so *tired*.

"I graduated with honors with a dual degree in mathematics and engineering." Not that it should matter. "I'm a baker and a small business owner, and I bet I do more in an hour than you do in a day."

He scoffs.

I set my fork down on the table. This evening just rocketed to the top of my Worst Dates Ever list, and the competition is robust. I can't believe I put on my green dress for this. What a freaking waste. "I think you should go grab the check."

He holds up both hands, his eyes wide. "Woah, don't be so sensitive. I didn't mean to offend."

I ignore him and slip another bite of coconut into my mouth. This rum sauce really is life-changing. Maybe after we wrap up here, I'll sneak back into the kitchen and sweet talk the chef into sharing his recipe. I bet he's better company than bampot Bryce.

He makes no move to get the check, as requested. I

whip the napkin off my lap and drop it on the table. "That's fine. I'll go settle the bill at the bar."

He rolls his eyes. "I was getting to it. You don't have to be so rude."

Alright. I'm the rude one. Okay.

I push my chair back and head towards the bar at the edge of the surf. I don't usually come this far out for a date, but Bryce had been insistent about trying a new tiki bar right on the coast. Low hanging string lights. A couple of fires burning in large, round pits. The tide rolls in behind bottles stacked on old wine barrels. Bartenders move back and forth behind a small row boat that's been flipped over and converted into bench seating.

It would be a romantic spot if my date was not a complete and total asshole.

Our waitress, Celia, waits behind the bar with her lips in a thin line, her eyes kind and understanding. She hands me the bill before I can even ask.

"Did the dessert help, at least?" she asks.

I snort a laugh and flip open the bill. "It was the best part of my evening."

"I can get you another one," she offers. When I shake my head, she makes a short, contemplative sound. "I wasn't going to say anything, but that guy is a jerk. You can do better."

"Yeah, you're not wrong." Unfortunately for me, I haven't seen better on any of the dating websites I pay an unseemly monthly membership for. Bryce is pretty par for the course. "Any ideas on where to look?"

Her gaze trips over my shoulder as she pulls a thick evergreen rag out of her back pocket, shining the edge of a tumbler. Her face morphs into something glassy, appreciative, and she tilts her head behind me. "That looks like a good place to start."

TWO

LAYLA

I FINISH SIGNING the check and follow her line of sight, straight to the man effortlessly moving through the crowded tables clustered together on the beach. Not my date. Of course not. Bryce is about as memorable as a crumpled up gum wrapper shoved in the bottom of my purse.

No, the man making his way towards us is tall. Easily over six feet. Brown, glowing, gorgeous skin. I don't get a good look at his face because he's busy looking over his shoulder at the group he just wandered away from, shouting something with a laugh. He's wearing a colorful Hawaiian shirt that should be ridiculous, but with the top three buttons undone I can only focus on the jut of his collarbones, the material of the sleeves clinging to the curve of his biceps. The fabric is stretched too tight there, like the shirt can't possibly contain the strength of him.

I stare at the dancing pineapples on his broad chest,

distracted. I keep staring at them as he slides right up to the bar next to me and places both his hands flat on the bartop. His forearms flex and I resist the urge to drag both of my palms down the sides of my face.

What is it about *forearms*?

Je-*sus*.

"I'd like another piña colada, if it's not too much trouble. The birthday boy is getting antsy."

Celia looks like she'll happily give him more than a piña colada. I hide my smile behind my fingertips and finally glance at his face. I almost sputter in surprise.

"Caleb?"

Caleb Alvarez. The same man I've seen at least twice a week for the past five years without thinking about his chest once. He comes in every Monday, Wednesday, and Friday and orders exactly one croissant and a coffee. Just cream.

Caleb is *here*, so far away from our little town.

At a beach bar.

Wearing an almost indecently unbuttoned Hawaiian shirt.

His head snaps to the side and his brown eyes widen. I watch in fascination as the deep rich brown grows warmer in recognition, a ring of amber around his iris. Never in my life have I noticed the color of this man's eyes. I'm really having a moment, taking him in like this. Hair ruffled by the ocean breeze and all that warm, olive skin on display. A smile kicks up the corner of his mouth and I have to swallow compulsively three times in a row.

"Layla," he says, a sweet combination of surprised and delighted. It's the exact same way he's always said my name, but it sounds different here with the salt and the sand. My mouth goes dry.

"Hey, Caleb." I gesture to one of the pineapples ringed in bright orange flowers on his chest. My mind is blank—wiped completely clean by three tiny buttons. "Nice shirt."

I've seen Caleb in a crewneck sweatshirt a couple of times. Worn jeans and boots that lace at the ankles. T-shirts, in the summer. I never had an ... event ... over any of that.

He smooths his hand down the buttons, a faint pink lighting up his cheeks. "Ah, well. Alex insisted."

He jerks his chin over the tables. I follow his gaze and spot Alex Alvarez—our quiet, unassuming, small town bookstore owner—doing some drunken version of a salsa with a beautiful redhead, the both of them in equally terrifying Hawaiian shirts.

"We have a tradition," Caleb explains.

"Clearly."

"He loves a strong pattern. And a cohesive theme."

I guess that makes sense. I've seen Alex's window displays. They're always a bold look. Last Halloween, there was a town petition about the graphic interpretation of *The Rocky Horror Picture Show*. I blink back to Caleb's shirt.

"I can see that."

"He also likes making his entire family look like a bunch of idiots in public places." Caleb curls his hand around the glass Celia slides over to him and gives her a thankful smile. We sigh in unison.

"What are the chances, huh?" He leans one elbow up on the bartop and gives me a slow, unfurling smile. W*hew*—okay. I definitely haven't noticed those dimples before either. "Out of all the bars."

"Yeah," I say, still distracted. My brain is trying to align this version of Caleb with the one in my head. It's ... not working out so well.

What sort of voodoo is this Hawaiian shirt?

His eyes flick briefly over my green dress and his smile melts into something earnest and sincere, the faint pink on his cheeks deepening into a rich, ruby red. "You look beautiful."

"Thank you," I manage, resisting the urge to clear my throat. I don't think Bryce told me once that I looked nice tonight, beyond his comment about me being prettier than my profile picture let on. And what a compliment that was.

I put effort into tonight. I wore my mint green dress with the thin straps, a slit in the side up to my thigh. I wanted to look nice. To feel pretty and cherished and desired.

And I wasted all of it on Bryce.

"Are you here with Stella and Beckett?"

I amuse myself for a moment with the mental image of Beckett, our resident grumpy head farmer, frowning with a coconut drink in his hand. But then I finger the strap of my dress and let out a blustery sigh, glancing back over to the table I abandoned. "I'm here on a date. Well, I guess I *was* on a date."

Because Bryce is nowhere to be seen. Our table is empty and I swear some of the silverware is missing. My dessert plate, too.

Asshole.

Caleb is confused. "With, uh, with yourself?"

"No. With a big ol' turd who dines and dashes, apparently." I frown as I think about what will inevitably be a very long and very expensive Lyft back to Inglewild. "Shoot. He picked me up for dinner."

"And he left?" Caleb's face turns into a storm cloud. His jaw clenches, dimples evaporating as quickly as they appeared.

"Believe me," I offer. "This is an improvement."

I cannot imagine sitting in Bryce's car for the thirty-minute drive back to Inglewild, staring balefully at the hamster bobblehead on the dash. He'd probably play Ace of Base. Or worse, Nickelback.

"He shouldn't have left you," is all Caleb says, still staring unseeingly at the empty table. He looks like he's about to charge out in the parking lot and exact some vigilante justice. The thought is oddly delightful.

"It's alright. I'll just grab a Lyft home." I turn to look at Celia still standing behind the bar, her eyes darting back and forth between Caleb and I. "I'll take that extra slice to go, I think."

"Hold on a sec." Caleb wraps his long fingers right

above my elbow and squeezes once. His touch is gentle, his palm warm. "I'll drive you back."

"No, no. That's okay." I look over to the far end of the bar where Alex is being dipped by his dancing partner, both of them laughing so hard they can barely stand up. Their table is surrounded by a collection of people in various matching Hawaiian shirts. The entire Alvarez family, I finally realize. Their uncle Benjamín is wearing his shirt tied high around his waist in a weird bastardization of a crop top. I grin. "You can't leave. It's your brother's birthday."

I squint, focusing on one dark-haired man with a coconut bra at the far end of their little group. He stands a little bit taller than the rest. "Is that Charlie?"

Caleb doesn't bother following my stare. "Yeah, it is."

I watch as Stella's half-brother shimmies, a drink in each hand. "He drove down from New York?"

"You know him. He never misses a party." Caleb keeps his hand and his eyes on me. "Alex won't remember anything past an hour ago. I promise. Let me drive you home."

"But his drink."

"I'll drop it off and then we can go."

"How will he get home?"

"We rented a Margaritaville bus." Of course they did. Caleb gives me another bashful look, his blush deepening to a deep crimson. "He really loves a tropical theme," he mumbles.

I roll my lips against a smile. "Will we be stealing the bus, then?"

"What? No." He looks alarmed. "I drove separately."

"Do you hate Jimmy Buffett?"

A smile hooks the corner of his mouth. "I think everyone hates Jimmy Buffett a little bit."

"Except Alex."

"Except Alex, of course."

His smile tumbles headfirst into a grin, so bright and sudden and beautiful that I have to remind myself to breathe. Those dimples blink back to life in his cheeks and it's a good thing he's holding on to my arm. His thumb rubs once against the inside of my elbow—an aimless, unthinking touch. Caleb tilts his head forward and a lock of dark hair falls over his forehead. Some far recess of my mind is still whispering, *what in the hell is going on?*

When did Caleb Alvarez get so *hot?*

"If you're sure," I murmur.

I'm not sure. I'm probably the least sure I've ever been. What secret will Caleb reveal next? Can he play the harmonica? Does he also have a strange animal bobblehead on the dash of his car? Is he sneaky hot but also a terrible driver? Oh god, does he drive in *silence?* Does he hate music? I have no idea. I'm truly just along for the ride at this point, my mind sufficiently blown by a set of strong biceps and a shirt with rotating palm trees.

"I'm sure." He is resolute as he uncurls his fingers from around my arm and picks up the fruity concoction in front of him. I watch the way his shirt stretches across his chest with rabid interest. I feel like I'm in an alternate dimension where the nice, unassuming guy who comes into my bakery with almost militant precision is suddenly a dreamboat in a Hawaiian shirt. "Just give me a second to talk to Alex and we'll get going."

He ambles away, crossing through the tables, somehow managing to not look ridiculous. I watch him go.

So does every other woman in the establishment. A few men, too.

Celia whistles low. Damn, I didn't even realize she was still standing there. "You made quick work of that."

I scratch once at my eyebrow and watch as Caleb attempts to extricate Alex out of his sloppy salsa routine. Alex pulls an evasive maneuver while Charlie fist-pumps aggressively. "We live in the same town. I know him."

"I'd like to get to know him," she mumbles under her breath.

I turn to look at her and raise both eyebrows. "Don't hold back on my account."

She waves her hand. "Nah. I sensed vibes."

"There were no vibes. He's just a really nice guy."

The nicest. I routinely watch him help little old ladies cross the street. He volunteers every year for dig day at the farm, when residents of the town help us prep the fields for the new season. Half of the time I can't tell if he genuinely enjoys the butter croissants he religiously orders, or if he just wants to support a local business. Stella once referred to him as chronically kind. He is sweet and funny and is never too busy to stop and help load seven 50-pound bags of sugar into the back of my hatchback.

Dane, our town Sheriff, fired him from his deputy position four months ago for being *too nice*. From what I hear, he accepted one too many parking ticket payments in the form of IOU's written on the back of old receipts. I heard from Matty at the pizza shop that some of them got pretty explicit.

He's been substitute teaching at the high school ever since.

I watch as Alex attempts to dip his older brother. All of the people gathered around the table cheer. I grin. "Like, a really nice guy."

"Sure, sure." Celia sets the glass she's been polishing for close to fifteen minutes to the side. Picks up another. "I'll make it two slices to go."

Caleb finally wrestles Alex into a stationary position. I watch them with their heads huddled together. Caleb says something that makes Alex brighten and then he's trying to get on top of the table again, hand shielded against his eyes even though the sun set hours ago. He spots me by the bar.

And then he screams at the top of his lungs.

"LAAAAAAAYLA."

Caleb looks mortified.

I make my way over to the table before he can begin launching projectiles across the beach bar. As soon as I'm close enough, he makes a spectacular swan dive off the top of the table and lands somewhere near my feet. He wraps both of his arms around my legs.

"Laylaaaaaaa," he drags out the syllables of my name on a warble in his best Eric Clapton impersonation. "You came to my birthday party!"

I try to haul him up with my arms beneath his, but we're impeded by the six-foot-five wall of muscle suddenly bear-hugging us both. Charlie smells like an entire shelf of liquor, his big, dumb face pressed into my shoulder.

"Layla." He sounds suspiciously close to tears. "It's so good to see you."

I press my palm to his forehead and push him off me. "You saw me last weekend, you brute."

Stella and her boyfriend Luka had dinner at their place and I had the distinct pleasure of watching my best friends and their significant others fawn over each other. Charlie left after fifteen minutes claiming a stomach ache and I concluded my evening with the best date I've had in months—a shiny bottle of sauvignon blanc and a plate of peanut butter fudge cookies I made myself.

"Still," Charlie slurs. He pulls back, his big blue eyes wide as saucers. He's wearing a coconut bra and a flower behind his ear. He looks ridiculous. "Wanna do a shot?"

Alex lets out that high pitched screech again. A chant of *shots, shots, shots* starts up amongst the entire Alvarez group. I feel two strong hands on my shoulders, gently guiding me away from the drunk love bugs hanging all over me.

"Maybe we shouldn't have said goodbye," Caleb

mutters. One of his uncles tries to hand him a tiny shot glass. Caleb makes a face and shakes his head, then looks overtop of my head. "Christ. I think Charlie is encouraging people to take body shots off of him."

I don't even want to look. "I'll take your word for it."

"Right. Time to go."

He holds his hand out to me, palm up.

I twist my fingers through his and together we dash through the sand.

THREE

LAYLA

THANKFULLY, Caleb does not have any strange bobbleheads on the dash of his car.

Just one of the pine tree air fresheners with the Lovelight logo that Stella started selling at the farm a couple of months ago. An old newspaper wedged between the center console and the driver's seat. A box from my bakery that he tries to hide as soon I slip into his Jeep.

I stare at him as he gets situated in the driver's seat, adjusting the air vents so they blow on my legs and not my face. He checks his rear view and side mirrors and I smile. Of course Caleb checks his mirrors every time he gets in the car. I bet he knows his tire pressure, too.

I narrow my eyes and watch him, a restless feeling under my skin.

"Did you get a haircut?"

He drags his fingers through his hair, self-conscious. "No."

"Did you grow, maybe? Taller?"

He snorts. "I haven't grown an inch since I turned eighteen." He narrows his eyes right back at me. "Why?"

"A nose job?"

He looks offended. "No."

"Hip replacement?"

He laughs at that. "No. What's gotten into you?"

"You just seem ... different, is all." Hotter, my brain screams at me. Level-ten attractive. I swear on my butter and jam baguettes that I have never noticed Caleb looking like ... this ... before. A passing attraction, maybe. An—*oh, he's cute*—in an unassuming sort of way.

This is ... not cute.

This is violently attractive.

I'm rattled by it.

I settle back into my seat and watch as Caleb continues adjusting his driver settings like he's about to launch us into space.

It's the Hawaiian shirt.

It has to be.

"I'm surprised."

He gives me a hesitant look out of the corner of his eye, making sure I have my seatbelt on before he guides the car out of park. I think he's regretting offering me a ride home. "By what?"

"That you didn't want to take the Margaritaville bus."

Another laugh rumbles out of him. Caleb's smiles are frequent but his laughs are rare and I find myself sinking lower into my seat at the sound of it. His laugh is nice.

Warm. "Nah. The lights give me a headache. Plus, I got out late from school today. I missed the bus."

There's irony in that statement somewhere. "How is that going? The teaching?"

"It's good. Different. I'm learning. I'm lucky Katie Metzler decided to go on that soul searching trip in the Florida Keys."

An odd choice for a self-discovery trip, but okay.

"The school was pretty desperate for a Spanish teacher for their summer session and they didn't care that I basically had zero qualifications. I'm getting my certification while I fill in. Hopefully I'll be a full-time staff member by the start of the new school year. It couldn't have been better timing, all things considered."

"Were you upset? With what happened at the Sheriff's station?"

"You mean when Dane fired me?" He huffs out a laugh. "No, not at all. It was time. We both knew being a deputy wasn't a good fit for me anymore. He only fired me so I could get the severance package." Caleb glances at me briefly. "Maybe I should have been upset, but I don't know. I was mainly relieved. I think I can help more people as a teacher. More kids, at least."

Especially in our tiny town, where Caleb spent more time keeping Ms. Beatrice from using her car as a battering ram outside of her coffee shop than preventing any sort of major crime. I'm sure Dane has it handled on his own.

"Alex keeps telling me I should forget about the certification and just show the kids old reruns of the telenovela my abuela always made us watch. She never missed an episode of *Corazón Salvaje*."

I grin. I see him around town with his grandma sometimes. He towers over her, and she's usually bossing him around, making him carry her groceries. "Wild Heart?"

"That's the one."

I hum in consideration. "It's not a bad idea."

"The school board might have something to say about it."

I snort a laugh and peer over my shoulder at his backseat. His car is tidier than the mess of crumpled receipts, old mixing bowls, and expired candy canes that litters mine. It smells like cinnamon in here, like he's got a whole batch of gingersnaps somewhere. I reach for the edge of the pastry box half wedged beneath my seat, hoping there's something sweet inside. I forgot my damn slices of cake at the bar, distracted by Caleb trying to herd the entire Alvarez group like a bunch of drunk cats.

I rattle the white box I rip out from beneath the seat with a yank. I'm conscious of the fact that I'm wearing a very tight green dress and the material is probably all the way up around my waist at this point, but Caleb's eyes are firmly on the road. Thank god. "Is there anything left in here?"

"You think I have that kind of self-control?"

I give him a bland look. "I absolutely do."

Every week he comes in and eats exactly one croissant

while staring longingly at an entire case full of buttercream cronuts. His self-control is steel enforced. His hands flex and release on the steering wheel and I shimmy back in the seat. My gaze crawls up his arms to the slope of his shoulders, the hollow of his throat and the strong line of his jaw. One hand releases the steering wheel to card through his dark hair. With night pressing in around us, it almost looks like spilled ink. Chocolate melting on the stovetop.

Honestly. I've known Caleb for years. How have I never noticed how *handsome* he is?

Probably because I've been lost in my manic motivation to find a life partner. Or the string of lackluster men I've allowed to yank me around for the past couple of years. Or maybe my self-imposed rule to never, ever date someone within town limits. I think it made me have blinders.

Our town population is somewhere around seven. I can't imagine having to see a date-gone-bad everywhere I look. If I had to see Bryce on the regular, waiting in line at my bakery, ordering my favorite salted white chocolate oatmeal cookies—I'd die. I would simply cease to exist.

And I'd probably be arrested for murder.

Caleb clears his throat. "Can I ask you a question?"

"You saved me a hefty Lyft bill tonight. Not only can you ask me a question, you can also enjoy free coffee at the bakehouse all week."

A smirk curls at the edge of his mouth. "You already give me free coffee."

"Well, now you get coffee *and* a question."

He pauses for a second. "Just the one?"

"Does it matter?"

He looks shocked that I'd even ask. "Of course it matters."

"How so?"

"If I only get one question, I should pick something good."

"I guess you should," I say with a laugh.

He hums, the sound rich and low between us. I watch the streetlights paint his face in shadow. Golds and silvers and warm, warm red. The smile slips from his mouth and his gaze trips into something hesitant. His eyes dart to me and then back to the road.

"Why did you go to dinner with a guy like that?"

I fidget in my seat.

"A guy like what?"

He mumbles something I don't catch beneath his breath. "A guy that leaves you with the check and steals the silverware on his way out," he says louder, clearer.

I sigh and press two fingers to my forehead. "You noticed that too, huh?"

"I heard you talking to Stella in the bakeshop a couple of weeks ago," Caleb hesitates. "About a guy who used a lint roller on you before you got in his car."

Ah, yes. Peter. He also made me put those little disposable surgical booties on over my heels, but I keep that to myself. I glance out the window and tuck my hair behind my ears. I straightened it tonight, something sleek and shiny. I feel silly about the effort now.

"I've had some bad luck recently with dating," I finally manage as an explanation. It's an understatement, but how else could I possibly explain the dumpster fire that is my love life?

Peter and Bryce aren't even the worst of it. I had one guy ask me if we could pick up his mom after lunch and take her to her dry cleaner. I had another guy bring his best friend and proceed to act like I wasn't even there at all. They talked about fantasy football for forty-nine minutes and did seven pickleback shots.

Each.

"And that guy—what was his name—Justin?"

"Jacob," I supply quietly.

He's the one that hurts the most. All of the rest—I can play them off as amusing stories to entertain my friends. Forays into the wild and weird world of dating. But I had been with Jacob for months. I had given him so many pieces of myself in a desperate attempt for it to work. I wanted so badly for someone to just ... stick ... that I made excuses. Justified his crap behavior and told myself he would get better. His ambivalence. His indifference. I told myself that he just needed time to settle into a comfortable rhythm. He just needed some time to *like* me.

But the more time I spent with him, the more I felt like I was losing those bits of myself that I had given him so freely. He didn't prioritize me or our relationship. He was more committed to his phone than he ever was to me.

I deserved better than that. I *deserve* better than that.

"Jacob sucked," Caleb says. His jaw does that clenching thing again.

"He did."

"What's going on, then?" Caleb nudges the turn signal with his wrist and we merge off the highway, closer to home. "These guys all seem like—"

"Douchebags?" I offer. Assholes? Giant, humiliating wastes of my time?

He laughs, but it doesn't sound very funny at all. It's sharp at the edges. "Yeah," he agrees. "They all sound like douchebags."

I don't say anything in response. I don't need the reminder that my romantic life is a disaster. That the one thing I've always secretly, quietly hoped for is as much a mystery to me as dark matter and extraterrestrial life. It doesn't matter how many dates I go on, I'm as far away from it now as I've ever been.

I don't understand how something so easy for everyone else can be so difficult for me.

"Layla." Caleb presses out my name with a sigh. When he says my name like that, it feels like two hands curled around my shoulders, a gentle shake. "Why are you giving these guys your time? Why are you settling for crumbs when you deserve the whole damn cake?"

My chest pulls tight. An ache, right in the middle of me. "That's a really lovely thought, but sometimes crumbs are all you've got."

I can tell he doesn't like my response, so I turn and

stare out the window, watching the land slowly change as we move away from the coast. Everything here is rich and vibrant, late summer settling in earnest. Lightning bugs dance outside my window, quick flashes of gold as we speed past.

I wait for him to try and talk me out of my sad little conviction. When he doesn't, when he just patiently waits for me to go on, something unlatches, and my words tumble out.

"I don't know. I guess—I guess I'm just looking in all of the wrong places. I want someone to be mine. And not everyone is perfect right off the bat, you know? Sometimes people need a little time before they shine. Everyone deserves a chance." I shrug again, feeling naive in the worst of ways. I mean, Peter stepped out of his car with a lint roller. Not so sure he deserved any of my attention after that. "And with Stella and Luka together, and Beckett and Evie, I'm kind of surrounded by it. I guess I've been thinking that crumbs are better than nothing." I rest my forehead against the cool glass of the window. "Maybe that's my problem. Maybe I should swear off cake altogether for a little bit, crumbs and all."

Caleb is silent, the rumble of his Jeep beneath us the only sound. Wind at the windows and the low hum of voices on the radio.

"This analogy got weird," he finally says.

"It really did."

The truth is I watched Stella fall in love with Luka, a man she harbored a crush on for close to ten years. Then I watched Beckett begrudgingly fall in love with Evelyn, a woman who couldn't be more his opposite. And after Beckett declared his love via social media—a shock to literally everyone, Beckett included, probably—our little Christmas tree farm became a destination for anyone hoping to snag a little romance for themselves. I have seen more proposals, first dates, and sickeningly affectionate couples in the past three months than any person stuck in a dating rut should have to endure.

I want that for myself.

"Didn't—" Caleb starts and then stops, hands flexing on the wheel. "Didn't Jesse ask you out a couple of months ago?"

I raise an eyebrow at him and I swear he blushes all the way to the tips of his ears. *Cute.* "It was trivia night," he mutters. "I'm pretty sure the whole town heard him ask you out."

That's right. He practically yelled it into the microphone while I was getting another pitcher of beer. I shrug. "I don't date anyone within town limits."

Caleb blinks. "Oh."

"With my track record, I'm not exactly eager to relive the ghosts of dating past every time I need an artichoke from the grocery store."

"Is that often?" Caleb's smile is a slow thing. It starts at one edge of his mouth and tugs until his whole face is alight with it. I can't stop staring at him, confused and captivated. I need a bucket of cold water over my head. "That you need artichokes?"

"You'd be surprised."

"I'm sure I would."

We lapse into silence again, the steady rumble of the road beneath us and the hum of something slow and soft on the radio. Exhaustion settles deep in my bones and my shoulders curl in. I am so, so tired. Tired of doing the same thing over and over and getting nothing in return. Caleb is right. I am settling for crumbs.

"I think I'm done," I declare. These dates are getting me nowhere. Just hardening my heart more and more with every failure. I don't understand why finding someone is so difficult for me. "No more cake for me. No cupcakes or even ... jelly rolls. Strictly vegetables for this gal."

Caleb doesn't comment on my determination to carry on with his analogy. He just props his elbow up against the window and rubs his knuckles against his jaw. "If it makes you feel better," he says. "I haven't had much luck with dating either."

I can't help it. I snort. Caleb with the hair and the face and the dimples and the shoulders. Any of the women at the tiki bar tonight would have happily had dinner with him. I bet when he unbuttons that ridiculous Hawaiian shirt when he gets home, phone numbers fall from it like tiny pieces of confetti.

"I find that very hard to believe."

"What? Why?" He is the very picture of confusion.

"Look at you."

"Look at me?"

I broadly gesture at the whole of him. Like Vanna

White. Or one of those pretty ladies at the car shows. I feel like I should be holding a cardboard number over my head. Tens across the board. "Look at you."

A confused smile twists his mouth. He clears his throat. "When was the last time you saw me with someone around town?"

"Besides Alex?"

"Yes, besides my brother."

I usually see him with his tiny grandmother. His mom and dad, too, at the farmer's markets on Sundays. An entire fleet of cousins that always seem to be bickering, Caleb trudging along at the very front of the group, trying to keep everyone organized.

"I'm not someone that's—" He stops abruptly and sighs. "I can't believe I'm telling you this," he mumbles, embarrassed. He takes a deep, fortifying breath and blows it out. "Okay. I'm really bad at dating, I think. Not Peter-with-the-lint-roller bad, but I don't really know what I'm doing."

"What do you mean?"

"Maybe I say the wrong thing, or maybe I'm too hesitant. Or too forward. I have no idea if I'm doing too much or too little. All of my relationships, if you can even call them that, stall out around the fourth date. Even when I think it's going well."

"Every time?"

He nods. "Yeah. Every time. Give or take a date."

"Huh."

"Yeah." He looks like he wants to open his door and

roll right out of this car. He releases a sigh from the very depths of his soul. "I think I'm—I think I might be too much. For some people."

Something in his voice loops around my chest and squeezes. "Too much?"

Pink lights up his cheeks again and climbs all the way to the tips of his ears. "I have trouble reading cues. I get ahead of myself, probably. The last woman I dated, she told me I was a nice guy. But she said it like it was a bad thing. Alex tells me I'm a doormat in relationships, that I put people on a pedestal they don't necessarily deserve, but—I don't know. I don't think seeing the best in someone is a bad thing. I don't think being nice is a bad thing, either."

"It's not." I think about that time he gave a tiny little girl his untouched croissant after she dropped her cake pop on the ground right outside the bakehouse and burst into tears. The way he got down on one knee so he could wipe her tears with the sleeve of his shirt. "Being nice is the best thing."

He shrugs like he wants to disagree. I feel that like a pluck to my heart. Caleb shouldn't change a thing about himself, his kindness especially. I frown at his profile, the clench of his jaw.

He shouldn't be wasting his time on crumbs either.

We rumble past the Inglewild town sign, an old faded thing with hand painted lettering. *Home*. Finally.

The stars are cast like gemstones across the night sky, brighter now that we're with the grass and the trees and the fields. I think about Caleb and I think about me, the both of us stumbling through our respective love lives.

"What a pair we make," I say, just for us and the moonlight. "We really have no idea what we're doing, huh?"

"It's nice to know that I'm not alone in the struggle." He tilts his head to the side, thoughtful. "Maybe that's the answer."

"You're absolutely right," I say with a nod. "Let's drown our feelings in dessert."

"That is … not what I said."

"Oh." That must have been what I was thinking about. I spent the last half of my date with Bryce daydreaming about what I'd eat when I got home. Chocolate cake with a thin mint drizzle. Strawberry shortcake and ice cold lemonade. Peach cobbler. Blueberry crumble. My options are limitless.

Caleb drums his fingers against the steering wheel. That damn Hawaiian shirt stretches over his bicep again. Thank you, Alex Alvarez, for your commitment to a theme. "Maybe we should date each other."

My grin falters. I probably look like one of those freeze frame photos you get at the end of a roller coaster—the shot after that first big plunge. A little bit delighted and slightly confused. Kind of terrified. I was never prepared for those pictures as a kid.

I'm not prepared for Caleb's suggestion either.

"Are you—" Something cold steals over my chest and presses down on my lungs. "Are you making fun of me?"

"What? No!" His eyes dart between me and the road.

Thankfully we've slowed to a crawl within town limits. "No, Layla. I am not making fun of you. Think about it for a second."

"I'm thinking about it." And coming up blank. I'm not exactly sure how he arrived at *we should date* from *wow, we're both really bad at this.*

Caleb's face falls at my lackluster response. "Is it that unbelievable of an idea? To date me?"

No. Maybe? Okay, probably yes. I have never once entertained the idea. Not for a fraction of a second. My rule about dating in town, certainly. But, also ...

He's Caleb. The guy who comes into my bakeshop and hits his elbow on my counter display. The guy who leans up against my counter with his legs crossed at the ankles and makes dumb jokes about donuts. He has always been firmly—perfectly—in the acquaintance column. A friend, even. I've never once considered exploring anything else with him.

But could I?

"It's not you," I offer and he huffs a sound that should be a laugh but sounds too self-mocking to contain any humor. "Caleb. You caught me off guard. I wasn't expecting you to say that."

"That's fair," he concedes. His shoulders relax from where they're pressed by his ears with a gusting breath. "I was just thinking. We're both fed up with dating. It could be like a—like a social experiment."

A laugh bursts out of me, bright and loud. "Just what every woman wants to hear."

He tosses a grin in my direction and okay, maybe it's not such an insane idea. To date Caleb. Experimentally date Caleb? Whatever this is. "Wouldn't it be easier, though? To go on a date and get actual feedback? Maybe we can both figure out what we're doing wrong."

"If you suggest a survey, I might punch you in the face."

"If I suggest a survey, I might punch myself in the face."

I arch an eyebrow at him. "So, what. We'll go on a date and you'll tell me all the things I'm doing wrong?"

My voice wobbles around the edges. An old, tender bruise flares to life in the center of my chest. An aching insecurity that I'm the reason none of these relationships are working out. That I somehow manage to attract the worst kind of men. That these disappointments are somehow my fault and exactly what I deserve.

"No," he replies quickly, voice sure in the quiet between us. "That's not it at all. I think you need to be treated right by someone. I think you need to see that you *can* be treated right by someone. We'll go on a couple of dates. I'll help you into your jacket. I'll hold your hand and listen about your day. We'll go to dinner. Eat spaghetti, or whatever you want." A sly smile tugs at his bottom lip. "I won't steal the silverware on the way out."

Well, damn. Okay. That actually sounds really nice.

"And what do you get out of this little arrangement?"

"Besides time with a beautiful woman?" Heat flushes the back of my neck and I shift in my seat. "Hopefully you can tell me why I'm so bad at dating."

"A social experiment."

"Yes."

He slows to a stop in front of my little house. I painted it a pale pink last spring and planted enough flowers in the gardens to make it look like Mother Nature threw up all over it. Lilies and gardenias and big, bright sunflowers. I like to sit on the front porch in the evenings and smell the lavender. Sink my toes into the cool grass and watch the sky blink awake with the stars.

I unbuckle my seatbelt and slip from Caleb's car, holding the door open with the palm of my hand. I stare at him sitting there in his dancing pineapple shirt, hair in disarray, sticky summer heat clinging to my shoulders and the backs of my knees. He stares right back, a smile in his eyes, his gaze nowhere but right on me.

Caleb Alvarez. Who knew?

"For someone who is supposedly bad at dating, you're awfully smooth."

The smile in his eyes slips to his mouth. I trace the angles of his face in the moonlight. "Just with you, Layla."

Bad at dating, my ass.

"I'll think about it," I promise with a laugh.

He looks like he wants to say something else, but he swallows it back and gives me a nod instead. "I'll see you on Monday?"

A butter croissant and a coffee with just cream. He sure will.

"I'll see you on Monday." I tap the hood of his Jeep twice. "Thanks for the ride."

His smile spreads into a grin and those brown eyes sparkle. Oh, boy.

I've got a feeling I'll be thinking about a lot of things where Caleb Alvarez is concerned.

Starting with those three damn buttons and the smile lines by his eyes.

FOUR

CALEB

I DON'T SEE Layla on Monday.

Darlene from dispatch calls me on my cell and informs me that my brother is seven minutes late opening up his bookstore. Why this is my problem, I have no idea. She still hasn't gotten the memo that I no longer work for the Sheriff's department and calling me sixteen times a day with the random happenings around town does not fall under my responsibility anymore.

That's great, Darlene. I'm glad they have hazelnut lattes at Ms. Beatrice's again.

I'm sorry to hear that Mabel cut you off in front of the hardware store.

I can't do anything about whoever is dumping hundreds of plastic ducks in the fountain in the middle of the night. The kids love it, though.

No, I did not catch the latest episode of The Bachelor. I have never watched The Bachelor in my life.

I hang up my phone and flex my hands on the wheel, staring hard at the road that leads down to Lovelight Farms. Alex is hungover. I know he is. But if my mother finds out I left Alex alone on the floor of his kitchen, she'll smack me all the way down the driveway and back up again.

"Shit," I sigh. I turn left instead of going straight, heading back towards town and my idiot, indulgent brother. The massive weeping willows that hug either side of the road mock me in my rearview mirror, their branches swaying softly in the breeze that drifts in from the fields. *You're late,* they whisper. *She's going to change her mind.*

Great. In addition to impulsively proposing dating experiments to pretty bakery owners, I am now talking to trees.

I had hoped to see Layla this morning. I wanted to salvage ... something ... from our conversation Saturday night. I blame the sad look on her face and the way she kept trying to smile her way through it. I also blame that dress she was wearing and the way the mint green material hugged her thighs in the passenger seat of my car. I couldn't think when she was sitting there, looking like that. I couldn't think when I saw her at the bar either.

I am ninety-nine percent sure I made a total ass of myself, sharing the dismal state of my romantic life. With a set-up like that, the chances of her agreeing to my proposition are slim to none.

Date me, Layla, I basically said. *I'm really fucking terrible at it.*

I pinch the bridge of my nose.

I was joking.

Kind of.

Not really.

Alright, I wasn't joking at all, but I'm prepared to sell that lie if I need to.

I do struggle with dating. That's the truth. I can never seem to figure out the right thing to say at exactly the right time. I overthink and then overcompensate for over-thinking and then overthink myself overcompensating. It's a vicious cycle.

But there's another reason, too. I'm convinced I'm picking the wrong type of person. Because the right type of person is about five-foot-three, has cropped brown hair and hazel eyes—a collection of ridiculous aprons and absolutely no clue about my crush. I'm not sure she's ever thought of me as anything more than the guy with a crois-sant problem, ambling into her bakery three times a week for the exact same order.

I'm not so sure explicitly telling her I'm bad at dating is going to help her see me in a different light, but here we are.

I've always had a thing for sweeping love stories. I used to sit at the little wooden table in my grandparents' kitchen when I was a kid and listen to my abuelo talk about the exact moment he met my grandmother, the love of his life. I'd scuff my shoes across the floor and watch my abuelo's face change. I'd watch every bit of him light up.

The first time my grandfather saw my grandmother, he

was buying fish at their local market. She had her hair pulled back in one long braid and was selling huaraches from a tiny wooden stand. He said he took one look at her and bought everything she had. What he intended to do with over thirty pairs of women's sandals, I have no idea. But she walked him home with bags hanging off both their elbows and they were married one month later. *Love at first sight*, he said.

My dad met my mom when he was standing on the balcony of his apartment. He was watering his plants and saw her standing on hers. *Una santa,* he'd always tell us when we were kids, climbing all over him, asking to hear the story again. He thought she was a saint. He would whistle from his open window to hers and she would appear there with a bottle of wine and a cork between her teeth. They'd talk until the sun was low in the sky, both of them in their windows, the wine bottle passed back and forth.

I grew up with these stories. Tender and romantic and absolutely useless at helping maintain my expectations for relationships. I know what I want and what I don't and I'm not willing to settle.

Layla should feel that way, too. She shouldn't settle. She shouldn't be out on dates with guys that steal the silverware. Guys that leave her standing at the bar by herself with a pen between her teeth, paying for a mediocre dinner and bad company. I saw her once at the farmer's market with that Jacob guy she was with for a while. She was holding up a bouquet of flowers, trying to show him the different blooms. He ignored her completely, busy on his phone. I can still remember the way her face fell. The way she carefully put the flowers back and curled in on herself.

Anger burns sharp in my gut and I slap at my turn signal harder than I mean to.

She deserves better.

I'd like to try my best to show her that.

If she'll let me.

Alex's car is in the driveway when I park, the curtains drawn over the windows. I don't bother knocking. I just grab the key from where it's wedged under a small statue of the Virgin Mary in his garden and elbow my way through the door. Our grandmother bought him that statue four years ago and we're both afraid to move it. Every time we so much as stare at it for too long, our abuela appears at the front door as if we summoned her.

"Rise and shine," I shout down the short hallway. I make sure to slam the door behind me. A groan echoes from the depths of the house.

I hear his voice in the kitchen, faint but there. "Solo déjame morir."

Alex always reverts to Spanish when he's feeling dramatic. I grin as I follow the sound of his wheezing and find him sprawled across the floor in front of the fridge, his glasses on his chest and a bottle of Gatorade clutched in his hand. His bag is still over his shoulder and his shirt is half tucked in, shoes unlaced on his feet. It looks like he made a valiant attempt to get out the door this morning, but had a change of heart halfway across his kitchen.

"I'm not going to leave you here to die," I reply. He makes a pitiful whimpering sound and rolls onto his side, his knees to his chest.

"I sat down for a minute," he whines. "I don't think I can get up again."

"You can."

He groans. Long and loud and obnoxious. "Fine. I don't want to."

"You're supposed to open the store." I nudge him with my foot and he swats at my ankle. I kind of expect him to snap his teeth at me, too. He's always the worst when he's hungover. "And I have to get to school. Let's go."

"I am ten—" He turns slightly and squints at the clock above the microwave. "—I am twelve minutes late. I own the store. This is my right."

"People are worried."

"Darlene doesn't count as people. The old bat."

I snicker. She is an old bat. "I'll tell her you said that if you don't get your ass in gear."

He glares at me and slips his glasses on. "It's nothing I haven't said to her face. The only reason she knows the store isn't open yet is because she shows up every Monday and sits in the back and reads all of the saucy parts of my paranormal romance novels without paying for them. I caught her taking pictures on her phone a few weeks ago." He sits up with a huff. "It is not out of the goodness of her heart, I promise you."

"Either way, I need to get to school." And panic about my life choices and the bargains I make with pretty women in the passenger seat of my car. Not scoop him off the floor. "I'll drop you on my way."

"Isn't it summer? Why are these kids in school?"

"Summer school, Alex."

He gives me a baleful look, hunched over in a half-standing version of the fetal position. "There is a seventy-five percent chance I'll throw up in your car."

I blow out a sigh. "I'll roll down the window."

"Fair enough." He pushes up to his knees and dry heaves into his fist. "*Dios*. I think I might die today."

I frown. "How are you still this hungover?"

"Luis, Aaron, Charlie and Sofia stayed over the whole weekend. Tio Benjamín, too. There was tequila involved." He squints. "I think."

"Ah."

Alex shudders as he unrolls himself to his full height, hands braced on his hips. "You didn't see Benjamín when you came in?"

"I didn't."

I'm surprised he wasn't in the bushes when I pulled up. It wouldn't be the first time.

Alex frowns. "I could have sworn he was still here."

My mother's youngest brother never misses a celebration and never forgets to bring the tequila. I'm not interested enough to solve the mystery as to where he's disappeared to this time, already annoyed with having to stop by in the first place.

I promised Layla I'd see her today. I don't want to start out ... whatever this is ... with a broken promise.

Alex finally manages to pick himself up off the floor and begin a slow, creeping shuffle to the front door. He's halfway down the hallway when he trips on something and tumbles head first into the wall. A picture of us from when we were kids rattles in the frame as he catches himself.

A pained moan floats out from the coat closet. We both look down. Two legs stick out from a crack in the door. I don't know how I missed them when I first came in.

"Leave me here to die," warbles Charlie's voice from inside.

Alex laughs and wedges the door open further. He tosses his bottle of Gatorade inside without bothering to look where it might land. There's a thud, another groan, and the two legs laying out into the middle of the hallway shift slightly.

"Stay as long as you'd like but lock up when you leave, yeah?"

There's silence for half a second. "I'm eating all of the leftovers in the fridge before I go," Charlie grumbles.

Alex rolls his eyes. "I assumed you would."

Neither of us care to hear his response. We make our way to my Jeep, Alex's walk more of a stagger than anything coordinated and purposeful. The third time I check my watch, he grunts at me and slides into the passenger seat like his entire body might combust at any moment. Given the pale color of his usually dark skin and the sweat beading at his temples, it's likely.

I offer him the empty pastry box Layla was messing with the other night.

"In case you get sick," I say.

His mouth settles into a grim line. "Not a bad idea."

It's a silent drive as Alex does his best to keep himself together in his seat and I do my best not to catastrophize in mine. Was Layla waiting for me this morning? Did she already make a decision? Is she going to laugh in my face? Or worse, will she pretend like we never had the conversation in the first place? I won't be able to walk into her bakery ever again.

Christ, that would mean I have to give up croissants.

I can feel Alex staring at the side of my face. I meet his stare as soon as we hit a stop sign. He used to get the same look on his face when we were kids and he was about to con me out of the last concha.

"What?" I ask.

He slumps down further in his seat. "Did I see Layla at the bar on Saturday, or was that the influence of seven daiquiris and a platter of crab dip?"

"She was there."

"Did I also see you leave with her?"

"We talked about this with you before we left. We both said goodbye."

"Do I need to remind you how much alcohol I consumed on Saturday?"

Fair point. "I drove her home. Her date ditched her and she needed a ride."

Alex makes a grumbling, disapproving noise. "What an asshole."

"Yup." I haven't been so kind when thinking of the man she had dinner with. I'll never understand how anyone could sit across from Layla and be anything other than mesmerized. Her smile. Her wry humor. The absolute joy she radiates when she talks about ... anything. Did he even realize how lucky he was to have all of her attention? I've seen her three days a week for the past five years and I don't think she's noticed me once.

Although, maybe she has. I don't know. I didn't realize she had a rule about not dating people in town. That makes me feel slightly better.

"So you ... drove her home."

"I did."

Alex hums, somehow managing to infuse those three syllables with enough smug satisfaction to make my teeth clench.

We roll to a stop at a red light. The only red light, really, in this tiny town. I usually like living in a small town, close to all of my family. But on days like today, I'd really love to be a little anonymous.

Alex's face is fully against the passenger side window, his hands clenched tight around the straps of his bag. And yet he's still smiling like he knows something I don't.

"What?"

He shrugs. "Nothing."

I regret not leaving him on the kitchen floor. "What, Alex?"

"Did you place an order for a custom cake on your drive back?"

I punch him in the arm as hard as I can while maintaining a grip on the steering wheel. He cackles in delight and rubs at his bicep.

I went through a ... phase ... not too long ago. A phase where I ordered a custom cake from Layla's bakery every two weeks.

I hadn't even realized I was doing it. Not really. I just liked seeing her, spending time with her. Ten pounds later, I decided I needed to let that little buttercream addiction go.

I shift in my seat. "She makes a really good cake."

"I'm sure she does."

"The icing," I mumble, and stop myself halfway through the thought. It's not worth it. "Shut your mouth."

Alex snickers and I deliberately hit a speed bump too fast, sending him tipping back and forth in his seat. He groans and claps his hand over his mouth.

"We both suffer if I throw up, you know."

I DROP Alex off at the curb of his bookstore and hightail it over to the high school, barely managing to skid into my classroom before the warning bell. I slip into the day, grateful for the distraction of twenty-eight angst-ridden teenagers pissed off about being in summer school. I spend more time intercepting notes between the McAllister twins than in my spiraling thoughts. It's the best diversion I could ask for, all things considered.

I like working with kids. It's the change I needed. The only reason I ever became a police officer in the first place was to get financial help for my degree. It wasn't a calling, or a job I felt particularly passionate about. I liked helping people, and I get to do that here, too.

The conversations I have with my students are the best part of being a teacher.

"Can you help me translate this, Mr. Alvarez?"

I take the slip of paper out of Jeremy Roughman's hand and glance down at his chicken scratch scribble across a piece of notebook paper. I sigh.

The conversations I have with my students are the worst part of being a teacher.

"No, I can't." I crumple the paper in a ball and toss it in the wastebasket under my desk. I feel like throwing it away isn't enough. I need some lighter fluid. Maybe a box of matches. "Who are you even saying that to?"

He looks down at his feet and mumbles something under his breath.

"What was that?"

"I was gonna ask Lydia to the dance."

My lips twitch. "And you thought reciting 90's rap in Spanish would accomplish that particular goal?"

He shrugs his shoulders. "It works for you."

I blink. I have no idea where he came up with that idea. "I am not reciting rap lyrics to anyone."

"No, the Spanish thing. How'd you get so good at it? You're a way better teacher than Ms. Metzler."

Probably because Ms. Metzler didn't speak any Spanish and only taught the kids how to order a quesadilla con chorizo from the culturally appropriative restaurant two towns over. And tres leches. I'm confident her approach to teaching Spanish was just reciting her dinner orders over and over again. It was a very low bar.

"Thank you." I think. There's always a lot to unpack every time Jeremy opens his mouth. "I grew up speaking Spanish. My whole family speaks it. My grandmother is from Todos Santos." I have told this to the class no less than thirty-seven times.

He stares at me blankly. I rub the palm of my hand across my forehead. "It's a town in Mexico, Jeremy. We were literally talking about it three days ago."

"Oh, that's right." He snaps his fingers with a grin. "Those pictures with the girls in bikinis."

I sigh again. If you zoomed in on my presentation, maybe. I guess I'll have to go through and replace those slides. "The pictures with the *beaches*, Jeremy."

"Yeah, yeah. That's what I meant." He stares longingly at the basket I tossed his inspiration into. "You really won't translate that for me?"

"I really won't." I cross my arms over my chest and lean back in my chair. "But how about you come up with something you want to say, and I'll work on it with you."

He opens his mouth.

"Something that isn't vulgar, or a liberal interpretation of rap lyrics."

He snaps his mouth shut with a grimace.

"Is this graded?"

I hide my grin behind a closed fist. This kid, I swear. "No, it's not graded. You asked for help. This is me helping you."

He looks like he regrets ever coming into this classroom at all. "I didn't expect to get more homework out of it," he complains. He sighs with all the drama of a prepubescent male and drags his hand through his hair. "Later, Mr. Alvarez."

I watch him saunter into the hallway with all of the confidence of an adolescent man. I don't even want to know the trouble that kid is off to get into now. I collect my things and reach for my bag. If I hurry and no one asks me to translate anything else, I should still be able to catch Layla at the bakery before she leaves for the day.

Maybe we should date each other.

I might as well be Jeremy reciting horrible rap lyrics in Spanish.

"That was an interesting assignment, Mr. Alvarez."

I slam my knee on the underside of my desk and my bag goes toppling to the floor. It takes a cup of pens and a tiny ceramic turtle in a sombrero with it. Alex bought it for me my first week of teaching—said it would make me seem cooler. I'm starting to think he was making fun of me.

Emma, the eighth grade English teacher, winces from the doorway.

"Sorry. I didn't mean to startle you."

"It's fine," I say, as I heave myself out of my chair and start collecting the pens scattered across the floor like a school supply firework blast. "My mind was somewhere else."

On Layla, specifically. On the butter croissant I should have had for breakfast and the way her laugh sounds when she's covered in flour and sugar up to her elbows.

Maybe I'm not over my custom cake crush.

Emma comes further in the room, bending gracefully to her knees to help collect pens. "Must have been. I wasn't even trying to be sneaky."

A pluck of apprehension nudges at me. I wonder how much of my conversation with Jeremy she heard. "I probably shouldn't have done that, huh?"

She peers up at me, her bright blonde hair pulled back in a neat bun. "Thrown this little cutie?" She picks up my turtle and taps at the hat on his head. "Probably not."

I huff a laugh and collect the knick knack, placing him back on his rightful throne at the corner of my desk. Joke or not, I've become attached to Fernando. "Real teachers probably don't encourage their students to write love letters as an assignment."

Emma stands and hands me the rest of my pens, a fistful of red and blue. This is the fourth time this month she's stopped by my classroom. She tells me it's because she wants to make sure I'm settling in, that the kids are behaving, but it feels like something else. Her check-ins are a little too consistent. Maybe Principal Waller is having her drop in as some sort of evaluation.

"Real teachers help their students learn, however they can." She gives me a gentle smile. "You're doing great, Caleb. Really. If Jeremy of all people is showing interest, then you're doing a fine job."

"Okay, good." If I could get that same sort of endorsement on how I'm handling the rest of my life, that would be great. I shove all of the pens into an empty desk drawer and glance at the clock. "Ah, shit."

Emma follows my eyes and frowns. "Somewhere you need to be?"

By the time I make it to Lovelight, Layla will be gone for the day, the bakery in the hands of her support staff for the rest of the evening. I could visit her at her house, but I don't know. It feels like too much.

I don't want to make her uncomfortable.

I think I might be too much. For some people.

"I was going to try—" I swallow back the words. I was going to try *what*? Try to convince Layla to take me up on my ridiculous idea? Beg her to forget about it? I don't even know.

"I'm sorry, yeah. I do have somewhere to be." I give Emma a tight smile and sling my bag over my shoulder. "I'll see you later this week?"

She smoothes her palms over her skirt. "Sure, yeah. Of course. Same school and all."

I hesitate at her tone. "Was there something else you needed?"

"No, no." She waves me off. "Just saying hello."

I give her another forced smile on my way out. I barely manage three steps down the hallway before a body slams into mine, a shower of manila folders and looseleaf paper raining down on me.

"Ah, my bad, Caleb." Gabe, the biology teacher, adjusts his glasses and snatches a piece of paper slowly floating its way to the ground. Too bad the rest of his files are strewn across the hallway. "I wasn't paying attention."

"Neither was I," I sigh. I collect a couple of loose sheets by my feet, a frankly terrifying drawing of a frog dissection staring back at me. I am very glad a language position became available, and not something in the practical sciences.

"You know, I'm actually glad I ran into you. I was in the teacher's lounge the other day and—"

I stack the papers in a haphazard collection and shove them in Gabe's general direction, ignoring whatever it is he's talking about as I head past him to the exit. I'll find him tomorrow and apologize. All I want to do is get in my car, drive to the farm, and talk to Layla. Even if it's just for five minutes. I need her to know I didn't forget about her.

"Caleb!"

I want to slam my head into the emergency door. At this rate, I'll never leave this school. Might as well make myself cozy on the linoleum floor and set up a velvet rope walkway for anyone who might need something from me. I collect my frustration like Gabe's wayward assignments and stack it into something neat and tidy in my chest. I blow out a deep breath and turn to watch Mrs. Peters march her way towards me.

"What can I do for you, Mrs. Peters?"

She waves away the formality. "Carina, please. We work together now, Caleb."

"Habit," I explain. "You'll always be Luka's mom to me."

"As it should be, I suppose." A smile lights up her face, chestnut hair swinging behind her shoulders. Luka looks just like her, down to the freckles over his nose and the smile that spells nothing but trouble.

She clasps her hands behind her back. "I wanted to remind you that you're on bus duty Wednesday morning. I think this is the first time you're on the schedule."

Shit. I did forget about that. "Ah, yes. Thank you for the reminder."

Maybe I can stop by Layla's tomorrow morning instead. I might break my self-control streak and get something with dark chocolate. Go crazy and get peanut butter. I feel like I've earned it.

"Will you be stopping by the farm this week?"

It's like she's read my mind. I blink and try to stop the heat from rising to my cheeks. Judging by her smile, I'm entirely unsuccessful. My blush has always given me away.

"I'm going to try," I manage. "I can't seem to get through my week without something from Layla's."

My blush deepens. Mercifully, Mrs. Peters doesn't comment on it.

"If you see my son while you're there, remind him he has all of my good Tupperware." She clicks her tongue once. "He finally moves closer to his mother and I suddenly see him less than when he lived in New York."

"Ah, well. I'm sure Stella is keeping him busy."

"As it should be, I suppose," she repeats with another grin. She turns on her heel and heads back in the direction she came from. She hosts a cooking class after school for some of the kids whose parents work late. Easy recipes they can make on their own with enough leftovers to bring to their siblings. I've always thought it was incredibly kind of her.

"Oh, and Caleb?"

I sigh. "Yes, Mrs. Peters?"

"Tell Layla I say hello."

FIVE

LAYLA

"HONEY, I just want you to know that you're the best thing that's ever happened to me—"

I clench my teeth and pointedly ignore the couple standing less than two feet away from me, their noses rubbing together, their hands clasped tightly between them.

"—and I'm so happy we could come here together. It really feels like our love has grown deeper and—"

I make a choking sound and duck down further behind the counter. Every day. This happens *every day.*

"—coming to this place, feeling this magic, I know I'm supposed to be with you for the rest of our lives."

I know what comes next. The gentle thud of someone's knee hitting the hardwood floor and the breathy gasp in response. I have seen seventeen proposals in the last six months.

Nice, I guess, in some ways. But in other, more important ways—the absolute worst.

I pop back up from behind the counter just in time to see two people frantically making out against my display case, a big diamond sparkling on the appropriate finger. I ignore them and turn back to my cupcakes. I have bigger things on my mind than potential public indecency right where all my salted caramel cookies can see.

Caleb didn't show up on Monday.

Or Tuesday.

It's Wednesday afternoon and I have yet to see even a hint of him. He's missed two butter croissants and all of his promised free coffee.

I tell myself it's fine. Our conversation over the weekend was purely hypothetical—two people who casually know each other killing time during a long drive back home. There's no reason to be embarrassed that I spent all of Sunday turning the idea over and over again in my head, examining it from every angle while I drew up the bakery menu for the week. I don't need to be ashamed that I sat there in my big, fluffy, lilac robe and entertained the idea of dating Caleb Alvarez in his quest to be better at wooing women.

Whatever that means.

I'm starting to think he meant it as a joke and that is— that is *fine*. More than. He doesn't need to avoid the bakehouse. He doesn't need to avoid me.

I fill my piping bag with icing and watch as the happy couple leaves the bakery, my wreath of peonies on the front door swinging lightly with their exit. It's not disappointment that lodges firmly in the back of my throat—just a bad batch of coffee. I kept it too long on the warmer this morning and I didn't bother to use the good beans from Ms. Beatrice.

He wouldn't, though. Would he? Make a joke of it. I can't imagine he would. He once stuttered his way through the duration of a town meeting after Ms. Beatrice accused him of cutting her off mid-sentence. He had been so embarrassed, his face was practically purple at the front of the room. I watched him fold the same piece of paper seven times. He never volunteered to lead a town meeting again.

No, he wasn't making fun of me. Maybe he just got held up somewhere. Doing ... something.

For three days in a row.

"Are you waiting for someone?"

Stella appears out of nowhere right in front of me. My entire body jolts and my elbow knocks my tray of cupcakes to the side. She helps me correct it, and then plucks a dried orange slice off the top of one that took a tumble. I roll my eyes and hand her the rest of it. The amount of food I lose to Stella and Beckett's grazing is astounding.

"Where did you come from?"

"The back, Miss Jumpy. I was calling for you." Stella carefully peels the paper liner away from the cupcake. "You keep looking at the door. Are you expecting a shipment? I didn't see any paperwork."

"What?"

"Who are you waiting for?"

I glance at the door again. I see nothing but trees out the front wall of windows, the branches thick and full and green. They press in on the floor-to-ceiling glass windows in the front, hiding the bakehouse almost entirely from view. I don't see a single sign of a six-foot-three man with dimples for days.

Ugh.

"No. No, I'm not." I compulsively squeeze my icing bag. "I am not. I am not waiting for anyone."

Stella narrows her eyes at me, her mouth full of cupcake. "That was an enthusiastic denial."

I bend at the waist to resume my icing, a perfect ring of white buttercream around the top of an orange sponge cake. I'm calling these little cuties Orange Crush. I'd like to crush one right into Stella's face, if only to keep her from pestering me.

"It was not," I mumble.

"You have checked the door twenty-one times since I got here. Which has been about three minutes."

I narrow my eyes and keep my gaze firmly away from the door. My left eye twitches. "I have not."

"You almost upended your Kitchen-Aid when I said hello."

"You surprised me."

"Hm."

Stella has always been good at this. Waiting patiently for me to spill whatever is running circles in my mind. It became an art form to her in college, when we were both awkward girls trying to find our way into adulthood. We spent plenty of nights huddled together in our dorm's common room, laughing about nothing and talking about everything. Making cake out of a *box*. When we graduated, I followed her back to the tiny town she grew up in, not ready to leave my best friend quite yet. I made some chocolate chip cookies for the firehouse bake sale and Stella got a manic gleam in her eyes as soon as she tasted them, exploding into a frenzy of Christmas tree farm-related business plans.

I've been here ever since.

Apparently, baking is an excellent use of a mathematics degree.

My hand wobbles and my perfect icing goes trailing down the side of the cupcake. I sigh, pluck it from the tray, and place it in front of Stella.

"You're distracting me."

"I think you're distracting yourself."

"Fine." I set my icing bag to the side and sweep my eyes across the space, making sure there's no one close enough to overhear me. It's empty enough on a Wednesday afternoon, but our town is stuffed to the brim with busybodies that love to snoop. I narrow my eyes at Gus in the corner, the handsome young firefighter who might be the biggest gossip monger of them all. I know for a fact that he's near the top of the town phone tree that distributes gossip instead of important town information. I know about the betting board in the back of the firehouse, too. For a while, it was listing the odds on when Stella and Luka would finally get together. Now I think it's a betting list based on when Beckett will adopt his next animal.

Satisfied Gus isn't listening, I look at Stella and prop my hands on my hips. "I saw Caleb this weekend," I whisper.

"What? Like around town?" She frowns and takes another bite of cupcake. "That's nothing new. Why are you whispering?"

Oh my god. "Why are you yelling?"

"I'm not yelling. I'm talking at a reasonable level." She gives me a strange look and takes another obscene bite of cupcake. "You're freaking out."

"I don't want Gus to hear what we're talking about," I tell her, still whispering. The entire town doesn't need to know that I've been waiting for Caleb to walk through those doors. They'd probably bring it up at the next town meeting.

"I can't hear anything," Gus calls from the booth in the corner, his back propped up against the window, a plaid pillow on his lap. He doesn't bother looking up from his slice of pecan pie. "Carry on."

"You remember where the door is, don't you Gus?"

He shoots me a wink. "Sure do, Laylabug."

"Don't call me that."

I grab Stella by the elbow and drag her into the back kitchen. She abandons her cupcake on my prep table and grabs both of my hands in hers. Squeezes tight.

"What's going on? Was it your date this weekend? Did he do something weird?" Her hands hold onto mine even tighter, a white-knuckle grip. "Should I call Beckett and Luka? I bet Dane could use his Sheriff connections to find his address. I've always wanted to slash someone's tires."

"Calm down, Rambo. We don't need to slash anyone's tires. I told you. I saw Caleb this weekend."

Stella raises both eyebrows at me. "Okay. And? He lives here. We see him all of the time."

"No. I saw him at the bar."

She stares at me, confused. "Layla, I honestly don't understand the level of urgency you have right now but I'm going to match it because that's what friends do. What bar?"

"I went to that beach bar over in Rehoboth for my date with Bryce."

She makes a face like I just forced a lemon in her mouth. "Bryce. What a douche-y name."

"Well, he was a douche. So it's appropriate." I release her hands and rub my palms against my thighs. "He ended up ditching me, and I ran into Caleb when I was trying to figure out what to do."

"Bryce left you there? At the bar?" Stella's jaw does the same clench thing that Caleb's did. Her pretty blue eyes narrow into slits and her hands curl into fists. She looks like she wants to cut down one of our trees and go out swinging. "Where does he live again?"

I ignore her. "It doesn't matter. Caleb was at the bar, and Stella—he was wearing a Hawaiian shirt."

That shirt is all I can think about. I've been icing orange hibiscus flowers on everything all week.

The shirt has been on heavy rotation with his biceps. His dimples. His voice when he said, *Maybe we should date each other.*

I'm a mess.

"Okay." Stella gives me a concerned look. "That's a … choice."

"He said we should date each other," I add as an afterthought, my brain still stuck on tan skin and the jut of his collarbones beneath his unbuttoned collar. I would love to stop thinking about this shirt. I really would.

Stella reaches out and smacks me in the arm. I jolt backwards, right into a metal shelf filled with cupcake toppings. A jar of mini chocolate chips goes tumbling to the floor.

"What the hell was that for?" I ask, rubbing at my bare skin.

"Way to bury the damn lead!" Stella looks like she's going to swat me again. "Layla, I swear to god. Why didn't you start with that?"

I shrug. "I don't know." Probably because he's skipped his regular morning stop-in two days in a row and I don't think he's gone a week without a baked good since I opened up the shop. Is he getting his croissants somewhere else? The thought settles like a rock in my stomach. No one makes better croissants than me. No one. "I'm not sure he was serious. I haven't seen him since."

"What do you mean?"

"I mean—" I peer over her shoulder through the tiny window in the door and make sure Gus is still occupied. I wouldn't put it past him to press his ear right up against this door. "I mean he told me when he dropped me off at home that I would see him on Monday, and I haven't seen him since."

Stella searches my face. "Did you want him to be serious?"

"I don't know." It did sound nice, the things he was talking about. To have a dating experience that didn't leave me embarrassed and hopeless. "It wouldn't be real dating. But that might be a nice change of pace."

Stella's entire face collapses into confusion. "I feel like I need a roadmap for this conversation. What do you mean it wouldn't be real dating? Start from the beginning."

So I do. I tell her about my failed date with Bryce, about the stolen silverware, about Caleb at the bar and the Margaritaville bus. I tell her about Alex and Charlie and the sloppy dancing on the table. I tell her about our drive home, how Caleb told me he's bad at dating. His suggestion that maybe we should date each other and help one another out.

"So what are you going to say?"

"Nothing if he keeps avoiding me." I reach for her abandoned cupcake and pluck a bit of icing off the top. "If this is how it's going to be, maybe it's for the best if we pretend that conversation never happened."

"No," Stella breathes, her eyes as wide as saucers. Oh, boy. I know this face. She is *invested*. Like suddenly-buy-a-Christmas-tree-farm-and-demo-half-the-buildings invested. Binge-watch-all-of-*Deadliest-Catch*-after-reading-one-book-about-crab-fishermen invested.

She bounces up and down on her toes. "No, no, no. You have to say yes."

"I do?"

"Obviously."

It is not obvious to me. "Why?"

"It's the perfect situation. A gorgeous man with dimples—"

"You've noticed his dimples, too?" I swear I never once noticed his dimples prior to this weekend.

"You mentioned them several times during that short story."

"Oh, okay."

"Anyway, a gorgeous, kind man with dimples wants to take you out." She lifts up one finger like she's ticking off her grocery list. "He wants to shower you in the affection you deserve." Another finger. "And he wants you to critique him while he does it. I quite honestly do not see a downside."

I take another nibble of my cupcake and consider. She's right. I've put in my time with asshole men. There may be plenty of fish in the sea, but most of those fish are bottom-dwellers with weird lanterns hanging off the front of their faces. They lure you in and steal your brownies.

I deserve to have some fun. I've earned that.

"He has to stop avoiding me first," I say, circling back to the original problem. I can't take him up on his offer if I never see him again. I don't think it's a coincidence that he's suddenly broken his long standing croissant habit right after our conversation.

And just like that, my anxiety and unease at being ghosted takes a nosedive into irritation.

Typical. To be left hanging by a man.

"That's an easy fix." Stella pulls her phone out of her back pocket. "I'll just ring the phone tree and see if anyone has seen him around town."

Absolutely not. Initiating the phone tree about Caleb would result in the entire town showing up on my doorstep with their opinions on the situation. I slap the phone out of her hand so fast it goes flying into a bowl of fluffy, white shortcake filling.

Shoot. I was going to pipe that into some donuts later.

We both stare at it as the door swings open and Beckett comes strolling in, his hat on backwards and the sleeves of his t-shirt slightly rolled. He's covered head to toe in dirt and sweat and—

"Is that blood?"

"What?" He looks down at his shirt. "Oh. No. It's strawberry filling. I grabbed a donut from the display case on my way in."

Of course he did. I drop my head back to the ceiling and groan. "And what were you doing before you came in here?"

As head of farm operations, it's not exactly suspicious

that Beckett looks like he spent all morning rolling around in a puddle of mud. But he's been trying to convince me for the past month and half that I should adopt a bunch of chickens from the produce farm down the road. I have a sneaking suspicion that he's building a chicken coop in the tree field right next to the bakehouse despite me telling him specifically not to do that.

I don't want any chickens, and I don't want to hear Beckett talking about chickens for the foreseeable future. The man has a problem.

His silence is answer enough. I don't bother opening my eyes. I want to crawl under one of the prep tables and take a very long nap with a very big bottle of wine.

"I wasn't doing anything," he mumbles.

"Mmhmm."

I hear the door swing open again and my entire body goes taut. I am a rubber band stretched way too tight, two seconds away from snapping.

"Woah." It's Luka's voice this time, his boots stuttering against the hardwood. "Weird vibes in here."

I open my eyes just in time to watch him press a lingering kiss to the back of Stella's head, his arm curling around her shoulders, his palm pressed flat over her heart. She loops her hand around his wrist and squeezes. Something in my chest squeezes, too.

I am happy for them. So, so happy for them. It took them ten years to get to this place with easy affection and whispered words. No one deserves it more than them.

But I'm sad for me, too. A little bit weary. Tired in my head and in my heart.

I breathe in deep through my nose. Out again. Beckett watches my breathing exercises with consideration. His face gets more and more grim the longer I try to collect myself.

"Luka," he says without bothering to look at the man he's commanding. Which is good, because Luka is busy pretending that we can't all see the palm of his hand inching down over the swell of Stella's ass.

"What?" Luka mumbles, his nose behind Stella's ear.

"Get the Gator."

"Why?"

Beckett's eyes narrow until they're two tiny slits. He looks like Clint Eastwood gazing into the sun. The only thing missing is a toothpick hanging out of his mouth. Evie has been gone for two weeks on a work trip and the man is a walking storm cloud.

"We're going out."

Luka, bless him, doesn't move a muscle. "Where are we going?"

Beckett turns his head slowly. "Do you still have that face paint?"

Luka grins. Stella groans. I snort a laugh.

Luka and Beckett's favorite problem-solving method is to sit in bushes with green and black paint smeared over their faces and intimidate whatever is causing the issue. The last time they did it, Dane put them in the drunk tank for 48 minutes and made them watch *Keeping Up With The Kardashians* as punishment. Beckett almost cried. Stella and I had to bail them out with fresh baked donuts with custard cream filling—Dane's favorite.

A smile ticks at the corner of my mouth. "No. This is not a face paint situation."

"Then why do you look upset? And why is Stella's phone in a bowl of icing?"

"It's shortcake filling," I mutter, feeling petulant. I reach for the bowl and fish out the device, tapping off the excess cream and wiping at the edges with a dishtowel. I can feel three sets of eyes on me.

"I'm just—" I hand Stella her phone. She takes it, but she grabs my wrist and holds on, too. Luka shifts his body so he can sling his arm over my shoulder. We stand there, a weird semi-group hug thing happening. I don't hate it.

"I'm just tired of being disappointed," I whisper. I try to clear my throat but sadness sticks there, clinging, making my voice thick.

I'm tired of being alone, I want to say.

No one says anything in response to that. It's quiet in the kitchen, nothing but the tick of the timer in the corner and the hum of the oven. I put some mini pies in there not too long ago. Blueberry and rhubarb with little stars cut into the crust. They'll need to come out soon. But before I can even think of extricating myself from Luka and Stella, Beckett grunts behind me and then all three of us are wrapped in strong, sweaty arms. It's disgusting. I'm going to need to change my apron.

Stella curls her arms around my waist.

It's also the very best thing.

"This is weird," Luka mutters somewhere above my head. Beckett makes an aggravated noise and there's a scuffle. Luka grunts and his arm jostles my shoulders. "But also nice! Beckett, christ, why do you have to kick me? I was going to say it's nice."

"No, you weren't."

"I was. I was going to say we should group hug every day." A pause. A thoughtful hum. "Evelyn has been a good influence on you. You're more in tune with your need for affection."

Beckett grumbles again. I press my face into Stella's shoulder with a snicker.

"No matter what," she whispers while Beckett and Luka continue to argue over our heads. "You've always got us, Layla. You'll never be alone."

She leans back and grins at me. "Whether you like it or not."

CALEB FINALLY APPEARS on Thursday morning.

He emerges from the grove of trees surrounding the bakehouse like a hot, vengeful spirit, striding up my stone steps like he's thought of little else since I last saw him. I pause with my tray of bear claws halfway behind the counter as he swings open the door with force, my poor floral wreath flying across the cozy dining space.

Everything about Caleb looks like a physical study of

impatience. Stiff shoulders. Fierce frown. Hands struggling with the strap of his bag looped around the handle of the door.

I watch with interest as he untangles himself, cursing beneath his breath the entire time.

He looks like he ran here. Maybe got hit by a tornado on the way. I don't think I've ever seen him this disheveled.

Or grumpy.

"Give me your phone," he says once he's freed himself from the door. No *hello*. No *how are you*. No *sorry I ignored you and your croissants for three days.*

"What?" I'm still ten steps behind, I guess, my hand frozen halfway between the counter and the display case. A pastry hangs precariously in the balance. If Caleb is *impatience,* then I am *confusion. Bewilderment.* "Why?"

He crosses the distance from the door to the countertop in three long strides. "This week has been one thing after another. I've tried to come every day, but Alex was hungover and then my abuela needed help with her dishtowels, and Jeremy has this love note thing. It's just been —" He presses two fingers between his dark eyebrows and exhales a heavy sigh, tension on his face and in the way he's holding himself contained in the space in front of me. "I'm sorry I wasn't here. I should have been. I wanted to be. I tried to text, but I don't have your number."

I frown and focus on the last bit. "How is that possible?"

It's strange that someone I've been at least peripherally

aware of for the past couple of years doesn't have my phone number. I think Clint at the firehouse has my number.

Caleb is frustrated. "I don't know."

"You could have called the bakehouse."

His face tightens. It is very clear that he didn't think of that. "I suppose I could have." He drops his hand from his face and beckons two fingers impatiently. My gaze sticks on that small, incremental movement. "Phone. Please."

I put down my tray of baked goodness and slide my phone across the countertop. The tips of his fingers graze my knuckles as he grabs it, his touch gentle. He smiles faintly at my pink cupcake phone case, his thundercloud expression clearing.

"I'm taking you out on Friday," he tells me.

I raise an eyebrow and blink away from where he's tip tapping across my screen. "Oh yeah?"

He hums in the affirmative. "I'll pick you up at 6:30." He hands my phone back to me, dark brown eyes searching mine. I can make out flecks of gold in the afternoon light that slants through the giant windows. A smile curls at the corner of his mouth.

I tuck a strand of hair behind my ear. I'm having trouble catching up. One second I'm restocking my baked goods, and the next Caleb is swinging through my front door. I didn't think I'd see him again for another four to six months, when we could pretend the ride in his Jeep never happened.

I watch him, watching me. "What?"

"Nothing," he says, and his smile tips into something wider. "You look nice today."

"I look nice every day."

His thumb brushes against his bottom lip and his stare slips from my eyes to the curve of my chin. The slope of my neck. My bright red apron with cartoon strawberries printed all over it.

"You really do," he says faintly.

He clears his throat and blinks away towards my clear glass display case. A deep, rumbling groan slips out of his mouth. It is a sound of pure, unadulterated appreciation. A lick of heat caresses the back of my neck.

"Are those bear claws?"

I brush my palms against my apron, my face hot. "Yes, they are." My sudden appreciation for how Caleb looks and sounds and acts is jarring. It's all jumbled up with our friendly banter, my peripheral awareness of him. I'm turned completely upside down and left scrambling. I clear my throat. "Would you like one?"

His face says he would like several. But all he does is lick at his bottom lip and continue staring at my baked goods. I pick up my tongs and carefully transfer a bear claw that's still warm from the oven. I wave it back and forth in front of his face.

"Caramel and sea salt," I sing-song.

"I shouldn't." He's already swaying closer like a lust-drunk sailor.

"You absolutely should."

Caleb stares at the bear claw like he's never seen anything so tempting in the entirety of his life. He is heavy eyes and a deep breath that starts in his chest and rolls down over his shoulders. Pink cheeks. This is a look meant for the dead of night. For grasping palms and sweaty skin. His tongue appears at the corner of his mouth again, the palm of his hand working at his jaw. His other hand braces his weight against the counter, forearm flexing. I stare hard at the two inches of skin exposed by his rolled sleeve.

"Why are you restricting yourself to butter croissants, Caleb?" I keep my voice low. Lilting. Teasing. He makes another soft groaning sound. "There's a whole world of fried dough waiting for you."

He blinks away from the treat in my hand and shakes himself out of his stupor. He levels me with a look. "You're playing dirty."

I snicker and plop the dessert in a to-go bag. "You have no idea." There are few things I enjoy more than feeding people. I hold the bag over the counter for him to grab. "Yes, I'll go out with you tomorrow. But if you leave me hanging again, we will explore this arrangement no further. I don't want to be jerked around."

Not by you. I keep that part to myself.

"I won't," he tells me, his eyes losing a little bit of their caramel and sea salt haze. "I promise I won't. I never meant to in the first place."

Something right beneath my lungs twists and tugs.

"I'm going out on a limb, suspending my *no dating in town* rule."

He looks amused, but he doesn't laugh. "Well—" He stops abruptly and scratches once behind his ear.

"Well, what?"

"We're not technically dating, right?"

"Fine." I wiggle his paper bag back and forth, probably a little bit more aggressively than I should. "I am suspending my *no going on dates with men I know from town* rule."

"Ah, I see. I understand now."

"Okay then."

"Okay," he agrees. "I'll pick you up tomorrow."

He snatches the bag out of my hand and turns away.

Bemused, I watch him give the handle on my door a wide berth. "See you then!"

He waves a hand over his head and disappears down the steps. He weaves between the trees that hug the walkway, each step sure on the stone slabs. He unbuttons his collar as he moves through the summer heat and I get a flashback to that damned Hawaiian shirt.

Pineapples.

Flowers.

Collar bones.

My phone vibrates on the counter.

I flick open the message and find a picture of Caleb, his face half in the frame, most of it taken up by a bear claw with a monstrous bite missing. His cheek bulges with fried pastry dough, the crinkles by his eyes deeper with his smile.

A soft *oh* comes out of my mouth without permission.

And he thinks I'm the dangerous one.

Caleb Alvarez

Best I ever had.

A laugh bursts out of me.

I text right back.

You're damn right.

SIX

CALEB

"YOU ARE FULL OF SURPRISES," Layla tells me, her hands propped on her hips as she stares at our destination. I'm staring too, but I'm more focused on the banner that is barely hanging on. Its listing slightly to the left, *Skate It Easy* stenciled in neon letters. *Skating rink and fun park* in bold just below.

But then Layla bites her bottom lip and I'm distracted for a solid twelve seconds.

She swivels to look up at me. "I don't think I've ever been here before. Solid score on originality."

A swell of unease punches me right in the chest. "There's scoring involved?"

"Oh, definitely. You said you wanted feedback and I intend to be very thorough."

"I was hoping you'd forget about that part," I mumble, more to myself than her. I've been a solid, tangled up mess since I stormed into her bakery and demanded her phone.

I haven't quite calmed down since. "What else am I being scored on?"

A sly smile curls the edge of her lips. "Wouldn't you like to know."

"I would, actually. That's why I'm asking."

She shrugs. "Tough cookies."

"Not even a hint?"

She shakes her head.

I rock back on my heels and shove my hands in my back pockets. It's a good look on her, this smile—the teasing. Much better than that sad, reserved look she was wearing at the beach bar that dimmed her light and made her seem small.

I guess I'm doing something right, if I can make her smile like that.

Some of the anxiety strumming in my chest fades.

Only to rocket right back up when a group of teenagers rush past us. I frown as I watch them dart in through the doors. There shouldn't be anyone but us here tonight. I called in a favor and reserved the rink for the two of us.

I thought I had, anyway.

I distinctly remember having that conversation on the phone with Oliver, the owner. Promises were made. Dates were set.

The doors to the roller rink open and a burst of noise echoes out. Teenagers screaming and something that sounds vaguely like Flo Rida.

I guess promises were not made. Dates were not set.

Oliver had simple instructions. The rink private for

one hour. The sound system hooked up to my phone. Two pairs of skates and dinner behind the snack bar.

26,000 hormone-addled teenagers were not included in that directive.

I frown at the door.

"Is this—" Layla is confused. "Is this not what you had planned?"

"Not exactly." Last year I helped Oliver push through all of his permits to get the place up and running for the roller derby season. He tried to give me a season pass to *Skate It Easy* as a thank you, but I didn't see the need. This was supposed to be the favor he owed me. "Ah, it was supposed to be closed for everyone else."

"For just me and you?" Layla's eyebrows raise high.

I nod. "Yup."

She looks at me for a beat, and then back to the front of the skating rink. "I don't think anyone has ever reserved anything for me before," she says quietly.

Did I overdo it? I scratch roughly at the back of my head and then try to smooth my hair back down. I didn't think a roller rink for one hour on a Friday night was that impressive. Or maybe it is, I don't know. Maybe it's too much.

Maybe I'm trying too hard.

"What you deserve, remember?" I ask gently.

She beams at me, the hazy summer sun making her glow.

"It is," she says with a quiet sort of joy.

My feet move without my explicit consent—two steps

forward until I can make out the faint freckles over the bridge of her nose. She tips her head back and welcomes me in her space. I nod towards the doors. "We can do something else if you want. We'll probably see something traumatizing in there."

"How bad could it possibly be? You'll be with me." Her chin lifts half an inch and I get a whiff of golden, flaky pastry dough, fresh from the oven. Cotton candy and rainbow sprinkles. Christ, she smells like *dessert.*

"I will be," I assure her. "Though I guess I should have asked if you can skate."

"I haven't skated since I was a kid." She shrugs like it's no big deal. "But we'll figure it out together."

At least she's wearing something appropriate for roller skating, if not completely inappropriate for me to maintain the guard rails around this situation. Cutoff shorts with frayed edges. A bright orange tank top and a teal scarf twisted through her cropped hair. Layers of gold necklaces that catch the light and scatter it. Living, breathing technicolor.

"We can play arcade games instead," I try.

"The night is young. We'll see how it goes."

Her hand reaches for me and loops around my arm, tugging me hard towards the building. The closer we get, the louder the thumping pulse of bass pounds. I wince again. It sounds like ... *The Electric Slide*? Maybe?

Layla opens the door and I'm overwhelmed by the smell of fried chicken and disinfectant spray. Leather and popcorn. The rink is filled with what looks like the entire population of Inglewild High. I see Jeremy cruise by, weaving in and out of the other skaters at breakneck speed. I bite back a groan.

"Please don't evaluate me on this."

"No promises," Layla laughs. Her hand on my arm squeezes again. I like it probably too much. "You're doing fine, Caleb. You didn't try to lint roll me or whip out a blindfold from your back pocket. So far, so good."

I look down at the top of her head in concern. "Who tried to blindfold you?"

She ignores me and moves us forward. "Let's just go skate."

Making our way through the crowd of teenagers, it feels like everyone is either glued to their phone, crying in clusters, or screaming at the top of their lungs. By the time we reach Oliver at the counter, I'm agitated and irritated. Oliver takes one look at me and his eyes widen.

"Oh shit," he whispers. "You meant *this* Friday."

Layla hums and takes her skates from the top of the counter, patting me once on my hip before disappearing to find a bench for her shoe change. I probably like that too much, too. I need to find some sort of pressure relief valve in my brain if I'm getting this worked up over an arm grab and a hip pat.

I turn back to Oliver and try to keep a lid on my frustration. "Of course I meant this Friday. Those are the exact words I used. This Friday."

"I'm sorry, dude. It's high school night."

I look over my shoulder and count at least seven of my

students. Jeremy is already hanging over the rail waving like a lunatic. A headache starts to pound right behind my eyes to the beat of *boogie woogie, woogie.*

"Did you at least remember to put the food in the oven like I asked?"

Oliver winces and scratches at the corner of his mouth. There's a red stain by his collar that looks suspiciously like the marinara sauce from Matty's. Specifically the marinara sauce Matty uses in his eggplant parmesan. The kind that I bought, brought over here, and stashed in the fridge behind the snack bar for dinner later.

"I thought you brought me a snack."

I stare at Oliver. "You thought I brought you a snack?"

I like to think I'm a patient person. Kind, for the most part. But I've never had more dark and dangerous thoughts than I've had this week. When it feels like my family, the population of the high school, the skate rink owner, and the rest of the living world is conspiring against me.

Oliver takes two steps away from the skate rental counter.

"Caleb." Layla calls to me from her bench, one skate on her foot and the other in her hand. She picked a pair with tiny skulls and crossbones, bright pink laces and neon purple wheels.

They suit her.

I pick up my skates. Mine have dancing hot dogs, because of course they do. I narrow my eyes at Oliver. "You owe me two favors now. Three if we include the eggplant parmesan."

He swallows and nods nervously. "You got it, man. Enjoy your skate."

I don't bother responding. I'd enjoy my skate more if it were the private rink I asked for, and I could try and hold Layla's hand without Jeremy Roughman bellowing at me from the other side of the room. Now I'm going to have to dodge my third period Spanish class and yell over the Cupid Shuffle.

I collapse in the seat next to Layla. "I'm really sorry."

I'm supposed to be showing her how good things can be. Not giving her incentive to dive right back into the dating pool.

"They have nachos here, Caleb." She slips her foot into her other skate and fumbles with the laces. I nudge her hand away and prop her ankle up against my knee, untangling the knot of string. She exhales a shaky breath and watches me. "Your score is holding strong."

I tug and tighten her laces until they're perfect, focusing on the task instead of my hand looped around the bare skin of her ankle to hold her steady. "That's good, I guess."

Layla nudges me with her perfectly tied skate. "Seriously, Caleb. Everything is great. Let's have some fun, okay?"

Unfortunately for me, I can't quite figure out how to do that.

I don't know who to blame. Oliver, for not doing exactly what I told him to do. Or myself, for thinking this was a good idea in the first place.

Or Jeremy, for skating approximately three feet behind me and Layla the entire time, offering his colorful commentary and suggestions.

"My dude, you have to balance. *Balance.* It's four wheels under your foot, I don't understand why this is so difficult for you."

I ignore him and lever myself into a seated position, arms hung loosely over my knees. Layla skids to a stop in front of me and then backtracks to where I'm splayed on the floor.

Again.

"Why did you bring me to a skating rink if you don't know how to skate?" Layla asks, trying to help me up. But she's laughing too hard and my feet slip out from under me every time I get a bit of leverage, like one of those cartoon characters stuck in place, legs spinning beneath them.

"I thought it would be easy to figure out," I pant, slapping her hands away and rolling onto my side. I brace myself on my knees and try to find my balance. I might stay down here. Live out my days on this greasy, shiny floor.

I'm going to have bruises on my ass for the next two to five years. I'll consider it a win if I make it out of this rink alive. Death, frankly, sounds more appealing than this continued humiliation.

"Use your arms," Jeremy bellows from the opposite side of the rink, his hands cupped around his mouth. "It's about baaaaalance."

Christ.

I ignore him and tilt my head towards Layla. Layla who is standing perfectly balanced—perfectly still—at my side.

"I read online that roller skating rinks are nostalgic and romantic," I confess. In retrospect, I probably spent way too much time on this idea. "I thought you'd like it."

A kid from my third period Spanish class skates a little too close to my fanned fingers and I curl them into fists. Somewhere in the distance, there's a chant beginning among my students. *Get up, Señor Alvarez. Get up.*

Wonderful.

"I do like it."

Layla's hands hold my wrists as she helps me up, wedging her hip up against the wall to hold us steady. She keeps holding onto me as I find my balance, my body hunched over in front of her. Like this, my chin almost meets the top of her head. Her feet are still, somehow. Infuriatingly stable. I stare at the little flowers on the teal scarf twisted through her hair and try to focus.

I'm no better than that guy with the lint roller. The guy who made her drive all the way to that beach bar and then left her on her own. I brought her to a crowded roller rink on *high school night* and they've played *Call Me Maybe* twenty-six times. It smells like feet in here. Like hormones and the Axe aisle of a big box store. I might as well have driven her directly to hell.

She blinks up at me, her hazel eyes shining brighter than the damned disco ball. An unnamed emotion curls at the corners of her lips, but I'm too focused on not breaking every bone in my body—and subsequently hers, when I inevitably take us both to the ground—to figure it out.

She's probably wondering how many more laps she needs to take before she can leave. If it's worth staying for a soft pretzel or if she can just microwave something when she gets home.

Her grip adjusts until her palms are pressed to mine. She squeezes once and starts moving slowly backwards.

"Let's talk about this research you did."

"Let's not."

"Was it a Buzzfeed article?"

I glance at our feet, guilty. "It was a very qualified, academic article."

"About roller rinks."

"Yes. There were sources listed." I hesitate. "I wanted you to have a good time, but I probably overdid it."

Again.

She doesn't say anything in response. Her face settles into something soft, contemplative. I've seen that look before. Usually when she has a spatula the size of a half dollar in her hand and her tongue between her teeth, her face level with a cake sitting at the edge of the counter.

She skates around a curve, still backwards, tugging me along with her. Slow, slow, slow. Jeremy whips by and shouts something vaguely encouraging. *Go the distance.* I glare at nothing in particular.

"Caleb?"

"What?"

She squeezes my hands.

"Caleb." Again. Gentler this time. A laugh on the tip of her tongue.

I stop trying to burn a hole in the strobe lights and look at Layla instead, her face tilted up towards mine. Her skin shimmers beneath the erratic lights, a brush of pale pink across her high cheekbones. Her eyes look almost green in the dark of the rink, her hair brushing the tops of her bare shoulders. She looks happy.

"What?" I ask, dazed by that look. I want to fold it up and slip it into the back pocket of my wallet. The spot where I keep a rubbed down penny my abuelo gave me and my loyalty card for the snowball stand.

"I like the roller rink." Layla's thumbs rub over my knuckles. "Solid tens across the board."

"STOP."

"I'm sorry," she wheezes around another laugh. "I can't help it."

Layla hasn't stopped laughing since my last spectacular fall, when my elbow went through one of the wooden sideboards and I wedged myself so firmly, Oliver had to practically cut me out. I saw six teenagers with their cellphones directed right at me. I don't even want to know what will be on social media in twenty minutes.

I roll my lips against a smile and grab a nacho from her tray. She tries to calm herself, but all it takes is one look at my elbow for her to peel off into bright, bursting giggles again. She collapses onto her back in the tall grass behind the roller rink, her hands clutching her stomach.

"Alright, that's enough."

"I don't think it is," she manages around two gasping, wheezing breaths.

I squint out at the parking lot and bite into my chip.

"It's the Band-Aids that do it," she says with a sigh. She reaches out and traces her finger along the edge of a bright yellow, Big Bird bandage. One of several along the length of my arm. "You kept saying you didn't need them, and Oliver kept insisting."

"What kind of roller rink doesn't have regular bandages?"

"I don't know. Grover suits you." Her touch moves down to my forearm, where three other bandages are slapped together. She taps at the bright blue Sesame Street face right above my wrist. I don't even have a cut there. I don't know what Oliver was thinking.

I grab another chip. "Tonight was not my best showing."

"I wouldn't say that," she muses. "There was entertainment. Dinner." She nods at the tray of nachos between us. "Dessert if you take me back inside for a churro. It's a better date than I normally have, pending you not leaving me in the parking lot at the end of it."

I narrow my eyes at her. "This shouldn't rank anywhere close to the top of your list, Layla."

She shrugs. "That's for me to decide. Not you."

She leans back on her elbows, her body a smooth

curve against the grass. We're caught in the endless evening of late summer, the sun hanging heavy in the sky just above the horizon. A warm wind blows through the little patch of grass we're situated in, the weeds and the flowers dancing around us. It lifts the edge of the scarf in her hair and trails it across her bare throat, a temptation if I've ever seen one.

I wonder if the skin there tastes as sweet as the sticky honey glaze she uses. Or if the taste of her is more indulgent like the heavy, rich chocolate ganache she uses on some of her cakes. I wonder if I'd taste her on my tongue for hours. If I'd crave her the same way.

"Caleb."

I force my gaze away from the hollow of her throat, heat rushing to my cheeks. I look up at the sky instead, the fluffy, white clouds floating slowly by. That's not the sort of relationship we're going to have, Layla and I. It's an arrangement.

"What?"

"I said, we should probably talk about how we're doing this."

"How we're doing, what? Sharing these nachos?" I nudge the tray towards her. "I already told you that you can have the cheese."

"No." She looks amused. "Our arrangement. The last time we talked about it, you came into my bakery and barked at me about my phone."

"Oh." I rub one finger across my eyebrow. That's

exactly what I did. "Yeah, you're right. I'm sorry about that, by the way. I was ... stressed this week."

"Is everything okay?"

"Everything is fine." Everything is *fine*. Assuming that my tumble through the skate rink wall didn't give me blood poisoning. "What did you want to discuss? Do you think we should make some rules?"

Her face pinches in distaste. "No. I don't think we need to do that. That makes it feel like something—" She trails off, looking for the right words.

"Fake?"

Her face eases, soft lines and bright eyes. Out in the sunlight, they match the grass around us. Forest green. Flecks of brown in the middle. "Yes. Exactly. I don't want that."

"I don't either."

"Good."

Layla plucks a blade of grass and holds it between her thumb and forefinger, watching me the entire time. "Why are you doing this, Caleb?"

"I told you," I make sure I keep my eyes on hers. It's important that she believes me. That she understands I'm telling the *truth*. "I've been, ah, struggling on dates lately. And I need your help to figure out why."

She cocks her head to the side and searches my face. I feel the drag of her gaze like a finger against my cheek, turning my face into the light to evaluate. "Have you taken anyone roller skating recently?"

"Just you."

"Hm."

"What's that?" I ask. "That *hm*."

"It means I haven't reached a conclusion yet. It means we have more work to do. More dates to go on, to figure it out."

I fight against my smile. "I think so."

"Good."

This time I don't do anything to restrain my grin. It tumbles right out of me. "Great."

She reaches for another chip and puts an unholy amount of liquid cheese on it. "What do you think? A month?"

How she manages to take a dainty bite of that monstrosity, I'll never know.

"A month sounds good."

So does two. So does four. Few things sound better than sitting next to Layla, eating slightly stale chips in a field behind the *Skate It Easy*.

But that's the exact impulse I'm trying to curb with this little experiment. I jump in with two feet when there's even a hint of something, pouring all of myself into everything. And then I second guess. I overthink. I try to rent out a roller rink for a single date with a girl I like.

Too much. Way too fast.

"And if either of us wants to end it, for whatever reason, that's it. No explanation necessary."

"Fair enough." I scoop some salsa and somehow manage to spill it all over my chest. I flick off an onion and watch it sail over the side of the hill. "And it's only us, during our month. I won't be going on dates with anyone else."

I don't mention that no one's caught my interest for a while now. I've been too busy eating butter croissants and ordering ridiculous, custom-made buttercream cakes. Layla watches me, a strand of hair dancing across her cheek. I want to tuck it carefully behind her ear. I want to brush my knuckles against her skin and feel how soft she is.

"I won't date anyone either," she says. Experiment, I remind myself. *This is an experiment.* The rush of pleasure I feel over the idea of Layla only spending time with me is not appropriate.

"I'm not sacrificing a whole heck of a lot there," she continues. "My dates have been miserable lately."

"Hopefully we can fix that, skate disasters notwithstanding."

She brightens considerably. "This skate disaster was a delight, thank you very much."

I busy myself with another chip from the tray while I watch the melting sunlight slip over her skin. Reds and golds and a deep burnished orange. She looks like she was meant to be exactly here, sprawled out in the grass next to me, the frayed hem of her shorts high against the creamy skin of her thighs. There's a throb down my entire left side from hitting the floor one too many times, but there's one at the base of my spine, too. In the palms of my hands.

"One last question."

I blink back to her face. I'm used to three feet of countertop between us and her colorful aprons that tie at her neck. Sitting this close to Layla and having all of her attention focused on me is an exercise in resistance.

"Shoot." It comes out hoarse. I clear my throat.

Layla's grin tips into something unrestrained. Brighter than the colors dancing ribbons through the sky.

"When are you taking me out again?"

SEVEN

LAYLA

"WHAT IN THE hell are you doing?"

Beckett jumps as I lean my shoulder up against the back door of the bakery, a mug of coffee in my hand. I bet he didn't expect me to be here today. I'm guessing he was counting on exactly that, given the chicken wire bundled in his arms and the guilty expression half-shadowed by the bill of his baseball cap.

He blinks at me. I take a sip out of my mug. This is how ninety percent of our conversations begin and end.

"I'm not doing anything," he says, like there isn't a two-by-four over his shoulder.

"Hm."

I don't say anything else. He fidgets. Well, as much as a man his size holding all the supplies for a chicken coop between his huge, tattooed arms can fidget.

He sighs and lets everything drop to the ground in a

clatter. He crosses his arms over his chest and scowls at me.

"What are you even doing here?" he demands.

"I work here," I reply calmly.

"Not on Saturday mornings."

I take another long pull of coffee out of my mug. Beckett squirms in the silence.

I take my time when I say, "Good to know this was premeditated."

"The chickens need somewhere to go, okay? I don't want to be at the grocery store and wonder if Delilah is in the poultry aisle."

"Delilah?"

He glares at me. "That's her name."

Of course it is. "Why don't you build Delilah a new home in your backyard?"

He mumbles something.

"What was that?"

He rolls his eyes skyward, up to the big, fluffy white clouds sinking low across the sky. It's hot already, the heat pressing at the bare skin of my arms, inching up over my neck. Beckett scratches at the back of his head and adjusts his baseball cap until it faces backwards.

"Evelyn cut me off," he explains. "After Clarabelle."

That's right. The cow he rescued from that dilapidated farm down in Virginia. They were keeping her in a concrete pen, blisters all over her belly and back. She lives in the pasture behind Beckett's house now, grazing to her heart's content. He makes her flower crowns, I'm pretty sure.

He hesitates. "And Zelma."

Another duck. In addition to the four cats he previously adopted and the duck that already lives in his greenhouse. It's a good thing his house is so big over on the far edge of the Lovelight land. He's running his own animal sanctuary over there.

"When does Evelyn come back?"

"Tomorrow."

Good. Maybe he'll stop sneaking around the grounds then. I push off the edge of the door and beckon him inside. "Come on. I made zucchini bread."

He follows after me without another word, leaving his pile of wood and wire and god knows what else in a heap on the ground. Maybe I can get Luka to hide it while Beckett is occupied with baked goods. Though Luka is probably under forty-seven comforters over at Stella's place, snoring happily through his Saturday morning.

Beckett collapses on a bar stool at the opposite edge of my work table, his chin in his hand, the tattoos twisting up and down his arms on full display in the early morning light. His eyes bounce around the kitchen, looking for the zucchini bread I tempted him in here with.

Part of me wants to withhold it until I can get him to agree to stop trying to build a chicken coop in my backyard, but the bigger part of me wants to clear out some of these leftovers for the new batch of stuff I'll be baking this morning. I've always valued practicality over retribution.

"In there." I gesture towards a small metal tin covered in foil at the edge of the counter, dancing trees printed along the sides. "No chocolate chips this time. Sorry."

Beckett would do just about anything for a slice of zucchini bread. Once when Stella smugly declared she had the second-to-last slice, he pushed Luka headfirst into an overgrown tree to make it up the steps before him.

We sit in silence, Beckett with his bread, me with the donut batter I was working on before I heard him in the back. I don't usually come in on Saturday mornings, that's true, but I was feeling restless. I woke up and immediately thought of Caleb. His blush-stained cheeks and his wide smile. That damned dimple in his cheek. I was pouring my coffee and kept picturing him after his last fall, starfished out on the floor of the roller rink, a long arm slung over his eyes.

Images kept flickering like the ends of a film strip. The line of his jaw. His thumb at his bottom lip and a glob of salsa on the front of his t-shirt. Long legs spread out in the grass. He is nothing like I expected him to be.

It was the most fun I've ever had on a date.

"Why are you making that face?"

I go back to mixing my batter. "What face?"

Beckett narrows his eyes at me. "That weird smile thing." He tries to mimic a grin, zucchini bread bulging in his cheeks. He looks absurd. "I've never seen that look on your face before."

"Well, I can't see my own face, can I?" I snap.

"Fine." He rolls his eyes and goes back to his bread. I

whip my batter until my arm begins to ache. He mutters something under his breath that sounds vaguely like *touchy*.

"Did you—" I hesitate, not sure I want to ask Beckett the question that's prodding at the edges of my mind. The question that I hear the loudest whenever I'm with him and Evelyn and Stella and Luka. Every single time I watch a couple move together in perfect, easy synchronicity through the front doors of my bakery.

Beckett watches me with a level of patience I probably don't deserve, the tray of bread clutched between his hands. "Did I, what?"

"Did you ever think you'd find someone?" I swallow around the lump in my throat. "Did you think you'd find Evelyn?"

His face eases when he hears her name, a calm settling over his shoulders.

"No," he says. His head tilts to the side and he drags his palm against his chin. "I didn't. I'm not exactly a social butterfly and I—I struggle with people. You know that."

Beckett has trouble with interactions—with small spaces and loud noises. It takes him some time to warm up to people, to ease into conversation. It's why, I suspect, he spends so much time out in the fields. In the quiet, he can pull the edges of himself back together.

"But Evelyn saw the pieces of me that no one else did and decided she wanted to keep them. I wanted to keep hers, too. I'm—" He clears his throat. "I'm grateful for that.

And I, uh, I guess you've noticed I have some trouble when she's gone."

The man has been stomping around the farm like someone took his favorite toy away. Evelyn travels for her work with the U.S. Small Business Coalition, helping little places like ours all over the country get their digital legs beneath them. She's incredible at what she does. It just leaves a grumpy-ass farmer for the rest of us whenever she goes.

I give him a droll look, arm still working at the batter. These better be the best damned donuts on the East Coast by the time I'm done.

Beckett gives me a half-smile, fingers collecting the crumbs he missed at the bottom of the tray. "You'll find someone, Layla."

"Everyone keeps saying that, but I'm not so sure," I confess. "I'd like something to be mine. Someone, maybe." Mine and mine alone. Secret smiles and easy touches and lips pressed against the back of my neck. Easy affection and comfort in the mundane. I set my mixing bowl aside and reach for a tray. "You really think someone will want my pieces?"

He shrugs. "At the very least, they'll want this bread."

I flick a spatula at his head.

STELLA INTERRUPTS me during my third batch of donuts, swinging through the back door hard enough for it to bounce off the wall. A cascade of aprons and head scarves come tumbling down on top of her, pale pink and bright purple and a thick canvas with dancing nutcrackers on it that I'm sure was a joke but I love to wear year-round anyway. She fights her way through the fabrics.

"Big news," she tells me with an orange scarf over the top half of her face. It's a shame Beckett left already. He'd probably enjoy this more than my zucchini bread.

"You discovered a filing system that doesn't involve chucking all your paperwork into the bottom drawer of your desk and hoping for the best."

"Ha." She bats away the orange scarf and wrestles with a pale blue one. "No. Though Luka continues to try his best."

It'll be the culmination of Luka's life's work when he finally gets Stella organized. Sometimes he waits until she's out of the house and reorganizes all her closets. The last time she went to Annapolis for a shipment, he reorganized her book collection by genre and color.

A thrill of excitement rockets through my chest. I straighten from my standard curved-over-the-table position and almost send my donut tray flying. "Did Luka propose?"

I might have misgivings about my own love life, but I am firmly invested in the happiness of my best friends. The tickle of sadness in the corners of my heart is easy enough to ignore, bursting as it is with absolute joy.

"What? No." One pale blue eye peeks out at me through gauzy fabric. I have no idea how she's still tangled up over there. She swats the last piece away with a relieved sigh. "We just moved in together."

After a lengthy construction on the back of Stella's tiny cottage so Luka has space to work and Stella has more space to hoard pine tree air fresheners and novelty tea towels and goodness knows what else.

"You've been in love with each other for a decade," I reason.

She scratches behind her ear. "But only dating for a year and some change. I know I'm going to be with Luka forever. I'm not in any rush."

Only Stella would think of a decade as a rush. I fill a piping bag with batter. "My best colors are a sienna or a dusty pink, so a fall wedding would work best for me."

"I'll take that into consideration. But that's not what I have to tell you." Stella hops up and down on her toes on the opposite side of my table. I pause with my hand curled around my bag.

"What?"

"The news!"

"Right. Please proceed."

She flops down on the stool Beckett abandoned three hours ago after he consumed all of the goodies within his direct line of sight. "I really expected more enthusiasm."

"From me?"

"Yes."

"For an announcement you have given me no context on?"

Stella nods. "Yes."

"Okay." I raise one arm up in the air and let out a whoop. I drop it back down to my side. "Good?"

"Better." Stella nods with a grin. "Because I just got a call from *Baltimore Magazine* and they want to run a feature on you for their 'Best Of' issue."

I blink at Stella. "What?"

She's back to bouncing up and down in her seat, practically vibrating on the other end of the island. "They called a little bit ago. I ran all the way here from the office and you know how much I hate cardio endurance. They said they've been seeing the bakehouse all over social media and monitoring reviews and not only will you be included in their list of best bakeries in Maryland, but they want to do a feature on you as well. A full spread. A photoshoot!"

She practically screams the last two words at me.

"Of me?" I point at my chest, a smudge of powdered sugar against my t-shirt.

"Of you!" Stella shrieks, launching herself halfway over the counter and into my arms. Her elbow lands in my bowl of batter. Her knee edges the tray right off the table and onto the floor. She holds me tight with both arms around my shoulders. Her bony little elbow is digging into my neck.

"Are you sure?" I ask into her hair. I can't comprehend it. My bakehouse doesn't even have a *name*. Just *the bakehouse*. And they want— "You're sure they want me?"

"They mentioned you by name and talked at length about your blueberry crumble scones. They'll be here in a couple of weeks for your interview and photoshoot." Stella pulls back and shakes my shoulders lightly. "Of course they want you. *You* are amazing."

"They want me for a feature." I try the words out. It still sounds too incredible to believe. "They want to put me in a magazine."

Stella grins, her eyes soft. Her hands squeeze my arms in the one-two-three I always see Luka give her. Shoulders, elbows, hands.

"Of course they do."

I'M STILL RIDING a high of endorphins and far too much sugar by the time I leave the bakehouse, rumbling down the long road that leads back to town. Stella gave me the rest of the details in barely tempered excitement, yelling every third word, stopping repeatedly to smack me in the arm with her own enthusiastic brand of support.

They want *me*. My little bakehouse. The girl who never studied baking in any formal capacity and tripped right into this profession. I've never needed anyone's validation other than my own to feel good about what I do—to be happy in my little glass house in the middle of all the pine trees—but it feels nice to be noticed. To be recognized.

I swing by the liquor store on a whim, winding my way through stacks of Natty Boh and an impressive arrangement of vodka bottles in the shape of a Maryland blue crab. I stop on my way to the boxed wine and peer up at the bottles of champagne stacked high on the shelf, the orange ones at the top glowing beneath the terrible, flickering lighting in this place.

It's like a sun beam broke through the clouds and illuminated them on the shelf. Kismet. It's the universe telling me I deserve the damn champagne.

"I do deserve it," I reason. It's not every day I snag a magazine feature in one of the most widespread issues *Baltimore Magazine* publishes. Local networks make television specials for the *Best Of* issue. Most of the restaurants down on the shore get their features framed and hung on the wall. Not a single Inglewild business has ever been recognized before.

I search the floor for one of the step stools Juliette keeps for restock so I can reach my celebratory champagne. No luck. I sigh and scratch once at my temple. "No problem. I can still reach it."

"Why does it sound like you're issuing yourself a challenge?"

I peek over my shoulder to the owner of that deep and rumbling voice, Caleb standing at the end of the aisle, arms crossed over his chest and a smile hitching at his mouth. He's wearing a plain white t-shirt today. Faded jeans with a tear just above the knee. Black sunglasses pushed back over his hair.

He looks delicious.

Even more so than he did last night when he picked me up at the house, his hands clasped behind his back and a lock of dark hair falling over his forehead. No lint roller for Caleb. Nope, he walked all the way to my front door and knocked politely, hovered his hand over the small of my back as he opened the passenger side door of his Jeep.

He gestures towards the shelf. "What was your approach going to be?"

I extend my leg and point at the bottom with my foot like I'm a ballerina and this shelf is my stage. Caleb swallows heavily. "I was going to scurry on up like a squirrel."

He pushes himself off the end cap, lazily making his way over to me. It looks like he's recovered from our little roller skating adventure. All of the bandages are missing from his arms, though there's a pretty nasty bruise just above his elbow. I frown at it as he moves closer.

"While I'm sure that would have been entertaining, let me help you out." Caleb stops right next to me and reaches up, up, up. I get a whiff of sunscreen and cinnamon, rich coffee and sweet cream. I want to press my nose to his shoulder and breathe in deep. Maybe climb him instead of the shelf.

He arches an eyebrow down at me with his arm still extended. I grin, unashamed.

"Why do I get the feeling you're plotting something?" he says, voice low.

"Me?" I point a finger at my chest. "Never."

"Sure." He huffs a laugh and curls his hand around the bottle I had my eye on, pulling it down without even resorting to tip-toes. He offers it to me, whistling when he sees the label. "What're you celebrating?"

I hold the bottle close to my chest, grinning so hard my

cheeks ache with it. "*Baltimore Magazine* wants to feature the bakehouse in an upcoming issue."

"Layla." I've never heard anyone say my name like that. Like they don't want to say anything else ever again. His smile spreads wide until the crinkles at the edge of his eyes wink at me. I stare at him until my own lips tip up at the corners and we're grinning at each other in the middle of the liquor store aisle like two silly idiots. He hesitates, and then smooths his hands over my arms to grip my shoulders. A half-hug. A hand-hug. His fingers squeeze. "That's incredible."

The heat of his palms bleeds through my thin tank top and I lean into his touch. "It is, isn't it?"

He nods. "Way overdue."

I beam at him. The invitation is there, on the tip of my tongue. *Come over,* I want to say. *We'll eat the cupcakes that I stress baked last week when I thought you were avoiding me and we'll drink this champagne. We'll watch something stupid on TV and I won't have to be alone.*

But it feels like too much. Like it's maybe crossing a line in this strange arrangement we've made for ourselves. So I swallow it down and tuck my smile into something restrained and try not to feel any type of way about his hands on my skin. His pinky just barely edging under the strap of my tank top.

He clears his throat and lets go, thrusting his hands into his pockets.

I scramble for something to keep Caleb in front of me. For just one more second. I tip my head to the side and scuff the tip of my shoe across the floor. "You know, you never answered me yesterday."

"What's that?"

I push past him to the check-out, noticing for the first time the six pack of Natty Boh waiting by his feet. He picks it up as he follows me.

"When are you taking me out again?"

"Ah." A blush darkens his cheeks and he scratches behind his ear. I wedge my champagne bottle under my arm and grab a bag of Old Bay chips to add to my celebratory feast. Caleb grins at my collection of items. "Are you free on Tuesday?"

"I sure am."

"Good. Ah, great. I'll pick you up at the same time?"

I nod. "Will I need wheels? Maybe some knee pads?" I poke him once in the ribs. "You want to give me any clues?"

He glances down at me, one dark eyebrow rising on his forehead. A smirk plucks at his mouth and oh, I like this version of Caleb, too. When the smooth, easy confidence edges out over his quiet bashfulness. When I can see a hint of something else—something teasing and delicious.

"Now where would be the fun in that?"

EIGHT

CALEB

"HOW DID YOU KNOW?" she breathes as soon as we arrive.

It had been another gamble, coming here, but Stella had sent me a string of vague text messages after I ran into Layla at the liquor store with a list of seemingly unrelated items. Things like: *Lavender. Deep dish pizza with spinach and ricotta. Plants in terracotta bowls. Scarves. The color orange.*

Escape rooms.

It didn't take a genius to figure out that Stella thought I could benefit from a list of Layla's favorite things, though the escape room addition had been surprising. Part of me thought Stella was setting me up, deliberately giving me something Layla would hate. That worry has evaporated, given the barely restrained glee Layla is broadcasting at the front doors.

She looks like a little firecracker over there, lit up and ready to shoot into the sky.

I rub my thumb against my bottom lip, trying not to smile. At the bakehouse, she's reserved. Friendly, but quiet. I like getting to see these other pieces of her. Untempered enthusiasm and unadulterated joy.

"How did I know, what?"

"My deep love and appreciation for a good escape room."

"Well." Best to come clean, I guess. "Stella did text me a comprehensive list of your favorite things."

Layla turns to look at me, confused. She's wearing another scarf twisted through her hair today, a bright cherry red with little strawberries printed on the fabric. It matches the apron she was wearing the other day and I smile thinking of her wearing them together.

I want to feel it slip through my fingers. I want to twist it around and around my fist until I can tilt her head back and guide her mouth to mine. I wonder if she'd taste like strawberries or that sugar sweet glaze she uses on everything.

I veer sharply away from that thought.

"Stella did what?"

"To be fair, I knew most of the things on that list already."

"Like what?" It's a challenge, that question. I watch as an ambling summer wind catches the end of her scarf and lifts it. I give in to temptation and slip my palm along the material, feel it between my thumb and forefinger. I rub it once and tug her half an inch closer.

I'll settle for having her in increments, if that's what it takes to make it through this arrangement. Probably better for my sanity that way, too.

She sways into me with a smile.

"Lavender," I say. She has it planted all over her front yard, a big bundle of it right below the little window in her kitchen that always seems to be open. "Scarves." I let the length of the silky material slip against my hand, my knuckles brushing against her neck. She sucks in a sharp breath and I drop my hand to my side. "Expensive champagne and cheap crab chips."

She grins at the last two. "I can't tell if I'm offended or impressed. I don't think any of my dates have received inside information before. She must like you."

I shrug. "I think it just proves how much she likes *you*."

Layla's smile is quiet this time, thoughtful. But her eyes shine bright as she slips her hand in mine. I like how easily she reaches for me, how well we fit together. I like how she threads her fingers through mine and squeezes. I'm starting to see that she relies on touch to communicate, and I rely on it to understand.

"Enough of that." She swings our linked hands between us. "Let's get inside so I can kick your ass."

I trail after her, confused. "Isn't this a team activity?"

My confusion quickly settles into a low sense of foreboding. The lobby of *Quest For Escape* is painted almost entirely in black, a single desk against the back wall. Above the desk are what I hope are props, rows and rows of various weapons and masks and leather bound books painted gold. I stare hard at what looks like a machete. It's the first indication that I am wholly unprepared for what I signed us up for.

Layla has an entire list of questions she rattles through with the teenager behind the desk. Things I would have never thought to ask, like:

Is the game linear?

Are there any secret rooms?

Will anyone jump out at us?

I startle at the last question and glance down at Layla. "Is that a thing that happens?"

She shrugs. "It can."

The kid behind the desk shakes his head, swiping through a checklist on the iPad in front of him. He has an earpiece, too, and what looks like three cell phones on the desk in front of him. This is a more complex set-up than most spy movies. I vaguely recognize him from the school. Eric, his nametag tells me. "Not here. We haven't had characters in the room since Gus punched the last one in the face."

Layla and I snort in unison.

"There's an intercom in the room," he says. "I'll be able to talk to you and you can shout if you need me." He taps at a line of monitors on the other side of the desk. "I'll keep an eye on things too, just to make sure."

"What are you making sure of?"

Eric stares hard at me from the other side of the desk.

It's a battle-weary stare, that look. The look of a man who has seen too many things. "Just to make sure."

Alright, then. I'm starting to get the feeling that this might be another date disaster. Not as bad as the last one, I hope. I'm not sure anything can top the compilation video of my roller skating falls, set to some ridiculous song with a heavy beat. The kids have been sharing them back and forth all week. I got two in my work email. Alex sent me one that had over twenty thousand views with a string of crying, laughing face emojis.

I drag my palm over the back of my head, anxiety curling in my gut. "We're in the tropical island room, right?"

"Uh, no." Eric continues scrolling on his device. I have no idea what he's looking for. "We had to put you in the zombie apocalypse room."

"The what?"

"The zombie apocalypse room."

"Why?"

"Because someone was doing weird stuff in the tropical room and we needed to sanitize it."

Layla tries to cover her laugh with a cough.

"Do you have anything other than ... zombie apocalypse?"

An end of the world scenario featuring flesh-eating, undead creatures is not the setting I was hoping for.

"We have an outbreak room."

"An outbreak room and a zombie apocalypse room?"

Eric nods. "Billy is super into the undead."

I forgot Billy owns this place. He used to work part-time at the funeral home two towns over. I guess he found a new spot to channel all of his ... enthusiasm.

"Didn't Billy used to wear all black leather?" Layla whispers to me.

"Still does," Eric supplies. "Some days he wears fake vampire teeth, too."

Layla's smile falters. "That's ... great, I guess?"

"It's a choice is what it is," Eric grumbles. "Alright, I'll show you to your room. You'll have an hour to escape. Everything you need is hidden within, but you get three clues. Give a shout if you need one and I'll come over the speaker. I'll be monitoring you the whole time, so please don't destroy anything while you're in the room. Any furniture nailed to the floor should remain that way."

Layla nods along, her face set in grim determination. I didn't realize furniture adjustment was a concern. "Um, what?"

Eric waves us behind the desk and through a small entrance way. We wind our way down a narrow, dark hallway lined with nondescript black doors. I have to duck to keep my head from smacking into the low hanging lights, Layla barely visible in front of me. Sounds are muffled back here, like we're underground.

I can see why Billy likes it so much.

Eric continues his instruction as we walk. "Like I said, I'll be monitoring you, so please don't do anything weird."

Layla is interested, I can tell. "Can you define weird?"

Eric's face is half in shadow when he turns. "You'd be surprised by the things I've seen."

Layla snickers into her hand. I swallow around my unease. This is not what I expected. Eric stops in front of a door that's wider than the rest, a bloody handprint right above the handle. A scream echoes from inside.

I curl my hand around Layla's wrist and she tips her head back to look at me. It's the closest we've been since we started this thing and I'm dazed by the feel of her. Like this, I could wrap both of my arms around her shoulders and tuck her close. Press a kiss to her temple and drag my lips down the line of her jaw. Slip my hand in the collar of her shirt and feel the delicate skin beneath. Work at the place between her shoulder and neck with my mouth. I want so many things with Layla.

Right now, I'd settle for a normal date.

"What's up?" she whispers.

I swallow. "Nothing. I just wanted to be sure you're okay with this."

Her face breaks out into a wide grin. That smile is temptation and delight, topped with a sugary sweet glaze of distraction. She's wearing cutoff denim shorts again today, a white, billowing top that's tight around her arms and loose everywhere else. It looks impossibly soft and temptingly thin. I bet I could feel the heat of her skin through it. I bet the gauzy material would bunch at my wrists when I slipped my hands beneath.

I clear my throat and stare pointedly at the bloody

handprint on the door in an effort to distract myself. Layla's smile grows.

"Are you having second thoughts, Caleb?"

"No." Another scream erupts from behind the closed doors. I flinch. "Maybe."

Her megawatt smile dims. She turns in my arms until her front is pressed against mine. I'm distracted by the heat of her, the smell of sugar and butter and tart cherry jam.

Layla Dupree is *dangerous.*

"We don't have to go in," she whispers, the words just for me. "You could take me to get ice cream instead. If this is too much, I understand."

"No." Layla deserves this. For someone to try. Even if it's something as comically ridiculous as a zombie apocalypse escape room experience. *Especially* if it's a zombie apocalypse escape room experience, I guess. "We're going to escape this room."

That wide and excited smile blooms back to life on her face. It wedges in my chest, right under my ribs. God, she's beautiful. She should smile like this all of the time.

"Oh, I forgot to mention," Eric offers, pressing the door open with his shoulder. The sounds from inside intensify and Layla slips her hand back in mine. I'm more focused on that single point of contact than anything else, so I almost don't hear him when he says, "There's another party joining you. Our rooms have a four person minimum ... after the tropical island incident."

"Wait, what?"

He ushers us in the room, completely ignoring the

disembodied arm hanging from the ceiling above his head. "I'll bring them back as soon as they arrive."

And with that, Eric disappears back out the door and locks us into a zombie apocalypse.

I take in the space. I know Eric said no one will jump out at us, but it definitely feels like someone could. The room is set up to look like an old hospital. There's a wheelchair tipped over on its side, a medical cart with about forty-two thousand drawers, a couple of lab charts and haphazard coverings over the windows. But I'm fixated on the fake body parts littering the ground and parts of the ceiling, fake blood oozing around the edges. They're not hyper-realistic, thank god, but they're enough to make me grateful we didn't go to dinner before this little field trip.

I slip my hands into my back pockets and rock back on my heels, frowning at what looks like part of a fibula doused in ketchup.

"I really wish we were in the tropical room."

"I don't know," Layla pokes a dismembered head hanging from the ceiling. We watch it swing back and forth. "This has a certain ambiance."

I scratch at my neck, sifting my hand up into my hair and scrubbing roughly. She crosses the room and examines a splatter of fake blood on the wall like it's a priceless piece of art at the Met.

I feel like I'm ascending to new levels of absurd during this thing with Layla. I usually struggle with connection or conversation, not—body parts. I can't say I've ever brought a woman to be locked in a room with disembodied limbs before.

"Maybe we should count our next date as the first date," I hedge. We could start fresh. Maybe I won't be such a disaster.

Layla doesn't even bother looking at me as she picks up what looks like a syringe. She examines it, and then sets it down carefully on the table. "I don't think so. This is an excellent second date."

I wince. "Can we please not count the roller skating rink as our first, at least?"

"Why wouldn't we?"

I give her a look. "Because I still have a bruise that looks vaguely like Massachusetts on my ass."

She snickers. "Don't tease me about your ass, Caleb."

Before I can sink fully into the appreciation that comes with Layla talking about my ass, the door swings open behind us. Eric ushers three new people in, and I have to bite down around the edges of my groan. Gus, Clint, and Montgomery. Our three town firefighters and collectively the most obnoxious group of people I've ever met. They enter the room in matching t-shirts and blood red sweatbands around their foreheads. They look like they're about to run a marathon. Or maybe start a fight club.

Gus grins as soon as he sees us. "Well, well, well. What do we have here?"

"You know our names, Gus," Layla deadpans. "Why you insist on feigning surprise when you know exactly what's going on at all times eludes me."

"Are you implying something, Laylabug?"

I look at her and mouth *Laylabug* as a question, delighted. She winces and shakes her head.

"Don't call me that, and you know exactly what I'm talking about."

That makes one of us. I have no idea what they're talking about. Layla beckons me closer until her mouth is at my ear and my heart is in my throat. Fuck, she smells so good.

"Gus operates the phone tree," she whispers, her bottom lip just barely grazing the shell of my ear. "I'm pretty sure he runs the new text message gossip division, too."

Our town phone tree was intended for use in emergencies. That lasted maybe two weeks. Its sole purpose now is to share information on who cut whom in line at Ms. Beatrice's, where Evelyn is off to and how long we can expect Beckett to be grumbling around town, and when the good coffee is getting restocked at the grocery. I'm not surprised to hear Gus is at the head of it. Especially since I got a text message three days ago from an unknown number telling me Matty is trying his hand at stuffed crust pizza.

There's only one person who would be that invested in Matty's menu development.

"I don't know what you're talking about," Gus says archly.

Layla huffs.

Clint squints at the walls while Monty passes his hands over the frame of the door. Eric pokes Gus once in the arm, grabbing his attention. "No knives this time, Gus. I don't want you cutting anything open again."

"Again?"

Everyone ignores me. Gus holds up his hands, palms up. "How was I supposed to know there wasn't a clue in the mattress?"

"I thought me yelling *there is no clue in the mattress* repeatedly over the intercom might help."

This kid really isn't paid enough. Gus hides his chuckle behind the palm of his hand, fanning his fingers out over his stubble. "Fair point. Well made, as always, Eric. Do the usual rules apply?"

He cracks his knuckles. I glance at the ceiling in an effort to find patience and find a severed head instead. Layla shuffles closer to my side.

"It won't take us long to escape," she says. "I promise."

"GET IN THE CEILING, LAYLA!"

I sigh and loop my arm around Layla's waist, pulling her down from the top of the desk as she tries to follow Gus's instruction. It was cute, at first, how excited and enthusiastic she was. Now I'm just trying to keep her from long-term bodily harm.

"She's not getting in the ceiling, Gus."

Gus grips the front of my shirt in his fist and pulls until he's three inches away from my face. He is sweating ... a lot. "Do you want to live, Caleb?"

At this point? No. Not really.

"I'm happy to head out there and you know—" I make a vaguely motivational gesture. "Get the antidote or something. I'll take one for the team."

There was a snack bar off of the lobby. I will happily sit outside and eat a soft pretzel while this situation resolves itself. Layla and I can go get ice cream after and I can drown my sorrows in sugar and cream.

"If you leave the room, you're disqualified. You're gonna stay." Layla presses her palm flat to Gus's chest and pushes him away from me. "I could shimmy into one of the air vents I bet. The last clue said something about *flow*, didn't it? Maybe it meant air flow."

I like Layla a lot, but this is—this is chaos. This is complete mayhem. Why anyone chooses to do this for fun is truly beyond me.

Eric's tinny voice appears over the speakers. This is the fourth time in the past ten minutes. "Please do not climb into the ceiling or air ducts. There are no clues in there. And there are no clues within the body parts, so you can stop working on that arm, Montgomery."

Monty drops the piece of arm he was trying to dissect using a pair of tweezers and a piece of broken corkboard. It bounces across the floor and lets out a squeak.

"I think that was a dog toy," I mumble to no one in particular.

"What we need to do is focus," Clint yells at a volume that is not necessary. I don't think he realizes that no one can focus when he's gesturing wildly like that. "We need to find the third key, develop an antidote, and get the fuck out of here."

I pinch the bridge of my nose. Eric has steadily been increasing the ambient noise for the last twenty minutes. I'm going to be hearing the drag and thud of undead bodies in my nightmares for weeks. "This is insane."

"THIS IS LIFE OR DEATH, CALEB," Gus screams in my face.

"If this were life or death, we would have been dead seven minutes ago when you almost let an entire undead horde through the window," Layla snaps. "I don't want to hear it from you. Go over in the corner and work with Monty on the safe combination."

Gus stomps his way over to the corner, a parting look full of malice aimed in my direction. I haven't been the most helpful, sure, but I think Gus is overreacting.

I keep that thought to myself.

"Thank you," I say to Layla, resisting the urge to smooth my hands up and down her arms. If the fake zombies don't kill me, this shirt will. I caught a flash of bare skin when she lifted her arms to reach the top of the cabinet and I had to stare hard at a jar full of eyeballs to collect myself. "What happens if we don't escape the room?"

Layla gives me a fierce look. Her shoulders roll back, her chin tips up and those pretty eyes that look like a summer storm narrow. It tugs at something deep inside me and I am instantly, inexplicably, turned on.

Christ.

"We are escaping this room," she says with a steely level of determination. I don't doubt her for a second. I do, however, doubt the three idiots with their heads pressed together over the safe, trying to wedge it open with a fake foot.

"I should probably go help them."

I need a distraction or I'm going to escort Layla to the darkest corner of this room and give Eric some more material for his therapy sessions.

Layla nods. "I'll work on finding the key."

The key. The combination. The antidote. I keep forgetting all the pieces of this puzzle. I head over to where they've abandoned the foot and have started shaking the safe instead. There can't be much time left. I just need to endure the next half an hour, at most, and Layla and I can go somewhere quiet.

Alone.

Together.

With ice cream, preferably.

"How can I help?"

"I need you to stop flirting," Gus demands. "And focus on getting us the hell out of here."

"I'm not flirting," I grumble.

"You are."

"Here," Clint offers. He hands me something that looks like a poorly constructed hammer. "Start smacking this safe."

"Shouldn't we be trying to figure out the combination?"

Gus sighs and glares at the ceiling like I'm the dumbest

person on the planet. "The last clue was telling us we need to use brute force, obviously. The combination is a decoy."

"A decoy?"

"Yes, Caleb. A decoy."

"Sorry, it's difficult to hear you now that you're not screaming in my face every three minutes."

Monty hides his laugh in the crook of his arm. Gus cracks a smile. "You know, you're funnier than you let on." He nudges me forward. "Come on. Take a swing."

"You're sure?"

He is two seconds away from using my face as a hammer on this safe. He rolls his eyes. "I'm sure. Swing away, pretty boy." He adjusts one of the sweatbands cuffed around his forearm. "Unless you think you won't be able to manage it?"

I stare pointedly at the faux hammer hanging limply in his left hand. I can hear Layla somewhere behind us, muttering to herself about antidote ingredients. I want this to be a good date for Layla. I want to be someone she can have fun with.

I want to help us escape this room.

"I can manage it."

Gus holds his hand out in the direction of the safe, like he's offering me the best table at a fancy restaurant. If only. I bet I wouldn't have to look at severed toes if I decided to take Layla to dinner like a normal human being.

"Have at it."

I sigh and lift the hammer.

My first hit doesn't do much of anything. The hammer

bounces uselessly off the top edge. But then I swing again, and again, focusing on the hinge of the thick metal door. Something rattles and the whole thing gives a deep, ominous-sounding groan in response. Gus presses in closer to my side.

"You're almost there," he breathes.

"Could you back up? You're freaking me out."

He grabs for my wrist. "Here," he says. "I can help."

"I don't need your help." I try to pull my wrist away while Gus tries to swing my arm for me. It's clunky, and uncomfortable, and I'm not able to use any force whatsoever. "Gus, let go of my arm."

"If you just—"

"I know how to swing a hammer."

"Do you? Because it doesn't look like you do."

"Just back up."

Except Gus doesn't back up. He tries to swing my arm backwards again—to get some momentum or piss me off, I'm not sure which. But as he does it, he doesn't pay a single ounce of attention to his own movement.

It happens in slow motion. Layla lets out a triumphant yell from behind us and I turn halfway to see what she's up to. Gus doesn't do a thing to slow his motion and his arm rockets back as he tries to force me on the safe. In all of the chaos of the motion and the noise and the distraction, my face gets in the way.

A blinding pain explodes in my left eye. I go from standing next to Gus to flat on my back on the floor, my vision swimming. Hazy globes of light dance with the severed heads hanging from the ceiling until I'm so dizzy I think I might be sick. I close my eyes with a groan.

The bruises from the roller rink make themselves known.

I am a catastrophic mess.

The zombie soundtrack comes to an abrupt halt. I hear the frantic pounding of feet in the hallway and then the slam of the door being thrown open, a high-pitched screech of an airhorn. Four different sets of explicit words echo around my head.

Monty is the first to speak after the sound fizzles out.

"For fuck's sake, Eric. What the hell?"

"Injury on the floor!" Eric yells. There's really no need for that kind of yelling. "The game is suspended!"

"I think we can go ahead and call the game forfeited," I manage from the floor. There is no way I'm hauling myself up and finishing this thing. I'm tapped out. Completely and utterly done. For the second time in as many days, I roll to my side and lift up to my knees. I hold myself there, my head hanging limply between my shoulders. Layla's small hand presses gently at the base of my spine.

"Are you okay?"

"Fine," I mumble. Bruised, probably. Embarrassed as hell, definitely. I crawl my way to a standing position and avoid her eyes. Mainly because I can't see out of one of them.

It's a small consolation that Gus is shamefaced by the door, his big arms crossed over his chest. He's not the one that'll have to teach a class to a bunch of kids with a shiner for the next couple of weeks, though, so it's not too comforting.

"I'm really sorry, man. I tend to get lost in the heat of the moment."

That's an understatement if I've ever heard one. I glare at him with my one good eye. I recognize that he didn't intentionally try to punch me in the face, but I need to not be in this room anymore. I reach blindly behind me for Layla. "We're leaving now."

"Hold on a second!"

A closet I thought was locked swings open in the back right corner. Billy limps his way out of it, his face covered in zombie makeup.

We all stare at him as he picks his way over the props littered across the floor.

"I thought you said no one was going to pop out at us," Layla says.

"I didn't even know Billy was here." Eric is a combination of bewildered and resigned. I guess this isn't the first time Billy has randomly popped out of a closet in the middle of a session.

Billy stops right in front of me, his hand searching inside his jacket pocket. He has paint there, too—something grotesque that makes it look like his fingers have been chewed to the bone. I wish I were more surprised.

He hands me a piece of paper.

"What's this?"

"It says that you won't hold *Quest For Escape* liable in the event of an injury."

"Shouldn't I have filled this out before we started?"

Gus perks up in the corner. "Can I add my name to one of those paragraphs?"

"Enough." Layla snatches the paper out of my hand, loops her arm through mine, and starts tugging us towards the door that leads to the hallway. "We'll take a look, Billy. But no promises."

"But—"

"My date and I are leaving."

Gus gets a sly smile on his face. Well. As much of his face as I can see. "Date, huh?"

Layla flicks him on our exit. "You shut your mouth."

"Sure thing, Laylabug."

"I'M STARTING to think I'm the problem."

Layla and I are propped up against the back of my Jeep in the parking lot of the grocery store, a tub of ice cream balanced on the bumper between us, a bag of frozen corn over half of my face. Heat rises off the asphalt, a shimmer close to the ground where everything goes hazy. I tilt my head to the side so I can get a good look at her out of the eye not currently covered by produce.

"How do you figure?"

She pokes listlessly at the top of the ice cream with her spoon. "You've barely gotten out of these last two dates alive." She doesn't look at me. "Maybe you're not the one that's bad at dating."

"I'd hardly call our last date bad when we got to leave with this."

I hold up the picture that Eric made us take before we left *Quest For Escape.* Apparently it's part of the entrance fee to get a souvenir photo taken at the end of your hour. Now that I have a little distance, the photo is objectively hilarious. Layla is glaring at Gus, Gus is staring at the floor, I'm doing my best to smile with my eye swollen shut, and Clint is laughing so hard he's bent at the waist. Montgomery only got half of himself in the frame. Billy is lurking in the back corner, only his eyes visible through the facepaint.

I think I might put it on my desk. Right next to Fernando.

Layla doesn't respond. I nudge her shoulder with mine. "I don't think we're the problem here. I think it's ... everything else."

"Are you saying we're cosmically destined to be bad at dating forever?"

"No." I nod my head towards the grocery store where I can see at least five people by the windows who are pretending to be browsing but really they're just watching us in the parking lot. Cindy Croswell has been examining oranges for close to seventeen minutes. Bridget forgot to turn the flash off her phone when she aimed it at us ten minutes ago. "I'm saying this town has too much time on their hands."

Layla follows my line of sight. "Ah."

"Everyone knows us here," I explain. "We can't get any privacy."

Layla arches her eyebrow, spoon in her mouth. I stare a little too long at the way her bottom lip drags against the cheap plastic—her tongue at the corner of her lips. "And what are you going to do with privacy, huh?"

I adjust the bag of corn on my face. "Try not to get killed."

She snorts and kicks her legs back and forth, her toes barely skimming the pavement. She's quiet, another two spoonfuls of ice cream while I wait. "You want to leave town for our next date?"

I'm amazed she still wants to go on any dates at all with me at this point. My face must communicate something similar because her gaze softens. She digs her spoon into the ice cream carton and holds it up between us for me to take a bite. A reassurance in the form of caramel chocolate swirl.

"I think it's in our best interest."

I curl my fingers around her wrist and hold her hand steady as I take my bite, my thumb against the silky skin on the inside of her wrist. I can feel the steady beat of her pulse beneath my thumb, delicate and light.

I drop my hand. Layla keeps the spoon there between us, suspended, as her stare lingers on my mouth.

"Do I have chocolate on my face?"

She shakes her head and digs her spoon back into the carton, focused entirely on wedging a caramel out from the icy depths. "You'll text me this week?"

I peel the frozen corn from my face with a wince. "Yeah, of course. And I'll see you tomorrow for croissants and coffee."

She frowns at my face. "Maybe an ice pack to go, too."

"It doesn't look better?"

She shakes her head. I sigh.

"You win some, you lose some."

"It felt like a lose-lose tonight," Layla says. She hops off the back of my car and pops the lid on the ice cream.

"Nah, there was a win."

She loops around to the passenger side, watching me from overtop the cab of the car. "I know you don't like the picture that much."

I kind of do, but that's not what I'm talking about.

"I got to spend time with you, didn't I?"

She smiles, wide and bright and beautiful.

"Oh, Caleb," she sighs. She tugs open the door to my Jeep. "Ten out of ten."

NINE

LAYLA

THERE'S a secret at the bakehouse that not even the phone tree has uncovered yet. A confidential, classified, undisclosed piece of information that I've held close to my chest for years. Beckett doesn't know. Luka doesn't know. Evelyn doesn't have a clue. I think Stella suspects something, but she's never questioned me about it.

I think she realizes the enormity of the secret.

"Would you hurry up?" Ms. Beatrice struggles with the industrial-sized box of shortbread cookies in her arms. "I can't stand here like this all day."

"It's been twenty-three seconds," I whisper back. I fumble with the keys in my hand. "You don't have to hold them all day. Just until I get the key in the lock."

On the third Wednesday of every month, Ms. Beatrice and I have an exchange of goods. She brings me three dozen shortbread cookies and I give her six pies. We sit in my kitchen in complete darkness, consult on each other's recipes, and drink exactly two cups of coffee. She gives me a boatload of crap about how I prep my pie crusts and then she disappears back into the mist from whence she came.

It's all very clandestine.

The entire town thinks we're in competition with one another. We've carefully curated that reputation over the years with scripted conversations and intentional slights. Immature? Probably. Manipulative? Oh, certainly. We both do better business when it looks like we're feuding. People stop by Ms. B's in the morning to try her scones, and then come by the bakehouse in the afternoon and buy some of mine to compare. Little do they know they're the exact same recipe.

We are the Pat's and Geno's of baked goods.

The reality is a lot less exciting. Ms. Beatrice took me under her wing shortly after I moved into town. I think she got tired of me doom scrolling at her countertop while I frantically searched for a job. One day she demanded I help her in the back kitchen and that was it. I was hooked. I showed up every single day before the sun and Ms. B taught me everything she knew.

She's not nearly as scary as she likes to make everyone believe.

I finally manage to get the key in the lock and we shuffle through the back door of the bakehouse. She drops her cardboard box on the island and begins to unload it.

"Added some jelly thumbprint cookies, too," she tells me, tossing a bag of tiny round cookies colored with dots of strawberry and apricot jam right next to my mixer. "You never get those right."

I snort and flick on the coffee machine. "You know if people were to find out how nice you actually are, your entire persona would crumble."

Beatrice thrives on her threatening image. She serves up frowns with her coffee and doesn't bother with pleasantries when she drops a quiche on the table in front of you. But her lemon bars more than make up for it, so I suppose she can act however she wants.

"No one will ever find out." She settles into one of the stools, her long gray hair tumbling down her back, the lines of her face softer in the muted light of predawn. She's wearing her standard ripped up band t-shirt beneath denim overalls this morning, heavy black boots on her feet. She pulls a tattered-up spiral notebook out of the bag on the floor and pats the cover twice. "Let's talk rhubarb."

We sit in my kitchen and we talk about rhubarb and dark chocolate and hazelnut ganache. We discuss the consistency of shortcake batter and what we're going to make with the strawberry crop Beckett is almost ready to harvest. She criticizes my lemon custard and I give her grief about her homemade whipped cream.

It is an ordinary Wednesday morning.

Until someone starts pounding on my front door.

We freeze with our mugs halfway to our mouths. Ms. Beatrice's eyes dart to mine, accusing.

"Who is that?" Beatrice looks like she's ready to climb out the tiny narrow window above my work sink.

"I have no idea."

No one is ever here this early. No one except for us.

Another knock raps against the glass window in the front. I slip from my stool and crack open the door that leads to the front of the shop as Ms. Beatrice drops to the floor.

"What are you doing?" I whisper, incredulous.

"Hiding," she whispers back. She crawls two feet forward to get a look out the door and tilts her head to the side, a sly grin tipping her mouth. "That looks like Caleb."

I squint. It does look like Caleb, though I have no idea what he's doing here at five in the morning.

He knocks again, not realizing he's being watched by two creepy-ass women lurking in the back.

"Layla?" His voice is muffled by the thick glass of the front door. "It's me." He shifts on his feet and then glances over his shoulder at the dark cluster of trees behind him. "I brought you some breakfast."

"Does he realize you literally specialize in breakfast?"

"Shut up," I hush her. "Where did you park your car?"

"In the gravel lot Beckett uses for storage. The one behind the pine trees and the chicken coop he keeps insisting he's not building." She arches an eyebrow at me. "Do you think I'm an idiot?"

Kind of. With the way she's army crawling across the floor of my kitchen.

"Wait until I open the front door to slip out the back. I'll distract him."

She snickers. "I bet you will."

I don't bother dignifying that with a response. I smooth my palms over my hair, set down my coffee mug, and slip through the door to the front. Caleb straightens as soon as he sees me, a grin blossoming on his handsome face. A cascade of butterflies erupts low in my belly, my own smile as easy as breathing. I feel like I'm caught on the other end of a string, pulled closer and closer to wherever he is.

I flick down my row of locks, watching him through the glass. Khaki pants and a short sleeved button up today, ironed to perfection. My eyes travel from the jut of his collarbones to the dimple in his cheek. The straight line of his nose and the ... absolutely horrendous black and purple bruise around his eye.

I open the door and usher him in. "Your eye looks terrible."

But also really incredible, somehow. Attractive in a rough-and-tumble sort of way. With the khakis, its downright delightful—two drastically opposing looks on one man.

He touches the swell of his cheek with the tips of his fingers. "It does, doesn't it? It's why I wore the khakis. I thought they might help."

"Help you look like a 90's sitcom dad?"

He shrugs. "Help everyone be focused on something that isn't my face. The kids think it's hysterical when I wear khakis, for whatever reason. I don't know what I'm going to tell them about the eye, though. I can't tell them the truth."

Yeah, I'm not so sure Caleb should tell his students that he got a black eye after Gus elbowed him in the face while trying to use a fake foot to open a fake safe in a fake zombie apocalypse. I imagine the teenagers would have something to say about that.

Caleb frowns and steps past me to the countertop. He drops a plain brown paper bag on top. "Maybe I'll say it was something with a cougar."

"Oh?"

"Or a helicopter. I haven't decided yet."

"Both are good options." I peer over his shoulder at the bag, grease starting to bleed through the bottom. My stomach gives a ferocious rumble of appreciation. "What did you bring me?"

"A bacon and egg sandwich." He props his hip against the counter at my side. I stare hard at the khaki pants. They're distracting me from his face, but probably not for the reasons he's counting on. They fit him ... really well. "I figured you wouldn't want to cook something for yourself."

Something in my chest twists. A light pluck that echoes and shakes. I don't like cooking for myself. After spending most of my time making food for everyone else, I usually just eat the scraps of whatever is left over from the batch of what I'm working on.

It means something that he picked up on that.

"You brought it here for me?"

He nods, a bemused smile twisting his lips. "I did. Sorry it's so early. I wanted to catch you before I head over to the school."

"Early today?"

"Bus duty."

I can't stop looking at the bag on the countertop. He stopped somewhere. For me. Got up early, made an extra stop, and drove all the way out here.

"Thank you," I whisper.

He lifts his hand between us, but then seems to think better of it. He drops it back to his side. "It's no problem."

I want to know what he was going to do with that hand. "Still, I—"

Something clatters in the back kitchen—cookie sheets, by the sound of it. I stare at the back door with wide eyes and Caleb—Caleb is around the corner and through the back door before I can even think to stop him.

"Oh, shit," I whisper. I hope Beatrice is sprinting through the fields right now. Why did she take so long to leave? I'd bet all my chocolate croissants and my very favorite spatula that she was listening at the door, that nosy little troublemaker.

I follow after Caleb at a much slower pace and with a lot less enthusiasm. By the time I make it to the kitchen, he's standing in the middle of it with his hands on his hips, staring intently at the back door swinging wide open.

"We need to call Dane," he says in a stern, hard voice that zings right up my spine.

I ignore him and walk towards the door. I don't want a bunch of bugs buzzing around while I'm trying to make rhubarb pie. A heavy arm snakes around my waist and Caleb lifts me up and away like I'm one of my bags of sugar. He sets me back on my feet by the sink, his arm still firmly around my waist.

It is disturbing how much I enjoy it.

"Someone was in your kitchen," he tells me, his dark eyebrows in a low slant over his brown eyes. Specks of amber and gold dance as he gazes down at me, his hand clenching at my waist. It fans the little flame in my chest until I feel it ricocheting down to my palms. In the back of my knees and in the hollow of my throat.

I swallow hard.

"Caleb."

He gives me one slow blink. He's reluctant to stop scanning the place like an ax murderer is about to jump out from my walk-in fridge. The escape room experience really did a number on him. "What?"

"I have a—well, I have a confession."

That gets his attention. He looks down at me and his jaw clenches. "Yes?"

"It's not a big deal."

"Okay."

"I don't want you to freak out."

He swallows again, bracing his palm against the table at my hip. With the black eye and this—this look on his face, he almost looks like a different person. It's like the Hawaiian shirt revelation all over again. *Caleb is hot,* my brain supplies in a dreamy, singsong voice. *Caleb is really hot.*

Hot and protective and kind and sweet and he smells like fresh ground coffee. He brought me breakfast, practically kicked in the door to my kitchen, and he is standing so, so close.

Trouble.

"I hate to break it to you, Layla, but I'm about thirty percent of the way towards freaking out."

"Okay, so." Where do I even begin? *The year was 2013 and Beatrice and I decided to form a secret society where we share recipes and—*

"Layla."

Right.

"I had someone over for coffee this morning," I say in a rush.

Caleb blinks at me. His face slackens slightly and then he blinks again. He pushes away from the countertop and takes two steps back. He looks at the ceiling, then the floor. He clears his throat.

Awkward silence stretches between us and I clasp my hands together.

"Oh. That's—that's fine." A blush flares to life on his cheeks, a bright and ferocious red. But this isn't the same one he gets when he's quietly pleased, or when he's smiling so hard it looks like his face might stick that way. Or even when I trail my fingers down his arm. This is— he's *embarrassed*.

And I am hopelessly, terribly confused.

Caleb stands in the middle of my kitchen with his shoulders hunched, looking like he wants to be anywhere else but here. He stares hard at the island. The stools slightly out of their normal spots and the two coffee mugs on the countertop. I watch his throat bob with a swallow.

"I think I'm going to—" He hitches his thumb over his shoulder, still not looking at me. "I'm gonna go."

"What? No." I grab his arm as he tries to slide past me. He stops abruptly, but still refuses to look at my face. My shoes get the full force of his focused attention. The stack of mixing bowls on the bottom of my shelf. A row of colorful cupcake liners. "You brought me breakfast. Stay. Eat with me."

"I don't—"

"Please."

He sighs. A short, frustrated sound. "Layla."

"Caleb."

"I think I should go."

"I think you should stay."

He finally relents and looks at my face. I get a good look at his. I frown. I don't think I've ever seen him look so disappointed.

"I thought we said we'd tell each other if we wanted to end it," he offers in a low voice. "I wouldn't have minded, if you'd told me. I understand."

And, oh. *Oh.* He thought I had—he thought I had an early morning *date* over. He thought I was back in my kitchen having breakfast with someone else. A romantic someone else. I think about how long it took me to get to the front door. How he had to knock at least three times.

I wince.

Caleb tries to move past me again and I grip him hard with both hands. He could steamroll me if he wanted, but he stays perfectly still and stares holes into the floor by our feet.

"Caleb, I have another confession."

"I'm not sure I want to hear it."

"I—" I stumble over my words, searching for an explanation that makes sense.

"It's alright. Really, Layla. Third date is the charm for me, afterall." He laughs a little bit and I hate it. How it sounds like he's laughing at himself. "Please don't—you don't have to explain anything to me."

I ignore him. "On the third Wednesday of every month, I have a standing appointment with Ms. Beatrice."

Caleb's head slowly raises. He looks at me, his dark eyes watching. Cautious. "Ms. Beatrice?"

"Yes. She comes over and we sit here and we talk about all of the things we have planned for the rest of the month."

Caleb's mouth twists, confused. "Why doesn't she just —why was the door wide open?"

"Because it is a secret, Caleb," I say, deadly serious. "We heard you at the door and she ran. Can you imagine the utter destruction this news would rain down upon the town if people knew?"

"I don't think—"

"We have a reputation to uphold. Everyone thinks we hate each other. Secrecy is key."

His lips twitch again but this time it looks like a smile. A normal smile. "I see."

"Yes," I nod. "Now you see." I curl my hands around his

arms and shake him as much as I'm able. Which is ... not that much. "Did you really think I was two-timing you with some mystery breakfast date?"

"Maybe."

"You did."

"Alright, I did. But to be fair, you were being very suspicious."

I arch an eyebrow. "Who has a date at five in the morning?"

His blush lingers. "I'm here, aren't I?"

He smiles, gentle and slow and achingly careful. I want to trace it with my fingertips and press it deeper into his skin. I don't want him to have to be careful with me.

Caleb doubts himself in so many ways—big and small. He was so ready to believe that I was done with him. That he wasn't worth further consideration.

It makes me sad.

I slip my hands down his arms until my fingers are curled around his wrists. "Yes, you are here. And with a bagel, no less. All Ms. Beatrice brought were some short-bread cookies and a bunch of complaints."

"Hm." Caleb turns his hands until our palms are pressed together. Until his fingers are threaded through mine. We've gotten pretty good at this hand-holding thing. It's everything else that's a work in progress. "That raises an interesting point, actually."

I blink and watch the way the color on his cheeks fades to a light dusting of pink, his eyes becoming slightly calculating. My brain is moving a little slower than usual, standing this close to him. "What does? The cookies?"

"No, your clandestine early morning meetings."

"Oh. What's interesting about it?"

Caleb squeezes my hands and guides me closer until the toes of my tennis shoes are tucked neatly between his scuffed boots. My apron brushes up against the starchy material of his button-up. A breath shudders out of me.

"What's in it for me?" he whispers. He tugs our hands until both of my arms are wrapped low around his waist, his palms smoothing up my arms. His touch is intentional, slow—heavy and delicious. A beam of golden light slips through the gauzy white curtains of my kitchen and slants across his boots, working slowly up our legs as the sun rises with the rest of the world. I like him like this, here in the quiet. When it's just me and him and a bagel sandwich in a paper bag on the counter. Shortbread cookies in a tin and the warm puff of his breath against the skin of my neck. His nose nudges my chin and I tilt my head to the side, exposing more of my skin for him to explore.

"In it for you?" I ask hazily, too focused on the slow press of his body against mine.

"This is a secret, isn't it?" His voice is lower now, a deep rumble that I can practically feel. His bottom lip grazes the hollow just beneath my ear and I shiver. "What do I get for keeping your secrets, Layla Dupree?"

I hum and trace the curve of his jaw with my eyes. The fan of dark eyelashes across the apple of his cheeks. What color would they burn if I slipped another button free from this fancy shirt? I watch with interest as his lips part on a shaky sigh. It seems whatever game he just started is affecting him as much as it's affecting me.

I smile.

"What would you like, Caleb Alvarez?"

He tips his head forward and his nose bumps mine. One hand leaves the curve of my arm to settle between my shoulder blades instead, a gentle pressure until I arch into him. He lays his palm flat and drags down, down, down, fingers catching in the strings of my apron. A smile starts at the edge of his mouth. I want to bite it.

I clench my fist in his shirt.

"I want—" His fingers find a single apron string and he tugs.

The material against my chest begins to loosen. I'm more turned on than if he'd slipped his hand inside my shirt.

"What do you want?" I ask, voice catching.

His other hand cups my neck. He brushes his mouth lower against my jaw, and then back further, right against my pulse. Not quite a kiss. Just his lips grazing soft skin. His sigh tickles the delicate skin there, a low sound of appreciation under his breath. My knees go weak.

"I want some of those shortbread cookies," he whispers into my ear.

I groan and drop my forehead to his chest. He laughs in the quiet of my kitchen, rich and loud and deep. I tip my head back so I can glare at him. "Has anyone ever told you that you're a tease?"

He shakes his head, both of his arms looped low around my waist now. He rocks us back and forth and I can't help but smile, too. I like every version of himself that he shows me—the full spectrum of Caleb Alvarez. "Nope. You'd be the first."

"Lucky me." I rap my knuckles against his collarbone and push away, intent on getting a solid slab of countertop between us. I don't know when I started thinking about kissing Caleb, just that I have been. Incessantly. It's a buzzing under my skin and an echo in my blood.

Maybe it was at the roller rink, when I hauled him off the floor with both of my arms wrapped around his, cursing under his breath as we struggled together. Maybe it was in the escape room when he wrapped his arms around my hips and tugged me off that table.

Or maybe it was that first night at the bar, with his stupid Hawaiian shirt and messy hair, humidity making everything sticky and hot.

When he looked at me like he saw me.

I don't know. I only know that I want his mouth on mine. I want that smile of his that edges sharper on one side pressed into my skin. Greedy hands and those dimples winking to life. I want to unravel Caleb like one of my apron strings.

It's confusing. Surprising.

Wildly distracting.

"What're you thinking about?" he murmurs.

I'm thinking about how he'd taste after one of these

shortbread cookies. Whether he's had his coffee yet and if I'd be able to taste that, too.

I smile to myself. If he only knew.

I poke him in the chest and then spin away. "Something delicious."

TEN
CALEB

I THINK I pushed too hard with Layla.

After our moment in the bakery, she's been different. Not upset. Just—muted, I think.

She still gives me a grin that feels like it's only for me and her touch still lingers over my knuckles or wrist when I stop by for my coffee and croissant. We have plans for tomorrow night and she's responded to every single one of my text messages. But she feels far away.

"Tal vez deberías besarla, osezno."

To be clear, I did not ask my grandmother for advice.

She just took one look at me sitting at the tiny, rickety wooden table in her kitchen and decided to bestow it upon me. Along with an entire container of chilaquiles.

I came to her house for exactly one of those things.

"Do you have any hot sauce?"

She smacks me in the ear with her spoon.

"It does not need hot sauce. It is perfect as it is." She

mumbles something in Spanish under her breath that sounds vaguely like *spoiled* and *hot sauce*. I decide to keep my mouth shut.

"Where are you taking her tomorrow?" she asks.

"I don't know," I mumble around a mouthful of food. "She said she wanted to pick where we go this time."

Probably a good idea considering how the last two went. My black eye has faded to a muted yellow and the swelling is almost non-existent. I can walk without a limp now. Best not to tempt fate.

Even if it feels like I've messed up.

My grandmother nods in approval. "Good. A man who can take direction from a woman is a man worth keeping."

"Gracias, abuela."

"I was complimenting her, not you."

I roll my eyes to the ceiling. "Gracias, abuela."

"Cómete tus chilaquiles," she tells me, fussing with the dishwasher. I'd offer to help, but she'll probably smack me with her spoon again if I get up from this table before this whole container is empty. She has a thing about food. "You should have kissed her," she tells me again, in English this time.

I poke my fork around in my bowl. "I'm not so sure."

"Why?" My grandmother turns and arches an eyebrow at me, her hair piled in a loose bun. She's wearing the earrings my abuelo got her for their fiftieth wedding anniversary, two studs made to look like seashells, glowing in the light of the kitchen. Her bright red dress swings back and forth around her ankles, her face softened by age and gentle amusement. "Was I not married for almost seventy years? Do I not have sound advice?"

"Por supuesto que sí, abuela. I just—I think I made her uncomfortable," I mumble. I think I took it too far. I had wanted to tease her a little bit, but then it tumbled out of control.

I tumbled out of control.

I could smell sugar on her skin. Fresh strawberries and shortbread and her shampoo—something light and floral like rose petals. I slid my palm down her back and felt every ridge of her spine, the deep shuddering breath that she let out when her nose brushed against my neck. When I dipped my head, and she made a sound in the back of her throat, I almost picked her up and spread her out against the kitchen island.

"Who did you make uncomfortable?"

The screen door on the back of my grandmother's house creaks open and Charlie strolls into the kitchen like he's supposed to be here—like he does this every day—a bouquet of flowers in his hand and his suit jacket over one arm. He ignores my stupefied look and presents the flowers to my grandmother, a kiss on both of her cheeks.

"Hermosa como siempre, Mariana," he tells her.

She beams at him.

I frown, beyond confused. "What are you doing here?"

My grandmother makes a *tsch* sound and taps me between the shoulder blades with her spoon. A warning shot. "No seas grosero, osezno."

"Yeah, bear cub." Charlie raises both of his eyebrows,

delighted and smug. "Don't be rude."

Charlie lives in New York. Charlie works in New York. I don't understand why he's standing in my grandmother's kitchen on a weekday afternoon. I ignore my grandmother's use of my childhood nickname in front of Charlie and instead focus on the more important thing. Like why she has three Tupperware dishes for him when I only have one.

"Eres un ángel," Charlie croons, tossing what I assume is thousands of dollars in custom tailoring over the chair opposite of me. The guy is a study in contradictions. The last time I saw him, he was making my brother's coat closet his new home. I'm happy to see he's recovered. "Un tesoro. Una reina."

My grandmother flushes a brilliant shade of red. I guess that's where I got my blushing from. I stare at both of them, still dumbfounded.

"What is going on?"

Charlie collapses in his chair and folds his tie over his shoulder. He rearranges the bowl in front of him. "What does it look like? I'm having my monthly lunch with your grandma."

"Monthly lunch."

"Yes."

"With my grandma."

"Yes, Caleb. That is exactly what I just said. Very good."

"Since when?"

"Since he did my taxes for me last year," my grandmother offers from the stove. She's already cooking something else. Honestly, it's a miracle that Charlie is the only one who's walked in the door so far. Usually it's a constant stream of my cousins in and out. I think my Tio Benjamín still has a room here. "He is a good boy."

Charlie spears a tomato on his fork and brandishes it at me like a weapon. "Yeah, bear cub. I'm a good boy."

"Don't call me that."

"Too late. It's already imprinted on my mind. You are now *bear cub* forever."

I sigh and take another bite of my late lunch. Nevermind that chilaquiles are a breakfast dish and my grandmother told me this was all she had left. What a little liar. "Did you really drive all the way down here to have lunch with my grandmother?"

"Of course I did." I watch as my grandmother hands him a glass of lemonade and he whispers something to her in Spanish. She cackles, loud and bright, the sound bouncing off the walls and windows. A smile tugs at my lips before I can remind myself that I'm irritated. I've always loved her laugh.

"I had to bring some paperwork for Nova, too," he continues. "She's trying to expand her tattoo studio."

"That's right. She wants to buy that space behind the flower shop, right?"

"That's her plan." Charlie pops open another lid and lets out a deep, rumbling groan of appreciation. That bastard. My abuela made him tres leches.

"Abuela," I groan. "You told me you didn't have any left."

She only turns halfway from the stove, her face in profile. "I didn't."

"Then why does Charlie have half a cake?"

"Because he got what was left." She pulls her spoon from the massive pot on the stovetop and drags her finger along the edge. She tastes the sauce, makes a face, sprinkles in some chili powder, and goes back to stirring. "Now, are you a man or a child? Why are you sitting there whining?"

"Tu postre es mi favorito," I grumble. "You know I love tres leches."

"I was not talking about the dessert. I was talking about the woman."

Charlie props his chin in his hand and wiggles in his chair. A man of his size should look ridiculous doing that. But of course, he doesn't. He just looks eager and amused, his fork dangling from his hand and his cheeks bulging with whipped cream, cinnamon, and sponge cake. Asshole. That was my cake.

With his dark hair and bright blue eyes—he looks just like his half-sister, Stella.

They share a lack of subtlety, too.

"Let's talk more about this woman," Charlie says.

"No, thank you."

"Oh, relax." Charlie opens his third container and rolls out another string of compliments to my grandmother in Spanish. I didn't even know he could speak Spanish. "I know you and Layla have a thing."

"A thing?"

"A thing. I'll hand it to you, though. I think this is the first time I've seen the phone tree stumped. No one knows what's actually going on with the two of you. Gus had some ideas after the escape room incident, but—"

"What?"

"—but no one knows for sure."

Well, I suppose that makes two of us. Or ... however many people are on the phone tree at this point in time.

I deflect. "How did you get on the phone tree?"

Charlie makes a face. "Why wouldn't I be on the phone tree?"

"Because you don't live here."

He taps his fist over his chest twice. "My heart is here. That's what matters to the phone tree. Now stop stalling and explain what's going on with you and Layla."

"We're ... dating."

Charlie narrows his eyes at me. "You don't sound convinced."

I fidget in my seat. I guess I'm not. Especially after what happened the other day. Or, didn't happen. I don't know. "We are practice dating. For a month. There's an expiration date."

There has to be. I've only been on two dates with Layla, both of which ended in physical disaster, and I can still feel myself slipping. I like seeing her smile. I like hearing her laugh. I like holding her hand and ducking my chin against the top of her head. I like her dry humor and the way she calls me on my bullshit, every single time. I like getting to know the different parts of her. I like *her*.

One month. It'll be enough.

It has to be.

"Whose idea was that?"

"Mine." Maybe. "It makes sense like this."

"I hate to break this to you, my friend. This doesn't make any sense at all. But whatever helps you sleep at night."

"He didn't kiss her," my grandmother offers from the stove. "When she wanted to be kissed."

Charlie leans back in his seat with a heavy, disappointed exhale. "Dude." His eyes are like saucers. "You gotta kiss her when she wants to be kissed."

I busy myself with my silverware, staring hard at the tabletop. "I don't know if she wanted to be kissed."

Charlie and my grandmother make the same dismissive sound. My grandmother tacks on a few colorful curse words at the end of hers.

"You know," Charlie insists. "Think about it. Was she giving you the signs?"

Her hands clenched in the back of my shirt. Her nose against mine. That little sound she made, right in the back of her throat when I found her apron string and pulled.

"See?" Charlie points his fork at me again. "She wanted to be kissed."

I'M STILL THINKING about it as I walk up her driveway two hours later, some lavender clutched in my left hand. I'm thinking about it when I knock and I'm thinking about it when I hear faint steps down the hallway behind her front door.

Layla opens the door and smiles at me. She's wearing a short white sundress that makes her skin look golden and also makes me want to drop to my knees, curl my fingers around the hem, and drag it up around her belly button.

I swallow.

"This is for you."

She makes no move to grab the lavender, her smile flickering at the edges. "Is everything okay?"

I nod. And then I shake my head. She swings her door open a little more and beckons me in.

"Come on. We don't have to leave right away."

I step into her hallway and stop. Layla's house is perfectly, wonderfully her. There's color everywhere, from the pale pink rug across the worn hardwood floors to the deep, navy blue couch pressed up against the wall, covered with pillows of all shapes and sizes. There's at least fifty throw blankets of various colors and textures in a basket by her bookshelf, plants and books and picture frames competing for space.

I pick up a picture in a gilded golden frame, the metal shaped like vines twisted around the photo inside. Layla and three women that look just like her. The same hair and eyes and smile, but still Layla stands out from the rest. Her smile is a little bit more wild, a little bit more free.

"Your sisters?"

Layla nods. "When we were all together for my dad's birthday."

"You don't talk about them much."

She shrugs and picks up a blanket spread out across the ottoman and folds it into a neat square. "We're not as close as I'd like. When I went away to college, they stayed close to my parents." She tucks her hair behind her ears in a tic I've come to realize means she's uncomfortable. I frown. She shrugs and gives me a small smile. "We don't all have a horde of cousins willing to wear Hawaiian shirts for us."

I set the frame back down. "They haven't visited you here?"

She shakes her head. "Not yet, no. I think my dad is still hoping it's a phase. The baking thing."

What Layla does is so much more than baking. I hate for her to refer to the business she's created for herself as a *thing*. "The baking thing?"

She hums and collects a half empty jam jar from another side table. "Stole it from Beckett," she explains quietly. She blows out a puff of air, fortifying herself. "I went to school for mathematics and engineering. I don't know if you know that. I was always very good with numbers but, I don't know, I was never excited about it. I was feeling a little lost my senior year, a little alone, and Stella—Stella was my best friend. So I declined some of the job offers I had waiting and decided to follow her here instead. I don't think my dad has quite forgiven me for that."

"He wanted you to be an engineer?"

She nods. "I think he was holding out hope that I'd join

the Navy just like he did. My sisters are all involved in military life in some way, either with jobs themselves, supporting the base, or marrying military men. I think I'm a disappointment over here with my coffee and croissants."

I frown. "I'm never disappointed by your coffee and croissants."

She gives me a small, timid smile. "I know you're not."

"No, but Layla." It's important that she hears me. That she understands. "You know it's more than a bakery, right? What you do?"

She shrugs and I swallow down the rest of my burning curiosity. I have so many questions resting on the tip of my tongue. Why did she study engineering if she never enjoyed it? What did she want to do? Why did she feel like a small town on the coastal edge of Maryland was the only place she could go to? Is this why she feels like she only deserves the bare minimum from men?

It's reassuring, at least, that she seems happy here now. That she's found a home for herself in Inglewild. I glance at the picture of her and her sisters one more time and nudge it with my thumb until it's centered on her little table. Of course Layla would keep a picture of them in her home, despite the disappointments.

"Their loss," I whisper quietly. Too quiet for her to hear.

I watch her as she wanders into her kitchen, her white dress taunting me as it whispers against her thighs. It's so easy to picture her here, tucked in the couch with a mug of coffee. Working in the kitchen with her hair loose and one of her scarves fluttering down the bare skin of her back. Humming as she rolls out a pie crust, flour over every square inch of countertop.

"What's got that look on your face?"

You keep showing me pieces of yourself that I want to collect like seashells. I can't stop thinking about kissing you and I have no idea how you'd feel about blurring those lines. I don't want to scare you. I don't want to get myself in too deep.

Though I think it might be a little too late for that last one.

I shrug and slip onto a pale pink stool that looks like it came straight out of Candyland. I glance at the crossword puzzle she's left half-finished on the countertop. The answer for 7 across is HOPELESS, I'm pretty sure. That feels appropriate.

She pauses in her rearrangement of the vases on her countertop. Six of them, all filled with different sorts of flowers. It makes me smile. "Our arrangement means you can ask me things, Caleb. That's the whole point."

Our arrangement. I'm grateful for the reminder. I have nothing to lose by talking to Layla, except maybe some semblance of my sanity. I clear my throat and place the lavender down on the edge of the counter. "Did you want me to kiss you the other day?"

She fumbles the jam jar she just set to the side, sending it tumbling into her kitchen sink in a cacophony of sound. As soon as she rights it, she peeks at me over her shoulder.

"What?"

I rest my forearms on the counter and hold her eyes. "Did you want me to kiss you? In your bakehouse?"

"Well ..." She turns fully to face me, her hands busy with a dishrag. She hesitates and I watch her weigh her words. "I thought you might."

That doesn't exactly answer my question. Thinking someone might do something and wanting them to do it are two very different things. "Do you want me to kiss you, Layla?"

A low pulse begins somewhere near the base of my spine. I know my answer to that question. I want to kiss her. I want to kiss her more than I want another one of those cinnamon and sea salt bear claws, and that's saying something.

"People who date kiss each other, don't they?" Her voice is light, teasing. But her eyes hold a heat I've only seen in flashes before. I clench my hands on the edge of the countertop.

"They do."

"Then perhaps—" She reaches for the lavender I brought and her fingers graze the top of my hand. She dances them up to my wrist and taps there twice, continuing. Her voice drops to a husky rasp and goosebumps erupt along my skin. "—perhaps we should revisit the details of our arrangement."

Something in my chest unlocks, unravels, unspools. I flip my hand and catch hers with mine. I wrap my fingers around hers and squeeze. "Perhaps we should."

ELEVEN

LAYLA

I THOUGHT Caleb would kiss me right away.

After unexpectedly unloading some of my family baggage on him, I thought he'd get up from that stool, back me into my countertop, tangle his hand in my hair the same way he did with my apron strings, and give me one hell of a distraction. I thought he'd kiss me.

But he doesn't. Instead, he pulls his hand away from mine and ushers me out the door to the car like we just finished a conversation about the groceries, not the particulars of our physical boundaries.

He holds the door of his Jeep open for me and keeps his hand at the small of my back as I climb in. He lets me pick the radio station, and he keeps both hands on the wheel while I give him directions to the spot I've picked out for us. Wide open road, rolling green fields on either side of us. He kicks us up to seventy as soon as we hit the highway that leads straight to the coast, the warm wind whipping through my hair, my scarf twisting around me in a dance of pink and blue. I laugh as Caleb tries to tuck it behind my ear, but only manages to get it twisted around his wrist instead. I untangle it from my hair and leave it on his arm and he beams at me from the other side of the Jeep, pink on his cheeks.

The closer we get, the heavier the air gets. Sea salt and driftwood. Caramel from the taffy shop right on the corner of the boardwalk. The fields roll into soft dunes and willows, reaching their long green fingers to the sky, endless blue above us.

It's a perfect summer drive.

I just wish Caleb would kiss me.

I don't understand. I want Caleb to kiss me. I want to kiss Caleb. I thought I made that pretty clear. But he's driven us forty-five minutes down to the shore without a single press of his lips to mine and now I am confused.

"Are you going to kiss me or not?"

That's the beauty of our arrangement. I can ask whatever I want, whenever I want, without worrying that I might scare Caleb off. It's freeing in a way I never expected. I know that no matter what happens, we'll both be perfectly okay at the end of our month.

It's also an absolute delight to watch Caleb almost trip over his own feet as we walk through the parking lot to the beach, the gravel gradually changing to sand. We stopped for custard at the stand right before the beach, my hands curled around two orange creamsicle cones as Caleb attempts to tie my scarf back into my hair. The one in my left hand is starting to melt over my knuckles.

Caleb finishes with my hair and reaches for the hand with the slowly melting cone, unthinkingly guiding my messy fingers to his lips. My breath hitches when he lowers his mouth to my hand, bottom lip dragging across my knuckles, a slow drag of his tongue where the ice cream is sticky against my skin. He does it without hesitation—like we've been doing this for years—and now I'm the one tripping over my own feet.

"Not yet," he tells me, pulling his mouth away from my hand and steadying me with his arm over my shoulders. I certainly need it after that little performance. He tilts his custard cone to the side and saves some of the dripping ice cream with another obscene lick. Goosebumps erupt over every inch of my body. "I need to plan."

A laugh sputters out of me. "Oh yeah?"

He nods and takes another lick of his ice cream cone. "Yeah. You deserve a good kiss. A classic movie kind of kiss."

The tension I didn't even realize I was carrying disappears, just like that. Caleb wants to kiss me, too. Something tender and soft curls inside my chest. "Is that so?"

He nods and looks at me out of the corner of his eye. "Fireworks, shooting stars." He grins from behind a rapidly dwindling mountain of vanilla. "Et cetera."

"I'm interested in what et cetera means."

"I thought you might be."

"It sounds very complicated."

He shrugs, arm jostling against mine. His fingers trace a lazy pattern against the bare skin of my shoulder. I don't think he realizes he's doing it and it makes me like it even more, those hidden secrets written against my sun-kissed skin.

"Let me plan. I'll give you a heads up if that makes you feel better."

"I'd like that, thank you."

"My pleasure, Layla."

Something tells me it'll be my pleasure, too.

We stroll to a stop at the end of the reed fence that lines the small boardwalk down to the beach, the rolling dunes settling into soft, smooth sand. It's practically empty at this time of day, families packing up their chairs and umbrellas and towels and toys to head back to their hotels. We're the only ones on the beach moving closer to the surf, the crash of the rolling waves beckoning us forward.

I grab the blanket out of my bag and then the apple juice container, handing both to Caleb. He unfolds the blanket with one quick snap of his wrist as he stares at the apple juice container. I shouldn't find that so attractive.

"You brought apple juice?"

"Wine," I correct. "I didn't want to bring the bottle. Glass isn't allowed on the beach."

"Beautiful and smart," he tells me. He tries to peek into my bag. "What else do you have in there?"

A wedge of cheese. Some fresh baked bread wrapped in wax paper and tied with a scrap of bright pink string I found in the top drawer of my kitchen island. Some sopressata from Luka and—

"Is that strawberry shortcake?"

I hand him the container as he collapses to his knees on the blanket, hands reaching. I stay standing behind him as I sort through the rest of my bag. "It is."

"Can I eat this first?"

"We already had ice cream," I reason. "I think strawberry shortcake is the next logical step."

He makes a deeply appreciative sound and cracks open the top of the dish. I stop for a second and watch the top of his head as he reaches for a fork. Mussed hair and golden skin, the tips of his ears already a bit pink from the sun. I let my knuckles brush against the back of his neck and he tips his head until it's pressed to my thigh, his brown eyes smiling up at me. Sea salt air and the sound of the surf loud in my ears. Those lines by Caleb's eyes, crinkling just for me.

Well.

Me and my shortcake.

"If you don't sit down," he says, his smile deepening and laughter in his voice. "I'm going to eat all of this myself."

"It's a good thing I made it just for you, then."

I reach for my jug of apple juice and one of the paper cups I shoved in my bag and sit down next to him, my knee wedged against his thigh. He moves me slightly with his hand at my hip until I'm tucked against him—his big hand draped over my knee, our arms pressed cozily together.

He's looser with his affection now. It's like our conversation in my kitchen snipped the strings that were holding him back. It snipped some of mine, too. I know he worries about coming on too strong, but frankly I am starting to wish he'd come on a little stronger from time to time.

I offer him a sip from my dixie cup. "Tell me about your day?"

His smile deepens like it's the best question I could have possibly asked him. Like he's been waiting forever and ever for someone to ask him exactly that. For someone to care about the little details.

"Well, Jeremy handed in the first draft of his love poem assignment."

"Please, please, please tell me you brought it with you."

He pulls a folded up piece of paper out of his back pocket and hands it to me. I squeal in delight.

"No, no." I press the paper back into his hand. "I demand a dramatic reading."

Caleb snorts a laugh and unfolds it with one hand against the blanket while he takes a monstrous bite of shortcake with the other. I pay an unhealthy amount of attention to the way his jaw works, the bit of cream clinging at the corner of his lips. He scoops another forkful out and holds it in front of my mouth. I lean forward and curl my hand around his wrist, holding the fork steady between us. Tart strawberries, sweet and fluffy cream. A perfect bite that makes me hum with satisfaction.

I chance a look at Caleb's face. His eyes are heavy and

focused on my mouth, his chest rising and falling with a stuttered breath.

I swallow and swipe my fingertips across my bottom lip, making sure I didn't leave any cream behind. "Everything okay?"

"Fine," he says faintly. He shakes his head a little and looks back down at the container. "I'll, ah, I'll read the poem."

Delighted, I thread my fingers together and rest my chin on my clasped hands in eager anticipation. Caleb snorts at my attentive positioning and smooths the paper over his leg. My mind runs wild with possibilities. Jeremy helped me out last spring in the bakehouse and I'm well aware that he knows a frightening amount of Ja Rule lyrics.

He clears his throat and I watch his eyes scan the paper. A smile curls the edge of his mouth, bringing about a faint impression of his dimple.

"*Y yo me vo'a dar un shot por ti, espero que estés bien,*" he starts. "*Yo he estao con mile y tú sigue en el top ten.*" A fiery blush rises on his cheeks and he glances up at me quickly before darting his eyes back to the paper. "*No me lo niegue, baby, que yo también. Y yo me vo'a dar un shot por ti, espero que estés bien. Yo he estao con mile y tú sigue en el top ten. No me lo niegue, yo sé que yo también.*"

I stare at him, mouth slightly slack. I don't think I've heard Caleb speak that much Spanish before. I've heard him slip an odd word or two into conversation, but never something so ... extensive. I shift my legs against the blanket and press my fingertips to my throat, which suddenly feels dry. I feel like I need a tall glass of something strong. Maybe a cigarette.

I resist the urge to fan myself, and force myself to focus back on the poem. "I don't know much Spanish, but did you say something about *top ten*?"

Caleb folds up the piece of paper and puts it back in his pocket. "Sure did."

"Did I hear *baby put it on me* in there?"

"I can neither confirm nor deny." Caleb's cheeks flush a shade darker, but he's grinning with me. "It's a work in progress."

I snicker and reach for the bread, unwrapping it from the paper and breaking off a wedge. Caleb closes the shortcake with a final look of naked longing and then pours us some more wine. We move perfectly around one another, his fingertips against my shoulder, the small of my back, the curve of my neck. He smooths his palm beneath my hair and twists the silk scarf I'm wearing through his fingers, dragging it across his palm and gently tugging.

It's so easy being here with him. Sharing our days and watching the waves roll in. Toes tucked in the cool sand as the sun dips lower and lower in the sky, a blazing globe of orange casting gold in every direction.

It's almost scary, how easy it is.

"So we're halfway through our experiment," he tells me, his mouth two inches away from my shoulder. I shiver. "How am I doing?"

I want to lean back in his chest and feel his arms around me. I want to slip my fingers in between the buttons of his shirt and watch his blush stain his cheeks. I want a lot of things, more and more every day.

"I don't know." I arch my eyebrow and break off another piece of bread. "You haven't kissed me yet. I can't make an appropriate judgment."

The truth is I have no idea why all those other women let Caleb go. He's sweet. Kind. Caring in all the right ways. He might not have kissed me yet, but I see the way he looks at me sometimes. The slow heat. The careful consideration. Like he's plotting his path—every single spot he'd stop and worry over with his lips and tongue and teeth.

How in the world did I not notice this man before? How did everyone else let him go?

He gives me a heavy look, brown eyes heated to a liquid gold. "I told you."

"Yeah, yeah." I wave my hand between us. "Fireworks. Et cetera."

He stretches out his long legs and rests back on his palms, a secret smile curving his lips. He looks out over the water for a long moment and some of the heat between us simmers and banks. "Are you ready for your interview?"

I nod. The team from *Baltimore Magazine* visits the farm next week. I've been spending all of my free time organizing and reorganizing the bakeshop. Testing out new recipes. Practicing normal faces in the mirror so I don't look unhinged in the pictures. "Getting there. I'm trying to figure out what to make before they arrive." I pop a strawberry in my mouth. "I want to be impressive."

"Layla." Caleb laughs like I've made a joke. "You are impressive."

I shrug and busy myself with stacking our tiny paper cups into a pyramid. "I know. I just—I really want to blow them away, you know? I don't want them to think they've made a mistake when they arrive and see the place."

I've seen some of the bakeries they feature in their magazine. They're big and bold and beautiful. Custom light fixtures and hand-painted tiles and stoves that aren't rescued from the school cafeteria at Inglewild High.

I'm still not so sure this whole thing isn't one giant mix-up.

"Layla."

I open another container and pluck out a blueberry, not meeting his eyes. "I'm thinking I'll use edible flowers to make some custard tartlets. Maybe some macarons."

Caleb's fingers curl over my knee. His thumb presses at the soft skin beneath. "Layla. Why don't you think you deserve this?"

"I don't think that."

He arches a brow. A gust of wind blows in off the water and a single lock of dark hair falls over his forehead. I hesitate, and then smooth it back with my fingers.

"I don't think that," I say again, not sure if I am trying to convince myself or him. "I just worry—"

Hesitation steals the words from my lips. Caleb cups his entire hand around my thigh and tugs me closer. "What are you worried about?"

"I don't want it to be a mistake," I confess quietly. He

leans forward to hear me better over the rushing sound of the surf. I try to be brave. "I don't want them to see me and think there is something better out there for the magazine. I want my bakeshop to be enough. I want to be enough."

His hand releases my leg and his knuckles brush my chin. He tips my face up until I'm looking at him. "This isn't just about the magazine, is it?"

It's not. It's every failed date I've been on in the past three years. It's the eight months I spent with Jacob, trying to get him to love me. It's my parents, who feigned interest when I called and told them about the interview, but then asked me if I planned on going back to school to get my Master's degree. It's my sisters who can't be bothered to return my calls. It's watching everyone around me fall in love and struggling at finding the same for myself. It's every disappointment I've ever had, stacked one on top of the other like a trembling house of cards.

"No," I finally admit. "It's not."

Caleb's gaze is intent on mine. I've never seen him look so serious, not even when he thought someone was breaking into my bakery and he was thinking of using my oversized whisk as a weapon. "You deserve good things, sweetheart." He swallows hard, eyes searching mine. "Why can't you see yourself? Why can't you see how incredible you are?"

"Because," I say, my voice cracking at the edges. "Because no one else has bothered to."

He rubs his thumb against his bottom lip, brown eyes darkening. He looks back out over the waves, seeming to collect himself before turning back to me. "You know you wear orange on Tuesdays?

I blink at him, confused by the sudden change of subject. "What?"

"You wear orange," he says again. "On Tuesdays. Sometimes it's just a scarf in your hair, other times it's your dress or your shoes or your apron. Once you wore a bright orange t-shirt and these little orange shorts that I swear took two to seven years off my life." He blows out a deep, gusting breath and scrubs his hand against the back of his head. "And you drink chamomile tea in the afternoons. You get a line, right here," he says, dragging the tip of his finger at the corner of my mouth. "When you're excited and trying to hide it."

His thumb smooths over the curve of my cheek, down my jaw to the soft, secret space behind my ear that always makes me shiver. He strokes there once and then cups my face between both of his hands.

"You made something for yourself here—out of an old tractor shed. Something incredible for the rest of us, too. No one comes to your bakehouse by accident and no one likes you by accident. I see you, Layla Dupree." He says it so firmly, so resolute, that I can't help but believe him.

"Clear as day. I always have."

TWELVE

LAYLA

A STORM CHASES us off the beach.

One second Caleb has my face cradled between his hands and the next we're fumbling to collect the blanket as thunder rumbles above us, thick clouds rolling in quickly over the ocean. Caleb grabs the container with the short-cake and holds it close to his chest like it's a state secret as the first fat raindrops begin to fall.

A clap of thunder booms overhead. We both freeze and look at each other.

Caleb's mouth is set in a firm line, his shirt already starting to stick to his skin. "Make a run for it?"

I nod, the wind starting to pick up. I snatch the container of shortcake out of his hand and shove that in the bag, too, hoisting the entire thing over my shoulder. Caleb rolls his eyes.

"Give me the bag, Layla."

"No." I shake my head. "I can manage it."

"I know you can, but I want to help."

"I don't want to argue about the bag. I just want to get to the car."

The clouds above us settle heavy and dark and more than a little ominous. I'm embarrassed I didn't notice sooner, but I was distracted by Caleb's eyes and his hands and—

I see you. I always have.

How long have I been looking somewhere else when Caleb's been looking right at me?

A bolt of lightning splits the sky right over the churning surf. It's like Mother Nature decided to go from zero to sixty in the span of a minute.

"You're right," Caleb says. He bends down and bands his arm around the back of my legs, his hand warm against the bare skin of my thighs. He lifts until I'm slung over his shoulder like a sack of flour, my bag bumping against the small of his back. "Let's go."

I clutch tight to the sides of his t-shirt with a shriek.

"This isn't what I had in mind!"

He laughs, the sound lost in the wind and the rain and the rolling thunder. I grin like a lunatic and wrap my arms around his waist as he hauls us back to the parking lot. I don't know if I'm dizzy from the position or from the echo of his words. All I know is cold rain drops against heated skin and Caleb—his strength and his laugh as he runs us all the way back to the parking lot. He props me up against the side of his Jeep, fumbling for his keys in his pocket as rain begins to pelt us both, his dark hair sticking to his forehead. I brush it away and he smiles at me from beneath his thick lashes, small and shy and secretly pleased.

"Hop in," he orders, urging me up, his body blocking mine against the worst of the rain. As soon as my door shuts, he jogs around the front. Rain drums against the top of the car, a heavy beat that drowns out everything else. When Caleb finally manages to slip in next to me, he has beads of water sluicing down his arms, his neck, the side of his face. His pale blue shirt is soaked.

I clear my throat and tear my eyes away from the material clinging to his chest. I can see everything. A lot of … definition.

I clear my throat again.

"Do you, uh, do you have any towels in here?" My eyes keep flitting back to him and his wet t-shirt. I've been hypnotized by his broad chest. Rendered stupid by flexing biceps.

He drags his palm over his face in an effort to clear the rain from his eyes and blinks over to me, his gaze snagging on the collar of my dress. His cheeks flare a brilliant, burning red and he looks away, his eyes finding the dash and holding there like his radio has just exposed the secrets to the universe. I glance down at my dress—at where the rain has made the soft white material almost transparent. The lines of my pale pink bra are visible, a tease of lace through the top half of my dress.

Caleb reaches blindly towards the back seat.

"I have this," he says, his voice gruff. Tension fills the

space between us until I'm restless with it, my legs shifting against leather. I like it too much, the way he sounds. I want to know what that voice sounds like against the shell of my ear, the space beneath. How it might tense and tighten and grit when it's tucked against the soft skin of my stomach. Between my spread legs.

He hands me a black t-shirt, the material warm and threadbare between my fingers. I sit there dumbly with his shirt in my lap.

"It's clean," he tells me. "You can wear it over your dress."

"That's great, thanks." I pull my scarf from my hair and drop it in the cup holder between us. My elbows bump into the window, the center console—Caleb's shoulder— as I try to shimmy into his shirt. He huffs a laugh and then his hands are there, guiding the material over me. Arms, head, shoulders. My head breaks free and he lifts the hair from my collar, his touch lingering. He traces the column of my throat with his thumb down to the sleeve of the shirt. He smooths it down.

I'm not sure it was out of place to begin with.

"You look nice," he says, voice hoarse.

"I look like a drowned rat."

"A nice one, though."

Our eyes catch and hold. His jaw clenches.

It is not a polite look, the look he's giving me.

It would be so easy to close the six inches of space between us. I could twist my hand through the front of his wet t-shirt and drag him to me, the rain pounding down on the roof and the thunder rolling through the foggy glass of his windows. I'd catch his bottom lip between mine and kiss him like I wanted to in my kitchen. Taste the shortcake on his tongue and see what sort of sounds he makes when he *wants*.

"Layla." Something low catches in the back of his throat. Something that severely tests the limits of my restraint.

I lean forward and nudge my nose against his. I want this—*him*—desperately. The hand that's still pressed against me flexes.

"Fireworks?" I ask. "Et cetera?"

His laugh brushes against my lips. It's a low and husky thing and it tugs right at the center of me. "Not yet." He drops a kiss to the tip of my nose and leans back. "Put your seatbelt on, troublemaker."

I pout. "You're a tease, Caleb Alvarez."

He glances at me out of the corner of his eye as he starts the car and reaches for his seatbelt. He stares hard at the hem of his t-shirt against my bare thighs. I'm completely dwarfed in it—the thick, soft material almost down to my knees. It completely covers my dress, making it look like I don't have anything on beneath.

He heaves out a sigh like he's endured something.

"Right back at you, Layla Dupree."

"ALL I'M SAYING IS that vanilla is a poor choice."

"It's a classic."

"It's boring. I ask you if you could have one ice cream flavor for the rest of your life and you say vanilla." I shake my head as Caleb pulls into my driveway. "I'm almost offended."

He puts the car into park and grins unrepentantly at me. "Vanilla doesn't have to be boring. It's very adaptable. You can combine it with all sorts of things to make it delicious."

It doesn't sound like we're discussing ice cream flavors anymore. Something in my stomach twists and then plummets when he says the word *delicious*, a slow roll of heat through every inch of my body. Caleb's tongue licks at his bottom lip and his grin grows, that damned dimple appearing in his left cheek. I poke him once in the ribs, quick and hard.

He flinches and slaps at my hand. "Easy. This is the first date we've been on that hasn't resulted in my physical injury."

I make a show of checking my non-existent watch. "Yet."

"Here's hoping nothing happens between here and your door."

I look out the windshield. We left the storm behind us, but the rain has stayed close. Water rushes down over the windows, cloaking us in my driveway. It feels like we're in our own private bubble, tucked away from the rest of the world.

I like it. I like being tucked away with Caleb.

"Question for you," I say into the quiet of the car. Caleb

is busy fiddling with the radio, pretending like he hasn't been watching me out of the corner of his eye since we pulled into my driveway. I like his bashful approach to flirtation. I like that he has to work his way up to it sometimes. I like that he wears his emotions and thoughts and feelings so very plainly on his face.

I like a lot of things about Caleb.

"Let's hear it."

I fold my hands in my lap and arrange myself in the passenger seat. "Why do you need help with dating?"

I watch his smile falter and his jaw clench, his eyes darting to me then back to the radio. He presses a button and Rick Astley erupts over the speakers before he turns the whole thing off. "What do you mean?"

"I mean the roller rink, the escape room, the beach picnic—you might have had some hiccups with the location, but you've always been great." Great feels like a small word for some of the best dates I've ever been on in my life. "I don't really understand why you don't have a line of women around the block."

He shrugs, clearly uncomfortable. "I told you," he mutters. "I'm too much for some people."

"I don't understand what that means."

"It means," he sighs the words, glancing out the window at the rain falling in sheets. He shifts warm brown eyes back to me. "I haven't been entirely honest with you, Layla."

Oh, god. My entire body goes rigid in his nice leather seat. I knew Caleb was too good to be true. Is he going to pull out a tiny voodoo doll from the center console of his Jeep? Is he going to tell me he only likes having sex while wearing a full-size mascot costume? Is he a secret furry?

"What is it?" I whisper, bracing myself for the worst.

Caleb looks down at his legs. Back up at the ceiling. Over my shoulder through the window and then finally, reluctantly, back to my face. "I have a pretty good idea about why women don't go out with me."

"Please don't say you're a furry," I mutter to myself.

His eyebrows collapse in a heavy line. "What?"

"Nevermind. Please continue."

"I'm kind of a pushover," he finally tells me. "I tend to see only the good things and—" His mouth twitches with a small, self-deprecating smile that almost cracks my heart clean in two. "—and I gloss over the rest."

I frown, not seeing the problem. "There's nothing wrong with being an optimist. Especially when a relationship is just starting out."

"That's true. But no one wants a partner without an opinion, paralyzed by the fear that their true self is someone no one will ever want."

"Caleb." My chest pulls tight. "Is that what you think?"

He shrugs again. "I haven't had any luck with … anyone. It's why we started this arrangement, yeah? I guess I'm trying to figure out how to make my pieces fit with someone else's. You really don't have any tips for me?"

The earnest question urges the crack in my heart deeper. I think about Caleb on the dates we've been on, holding open every single door, his palm hovering over the small of my back. The eager, interested look on his face, anytime I've told him anything. How he remembers—my coffee order, how I don't really like seafood, my preference for oat milk over real dairy. My favorite ice cream flavor and what time I wake up in the morning to get to the bakehouse before the morning rush.

"No," I say faintly. "I really don't have any tips for you." I pause. "Except maybe double-check your health insurance before you start dating a woman. You are awfully accident prone."

He cracks a half smile, eyes stuck somewhere around his knees. "That's just with you," he mumbles.

"Caleb," I sigh his name and he looks up at me. I hate that this is how he sees himself, how he sees what he has to offer a partner. Because all I see is a man who is steady, kind and true, with a heart as wide as the ocean. "Maybe the reason why you haven't figured out how to fit your pieces with someone else is because you haven't found the right puzzle."

His lips quirk up at the corners as he studies me, weighing what I said. "You think?"

"I do." I nod once. "You've got to find your rare, one-of-a-kind, 808-piece puzzle with tiny pieces and frustrating colors."

A low laugh rumbles out of him and I'm ridiculously pleased. Every time I hear that laugh, I feel like I've won something.

"Alight, well." He drags his hand through his wet hair. I'm distracted by the stretch of his wet t-shirt over his bicep. Apparently the puzzle I'm offering is a penthouse pin-up. A centerfold, maybe. "I guess that's something."

"You have a lot to offer someone, Caleb. Don't settle."

His eyes are warm as he watches me. "I won't."

"Good."

I settle into the comfort of the silence between us, rain on the hood of the Jeep and the faint rumble of thunder in the distance. It smells like cinnamon in here. Cinnamon and coffee and Caleb, all twisted together. I'd like to stay for a long while in this car, just sitting next to him. Fog on the windows and his hand exactly two inches away from mine on the center console. It would be so easy to edge my fingers over. Trace his knuckles with the pad of my thumb.

Instead I sigh and squint out the window. "It's still raining."

"It is."

"I think I'm going to make a run for it."

I hear the click of his seatbelt. "I'll walk you."

"You are not walking me to the door."

I start to curl my hands around the hem of the borrowed shirt but Caleb stops me with gentle fingertips against the back of my hand. "Keep it." He looks like he's struggling with the thought of seeing my white dress again. Good, I am glad I'm not the only one suffering here. "And don't be ridiculous. Of course I'm walking you to your door."

"You are not."

"Who do you think I am? Peter?"

I pause. "Who is Peter?"

"The guy with the lint roller."

Ah, how quickly I've forgotten in the face of ridiculous Hawaiian shirts and dimples. I reach for the handle of the door. "There's no need for you to walk in the rain."

He sighs. "Layla. I'm going to walk you to your—"

I slip from the car before he can finish his sentence, slamming the door behind me and hopping from stone to stone on my walkway, my shoes tucked under my arm. The path is warm on my feet and the rain is cool on my skin, fresh cut grass and wet pavement and sunflowers rising up around me. I can smell the honeysuckle from the bushes at the edge of my yard. Wet earth and faint citrus.

Thunder rolls in the distance, a final farewell from the summer storm.

A car door slams. "Layla!"

I skip faster. The stubborn man can stand in the rain by himself if he wants to. I barely have my feet on the bottom step of my front porch when two strong arms wrap around my waist. A laugh bursts out of me as Caleb spins me around and around—the grass and the flowers and the rain and my pretty pink house blurring together beneath the evening sky. A swirl of color and sound and happiness. He sets me down on my top step, going still as I turn in his grip.

It's the easiest thing in the world, to loop my arms around his neck. To feel his broad palm settle warmly on the small of my back. I grin at him. "Your shirt is getting wet again."

Raindrops catch in his eyelashes. I watch as a drop of

water works its way down over his cheekbone. It slips through the day's worth of stubble on his jaw and down his tanned neck.

"I don't care about my shirt."

"No?"

He shakes his head.

"What do you care about?"

His arms tighten around my waist and the ghost of a smile tips his lips. It's a secret, that look. A promise. It's the only warning I get before he closes the inches between us and presses his mouth to mine.

I don't think I've ever been kissed with a smile before. I'm convinced I can taste it on his lips with the rainwater pouring down over us both—traces of strawberries and cream. Our lips brush and Caleb makes a soft sound in the back of his throat. Surprised, delighted, the very start of a laugh. He slips one hand up my spine and grips my hair, gently guiding my face to the side until he finds an angle he likes. His nose digs into my cheek as he continues to brush his lips against mine—once, twice, three times.

Sweet, tasting kisses.

He pulls away and drops his forehead to mine, his thumb tracing a line up my throat.

"What are you waiting for?" I whisper, dazed and hungry. My hands are two fists in the wet material over his shoulders. I'm greedy, absolutely ferocious with want.

He huffs a laugh as he brushes his lips against mine again. The perfect picture of control. The man who orders a single croissant with an entire buffet of sugar in front of him.

Right as I am about to combust, he takes a breath and presses his mouth to mine.

And oh. *Oh.* Caleb's kiss is the best sort of indulgence. He's slow. Contemplative. He kisses me with all of the self-restraint I accused him of having, but now it feels purposeful. It feels like I am being savored. He presses a kiss to the dip in my top lip, the corner of my mouth, the tiny white scar on the curve of my jaw from when I was seven and stupid and stole my big sister's scooter on a neighborhood joyride.

There, each kiss says. *There and there and there.*

I feel like his favorite butter croissant.

Each tiny, perfect kiss drives me higher until I'm desperate with wanting. My hand sifts into his hair and I tug, a whine caught in the back of my throat. I want more. I want everything.

I feel Caleb's careful restraint splinter beneath my hands and against my mouth. I want to grin in triumph.

But then he hitches me up with one arm wrapped low around my waist and tips me backwards until I'm clinging to him for dear life, my thighs squeezing at his hips for purchase. His wet jeans press against the bare skin on the inside of my knees, a rough drag that ignites my blood and has goosebumps erupting over every inch of bare skin.

Classic movie kiss, I think faintly, in some recess of my brain that is still capable of logical thought. He holds me steady with one strong arm beneath my ass as rain pours down on us both, his other hand cradling my face. I've never been held like this during a kiss before, never been touched with such ... necessity. Caleb catches my bottom lip between his teeth with a growl and my back arches, hands scraping against his shoulders. He tips my mouth open with his thumb at my chin until our tongues can slip together. Hot. Urgent. Wet.

Everything in my body clenches tight. Our hands move frantically between us, the both of us reaching for any bit of bare skin we can find. The smooth stretch of my thigh, the curve between his neck and shoulder—the small of my back and the slope of my arm. It's a fight to see who can claim new ground first. Who can touch the most.

When I slip my hand under the hem of his wet shirt and splay my palm flat against a stack of solid, surprising muscle, his whole body lurches against me. My nails scratch and his hand grabs mine, gently pausing my wandering exploration. He slows our mouths to something deep and wet, his fingers fanned against my throat, the back of my neck. He tastes like ice cream. Like sweetness and sugar and the bite of something dark, right at the edge. The cinnamon I sprinkle on top of my apple pies. Warm, dark chocolate.

His thumb trails down from my jaw to the hollow between my breasts. He lingers there, hesitating. I want him to go further. I want him to slip his hands beneath the soft, wet material of this borrowed shirt and drag that thumb against my nipples. Make me arch and cry out and tremble.

But he just kisses me. He kisses me until I can't breathe. Until I can't remember my own name.

"Layla."

It's a good thing he says it for me.

He guides my hand out from under his shirt and twists our fingers together. He squeezes gently, settling me. Settling us both. I squeeze back and press my forehead to his.

"Layla," he says again, voice low and a little hoarse.

"Hmm?" I have never been kissed like that in my life. I'm punch drunk. My whole body is numb.

He chuckles and helps me unwrap my legs from around his waist. I don't even remember how we got tangled up like this. He sets me down on the bottom step of my porch and my bare feet slip on the wet wood. He reaches out to steady me, almost falling over as he tries to keep me from doing a faceplant in the grass. It's messy and uncoordinated and a little bit perfect.

I find my footing, his hands on my hips and my heart in my throat. Caleb gently urges me back onto the steps until we're eye-to-eye. I've never been kissed like that, and I've never been taken care of like this. His borrowed shirt. His careful hands. His knuckles brushing under my chin.

I look at him standing there in the rain, droplets still cascading over his skin. His cheeks are flushed, his hair is wet, and his lips are bruised. Rain slips over his face and down his collarbone. I hope I remember him like this always.

"Tell me the truth," I try. My voice sounds like sandpaper. "You wanted to continue your injury streak, kissing me like that." I smooth his wet hair back from his face. I tug a little bit and his eyelashes flutter. Interesting. "You have a hurt/comfort kink."

He blinks at me. "A what?"

His voice is deliciously rough, a low rumble deep in his chest. I shiver and he notices, his eyes flashing a shade darker. Raw cocoa. Dark cherry.

"A hurt/comfort kink," I say, trying to hold myself back from hitching my knee at his hip again and grinding us both to something decadent and satisfying. Something with panting breaths and grabbing hands, his voice in my ear and my teeth against his neck. My gaze trips down his body. I can see two inches of bare stomach where his wet shirt has ridden up, a thick and heavy bulge at the front of his jeans. Now I'm the one who has to swallow hard.

Maybe I shouldn't have said the word *kink*.

Dark eyes consider me carefully as his fingers tuck a wet lock of hair behind my ear. His thumb traces my jaw and lingers on my chin, the swell of my bottom lip. It's like he's memorizing what that kiss made me look like. Flushed and breathless, I imagine. Gobsmacked.

Deliciously and deliriously happy.

"I'm going to go home now," he tells me, not moving.

I nod. "Okay." I don't unwrap my arms from around his waist.

He nuzzles my cheek. "I'll see you tomorrow."

"Okay." I still don't let him go.

He huffs a laugh. "Croissants and coffee. In the morning." It sounds like he's trying to convince himself.

I nod again and tip my face towards his, hoping for another kiss before he has to go. He chuckles and ducks down to press his mouth to mine.

This one is sweet. A cherry on top of a vanilla ice cream sundae. His tongue swipes slowly at my bottom lip and I feel like that ice cream cone he was eating on the beach. I sway into him.

"Goodnight, Layla," he says against my mouth.

I grin. "Goodnight, Caleb."

THIRTEEN

CALEB

THERE ARE twelve people in my kitchen when I let myself into my house.

Or I guess, when I float into my house.

Because I have no idea how I managed to get home from Layla's. I have no idea how I put one foot in front of the other and walked away from her. I probably shouldn't have been operating a moving vehicle. I don't even remember pulling into my driveway.

Warm skin. Panting breaths. Layla's mouth moving against mine.

I wanted to give her a classic movie kiss and instead Layla gave me an end of the world kiss. A mountain top kiss. A launched into space kiss.

I've never kissed a woman like that in my life. I've never been kissed like that, either.

I rub my fingertips over my lips and slip through the back door of my kitchen, my mind still somewhere at the bottom of Layla's porch steps, her body wrapped around mine. Her thighs around my hips and her hand against my stomach. I had been seven seconds away from pressing her up against her porch banister, slipping my hands beneath her borrowed shirt, and feeling all that lovely lace teasing me through the wet material of her dress.

I step into my kitchen and my entire family freezes, a comedic still-frame of dinner in progress. My mom is holding a large steak knife over a tomato. Luis is doing something bizarre with a dish towel and a corn cob. Sofia is digging around in my crisper. And in the middle of it all, like the center of a perfectly orchestrated storm, is my grandmother with her hands in a mixing bowl. She stops what she's doing and gives me a critical look, one stern eyebrow arching high on her forehead.

"Uh." I look over my shoulder to check that there's no one behind me—that I didn't inadvertently ruin a surprise party. At my own house. I lean back and double check the metal numbers above the door. Yeah. This is where I live. I step all the way in and pull the door shut. "What's going on?"

The room remains silent, a miracle when all of my cousins are wedged together in the same small place. This kitchen was not built for the full brunt of the Alvarez family.

My grandmother finally finds whatever she's looking for in my face. She nods once and continues mixing whatever it is she's got in that bowl, her sleeves rolled to her elbows. I hope it's pozole.

"Bien," she says. "You kissed her."

Like she's just snapped her fingers and issued an order, movement resumes in my kitchen. My cousin Sofia whoops from the fridge, her entire front half hidden as she rearranges my produce. My mom returns to her chopped tomatoes and onions. And Luis does—whatever it is he is doing with that corn cob.

I stand there, confused.

Alex appears at my side and hands me one of my beers that he got out of my fridge in my kitchen. The kitchen that he has been sitting in for an untold amount of time with the rest of my family while I was not here.

I am still so confused.

I scratch the back of my neck and frown. "Did I forget someone's birthday?"

"No." Alex takes a long pull from his beer. "Abuela called and said you were in crisis. That we all had to come to your house and feed you." He grimaces at my shirt. "Why are you all wet?"

I ignore his question. "How did you get in?"

"The key."

"What key?"

"Everyone has a key."

I blink. "Everyone?"

Alex nods. "Everyone."

Of course they do. My mom probably went to the hardware store where my cousin David works and cut copies as soon as I gave her my spare.

My phone buzzes in my back pocket and I almost fling

it through the window in my hurry to get it out of my pocket. It's difficult, my jeans wet and uncooperative. Alex snickers as I struggle.

I push him away with my hand on his face as I finally free my phone. It's a text from Layla.

Layla Dupree

Best I ever had.

I grin.

"Dios," my cousin Adriana moans from the corner. "You're already halfway in love again, aren't you?"

My cheeks flush hot and I pocket my phone. Alex shoots a glare to where she's sitting on a stool by the refrigerator. It looks like she's using one of my vases as a glass for her Corona. Great.

"No," I mumble. I can feel the eyes of everyone in the room. My throat tightens and I cough to clear it. "Of course not."

Adriana fixes me with a set of narrowed eyes that look a little too much like our grandmother. "You do this every time, osezno. You go on a couple of dates, you have a nice time, and then you think you're suddenly in lo—"

"Be quiet," Alex snaps at her. "You're just jealous because Frankie won't give you the time of day."

She raises one perfectly plucked eyebrow and brings

my flower vase to her lips. "He gives me plenty of time, and none of it is during the day." Another groan echoes through the room, this time laced with faint sounds of disgust. My aunt rolls her eyes and mutters something sharp and quick in Spanish. Adriana looks away.

"We will have this meal as a family," my grandmother says, a quiet command in her voice. "Basta con eso."

That's enough of that. There's a chorus of agreement in response. Someone turns on the radio and the low murmur of static and voices fills the space, the rise and fall of horns underneath it all. My mom's bright laugh rings out at something my dad whispers in her ear. Knives clack against a cutting board and someone pops the top of a wine bottle.

Alex hooks his arm around my shoulder and steers me into my dining room. My poor, unprepared dining room that can probably only fit half of the family. I'll have to get the folding table out from the basement. Some of the chairs from the garage. Adriana can stay in the kitchen to eat.

She made it sound like I fall in love twice a week with anyone who passes by. I know I can get ahead of myself sometimes, but this thing with Layla is different. We have very clear boundaries. Our expectations are set. I'm not— I'm not getting ahead of myself.

"Don't listen to her," Alex tells me, handing me a stack of clean plates from the cabinet against the wall. "She thinks love is a four letter word."

"Love *is* a four letter word," I grumble, feeling like a

teenager again, arguing with my cousins across the kitchen until my grandmother grabs us by the ear and makes us sit at the table together.

My wet t-shirt suctions to my chest and I pluck at it with my thumb and forefinger. The lightheaded, happy-dizzy feeling I walked into the house with is gone, swapped for a sinking one in my gut. Am I feeling too much from a single kiss? Should I have even kissed her? I honestly don't know.

Alex rolls his eyes. "You know what I mean."

I set out two place settings, the forks tilted a quarter inch to the right just like my abuela likes. My grandfather always did it that way and it makes her smile when we maintain that small tradition. "Still. What she said. It makes me sound like I'm some naive idiot."

Alex frowns at his table settings. He takes his time responding, and the sinking in my gut turns to a painful twist.

"It's not a bad thing," he finally says. "To want to be in love."

"Thank you."

"But I think you should be careful with this, Caleb. I know you. You lead with your heart. And this situation with Layla ..." He trails off, staring hard at the tablecloth my grandmother must have brought over with her. It's white and delicate and definitely not something I own.

"What about this situation with Layla?"

"You've had a crush on her for a while. You're getting to know her better now and I don't think—I don't want you to get the Layla in your head mixed up with the real Layla. Layla the actual person, with flaws and faults and imperfections."

I shake my head, frustrated. "That's not what's happening."

It's not. I'm getting to know her, understanding who she is beneath her quick smiles and easy laugh. I'm not projecting anything on to her.

"You looked like you had sunshine shoved right up your ass when you walked in your door tonight." He lets out a deep, worried sigh. "You have trouble holding boundaries sometimes, especially when it comes to feelings. I just—I want you to be careful. And I want you to be fair to Layla." He swallows. "It's difficult, sometimes. To be on your pedestal."

"You sound like Adriana."

"No. No, it's not like that. She is a—what does mama always say? Cangrejo enojón?"

I snicker. Adriana is the textbook definition of an angry little crab.

Alex grins at me and then flattens his mouth into a straight line. "I just mean, make sure you see this for what it is. You said this thing was temporary, yes?"

I nod.

"I think it'll be important to remind yourself of that," he says gently. "So you don't get your hopes up."

"Yeah." I picture Layla's face cupped between my hands, her eyes closed as raindrops painted her skin in sweeping strokes. The dazed smile on her lips and how she swayed into me at the bottom of her porch steps. I rub at my eyes and try to wipe that image away. "Wouldn't want that."

I glance down at my feet, at the puddle of water I'm leaving on the hardwood. My grandmother called everyone over here because she thought I needed emotional support. Adriana laughed in my face about my hopes for love. And my little brother is giving me a pep talk about boundaries. Resigned, I scrub my hand over the back of my wet hair. "I should go change."

"Caleb—"

I wave Alex off. "I'm fine."

I am. I'm fine. Perfectly and completely fine. I knew what I was getting into when I agreed to this thing with Layla. It was my idea. I can kiss her in the rain without catching feelings. Well. I guess I can kiss her in the rain without catching any more feelings than I already have. I can give her all of the things she deserves without doodling our names together in tiny little hearts in my notebook.

I'm an adult. She's an adult. I don't need to be coddled. I can handle the repercussions of my own damn actions.

I hand Alex the rest of the forks without looking at him and poke my head into the kitchen to let Sofia know where the salad bowl is. Instead I'm distracted by my parents, off in their own little world by the refrigerator. I watch as my dad tucks a lock of long hair behind my mom's ear, a whisper pressed into the skin just beneath. She laughs, loud and happy, and he sweeps her away. Her arms drape over his shoulders as he steps them into a light and easy rhythm, spinning around and around the tiny kitchen floor. She tips her head back and laughs even harder, my dad's eyes fixed intently on her.

Something in my chest squeezes, just shy of painful.

"Don't let Tio Benjamín know we have tequila," I mumble to Alex. "I'll be back in a minute."

I slip away before he can say anything else, clomping up the stairs to my room. My phone buzzes in my hand again and I swipe to open it, the glow bright in the darkness of the hallway.

Layla Dupree

I had a great time with you tonight.

I drag my thumb over the outline of her name before tossing the phone on my bed and peeling the damp clothes from my body.

I can finish this month with Layla without my feelings spiraling out of control. I can be everything she deserves without hurting myself in the process. Wasn't that the whole point of our arrangement to begin with? I'd give Layla a positive dating experience, and she'd give me some feedback on how to be more realistic.

Everything is exactly where it should be.

My heart included.

FOURTEEN

LAYLA

"HOW LONG HAS she been like this?"

"I don't know. I got here about half an hour ago."

I ignore the two people on the other end of the counter, carefully plucking a bright purple bloom from the edible flowers scattered across the metal surface of my counter. These things are delicate and I keep messing them up on the transfer.

"Is her face stuck?"

"Beckett."

"What? It's an honest question."

Evelyn sighs. "No, I don't think her face is stuck."

"You know I can hear you both." I straighten from my bent position and dig my palm into my lower back. Every inch of my body is aching. I glance around the kitchen. Almost all of my counter space is dedicated to the results of my photoshoot preparation. Tartlets and custards and miniature cannoli. Breads and brioches and bagels. An interesting interpretation of a soft pretzel. It looks like Candyland exploded back here.

"It's possible I overdid it."

Evelyn snorts. "You think? You've been in a baking haze for hours now. What are you even going to do with all of this stuff?"

Beckett's greedy fingers inch towards a chocolate walnut brownie and I slap at his wrist.

"I'm going to sell this, and then remake it all again next week when the people from Baltimore Magazine come. I think I've got my menu set." I rotate the tiny strawberry rhubarb tartlet in front of me, the edible flowers a pretty wreath around the bottom edge. "I think these will photograph well. What do you think?"

Beckett is busy frowning at me with his arms crossed over his chest, one of his legs propped up on the bottom of Evelyn's stool. He dragged her closer to him as soon as she came in fifteen minutes ago, his knee pressed to her thigh.

"I think what you had was fine."

I roll my eyes and bend back to eye level with my precious baby custards. I pluck a dried yellow petal from my flower collection and place it gently on top of another. "You sound like Caleb."

Evelyn grins and swivels back and forth in her seat. Her long dark hair flutters around her shoulders and Beckett becomes instantly distracted. His eyes turn into hearts and cartoon birds start flapping around his head. He twists his fingers through her midnight strands and tugs lightly. She brushes a quick kiss to the inside of his wrist.

"Tell me what else Caleb sounds like."

Beckett makes a choking noise. I flush red all the way down to my toes.

"Oh my god, you guys." Evelyn smacks her hand against Beckett's chest where he's still coughing into his fist. I don't think I've ever seen his face turn that color. "I meant, give me an update! You guys started dating when I was out of town. I feel like I missed all of the good stuff."

"We're not really dating," I mutter. "You know I pick shitty men to date."

But we are really kissing, apparently. I don't think we can call what happened that night on my porch practice. I haven't stopped thinking about it. Haven't stopped wanting it to happen again, either.

Caleb stopped by the morning after our date with a kiss brushed against my cheek and another greasy bacon, egg and cheese bagel clutched in his fist. He couldn't stop blushing every time he looked at me, pink on his cheeks and at the tips of his ears. I loved every second of it.

Beckett finally stops hacking up a lung and points at me, his finger making a circle in front of my face. "Your face says something different."

I slap his hand away again. "My face doesn't say anything."

"You've been smiling for three days."

"And, what? I don't smile?"

Beckett and Evelyn both shake their heads. Evelyn has

a giddy look on her face, her hands clasped under her chin.

"Not like that," Evelyn sighs, a little too dreamily for my liking. "Not for a long time."

I rub my fingertips against my bottom lip and stretch out my neck. It's been nice, spending time with Caleb. Dating someone that actually seems to care about me. Even if it's not exactly real. Even if after all of this, I'll have to go back to scouring through all the fish in the sea. I guess I'll have the memories.

I sigh and do what I do best. Deflect. "What are you two doing here anyway?"

They share a quick glance with one another. Evie's eyes widen and she bounces in her seat. Beckett clamps a hand down on her knee. "Not yet," he tells her.

I am immediately suspicious. "Not yet, what? What's not yet?"

"Nothing."

"Beckett."

"Relax, they'll be here in a second."

"Who will be here in a second?"

Stella bursts through my back door like she was waiting for the introduction from Beckett, Luka half a step behind her. They're both winded, cheeks pink from exertion. Stella's curls are absolutely out of control in the humidity. I narrow my eyes at them.

"Were you guys doing inappropriate things in the fields again?"

Luka snickers. "No. That's their thing, not ours." He

points at Evie and Beckett. Evie flushes red while Beckett shrugs, unrepentant.

"I told you not to look at the security cameras."

Evie's face flushes even darker. She ducks her head and tips closer to Beckett. "There are *cameras*?"

Beckett cups the nape of her neck with his hand and squeezes. "Not at our place, honey."

"Alright, I've heard enough, thank you." I don't need to know what weird exhibitionist things my friends are up to. "Why are you all here?"

Evie and Beckett stand from their stools. Stella hooks her arm through my elbow and starts tugging me towards the front of the bakeshop. "We have something to show you."

"That's great, but my custards—"

She shushes me, leading me forcefully around the counter and through the dining space, out the front door and down the steps. I stumble as I try to keep up with her, and slam into her back when she comes to an abrupt stop. She turns to face me and claps her hand over my eyes.

"Ow."

She ignores me. "We did something for your photoshoot next week."

Oh, god. The last time Beckett and Stella tried to help me with something baking-related, I ended up with three dozen burnt cookies, two shattered ceramic bowls, and sprinkles over every square inch of my kitchen floor. I love Stella to the moon and back, but she's hopeless when it comes to the kitchen. And Beckett has the patience of an irate three-year-old. "Who is *we*?"

"All of us," Luka says from somewhere behind me. That makes me feel incrementally better. If Luka is involved, it can't be too much of a disaster. He'd at least clean up the sprinkles first. I'm rearranged in front of the bakehouse, turned around and around until I have no idea which way I'm facing. "Caleb, too. Once we told him."

"Told him, what?"

Stella pulls her hand from my face. I blink against the bright summer sun sifting through the branches of the trees. I'm standing at the very bottom of the stone steps that lead up to the entrance, flowers and vines twisting up and around the heavy wooden frame of the shop. The blooms frame the entry like the prettiest of pictures, purple and gold and pale blue.

I focus on the bank of windows on the left.

"Um." My eyebrows knit in confusion. "Am I supposed to be watching Gus do inappropriate things to a quiche?"

Stella huffs. "No. Over there."

She directs my attention to the massive window on the opposite side of the door, thick clusters of Black-Eyed Susan on either side. I still remember planting those, the very first day Stella gave me the keys to the renovated barn. Dirt up to my elbows and a smile splitting my face. It finally felt like I was in the right place, at exactly the right time. An echo in my heart and in my blood.

Home.

I take in the new addition on the window.

Painted with care—in flowing gold script that takes up almost the entire space—is *Layla's Bakehouse.* A line curves beneath, dotted with small white flowers. And just above it is a brand new metal sign, swinging gently back and forth in the warm breeze. A bronze circle with the same flowing script, a pie etched beneath. I'd bet all of the croissants sitting in my workspace that Beckett made that.

I have to press my fingers beneath my eyes. My whole face feels suspiciously tight.

"You told me you wanted something to be yours," Beckett tells me quietly. His arm swings around my shoulder and he pulls me close. Stella piles in on my other side, and then Luka and Evie. I guess group hugs are officially a thing for us now.

"This has always been yours. Now it just says so."

CALEB IS WAITING on my front porch when I get home.

Sprawled across my bottom steps like the most delicious lawn ornament I've ever seen, Caleb looks sun-kissed and lazy. Half-smile on his face. One long leg stretched out in front of him. I have to stop and take a moment as I slip out of my car.

"I thought you were taking me out tonight," I call. I'm distracted by his white button-up, the sleeves rolled to his elbows and the collar undone. He must have come right from school, a light dusting of chalk against his left pants pocket where he probably leaned up against something.

"Change of plans," he says with a grin. He nudges the grocery bag at his hip.

I stroll to a stop at the very bottom of my stairs and tip my head back as he uncurls himself from his step. The last time we were standing here, I had my knees hugging his hips and his mouth against mine. He exhales slowly, a look of deep concentration on his face, the line between his eyebrows deepening the longer he looks. I think he's remembering, too.

"Thank you," I tell him, my voice softer than I mean for it to be.

One eyebrow arches on his forehead. "For what?"

He grabs his bag of groceries as I lead him up the stairs. He's warm at my back. Solid. I twist my key in the lock and usher us inside.

"For the sign," I say. "Beckett and Stella showed me today. They said you helped. Thank you."

"Oh. Yeah." Caleb sets the bag of groceries down on the countertop and begins to unpack. Tomatoes. Rice. A couple of limes and a bag of tortillas that look homemade. My stomach gives an appreciative rumble. "I'm not sure distracting you in the back while Beckett measured everything counts as helping."

I pull out a cutting board and take the produce to the sink. "When was that?"

"Friday," he says. He tears open a bag of tortilla chips and holds one in front of my face while my hands are in the sink. I bite down on the edge, my bottom lip against his thumb. His breath stutters in his chest as he pulls his hand away. "When you showed me that thing with the straw-berries."

That makes sense. Caleb kept acting like he'd never seen someone cut strawberries before. He must have asked me six times to show him how I slice them for garnish. I frown, a tickle of unease brushing against the back of my mind. I've had men pretend to be interested before, and it's never ended well for me. I know this is all practice, but I don't want to be a ... chore.

Caleb notices my fidgeting. He sets down the bag of chips and props his hip against the counter at my side, dark eyes mapping my face. "What is it?"

"Nothing." I shake my head and line up the limes on a clean dish towel. I nudge the water off with my elbow.

He's having none of my deflection. "Tell me."

I thought he wanted to be close to me, that he was making an excuse to notch his chin over my shoulder and press his body close to mine, watching intently as I sliced my way through a pile of fresh strawberries. I thought maybe he wanted to kiss me again, but he never did.

He hasn't, actually, since that night in the rain.

"I thought you were making an excuse to get close," I mumble, not quite meeting his eyes. "I didn't realize it was part of a plan."

He mirrors my frown and takes two steps forward, crowding me against the sink. His hands find the coun-tertop at my hips, his arms caging me in. He smells like summer rain and fresh coffee. I want to dip my nose in the notch at the base of his throat and breathe deep.

"Do I need an excuse to get close?"

I shake my head. He fingers a lock of my hair, his knuckles brushing against my neck. I shiver.

"What is it, Layla?"

"You haven't kissed me," I blurt out. I feel like an absolute idiot, but he hasn't made a single move to kiss me since our first. I peer up at him from under my lashes. "Did you—did the other night make you uncomfortable?"

He huffs a laugh and my stomach sinks. A sharp tug all the way down to my toes. I look down at the buttons on his shirt.

"I'm sorry, I didn't realize—"

"Layla, no." He nudges my chin up until I'm looking at him again. His eyes are gentle, a warm golden brown in the sunlight that spills through the windows of my kitchen. "If I've seemed uncomfortable, it's only because I've been wanting—" He swallows hard, his throat bobbing. It's his turn to hesitate.

"What have you been wanting?"

If he says he wants more space, I might walk right out my front door and keep walking. I don't think I've ever been so invested in a man wanting to kiss me before. It's an agonizing feeling, waiting on the ledge for his answer.

"I've been wanting to kiss you," Caleb says, his voice rough. My startled gaze swings to his. "I've been wanting to kiss you every single day."

Cool shock melts into something liquid and warm. "Really?"

"Yes, really." He drags his palm down his jaw and peers

down at me. A smile tugs at the corner of his mouth. He hesitates, just a moment, and then he leans down and nudges his nose against my forehead. "Haven't you noticed? I can't stop thinking about it. About you."

I drag him closer with two hands fisted in the white material of his shirt. I tip my face towards his. "Then why haven't you kissed me again?"

His hands flex on the edge of the countertop. "I don't know if it's such a good idea, Layla."

"Why?"

"Because every time I'm around you, I feel like I've got a balloon in my chest," he says right against my temple. He exhales, low and slow. "Because I'm pretty sure if I kiss you again, I'm going to want more."

My entire body flushes hot. Caleb cups my face with one shaking hand and trails his thumb beneath my ear. We stand there against my sink—held in the waiting. My heart hammers in my chest, my breathing uneven. I want more, too. The ghost of his kiss has been haunting me the past couple of days, warm lips and fleeting touches. I want to know what it feels like when his teeth find my neck. How his palms would feel on the bare skin of my thighs and the swell of my hips. What it feels like when Caleb finally lets himself go.

"What is it we said the other night?" I brush my lips over the curve of his jaw. His big body shudders against me and he pins my hips with his against the sink in a sudden, rough jerk. A moan catches in the back of my throat. "Maybe we should revisit the details of our arrangement."

FIFTEEN

CALEB

I CAN'T CATCH my breath.

I don't understand how I went from unloading the groceries to pinning Layla against her kitchen sink. *Patience,* I've been telling myself every day since the beach. *Restraint. She might not want you to kiss her again.*

Though I've certainly wanted to. That feels like an understatement. Everything in my body has been begging me to, every single time I've seen her. When I walked into the bakehouse the other day, she had a bright orange scarf twisted through her hair, an old, faded band t-shirt tied in a knot at her waist. She smiled as soon as she saw me and I wanted to hoist her up against the refrigerator in the back. I wanted to curl that scarf around my fist and *pull.*

I know I should be holding myself in check, reminding myself of the arrangement like Alex keeps telling me to, but fuck. It's hard to keep my distance when it feels so good to be close to her. When she looks at me and it feels like she could want this even half as much as I do. I can't pretend with Layla, and I don't want to.

I like this better, anyway. Layla doesn't deserve someone tucking away parts of themselves while they're with her. If I want to, I can kiss her at her kitchen sink and enjoy every damn second of it.

I smooth my hand down her back.

"Can I ask you a question?" Layla's voice is low, her hands toying with the top button of my shirt like it's personally offended her. She twists it one way, and then the other. Her pink fingernail scratches at the bare skin in the gap between and I almost fall to my knees.

I swallow hard. "You can ask me anything."

"What would we be doing if we didn't have an arrangement?" She slips one button free and moves to the next. "If I were someone else, tell me what you would have done the last time you wanted to kiss me."

"The last time?"

She hums and nods her head. "Yes."

"Well." I comb my fingers through her hair and hesitate, then gather it all up in my fist. She tugs against my grip and a small moan catches in the back of her throat. *Christ.* "I'd have waited on your front porch for you to get home from work with a bunch of groceries. So I could make you dinner at home. Because I wouldn't have been able to stand the idea of being somewhere I couldn't touch you. Because I would have wanted to be alone with you."

Layla's head lolls to the side and I press a lingering kiss against her pulse point, at the space below her ear. My restraint crumbles with my lips against her soft skin. She smells like caramel and sea salt. Like an entire tray of baked goods, fresh from the oven.

"I would have waited for you to shut the front door and then I would have put the groceries down by the steps. Helped you with your bag and backed you against that little window, right by your door."

Layla makes another small, wonderful sound, her hands clenching in my shirt. I want to lick that sound from the corners of her mouth, feel it with my lips in the space between her breasts. I want a thousand things in a thousand different combinations.

"I'd have picked you up and wrapped your legs around my waist. Like the other night, do you remember?"

She nods.

"I remember, too. We fit so well together like that," I mumble. I haven't been able to think of anything else since. I go to bed at night and think about how perfect Layla felt in my arms. How every inch of her lined up perfectly with every inch of me. "I would have held you there against me and kissed you hello." I brush my lips against hers teasingly. "I would have gotten carried away, I think. Dragged my mouth down your neck to the edge of this pretty shirt. I probably would have slipped my hands under your skirt to see if you wanted me as much as I wanted you."

Air rushes out of her. "Caleb."

I cling to the threads of my restraint and try to hold myself together. I lean back until our hips are no longer tucked tight, needing the space. She looks at me with heavy-lidded eyes, her gaze lazy as she catalogs me. Shoulders, chest, stomach—I feel her gaze like a fingertip against my bare skin, all the way down. She catches her tongue between her teeth when her eyes hit my belt. Lower, where I've thoroughly worked myself up.

I prop one hand against the countertop at her waist and ignore the need rushing through every inch of my body. "That's what I would have done."

She blinks at me. "All of that sounds very agreeable, for the record."

"Good to know." The kitchen suddenly feels like it is eight thousand degrees.

I turn back to the cutting board and the two freshly washed tomatoes sitting at the edge. I need something to do with my hands or I'm going to flip up Layla's little orange skirt and see what sounds she makes when my mouth is somewhere else.

I have to swallow against the sound caught in my throat.

"In the spirit of our agreement," Layla hesitates. "I have a confession to make."

"I'm all ears." I'm all *thumbs*, too, apparently, as the tomato rolls right out of my grip. I fumble with the kitchen knife and catch it before it can tumble its way to the sink.

"I've never had a partner who—" She trails off. I wait

for her to continue but she doesn't say anything. I look at her over my shoulder.

"You've never had a partner who, what?"

I don't know what I'm expecting her to say. Her history with men is storied, and after the lint roller thing, she really could say anything. Her cheeks flush and she smooths her hair behind her ears. She glances at me briefly and then stares over my shoulder. She shrugs half-heartedly.

"You know."

I don't know. Maybe I'm still drunk off the feel of her pressed against my body or maybe I'm just tired, but I don't have a clue as to what she's talking about.

I frown. "I don't know."

Her eyes lift to the ceiling and she blows out a deep breath. "I've never had a partner, um, you know, bring me to completion before."

She says the last bit of her sentence through gritted teeth, like it's being physically pulled out of her. When I do nothing but blink at her in response, she exhales sharply and crosses her arms over her chest.

"I've never—no one has ever made me come, Caleb."

The tomato in my hand goes flying halfway across the kitchen. It hits her refrigerator and then falls to the floor with a wet plop. Seeds and juice ooze out of its side.

Layla and I stare at it. A minute goes by in complete silence. Then another.

"I probably shouldn't have told you that," she mumbles under her breath.

"No. No, I'm just—" Reeling a bit. Having a medical event, more likely. My brain is stuck on an image of Layla spread out against crisp, white sheets, her body bare and her back arched. I'm thinking about her knees tipped open, her hand low on her stomach. My brain is record-scratching on the word *come* slipping out of those lips.

I clear my throat. Then I clear it again. "Never?"

She shakes her head and looks down at the tile of her kitchen floor. I can't see much of her face, but I can see her cheeks are a bright and brilliant red. I set the knife down. "Hey. Don't be embarrassed."

She digs her palms into her eyes. "I don't know why I just told you that. I've never told anyone that."

I hope she told me because she trusts me. That she feels comfortable enough with me now to tell me things. I close the space between us and rub my hands up and down her arms. "I'm glad you told me."

"It's embarrassing," she whispers. "It's just—for a long time, I thought something was wrong with me."

"There's nothing wrong with you." My hands squeeze against her arms reassuringly.

"I really don't know why I told you," she whispers again, her voice splintering in the middle. Her hands twist together between us. I still them with mine.

"Layla. It doesn't say anything about you, okay? It says everything about the people you've been with. Douchebags, remember?"

A small laugh slips out of her, but she keeps her face angled away from mine.

"Could you look at me? Please?"

She sighs but she does as I ask, tipping her head back and looking at me with shy, careful eyes. I can feel my heart pounding in my throat, at the base of my skull. This is either a terrible idea or a really fucking good one. I haven't decided yet.

I guess it depends how she responds. If she smacks me across the face or not.

"Is that something you want?"

Her eyebrows slant low. "What do you mean?"

"The point of our arrangement is for us to practice, yeah? We could practice this, too. You could tell me what you want." I swallow. "We could work together to figure out what you need and how you need it."

Christ. My mind goes wild with the possibilities. Layla beneath me. Layla up against the wall. Layla with both of her legs curled high around my back.

Her face is still etched in confusion. "Caleb, you're going to have to spell it out for me. I have no idea what you're talking about."

"Do you want to practice in bed?" I ask her. I try not to blush, but it's inevitable. I can't fight it back when I'm picturing us together, twisted in her sheets. I bet they have strawberries on them, too. Maybe tiny cupcakes. "Do you want our arrangement to be physical, too?"

Her mouth gapes open. She moves it soundlessly like the words she wants are somewhere out of reach. Far, far out of reach. That is ... probably not a great sign.

I try to pull away but she grabs my hands and holds on tight. "Why?" she manages.

"Because," I say. "Because you deserve to have someone try."

Her lips twitch at the corners and her hazel eyes narrow. "Any other reasons?"

This time when I untangle my fingers from hers, she lets me. I hover my hand over the smooth line of her jaw, watching the way she responds to me. Her head tilts to the side and I trace my knuckles down the soft skin of her neck, lower to the delicate jut of her collarbones. I trace one and then the other, dip my finger down to the warm skin between her breasts. I can feel the steady drum of her heartbeat. Every exquisite inhale.

I do have another reason. A selfish one.

"Because I want to watch you come undone," I tell her, my voice a rough scratch. I look up and make sure I'm holding her eyes. "Because I want to be the one to do it."

Fuck, I want it more than anything. I want to know what she looks like with my hands on her bare skin. I want to know what shapes my thumbs might make against her hips, her thighs, the curve of her ass. I want to know how she sounds with my mouth against her neck and her body flushed warm beneath mine. If she sighs or moans or bites down against sweat-slicked skin. I want to know all of the secrets she hasn't shared with me yet, everything I might unravel with our bodies together.

With Layla, I just *want.*

Her eyes pitch darker. Moss green. Thick branches in a

heaving summer storm. Her lips part as her eyes dance between mine, weighing the truth of my words.

"That's a good answer," she finally says.

I hum and take two steps back. I have to. If I don't, I'll tuck my hand beneath her thighs and urge her up on the countertop. I'll kiss her and kiss her and kiss her until I have my answer. I won't be the polite gentleman I want to be with her.

I turn to the cutting board and blindly grab another tomato. I start chopping with shaking hands. I feel like I've just been kicked out the side of an airplane without a parachute. I don't know if I'm breathing or just wheezing. I've never been so bold with a woman in my life.

I turn the tomato and chop from the other end. The pieces are horrendously misshapen. It's a wonder I don't slice my thumb clean off.

"I think I'd like that," Layla says over the sound of the knife. I pause and look at her over my shoulder. She's standing with her back to the sink, both of her hands tucked behind her and her eyes heavy on mine. Her hair is slightly mussed and the collar of her shirt is twisted to the side, the rise and fall of her chest tugging me into some sort of hypnotic trance. Again.

She looks gorgeous.

"With you," she clarifies and the rigid line pulling my shoulders tight eases, settles. The weight resting on my lungs lessens.

It matters that she wants this with me, specifically. That she trusts me enough.

Layla smiles at me softly and pushes herself off the sink. She scans the counter, looking for the produce she was in the middle of washing. Her eyes are contemplative. Thoughtful. Like she's making a list and checking it twice.

I swallow hard.

"With you, I think I'd like that a lot."

WE EAT OUR DINNER.

Layla sits at one side of the table and I sit at the other.

We make conversation like we didn't agree over a smashed tomato on the floor to make our relationship a physical one.

We talk about my classwork at the school. About Jeremy's progress with Lydia and how a couple of other kids have shown up asking for my help translating their notes. Layla calls it my *love club* with an adorable, snorting laugh that makes me feel like someone's trying to wrench my heart out of my chest through my throat. We talk about her upcoming photoshoot and the little custards that she's finally perfected. Beignets and brioche and baguettes with fig jam.

I only get hard twice when she uses fancy baking terms. I consider that a small miracle.

We don't talk about our conversation in the kitchen again.

Layla wants to. I can see it every time she looks at me, anticipation in her eyes and in the curl of her hands around her glass. One of her socked feet nudges mine beneath the table and my knee jolts so hard into the solid oak top that my glass goes tilting to the left. I catch it before it can spill.

Layla hides her smug smile behind her fingertips.

"Okay?" she asks just a little too innocently.

"Fine."

I'm fine. Totally fine. I just can't stop thinking about the way her breath slipped out of her when I had my knuckles against her neck. I can't stop picturing the soft swell of her breast and how she arched into me, chasing my touch without even realizing it.

She's so damn responsive. And the fact that no one has ever taken the time to reward her for that is a crime.

"Caleb?"

I shake my head. Distracted again. "Yeah?"

Her smile waivers, her eyes unsure. "I asked if you wanted dessert?"

I follow the line of her dress strap against her shoulder with my eyes. It's thin, a dusty orange that makes her skin glow. She was wearing a cropped button-up wrapped overtop of it before dinner, tied in a bow above her waist. She slipped it off slowly while she poured our wine, the material gliding over her shoulders to the bend of her elbows. It whispered against her skin when she tugged it off and draped it over a chair.

My hands had itched with the desire to do it for myself. I wanted to unwrap her like a present.

"You're drifting again."

"Sorry." I rub my hand across my forehead. "I know I am."

"Do you want any dessert?"

I shake my head and her face falls. "But I have Boston cream pie in the fridge."

It says something about how badly I want her that I don't even flinch. I push my chair back from the table. "Come here for a sec."

She doesn't move from her seat on the opposite end of the table. Her bottom lip is stained a deep red from the wine. "Why?"

"Because I want to kiss you," I tell her. Might as well be honest. I want to lick the wine from her lips and circle my hands around her waist. The only dessert I'm interested in having tonight is Layla, in any variation she's willing to serve up.

She blinks at me, owlish and slow. Her grin strikes quick though, like a bolt of heat lightning reaching its fingers out across the sky. She watches me for a second, and then she pushes her chair back.

"You could have told me that earlier," she quips. Earlier, I assume she means, when I had her plastered against her kitchen sink.

I pat my thigh and her eyebrow quirks. "Well, I'm telling you now."

She takes her time coming around the table to me, her hazel eyes blazing in the light of the setting sun. Warm golds and burnished reds light her up like she's a dancing flame, twisting closer and closer. I've never wanted to be burned so badly in my life.

Her fingertips skim my knee. The top of my thigh. She stills right in front of me and stands in the narrow space between my parted legs. I tip my head back and watch her.

"Caleb Alvarez, who knew you were so bossy." Her smile says that's not necessarily a bad thing. "It's gonna be like that, huh?"

I nod, my hands reaching for her hips. I help her settle on my lap, sitting sideways against my thighs. The curve of her ass is a delicious weight against me, her mouth hovering right over mine. I place a kiss under her chin. Another where her shoulder meets her neck.

"It's gonna be like that," I whisper, and then I kiss her.

I thought it might be different, kissing Layla for the second time. It's why I held off all week, still high off the adrenaline of our first. I thought our second might be more subdued—calm—the both of us settling into our respective roles.

Maybe the second time, I wouldn't feel so out of control.

But I'm an idiot, apparently.

Because the second I press my mouth to Layla's, I'm a goner. Everything drifts away until it's only me and her and panting breaths, our bodies creating delicious friction as her hands twist in my hair. She shifts in my lap and I grunt into her mouth, my tongue sliding hot and wet and slow against hers. She tastes so sweet. Like wine-soaked strawberries. Like the slices of oranges at the bottom of my glass she kept sneaking when she thought I wasn't looking.

I curl my hand around the bare skin of her ankle and grip her leg, adjusting it against my lap until her foot is pressed against the arm of the chair and my palm is tracing secrets up her calf. She jolts in my hold when my thumb smooths behind her knee. A huff of a laugh travels from her mouth into mine. That tastes sweet, too. Like champagne bubbles and the best goddamn buttercream icing I've ever had in my life.

I slip my hand higher and she tips her knees open slightly. I pause, my fingers curled possessively around her thigh.

"What do you want, Layla?" I ask her and then lick slowly below her ear. She tastes like powdered sugar. Like peaches with cream. Her whole body shivers and she scratches her nails against my scalp.

"I don't know. This is good."

"This is good," I agree. I press a sucking kiss to the column of her throat and her nails scratch harder. If she keeps moving on my lap like that, it's going to be better than good. I'm balancing on the razor edge of control and wild indulgence. "But I think you should tell me what you want."

"I don't—" She drags her nose against my cheek and rocks her forehead against mine. "I don't know what I want."

My thumb slips half an inch higher against the inside of her thigh. She makes a sound low in her throat and desire clenches a fist around my heart and squeezes. "Do you want—" I have to swallow twice to finish my question. "Do you want me to touch you?"

She nods her head eagerly and rocks her hips so they inch forward. I hold her body still against mine.

"I need your words, Layla."

"Yes." She turns her head and breathes her answer into my mouth with her hand cupped against my jaw. "Yes, I want you to touch me."

My fingers skim higher, toying with the flimsy material of her skirt. I watch their progress with fascination, my lungs burning. "How do you want me to touch you?"

She chokes on a laugh when my thumb slips over the top of her thigh to the naked skin of her hip, toying with a thin band of elastic. It feels like she's wearing dainty underwear made out of the softest cotton imaginable. I don't know why that makes me drag my teeth against her neck, just that it does. My control is hanging by a gossamer thread.

"I don't even know how I like to be touched." She's still smiling at her private joke, her head lolling back against her shoulders as she offers me more skin to bite and taste and suck. I take the invitation, worrying a mark just above her collarbone. *Mine*, it says.

Mine for now, a voice in the back of my mind reminds me.

I shove it away.

Layla cards her fingers back through my hair and shivers. "I want you to touch me. Isn't that—can that be enough for now?"

It's an easy enough decision. I urge her up and off my lap with my hands bracketing her waist. Confused, she frowns down at me, her hands rushing to tuck her hair neatly behind her ears. I grab them and set them against my chest instead. I don't want her to be unsure. I don't want her to hide.

Not with me. Not like this.

Her hands clench in the material of my shirt, eyes searching. "What's wrong? Did you change your mind?"

It's my turn to laugh.

"No," I say. "I didn't change my mind. Just finding a better position."

I bring her back to me, her knees on either side of my thighs on the narrow dining chair. Straddled above me, there's no missing the thick ridge of my erection beneath my worn denim jeans or how perfectly we line up. But I don't care. I want her to see how she affects me. I want her to know how wanted she is.

"Like this," I tell her, my voice rough.

There are better places to do this, probably, but I can't bear to walk the five feet to the couch. Or set her on the table in front of me. I want her chest pressed to mine. I want her breath on my neck and her knees hugging my hips.

I tug her down impatiently, her skirt caught between us. We both let out echoing, rumbling groans. Layla feels so good, even with layers of material between us. Warm and soft and fucking perfect. She rocks her hips as she settles above me and a shower of stars explodes behind my eyes. I have no idea how I'm going to last.

She traces her thumbs over the sides of my face. Lower to the curve of my bottom lip. I nip at the pad of her thumb and she huffs a laugh.

"What now?" she asks.

I grin and slip my hands back up her skirt. Her thighs tremble beneath my palms, her hips twitching into my touch. My thumbs find the thin straps at her waist and I snap the material.

"Now we figure out how you like to be touched."

SIXTEEN

LAYLA

I DIDN'T EXPECT to end the evening perched in Caleb's lap with his hands beneath my skirt, but here we are. I'm certainly not mad about it. His eyes are dark, his hair is every which way, and he has a hickey forming, just under his left ear from where I was a little too enthusiastic.

It's a good look for him.

His thumbs make another pass from the tops of my thighs to the inside of my knees and I almost launch us both out of the chair.

"I'm nervous," I whisper, deciding to be honest with him. I don't want him to get discouraged when I don't … respond to his touch. I've had partners get upset in the past. Frustrated. I learned quickly that faking it is usually an easier path without the complication of bruised egos.

But I don't want to fake anything with Caleb.

"Why are you nervous?" He slips his hands around to

the curve of my ass and squeezes, making sparks dance up my spine. "It's just me."

But that's the thing, isn't it? It turns out Caleb isn't *just* anything. He's careful touches and lingering looks. Roller skates on the very first date. Shared nachos and kisses in the rain. His hand on my elbow and the small of my back, his lips pressed against the back of my neck. Solid. Dependable. Kind. Smoking hot.

Caleb is turning out to be a whole lot of something for me.

"Sometimes—" I roll my eyes up and stare at the light fixture above my kitchen table instead of his face. "Sometimes it takes me a while. To get going."

A low sound slips out of him and his hips rock below mine. My eyes snap back to his.

He's panting, just a little bit, the buttons straining on his shirt. He looks a little wild, a little wrecked. Hungry for something other than dessert.

"That sounds like the opposite of a problem, Layla."

"Yeah?"

He nods with enthusiasm and then leans forward until his lips meet the spot where my dress cuts across my breasts. He presses a small kiss above my heart, and then licks a hot stripe all the way up my neck. Everything in my body clenches tight.

"I like to work for it," he whispers against my ear.

My breath gusts out of me, a small explosion.

Okay then.

He taps the side of my hip beneath my skirt, his face

still buried in my neck. "Up," he gently commands, and I rise on my knees above him so his hands can move. He traces the line of my underwear from one hip to the other with a single, deliberate fingertip.

"Do you like to be teased?" His knuckles brush over the front of the soft cotton covering me, just barely. I suck in a sharp breath as goosebumps break out over my skin. "Or do you like it fast?" His thumb presses hard over where I ache the most, and we let out twin sounds of appreciation —mine a gasping moan, his a low rumble.

"Teased." I pant the word into the top of his head, my voice breathy and thin. "I think."

I've never been asked that question before. I've never given it much thought, what I do and don't want when I'm with someone like this. But I like this build up, the low ache in my belly that swells when his touch is fleeting and soft. I like the brush of his thumb as he traces every inch of me below my skirt—slow, slow, slow. Like he's savoring. Like he's memorizing.

Like he wants it to last.

His thumb dips again and he grunts low in his chest when he feels the small patch of wet between my spread thighs.

"Christ," he curses. My whole body trembles like a leaf caught in the wind. "Tell me when it feels good, okay?"

I nod and rock into his hand. "Okay."

One of his hands slips out from beneath my skirt and he toys with the strap of my dress just as his knuckles drag over the center of me again. I bite back my moan and fist my hands in his hair, my hips pushing into his touch and then rocking away. This position is awkward, my body held suspended above his as he works me. I feel clumsy and off balance, everything pulled too tight.

"No, stay." Caleb's hand goes back to my hip and he pulls me back down onto him, encouraging a rhythm over his hand and his lap. More comfortable, I wind my arms around his neck and settle. A half smile tugs at his lips, teasing out that dimple I love, and I settle some more.

This is Caleb, and with Caleb I'm safe.

I watch him from beneath heavy-lidded eyes as I rock, his gaze fixed on me perched in his lap. I feel each touch of his eyes like the pad of his fingers against my bare skin. My shoulders. The swell of my breasts straining against my top, and the hem of my dress riding up against my thighs. He slouches back in the chair and kicks his legs wider, making mine spread, too. His fingers curl beneath my dress and my breath catches.

"You are so beautiful like this," he says on a low rumble. "Does it feel good?"

I hum happily in response and close my eyes. I tilt my head back as he pushes one of my dress straps down and then the other, both of them settling in the bend of my elbows. His lips brush against my collarbone, in the slight hollow between my breasts. The fabric of my dress holds there, constricted.

It feels amazing. A delicious tease—just like I wanted. Warmth collects low in my belly and every place my body is pressed to his. Knees, thighs—head and heart.

"Words, Layla." He adjusts his hand between my legs so I'm pressing directly into his thumb with each roll of my hips. My whole body shudders.

"It feels good," I tell him, my words slurred. It's the best it's ever felt with anyone ever and he hasn't bothered to remove any of my clothes. He hasn't touched the bare skin underneath them. One of his knuckles nudges the edge of my underwear and an erratic sound catches in the back of my throat.

"Do you like it when I talk to you?" His teeth clamp down on the edge of my bodice and he tugs the material an inch lower. The strain of my nipples against the soft fabric distracts him. He tongues at one through the flimsy material of my barely-hanging-on top until I'm arching in his lap.

"I like it when you talk," I manage between heaving breaths. I can't stop watching him. His tan arm flexing between my legs and his mouth at the tips of my breasts. He catches one between his teeth and heat licks up my spine. I've never—it's never felt like this. Not even when I'm by myself. I let out a shuddering exhale. "I like it when you—"

I break off, my thoughts scattered. He drops his forehead against my chest and grinds his hips up into mine, his hand trapped between us.

"What do you like?"

Heat blazes in my cheeks. I've never told anyone this, either. "I like it when you tell me what you like, too."

I like the praise, I think. I'd like to hear all of the good things I'm making him feel.

He groans, a helpless sound. He turns his hand so I'm rocking into his palm, the heel of his hand grinding into my clit with every rough jerk of my hips. He presses wet, sucking kisses to my neck.

"You want to know how good you feel?"

"Yes."

"You want to hear how I'm breaking apart, getting to see you like this?"

I nod, frantic. Yes, that's exactly what I need. I want to know that Caleb is feeling everything I'm feeling. That he feels just as wildly out of control. The tension inside me twists deeper—a spring coiled low in my belly. I rock my hips harder into his touch.

"You're doing so good, sweetheart. So good." The hand above my dress clamps down on my hip and he guides me against him. Everywhere I move, I feel a different decadent sensation. The button of his jeans when my hips jump. The hard press of his cock on the inside of my thigh when I grind down. His mouth on my chest and his messy hair against my neck.

"That's it," he encourages and I roll my hips harder. I grip the top of the chair we're balanced on and chase the feeling, making my legs twitch and shake. I chase that delicious, golden edge—right out of reach. "Just like that, Layla. Ride my hand until you feel good, yeah?"

"Jesus," I mutter. I think it's a combination of his steady touch and his low, murmuring words—praise whispered in my ear as I climb higher and higher. He doesn't waiver as I work myself against him, the rough material of his jeans chafing the inside of my thighs making everything better. I like the burn of it. I like the desperation.

I move and Caleb tells me how perfect I feel, how warm and wet I am through the thin material of my underwear. He tells me how already he can't wait to do this again, all of my clothes stripped off so he can watch my blush paint my skin pink.

"Just one of your pretty scarves," he mumbles with his mouth on the hollow of my throat, his pinky edging under the hem of my underwear. "Nothing else."

"I don't—" A whine lifts the edge of my voice. I'm so close, but I can't make myself tip over the edge. The harder I work myself against him, the further away it seems to drift. My pleasure flickers, hazy frustration dulling the sharp corners. I bite back a moan that sounds suspiciously like a sob.

Caleb carefully slows me down with gentle touches. His fingertips at the small of my back. A kiss between my shoulder and neck. "What do you need?" he whispers.

"I don't know," I mumble into his neck, scraping my teeth against his ear and forcing my hips harder into his hand. *I want to come. I want to come, I want to come, I want to come.* "I don't know what I need."

Caleb stills me above him and I wiggle in his hold, frantic. Need pulsates right beneath my skin, a frantic buzz deep in my bones. I suck at his neck, fumble with the buttons of his shirt. I'm a mess, tugging and grabbing at him beneath me. Patience is gone. Hesitation, too.

"Caleb, please," I beg, embarrassed that I'm pleading with him for an orgasm but also unable to stop. I'm so *close*. "Please keep going."

He smooths his hand down my back and cups my ass over my dress. He grabs a handful and lifts, holding me steady against the front of his body as he stands from the chair. I wrap my arms tight around his shoulders.

"I'm gonna keep going." He walks four steps to the couch and drops us both down onto it, rearranging our bodies until I'm pressed deep into the cushions and he's above me, my legs high around his waist. I cross my ankles and tug him into me, his cock heavy and hard against the space between my legs. "We're going to get you there, I promise. I think I figured out the problem."

"You stopped touching me," I point out, feeling petulant. Both of his hands circle my wrists, guiding my arms up above my head. I want them under my skirt. I want them on my skin. "That's the problem."

"I was making you work too hard," he says, watching the progress of his broad hands down my arms, over the sides of my ribcage. He hooks two fingers in the top of my dress and tugs until my breasts are bare beneath him. He makes a low, appreciative grunt and brushes lightly over my nipples with the palms of his hands. He teases me just like that, his chest heaving as he holds himself on his knees above me. When I slip my fingers through one of his belt loops and tug, he grabs my wrist and guides it back above my head, pressing me harder into the couch. My whole body shakes with need.

Eyes like burning coals glance up at me. "You're not supposed to work for it, sweetheart. I am."

And then Caleb goes to work.

He holds me down on the couch and moves against me like we're in a bed. Like we're in a bed and we're both naked and he's deep inside me and wants to get deeper. He rolls his hips and sucks at my neck and drags one palm down the line of my arm to my breast. He pinches my nipple as he grinds into me and everything erupts into bright colors. Shapes. Sensation and the panting sound of our breaths together.

"You look so damn pretty, Layla. Fuck." A lock of dark hair falls over his forehead as he reaches for my ankle. He curls his long fingers around the delicate bone and guides it higher against his back. My knees tip wider and I choke on the edge of a gasp.

"I bet you look prettier when you come. Can I see it?" He catches my earlobe with his teeth and tugs. "Will you show me?"

"Caleb." I say his name for no other reason than I want to. I want to taste the syllables on my tongue as I wind tighter. He hums and presses his thumb to my chin, guiding my mouth to his. He kisses me slow and deep and keeps his pace exactly the same. He doesn't speed up, he doesn't slow down, he just keeps rocking into me in that perfect, delicious, heavy rhythm.

"You almost there?"

I nod and then nod some more. I don't know how long we've been moving together like this, just that it feels so, so good. He feels so, so good. His teeth collar my ear just as his hand slips between our grinding hips, a heavy drag of his thumb that has me arching, gasping, whimpering beneath him.

"Tell me how you need it."

"Faster," I gasp. He takes my instruction beautifully and I whimper. "Two fingers, a little higher. Please—I—"

"Good. There it is," Caleb tells me. His hips bump into the back of his hand. "Chase it, Layla. Take it."

Maybe it's his encouragement or maybe it's his thumb slipping beneath my wet and twisted underwear. Maybe it's his first touch against my bare skin or the deep, appreciative sound he makes in response. The cut-off curse beneath his breath like he's unraveling just as thoroughly as I am. I don't know. I just know that in one breath I'm watching Caleb move above me and the next I am tumbling over the edge of my release.

It's sudden, a rough jerk right in the center of my chest. A rope being yanked. I cling to Caleb as it roars through me, a wildfire of pleasure and wild, messy sensation. It might have started suddenly, but it spreads slowly—the backs of my legs, the cradle of my hips, the tips of my breasts where they're pressed against the cool material of Caleb's shirt. I whimper and moan and make sounds I've never heard come out of my mouth before.

When I finally calm, Caleb is still above me, panting into my neck. I slide my palms down his back to the hem of his shirt and tuck my hands beneath. His hips jump and he nuzzles down into me, his skin warm beneath my touch. He feels like the heaviest, most delicious smelling blanket.

I grin at the ceiling. "I think that was the best idea you've ever had."

His nose nudges at my neck, and I can feel his lips curl into a smile. "Better than the roller rink?"

I wiggle beneath him, pleased as punch. "Oh, definitely."

He laughs and rests his hand at the base of my throat. His thumb traces over my skin. It's a comfort and a brand. A gentle reassurance that everything we just did was exactly right. "I agree."

"Do you—" I shift beneath him and trace the strong column of his spine, all the way down to the divots just above the band of his jeans. I want to strip this shirt off of him and trace pathways across all this gorgeous skin. I swallow hard. "Do you want me to touch you, too?"

Caleb leans up on his forearms, a delicious flush on his cheeks and throat and the tips of his ears. His lips are swollen and his hair is sweaty, tangled waves. I hope I think of him exactly like this, every single time he stands on the opposite side of my counter and orders a croissant.

Though I imagine that might be a challenge to my productivity.

"I, uh—" His teeth clamp down on his bottom lip with a wince.

"It's okay." I ignore the twist in my gut, the sting of his

rejection—kind and gentle as it was. It's okay that he doesn't want me to touch him the way he just touched me. It's fine.

I stare up at the ceiling and still my roving hands.

"Layla." Caleb sighs my name. "It's not like that. I already, uh—I already—"

I frown and watch his face twist in embarrassment. "What is it?"

He looks down at me with a timid, rueful smile. He lifts his hand and traces the lines of my face, the swell of my bottom lip. He looks captivated. That memorizing touch of his, all over again. I curl my hand around his wrist and press a smacking kiss right against the center of his palm.

He drops his forehead back to my collarbone and rocks it back and forth.

"I finished," he tells me with no shortage of reluctance. He rubs the hand I just kissed over his chest. "Watching you was enough. Touching you was—" He exhales slowly. *Incredible,* that sound says. Another sigh and a low, rumbling chuckle. "I feel like a teenager."

A surge of warmth replaces the hollow feeling in the center of my chest. Affection, steady and sure. "Teenage you must have been fun."

He shrugs and lifts himself up on his palms. "I was an awkward kid. I didn't really know how to talk to people. Girls, especially."

I find that hard to believe, since he was telling me to *take it* about three minutes ago. But I like it all the same. I like that he feels comfortable enough to be himself with me. That he doesn't censor or shape himself into something he thinks I want. I get Caleb in all his beautiful, imperfect shades.

He leverages himself up until his back is pressed to my couch and I stay sprawled across the cushions, my dress rucked around my middle, my arm flung above my head. Caleb's eyes travel a meandering path down my body, lingering on the curve of my breasts.

He blows out a deep breath, eyes hooded and heavy. Appreciation. Something softer, too.

I grin.

"Ten out of ten," I tell him, feeling off about assigning this a number on a scale. But I need to remember where the both of us stand, the foundation on which we're building. It won't do me any good to have the rug pulled out from beneath me at the end of this thing. Despite how incredible that just was. I ease out a breath and card my fingers through my sweaty hair. "Seven gold stars and a partridge in a pear tree."

He smiles, eyes crinkling at the corners. "Right back at you."

Caleb sits on my couch with his legs spread wide, one hand resting low on his belly, the other on the two inches of space between us. His gaze lingers everywhere my hands touch. The slope of my shoulders and the smooth expanse of my arms. The hollow between my breasts and the soft skin of my belly.

It's a simple thing, to have someone watch me piece

myself back together. Simple and beautifully, wonderfully intimate.

Another first for me tonight.

His hand skims around my ankle and he drums his fingers against my calf. He drags his palm up to the underside of my knee and back down again as I twist my arms back through the straps of my dress. A tap, tap, tap all the way back down.

"What?" I ask as I struggle with a stubborn, twisted strap.

Caleb's hand lifts from my knee and he finds the stubborn material, thumb dragging across my collarbone as he straightens it. He traces his palm lightly across my shoulders to the center of my chest. He rests his hand there until I'm sure he can feel the pounding of my heart beneath.

"Nothing," he says, his voice impossibly deep. "Just like looking at you."

I smile to myself and smooth my skirt back down over my thighs. I catch his hand with mine and twist our fingers together, snuggling into his side until we're wrapped together. We sit there on my blue couch and listen to the sounds of my house settling around us. The creak of hardwood and the crickets calling to one another through the open window above the sink. I don't think I've ever been so still with someone before. So content to just *be*.

I tilt my head and drop a kiss against Caleb's knuckles. He makes a pleased sound, low in his throat, and tips his head to look at me.

"Do you still have that pie?" he asks, his voice hopeful.

I laugh. "Yeah." I lean forward and kiss the curve of his smile. I feel like I'm floating. Like I'm in the middle of the pond that's on the very edge of the Lovelight grounds, staring up at the sun beams twisting through the trees. My lips trail down the sharp line of his jaw to his chin. I nuzzle into his chest and wrap both of my arms around him. "I still have some pie."

SEVENTEEN

CALEB

"WE SHOULD REALLY—*GOD,* CALEB—" Layla pants my name into my mouth, her teeth against my bottom lip and both of her flour-dusted hands clenched tight in my hair. I'm going to look like I dunked my head in a mixing bowl when I walk out of here. But I can't gather any of my usual control. I haven't been able to keep my hands to myself, really, since two nights ago on Layla's couch. Every time I close my eyes, I see that orange dress twisted around her middle. Bare skin and my hands pressing hers into the couch. I keep hearing the little sounds she made in the back of her throat as she moved on my lap and chased her pleasure.

If I thought the feeling of wanting her might fade with my first taste of her, I'm an idiot. It's only gotten worse.

Especially since she's wearing the apron with the strawberries today. There's something about the pop of red against her creamy skin, the strings looped twice around her waist and tied in a neat bow in the front. I want to undo them with my teeth.

Not to mention her cherry red lipstick and gold hoop earrings. The bright blue scarf with little yellow bananas twisted through her short hair. I walked in through the door and she glanced up from a tray of tiny vanilla crème brûlées, her smile cracking wide open at the sight of me. I had to stop for a moment and breathe deep through my nose. Rub the heel of my hand against the center of my chest and try to put everything back where it belongs.

I attempted to behave myself. I sat on my stool and pretended to drink my cup of coffee but I really just watched the curve of her body as she bent low over the countertop. I watched as she mixed and stirred and rolled out fresh dough for cinnamon rolls, ignoring the low pull in my gut when she pulled out a jar of cinnamon sugar. I couldn't help my faint moan when she stirred a bowl of melted butter, her brush painting the dough in wide stripes.

It was the buttercream icing that finally did it for me, though. One second she was pulling a bowl out of the fridge and the next she was holding out her hand in my direction, a perfect, pristine dollop of cream balanced on the pad of her finger. I sucked it into my mouth, her eyelashes fluttered, and then we were reaching for one other, mixing bowls and a display plate in the shape of a cupcake clattering to the floor.

"We should stop," she says, right before she drags her teeth up my neck and guides my mouth back to hers with her hand on my jaw, leaving more flour prints. I press her harder into the fridge and tighten my grip on her thighs.

"We should," I agree. I nudge my nose against her chin until she tilts her head back, until I can suck at her pulse point and taste the dusting of sugar on her skin. Her hips jump against mine and I am about four seconds from tucking my hands under this apron and finding out what sort of underwear Layla Dupree wears when she is in the kitchen.

I've always been meticulous with my control. Perfectly polite, always exactly what is expected of me. But Layla makes me feel unhinged. Untethered, unfocused, undone. I drag one of my palms up her leg and back down again, the hem of her dress brushing against my knuckles.

Her breath hitches and she tugs hard on my hair. Something slow and hot unfurls at the base of my spine, my breath shorter than it was a second ago. Her smile shifts into something delighted and surprised and she pulls again, angling my head back, her mouth on my Adam's apple. Her eyes right on me.

My whole body goes boneless against hers.

She laughs, a husky sound right below my ear. "I need to get back to work."

"Okay." I don't move from where I'm plastered against her, my face in her neck.

"Caleb." I can feel her smile against my shoulder. She circles her arms around my waist and gives me a squeeze. "Go sit on your stool."

"No, thank you."

I don't want to. I want to stay right here, wrapped around Layla, smelling flour and sugar and lilac on her skin, her heartbeat ricocheting against mine. Alex has been telling me I need to hold on to my expectations, but I don't see anything wrong with indulging myself in this.

I've always liked Layla—in the way anyone likes someone who is good and kind. Warm yet vaguely impersonal. I liked her smile. I liked her laugh. I liked the way she always worked the register herself, no matter how crowded the bakehouse got. I liked watching her decorate her cakes with her tongue between her teeth and that tiny little spatula held carefully in her hand.

But now that like is slipping into something deeper. I like how she leads with her heart no matter how many times it's been bruised. The way she tilts up her chin and does her best to be brave when she talks about her family. The unwavering loyalty she has for her friends and how proud she is of this place she's built.

I like the way she touches me too, how she mindlessly trails her fingers up and down my arm while we're sitting against the bumper of my Jeep. I like watching the sun paint the sky in a kaleidoscope of candy colors with Layla's head against my shoulder. The way her thumb digs into the soft skin at the base of my neck when she's excited about something, her voice tripping one octave higher, one beat faster.

She is all the things I thought she was and then some.

She hums the ambiguous beginning of a song beneath her breath and wiggles beneath me. Her fingertips play with the short hair at the back of my head as I sway us gently back and forth. A private dance for the two of us in the back kitchen of Layla's bakehouse. Flour in my hair and my heart pounding in my chest. Better than any date I could have ever planned.

"Do you think—" She swallows her sentence and scratches her nails lightly against my skin. A faintly embarrassing sound rumbles out of me and I lean harder into her touch.

"What?"

I can feel her hesitation in the way she holds herself against me. I sway us back and forth again as she collects her words. "Do you think things are working so well between us because of our arrangement?" Her voice is a whisper. "Or do you think it's us?"

I hum and let my mouth brush against her temple. "What do you mean?"

She tilts her face up towards mine, both of her palms pressed against my chest.

"Things between us feel—" A smile curls at the edge of her lips and I like it so much I bend my head to taste it. She huffs a laugh into my mouth and pushes me back again. "Stop distracting me." Her pretty eyes search mine and when she speaks again, her voice is soft. Shy. A lilt to it that I haven't heard before. "This feels really easy, Caleb. And I don't know how much of that is me and you, or the arrangement."

I trace my thumb down the curve of her jaw to the dip in her chin. "Can't it be both?"

She frowns. "What do you mean?"

I consider my words and voice a theory that's been nudging at me. "Maybe our arrangement has made it easier for us to be open with one another, but I don't think it's all of it. Maybe it's just ... a shove in the right direction."

At least, that's how I'm looking at it. The arrangement might have made it easier for us to find our way together, but the way I feel when I'm around her? That's one hundred percent Layla.

I keep her close to me with a firm hand at the base of her spine. She buries her face in the front of my shirt. Her short hair curtains around her cheeks until she's hiding as much as she can.

"How do you know?" she mumbles into my shirt.

I breathe out, low and slow, and then take a leap and make a confession. "February 17th."

She sighs, a little puff of warm air somewhere over my sternum. "What happened on February 17th?"

"I bought a cake."

I'm taunting her. Tempting her with too-short answers so she has to lean back and look at me. She holds steady though, raising one hand to knock against my ribs in admonishment. "If you tell me you bought a cake from the bakery of a supermarket store, I'm going to punch you right in the face, Caleb Alvarez."

A surprised laugh rumbles out of me. "What?"

"If it was out of a box or made by someone else, you're dead to me."

"I didn't buy a cake from the grocery store and I didn't

buy it from someone else," I tell her. "I bought this cake from you."

She doesn't say anything. I dance my fingertips down her back, along the ridge of her spine. She's so strong here, so steady. I don't think she even realizes.

"I bought a cake on February 17th. I remember the date because there was still a bunch of Valentine's Day stuff strung up around the front. You had this paper cupid thing that kept knocking into my head. I think you hang your decorations too low, sometimes."

"Or maybe you're too tall," she argues, somewhere below my collarbone.

"Yeah, maybe that. But there was someone giving you crap about a cake at the counter. They said you got the icing wrong and they didn't want it if it was wrong and you just—you looked so flustered and a little bit sad and I wanted to—" I remember the anger burning in my chest, the quick roll of it down my shoulders. A burn in the palms of my hands. "I was still Deputy and I figured punching the guy in the face wouldn't be appropriate, so. I waited. He left, and he left his cake too, and when I asked you what you were going to do with it, you sort of did this little shrug and looked at the pretty flowers on top like they were the worst thing you'd ever seen, and—" And it had broken my heart, a little bit, to watch her stand behind the counter and try not to cry. "So I bought the cake. And Layla, it was the best cake I'd ever had in my whole life."

Her hands rise from her sides and press against my ribs. Her fingers fan out.

"And I liked—" I halt. This is the hard part. The part I'm not so sure about. This is where I feel every failed conversation with a woman like a brand against my skin. I don't want to be too much right now, not for Layla.

I want to be just enough.

"I liked opening the fridge in the middle of the night for a glass of water and seeing your cake box there. I liked having a slice in the morning with my coffee and staring at the little flowers on top. Sometimes you bite the tip of your tongue when you're piping designs on the top of your cakes. Did you know that?"

I would sometimes come early to pick up my cake, just so I could watch her face transform in concentration. The careful and quiet joy that blossomed in her smile, like her tiny daisies piped in icing.

I keep that part to myself, though. "I kept it to one slice a day. When there was just a little bit of cake left, I started making the slices smaller. And then, when I had the last sliver with my coffee because I couldn't entertain the idea of waiting until after work, I stared at the empty box of crumbs and thought, *why don't I just order another?* I was—" I laugh, feeling self-conscious and stupid and a million other jumbled up things that sit heavy in my head and heart. "I was so nervous to call and order another one."

I called twice and hung up, stomped a lap around my kitchen, braced my hands on my hips and glared at my phone on the kitchen table. By the time I finally called, Layla wasn't even the one to take my order. I remember thinking how stupid I was being, over a *cake*.

"I thought you had a string of Alvarez birthday parties and you were responsible for the cake," she mumbles into the shoulder of my shirt, rubbing her nose back and forth against the material. Her voice sounds suspiciously thick.

"No. I was not responsible for the cake." I huff a laugh. I took sole ownership over those cakes, and I got a new waistline measurement to prove it. "I never knew why I kept ordering cakes. I just liked seeing you, I think. I liked being around you. I still like all of that, Layla."

She sniffles and clings to me tighter. Every pound of my heart feels like it's trying to fight its way through muscle and tendon and bone to get to her. I'm standing on a ledge here, hoping—

I don't know what I'm hoping for.

I guess I'm just hoping.

I drag my hand up the length of her back and sift my hand under her hair, cup my palm against the back of her neck. "So, yeah. I don't think all of this is because of our arrangement. I think some of this is me, and some of this is you, and some of this is us. All of this is good though, yeah?"

"Yeah," she whispers. "Yeah, it's good."

"I think we can figure this next part out together. Just— just keep telling me what you need."

She finally pulls away from my chest and tips her chin up, her eyes surprisingly clear and bright. She has a slight crease under her right eye to the apple of her cheek from where her face rested against my shirt, a delicate little line of where she bumped up against me. I like it too much, probably.

Her eyes search mine, back and forth. Her nose scrunches and I trace my thumb over the muted line.

"You tell me what you need, too," she finally says. "That's how we do this. We have to keep talking to each other."

"I like talking to you."

It feels like a stupid thing to say until her cheeks turn pink and a timid smile starts to bloom. I cup her face in my palm so I can watch as it blossoms into a grin. She turns her head and presses a kiss right in the middle of my hand. I wish I could curl my fingers around that, too.

"I like talking to you, too."

I sigh, feeling lighter than I have in ages, and take a step closer. "I do have a request, actually, now that you mention it."

"You do, huh?"

"I do."

"Let's hear it then."

I nudge under her ear with my nose and press a single, lingering kiss on the soft skin beneath. I grin when her hands clench in the front of my shirt and she tries to pull me closer. Layla might have trouble verbalizing what she needs, but she never has any problem showing me.

"More hand holding," I whisper. One of my hands reaches for hers and I tangle our fingers together. "More butter croissants."

More running through the rain. More beach picnics

with our feet in the sand, strawberry shortcake in containers. Less escape rooms and roller rinks, probably, but I'm flexible on that if it's something she wants.

A laugh bursts out of her. "More ice cream," she demands back. She drops a quick kiss to my jaw. "More kissing," she whispers.

I cup my hand around the back of her neck and brush my mouth against hers. "Should probably start that part right now."

She nods, her nose bumping mine. "Mmhm. I think so."

So I tip my head to hers and kiss her, slower than the last time and sweeter, too. It feels like something more, this kiss.

More of Layla. More of me.

More of us together.

More of everything.

EIGHTEEN

LAYLA

THREE DAYS LATER, Caleb is standing in the middle of my kitchen again. But this time his hands are deep in his pockets and he's staring at all of the fruit tarts crowded on the countertops like he's a step or two away from staging an intervention. He scratches at his chin and then drags his palm over the back of his neck. He glances at me and then back to the countertop.

Hesitation, personified.

It's cute.

"This is ... a lot of food," he says slowly, carefully. I think he's afraid I might spook. It's not an inappropriate reaction to my current mental state. He pokes lightly at the edge of a cupcake stand with his pinky finger, head tilted slightly to the side in consideration. That's a new cupcake tower and probably unnecessary, but my Bahama Mama cupcakes look real pretty on it and that's what matters.

Caleb turns to me and rocks back on his heels. I think

this is the first time we've been in the same space in days without mauling each other. Apparently our conversation the other day has largely translated to making out on and against every flat surface in my bakehouse and beyond. But kissing Caleb hasn't even entered my mind today, a testament to how nervous I am for my *Baltimore Magazine* interview tomorrow.

He's wearing a button up chambray shirt today, too. Loose with the sleeves rolled, two off-white buttons undone at the hollow of his throat. I wipe my hands down over my apron and look around my kitchen.

It's not as bad as the morning Evelyn and Beckett came to visit, but it's close. I toned it down slightly. If you squint, maybe. I still spent half of my day on six dozen custard tartlets, edible flowers lining the edges of every single one. Caleb had shown up during the last batch with another greasy breakfast sandwich and a kiss pressed to the back of my head. He slipped onto one of the stools and watched me with his chin against his fist, a lazy look on his handsome face every time I glanced up. Small smile, heavy eyes, just a hint of dimple. He looked like he wanted me more than the tartlets.

It didn't stop him from swiping one, though.

Things with Caleb are good. Better than good. Last night we got ice cream at a little wooden stand halfway out of town and sat in the parking lot with our feet swinging off his back bumper. Cotton candy skies and a warm summer breeze twisting through the fields. I sat with my knee tucked against his thigh and ate butter pecan ice cream and watched the way the willows danced in the breeze. Caleb's hand on top of my thigh, his thumb drifting back and forth on the sensitive skin beneath.

"More ice cream," he told me with a grin, echoing our discussion the other night. I smiled back and his eyes settled into something softer, more serious. He had thumbed at my cheek affectionately, leaned forward and pressed a kiss right at the corner of my mouth. "More of this smile," he added.

It's the most comfortable I've ever been with a man. It's liberating and lovely and terrifying and wonderful.

But mostly terrifying.

I keep waiting for the other shoe to drop. It's hard to believe that my dating disasters have suddenly evaporated. I loved Caleb's story about the cake, but I think—I think our arrangement has more to do with it than he thinks. Maybe the parameters of our pseudo relationship have given us both a pair of rose-colored glasses. Maybe the ticking clock is making sure we only see the best in each other, I don't know.

It just feels too easy right now.

I glance at him out of the corner of my eye, watching as he rearranges some of my clean spatulas in order of size. He saw me do it once, and now he does it every time he's back here with me. I found the aluminum foil organized in the closet the other day, too. Luka would be so proud.

He catches me staring and a smile quirks the corner of his mouth. The dimple in his left cheek flares back to life and my stomach swoops, an answering *thump* right in the center of my chest.

Maybe it's just chemistry. I've been fooled by that before. Or maybe it truly is the freedom of our arrangement. The ability to be exactly who we are without any sort of pressure from one another. A time clock, slowly ticking down. It has to be that, because this sort of thing doesn't just happen.

Not for me.

My heart sinks a bit and I busy myself with a square of parchment paper. If it's just the arrangement, all of these feelings should fade as soon as our month together is done. We'll part on good terms and go back to how things were before. Friendly conversation three times a week. A coffee with cream. Butter croissant.

I'll have a shiny new measuring stick to hold up against my dates, and Caleb will know exactly how to woo the next woman he sets his eyes on. It'll be like nothing ever happened between us at all.

The cookie I'm trying to wrap crumbles in my hands. I stare down at chunks of oatmeal and walnut and try to clear away the image of Caleb out with someone else. Would they get vanilla custard in cones on the beach? Would they sit behind the *Skate It Easy* and eat slightly stale nachos?

"Hey." Caleb taps the tip of my nose, suddenly right in front of me. "Where did you go?"

I blink and set the parchment paper down, rubbing a

palm against the tension pulling at the back of my neck. I don't need to be thinking about this right now. It's another worry for another day. A hill for Future Layla to climb. Right now, the only thing I need to be focused on is the interview and making this place look as beautiful as possible for the photoshoot.

"I was just thinking about flowers." It's easy enough to bend the truth. I was vaguely thinking about the flowers in the front of the shop, the massive canopy of peonies and lavender and daisies that Mabel helped me twist along the rafters. Now when you walk in the front door, it's like summer is pouring down through the ceiling. Blooms and blossoms everywhere.

"Well, they look great." Caleb leans his hip against the counter at my side and plucks a wayward chocolate chip off my parchment paper. "Did Mabel help you?"

I nod. Gus, too. A whole truckload of greenery before the sun was even up this morning. A thought occurs to me, a coincidence that's been nudging at the back of my mind. "Hey, have you heard from the phone tree lately?"

I usually hear from Matty when news is traveling down the branches, but it's been suspiciously silent the last couple of weeks. I don't even know if there's been an update on the rubber duck situation in the fountains.

Caleb's eyebrows collapse in a heavy line. "No. Now that you mention it, I haven't."

"That's kind of weird, isn't it?"

He nods and grabs another bite of cookie. He's lucky he's cute, Beckett would have gotten my spoon across his knuckles for that. "It is. I haven't heard from Darlene either, and she used to be a twice daily caller."

My suspicion deepens. "What do you think it means?"

"Does it have to mean something?" He shrugs. "Maybe there's no news."

I level him with a look. Oh, sweet Caleb. "Remember that time when there was a town-wide discussion about macaroni and cheese and Gus sent a decree that bow tie pasta was expressly forbidden as a method of distribution?"

Caleb chews thoughtfully. "Remember that time when Jesse ran out of cherries at the bar and tried to set up a phone-a-thon for donations?"

I snort. Beckett found out and changed the donation phone number to the local ASPCA when the tree got to him. I think they raised over seven-hundred dollars. "Exactly. So I don't think there's a lack of news or whatever interpretation thereof the phone tree specializes in." I pause for a yawn, the back of my hand against my mouth as my whole body shivers and shakes. "It's weird, is all."

I'm exhausted. I can feel my pulse at the base of my spine, my body angry with me for all the standing and lifting and baking. I don't remember the last time I stepped out of this kitchen, now that I think about it. Yesterday, maybe? The day before? I don't even know what time it is —if it's morning or night or mid-afternoon.

"Alright, sweetheart." Caleb abandons the cookie crumbs and curls both of his hands over my shoulders. "That's enough."

I sway on my feet, oatmeal chocolate chunk cookies dancing in front of my eyes. "What is?"

"The baking bootcamp you're putting yourself through."

He stands to his full height, fingertips spread out wide. His thumbs ease back and forth over my collarbones and slip under the collar of my shirt, just barely. It's a comforting touch, one that has warmth slipping over me like a blanket. *Tall,* my bake-drunk mind sighs happily. *Good.* His lips twist in amusement.

I hope I didn't say that outloud.

"You've made enough food to supply a small army. I think you should call it a night."

"It's night then, I guess." My bleary eyes scan my kitchen before looking back at the tall, handsome man holding me upright. "I was going to make peach dump cake next."

I watch as Caleb's eyes darken slightly, his pupils blowing out at the suggestion of peach cake. "Fuck," he mutters lowly, a deep grind of the words between clenched teeth. He flexes his hands on my shoulders. "I can't believe I'm saying this, but forget about the peach cake. You need to get some sleep."

"I just want everything to be perfect." I want the people from *Baltimore Magazine* to look around and see all of the things that make this place special. I want to be impressive. Memorable.

Someone worth sticking around for.

"Everything is perfect, Layla." He urges me closer until

my forehead tips against his chin. My eyes slip closed and I grab blindly at his shirt. He's so warm. Like a—like a—like a mocha fudge brownie. I sway in his arms and snicker into the buttons of his shirt. Maybe he's right. Maybe I do need some sleep. "Even without all of this stuff you've done, this place would look perfect. Let me take you home."

"Should I hang some cupcakes up first?" I lean back and rest my chin against his chest, my arms looped around his waist. "To go with the flowers?"

"Now I know you're delirious." He leans back until he can thumb at my chin, big hand cupping my face. "No, you don't need to waste cupcakes by hanging them from the ceiling."

I squint. "Are you sure?"

He smiles. A small one. "I'm sure."

"It looks okay?"

"It looks great."

"You're sure?"

His laugh rumbles low against my chest, right where I've got my chin pressed against him. He smooths his hand over my hair and presses his palm between my shoulder blades, soothing me. "Yeah, I'm sure."

I lean more of my body weight against his chest. He wraps both of his arms around my shoulders, cocooning me. I don't think I've ever been more comfortable in my life.

I hear the door to the kitchen swing open, heavy boots against the hardwood.

"Oh, shit. Sorry. Didn't mean to interrupt anything." Beckett sounds comically distressed. I don't bother looking but it sounds like he's talking with his back towards us. I bet he has his hands pressed over his eyes, too. Rich, coming from the man who I know loves a romantic interlude with Evie beneath the stars in the middle of our tree fields. I grin into the collar of Caleb's shirt, my eyes still closed. Am I asleep? Am I awake? I don't even know.

"Not interrupting," I mumble, my arms still locked around Caleb's waist. I want him to carry me to the car exactly like this. I want him to drive me home with me wrapped around him like a koala.

"That's illegal, sweetheart," he whispers into my hair, another smile in his voice. "Seatbelts are important."

"I can be your seatbelt," I slur.

Caleb laughs again and Beckett makes a gruff, grumbly sound that is a vague approximation of a laugh. "Is she bake wasted?"

"I called it bake bootcamp."

"That feels right."

"I can hear both of you." I just can't tell who is speaking. And why their voices sound like they're coming from the end of a very long tunnel. And is someone playing merengue music?

Steady hands work at the strings of my apron. I let Caleb manipulate my arms as he gently guides me out of the canvas contraption. I sway on my feet and slit my eyes open and watch as he traces his thumb over one of the strawberries, draping it carefully over the shelf by the door.

I turn my muddled attention to Beckett. I do feel like I'm drunk. Like I'm ten thousand leagues under the sea. "Did you need something?"

Beckett shakes his head, watching Caleb tidy up some of the bowls on my workspace and drop them in the industrial-sized dishwasher—the smaller ones tilted halfway on the top rack, just the way I like. A knowing smile starts in his eyes and he turns his hat around until the bill is backwards, a little embroidered Christmas tree above the snaps.

"Hey, man," he tips his chin towards Caleb. "How do you feel about dogs?"

Caleb glances over his shoulder. "In general, or a specific one?"

I narrow my eyes. "Don't even think about it."

Beckett ignores me. "I know a guy who is looking for a home for a dog that was abandoned—"

"Where do you find these people?"

"—and he thinks she was supposed to be a police dog. She's got all the commands down. He thinks she was dumped because she's a little small for it and not nearly aggressive enough. A real sweet girl. She loves pizza crust. Her name is Poppy."

Caleb pauses and tilts his head to the side, thinking about it. "I'm open to it."

I look at him, a little shocked. "You are?"

He shrugs. "Why not?"

Beckett nods and crosses his tattooed arms over his chest. "I'll let him know. Maybe the two of you can meet."

I try to picture Caleb with a little rescue dog who loves pizza crusts. A slightly hysterical laugh bubbles out of me. That's just what I need. Another reason to be attracted to the man.

Beckett's concerned gaze snaps towards me. "You good?"

"Did you really come all the way over here to try and get another animal adopted?"

He shrugs and reaches for one of the tarts I haven't packed in the fridge yet. I snap at his knuckles with a towel. "Ouch, Layla. Christ." He holds his hand against his chest. "I came over to check in. I wanted to make sure you actually leave this place tonight instead of making a tiny cocoon on the bottom shelf in your supply closet again."

I roll my eyes. "It happened once, and it was so I could keep an eye on my sourdough starter."

Caleb freezes with his back to me, hunched over the dishwasher. He turns his head to the side until I can see his face in profile. "You slept in the supply closet?"

I cross my arms over my chest, prepared to defend my commitment to my craft. "It was the bottom shelf, close to the floor, and it was very comfortable."

"You scared the shit out of me," Beckett grumbles. "I thought you were a vampire."

Beckett came in through the backdoor that night and I rolled right off the shelf. I think we both screamed at each other for close to seven minutes. No words, just incoherent shrieking.

Caleb finishes up with the dishwasher and comes over to me. He stands behind me and hooks an arm over my chest, tugging until my shoulder blades are pressed neatly to his front. I close my eyes and hum as he presses a kiss against the back of my head.

This is nice. I want to do this forever.

"How do you want to store all this food?" he asks. It's not a sexy question, but it feels like maybe it could be. I don't think I've ever had a man ask me what sort of containers he should use for cinnamon rolls before.

I give him some instructions and Beckett lends a hand. Together the three of us clean up the kitchen and pack everything away. I'm a little concerned about the state of my refrigerator, but I only need to make it through tomorrow. After that, I don't care about how many tartlets Beckett steals.

Beckett disappears with a grunt and a wave over his shoulder as soon as the last tray is put away, probably off to seduce Evelyn in a field somewhere. Hopefully this time out of camera view. I lean into Caleb's touch against the back of my neck and sigh. "I'm ready to go, I just want to look at the front one more time."

I want to make sure everything is exactly as it should be.

"Alright." His hand slips down my back and curls around my hip. "Follow me."

He leads me out of the back door with his fingers

tangled with mine, stepping along the stone walkway that winds around the bakehouse to the front. The path is lined with clusters of wildflowers, yellow and pink and bright purple against the weathered wood of the renovated tractor shed. When Stella bought the place, it was falling apart. I think Hank used it for storage. We cleared out the inside, made an addition of mostly windows off of the front, hooked up water and power, bought an obscene amount of paint—and the bakehouse was born.

Caleb's hand tightens around mine as he looks at me over his shoulder, the light from the moon slipping along the lines of his body. Shoulders. Jaw. Halfway smile. It ticks wider the longer he looks at me.

"Close your eyes."

"Why?"

He huffs and ducks his head down, guiding us carefully around a wayward lilac bush, one hand in mine and the other at my hip. He glances back up at me through his lashes, standing perfectly still as I drag my sleepy feet across the two stones between us. I bump into him, his arms circling my waist. My forehead drops against his chin and he laughs, husky and low.

"Do you trust me, Layla Dupree?"

I slip my fingers underneath the hem of his soft t-shirt until I find warm skin. He's like a furnace, warmer than the humid night air pressing in on us. I trace my fingertips at the base of his spine and he releases a shaky sounding sigh that I like very much.

"I trust you, Caleb Alvarez." My nose nudges under his

265

chin and he slips his fingers along the scarf in my hair. "A lot of other things, too."

"Oh, yeah?" His voice is gentle, amused, a low rumble somewhere above my head. "Want to share with the class?"

I rub my nose back and forth against his neck. I'm pretty sure he is supporting the entirety of my body weight. Again. "Not at the moment, no."

"Maybe another time, then. Come on. Not much further. We'll take a look and then we'll get you home."

Opening my eyes feels like a monumental effort. "Will you hold my hand?" My voice slurs around the edges.

"Yeah, sweetheart. I'll hold your hand."

He leads me the last three steps with my body practically plastered to his, my eyes obediently closed and our fingers tangled together. He stops me with a gentle touch against my shoulder, and turns me carefully on the biggest stone at the base of the stairs. The one I made Beckett haul halfway across the property with his tractor after I found it by the pond.

"Take a look," Caleb whispers, and I open my eyes.

The whole place is glowing. Warm yellow light spills out from the windows and dances along the stones in a shimmering shower of gold. The flowers hanging from the ceiling look picture perfect from out here. Snow white wisteria and pale pink peonies. Thick green garland that twists around and around the thick wooden beams across the ceiling. All of it floats above my cozy booths and neat little tables, mismatched chairs and old patterned vases.

Daisies and chamomile spill over the chipped edges of the colorful ceramic, a bundle for each table.

Magic. It looks like magic.

My foot slips in a patch of gravel and Caleb loops his arm around my waist again, tugging me closer until I'm pressed into his side. I cling to him as my eyes trail over every bloom. Every fleck of paint, every shingle, every last detail.

"Look at this." Caleb holds me tighter. Brushes his mouth against the apple of my cheek. "You made this, Layla."

"With a lot of help," I try to deflect, but my eyes are burning—thick pressure right between my eyebrows that lets me know I'm about to start blubbering on the front step of my bakehouse.

Caleb ignores me. "I'm so proud of you," he tells me, his voice hushed and earnest. His hands hold me tighter, and I wrap myself around him just as fiercely. Something in my chest shifts, realigns, and clicks into place.

A single tear slips from my lashes and glances along my cheek. When was the last time I heard that from anyone? When was the last time I believed it? I brush the wetness away with my knuckles and drop my forehead into his shoulder.

"I'm proud of me, too."

NINETEEN

CALEB

MORNING COMES FAR TOO QUICKLY.

Leaving Layla last night had been ... difficult. I dropped her off just as the sun was slipping below the horizon, the sky a pale lilac cascading into midnight blue. She had fallen asleep with her face pressed up against the passenger side window, both of her hands clutching one of mine tight to her chest. I pulled into her driveway and cut the engine—sat there with the sky swirling brilliant strokes of blue and purple and deep, deep navy and just watched her for a little bit. My hand in between hers, a smile flirting with the corners of her lips.

Then she jolted awake—screamed *WHAT* at me loud enough to have me rocket my head against my window—and almost gave me a concussion. It took her a while to stop laughing after that.

She had been pie punch drunk, donut delirious. I helped her into her house and she clung to my t-shirt like a tiny, persistent little barnacle. She twisted and tugged and tried to drag me back to her bedroom. I don't know when Layla got so damn strong, but it felt like I had to use all my physical and mental strength to resist her.

Come cuddle, Caleb, she had whispered in my ear, teeth grazing. *I'll be good, I promise.*

I almost tossed her over my shoulder and carried her there myself.

But today is important to her and I didn't want to be a distraction. Plus, she fell asleep as soon as her pretty head hit the pillow, a cute little snore with every inhale.

So I tugged off her boots and covered her with her blanket and slipped out the front door after making sure it locked behind me. I set my alarm for an atrociously early hour and now here I am, with one of my arms flung over my face, groaning curses at the incessant buzzing from my nightstand. I slap at it without looking and sigh when it stops.

I want to stop by the bakehouse before Layla's scheduled interview. I want to brush a kiss against her nose and get that nervous edge in her eyes to slip, just a little. She's got nothing to worry about. The bakery looks amazing. I'm pretty sure I had erotic dreams about those fruit tarts last night. *Baltimore Magazine* is going to have a field day with her little glass cottage in the middle of the woods. It's like something out of a book, like the stories parents tell their kids before they drift off to sleep.

Layla in the middle of the room, all of those flowers

surrounding her like a halo. A coy smile on her lips and pink in her cheeks. Bare skin. Strawberry shortcake.

My phone starts buzzing again.

I reach for it with one eye squinted shut, sitting up when I see the screen. It's not my alarm, but a phone call. I almost fumble it when I see Layla's name blinking across.

"Hey," I answer and try not to sound like I'm sporting a boner at the idea of her bare skin and shortcake. I arrange the blankets over my lap and clear my throat twice, like she can see me through the damn phone. "Good morning."

Her breath hitches on the other side of the phone and the lingering heat evaporates. Alarm punches me right in the chest instead, and I'm reaching for my sweatshirt before she can say a word.

"Caleb."

Her voice is thick and uneven. She sounds like she's been crying. I grab a random pair of jeans and shove my legs through, the phone held between my shoulder and ear. I listen to her try and collect herself and almost lose my fucking mind in the process.

"What is it?"

"There's—" Her breath hiccups and she lets out another shaky sigh. I charge through my house like I'm on my way to commit a felony. Which I might, as soon as I figure out what the hell is going on.

"Take a deep breath, sweetheart. Just tell me where you are, and I'll come to you."

I stop in the middle of my hallway and catch the

barely-there sound of a muffled sob. Like she turned her head away from the phone, like she's trying to stop crying long enough to talk. A flash of ferocious heat and then bone-chilling cold roars through my blood.

I like to think I'm a reasonable man. Controlled. But I'm feeling neither of those things right now.

"Layla," I plead. "Where are you?"

"The bakehouse," she finally whispers. "The power must have cut out overnight." A heavy swallow and a ragged exhale. "Everything is ruined."

IT'S WORSE than I thought.

With no climate control and the floor-to-ceiling glass windows welcoming in the heat from outside, all of the flowers in the front of the shop have wilted. Pristine and white last night, they're now hanging limp and faded, tinged with yellow. Petals with curled edges decorate the floor like little fallen soldiers, a haphazard battleground leading to Layla. Layla who is sitting on the floor of the bakehouse with her back to the front counter, her arms over her knees and her forehead tucked into her thighs.

"Sweetheart," I sigh. It feels like it's a hundred and ten degrees in here and the sun hasn't even fully risen yet. I glance at the countertop where she stacked her cookies last night. They look like an amorphous blob under the glass display case. I wince.

"The refrigerators stopped running," she mumbles without bothering to lift her face. I squat down in front of her and soothe my palms up and down her bare arms. Her fingers twitch, but she doesn't reach for me. "All of the tarts are ruined. Everything I—" She pulls in a shaky breath. "Everything I made yesterday is ruined. I don't know what to do."

"We can—" Two peony blooms fall from the ceiling and land with a soft thud at our side. Layla makes a sad, defeated huff that wedges right in the center of my chest. A knife under my ribs. "We can fix this."

Layla leans back and I get a look at her red-rimmed eyes, the tear tracks on her cheeks. I want to pull her in my lap and wrap both of my arms around her. I want to fight a defunct air conditioner, apparently.

"How?" she croaks. "How can we fix this? I don't have any power. My ovens won't turn on. None of my ingredients are usable." She blinks, her big hazel eyes filling with more tears. "The people from the magazine are supposed to be here at ten o'clock."

I glance at the clock above the counter before I remember it must have stopped working when the power went out. The hands are frozen at 10:12pm. Almost six full hours of no electricity. That explains the state of things.

I clear my throat and check my watch. "Then we have a few hours left to work with."

Layla's palms dig into her eyes. She has flower petals in her hair, a discarded, crumpled up apron at her hip. Like she came in and grabbed it off her hook like she always does, but didn't bother looping it over her neck. "To do what?"

I push up to my feet. "Is there anything you can make from what you've got? Anything you can get started on?"

She shakes her head, a shaky hand swiping underneath her eyes. "I don't—"

"Just the first step, Layla. You only need to start."

I hold out my hand to her. She blinks up at me from her spot on the floor, a frown twisting her lips and her shoulders hunched forward. She looks so small down there like that. Small and sad and diminished. I never want to see her like this again.

"I've seen you bake, Caleb," her voice is watery—scratchy and subdued. "Your cake batter is shit."

I huff a laugh. "My cake batter is fine."

"It's the worst cake batter I've ever seen in my entire life."

I tried baking with her once, and it ended with her laughing so hysterically she could barely hold herself up.

"Alright, well. How about you show me how it's done?" I beckon her forward with my fingers until she heaves out a deep breath and holds out her arms. I clasp my hands around her wrists and guide her up and into me. I brush a kiss against her temple and the bridge of her nose.

"You do the baking, sweetheart." I wipe the last of her tears away with my thumbs. "Let me take care of the rest."

BECKETT IS MY FIRST STOP.

I set Layla up in the back kitchen with a small battery-operated fan I find in the dash of my Jeep, clipping it to the edge of a shelf and angling it so it blows her hair off her neck. She gives me a thin, wobbly, grateful smile and I disappear out the back, hopping in my Jeep and tearing across the farm at a speed that tests the limits of my suspension on the bumpy, rocky dirt roads. I turn into Beckett's driveway and send a shower of gravel over the bottom two steps of his porch, narrowly missing the row of daffodils I'm pretty sure his sister Nova planted.

I pound on his front door with my fist until he answers with a ferocious scowl and a rose gold baseball bat clutched in his left hand. I spot Evelyn over his shoulder, swimming in an oversized flannel, two of the cats perched on her shoulders. Evelyn gives me a little wave.

Beckett drops the bat with a heaving sigh, hands on his knees. "What the fu—"

"Do you have a generator?" I'll apologize later this week and maybe ask a question or two about why he has a pink baseball bat covered in gold sparkles in his front closet. "Somewhere on the farm?"

"Caleb." Beckett straightens back to his full height and scratches roughly at the back of his head. He tosses the bat ... somewhere ... and stoops to stop one of the cats from dashing through the door. Prancer meows at me and bats her little paw in greeting. It's cute, but I do not have the time. "Why are you at my house at five in the morning asking about generators?"

Evelyn pads down the hall and nudges him out of the way. "Do you want some coffee? We've got a pot on already."

I shake my head and glance across the fields towards the bakery. A thick layer of humidity hangs heavy over the grass fields, blurring everything until it's just streaks of color. Evergreen. Copper and gold. Even now, I can feel the heat clinging to my skin. The back of my neck and the hollows of my wrists. It's going to be hot as hell today.

"Power went out in the bakehouse overnight." I turn back to Beckett and Evelyn. "She lost air conditioning, refrigerators, ovens. All of the food is scrapped."

Evelyn's eyes widen, just a touch. "The magazine people," she breathes. "That's today, right?"

I nod. Beckett's mouth settles into a firm, determined line. He props the cat up on his shoulder and turns to jog down the hall.

"I'll be there in fifteen minutes," he calls. He grabs a set of keys off a small hook by the back door. "Evie honey, I'll meet you there."

SANDY MEETS me at the grocery store with a faintly bewildered look, her keys jangling on the little cord at her wrist as she unlocks the series of deadbolts on the door. She ushers me inside as soon as the door is cracked, her small hand at my elbow.

"Is everything alright?" She looks over my shoulder at my Jeep parked half on the curb, half off of it. Her eyes dart to her cozy little sedan parked in the usual spot, a couple of feet from the doorway. Her brows collapse into a line.

"What on earth could you possibly need from the grocery store so early?"

"All of the butter, sugar, flour, and eggs you have in stock would be a good start, I think." I glance towards the produce section and make a decision. "Strawberries, too."

She blinks at me. "All of it?"

I nod. "All of it."

"Were you craving shortcake?" She glances at her watch. She wanders towards the registers and flicks on the lights, fluorescents buzzing to life above us. "At five-thirty in the morning?"

A smile I don't really feel hitches at the corner of my mouth. "Something like that."

By the time the bags are loaded in my trunk and I'm turning back onto Main Street, the sun is just starting to creep out from behind the trees. I watch light crawl across the pavement and feel like I'm in a race against time. I hope Beckett has the generator going. I hope Layla has her apron on. If I walk back into that bakehouse and see tears on her cheeks again, I might lose my mind. I'll probably start compulsively baking things in an effort to help and she's right. I'm absolute shit at making a decent cake batter.

I roll to a stop and lower the passenger side window. It only takes one bellow of her name across the sidewalk to get her attention from behind the counter.

Beatrice cracks open the front door of her bakery with a frown, long gray hair braided in a crown across her head.

She's wearing her combat boots again, a blood red sundress that falls below her knees.

"What?"

"Get in the car."

Her face cracks into a grin and she folds her arms over her chest. "While I love an invitation from a handsome man, I can't go joyriding with you through the sunrise today." She pushes off her front porch banister with her shoulder. "Come see me after closing," she says with a wink.

"It's Layla," I shout, before she can shut her door in my face. "She has her interview with the magazine today and she lost power. She needs an extra set of hands."

It's sort of incredible, the way Beatrice doesn't hesitate. She pulls a set of keys out of a hidden pocket in her dress and turns the lock on the front door. She hustles down the stone steps and practically flies into the passenger side of the Jeep, leveraging herself up with the handle above the door. She buckles her seatbelt and gives me an impatient look, her hand thrust forward out the window.

"What the hell are you waiting for, then? Let's go."

"One more thing." I hold my phone between my ear and shoulder, backing up into the alleyway between the buildings. It rings twice before I'm greeted with a flurry of Spanish. I wince when I look at the clock. It's likely I interrupted her morning re-run viewing.

Her huff sounds metallic on the other end of the phone as I turn towards Lovelight. "Lo siento, abuela. I need a favor."

TWENTY
LAYLA

I DON'T QUITE KNOW how he managed it, but I think Caleb's pulled off the impossible.

The entire bakehouse is a flurry of activity, from Gus aggressively pulling down dried blooms in the front to Beatrice whipping something into submission at my side. I haven't seen Caleb since he dropped Beatrice off at my backdoor and went running off through the trees again, but I know he's been in and out. I get a whiff every now and then of dark coffee. Hear the low sound of his voice over the steady thrum of organized chaos that's descended over my kitchen.

His grandmother arrived shortly after he left with a fleet of his cousins. She took one look at my face, grabbed both of my cheeks in her weathered hands, and said something fierce and determined in Spanish. She then smacked me on the ass and told me to chop some strawberries.

So I chopped the strawberries.

Beatrice drops another tray of shortcake in front of me and thrusts a small round cookie cutter against my chest.

"Cut these," she says. "Then hand 'em off."

I don't have my picture perfect miniature tartlets with an edible flower halo or the chocolate mousse cups I spent a painstaking amount of time on, but I do have six trays of warm shortcake and a generator pumping power into the place. I have functioning ovens and more helping hands than I know what to do with, a veritable conveyor belt of productivity made up of Stella, Evelyn, Beatrice, two of Caleb's cousins and a couple of other people from town. Barney, one of Beckett's farmhands, is shockingly good at cutting the strawberries into tiny flowers. And I've never seen anyone whip shortcake filling better than Alex Alvarez.

Hidden talents all around, apparently.

I cut the shortcake slices and then someone pipes the cream. Strawberries are sliced and placed and more shortcake is layered. On and on we go.

I won't have my full menu, but I will have food. That's more than I had an hour ago.

I knew something was wrong as soon as I stepped foot on the pathway this morning. The front light that is always on was snuffed out, the air conditioning unit silent. I wedged open the front door and stared for three long beats at the flower petals on the floor. I could feel the heat pressing against my skin, the slightly stale and sour smell of food left sitting out. My walk to the back felt like a thousand miles.

I checked the refrigerators, saw my destroyed desserts, sat on the floor and called Caleb.

It was the only thing I could think to do.

Which is terrifying in its own right. We have an arrangement with clear boundaries and safeguards in place but when I felt like I was bursting at the seams, Caleb was the only person I wanted to call. Not Stella. Not Beckett. Not Evie or Luka.

I wanted Caleb.

And he had shown up. Immediately. With his shirt on inside out and backwards, the tag just under his chin. Sleep rumpled and wearing two different shoes, he showed up for me.

That's definitely not included in our arrangement.

Stella nudges me with her elbow. "When do the scones come out?"

I blink and press another circle into the shortcake. I glance at the clock that Beckett fixed before he disappeared somewhere with Caleb and Luka. "Ten minutes."

Which gives me almost forty-five before the interview team shows up. It should be enough time to get these last shortcakes done and kick everyone out. Maybe I can pretend this is a normal morning and not the most categorically stressful moment of my life. Evie appears on my other side and starts toying with my hair.

"Not by the food," I mumble. That's the last thing I need.

"Then come over here for a second."

Beatrice swats me away with hands covered in flour

and aggressively yanks the shortcake out of my hands. Decision made for me, I roll my eyes and follow Evelyn obediently to the corner. If anyone has questions about why Beatrice and I are suddenly working together, they don't say a word. Maybe our portrayed rivalry isn't as fierce as I thought. Perhaps I should bodycheck her into the jam display the next time we're at the grocery store together just to reinforce the narrative. She'd get a kick out of that.

Evelyn blocks me in against the wall and immediately untangles the loose knot I tucked my strands into. She drags her fingers against my scalp, parting and fluffing. I blow out an anxious breath.

"I don't know if I have time for this."

"You're getting your picture taken today." She reminds me with an arch of one dark, perfect brow. "You'll thank me for this when your face is in a magazine."

She's right. I guess. It doesn't make it any easier to stand here though. At least with all of the activity, I've been able to keep my mind from running. I can hold back the thoughts that have lurked like shadows since Stella first told me about the opportunity. *I don't deserve this. They're going to show up and tell me it's all a misunderstanding. My scones aren't anything special. I'm not anything special.*

The intrusive thoughts haven't stopped since that first trickle, a couple of weeks ago. They've gotten worse, actually, an almost endless barrage of doubts and misgivings.

It's better with Caleb, though. When he's around. I try not to think too hard about that.

Evelyn pulls out some tinted lip stain out of the front

pocket of her overalls and unscrews the top, tap-tapping it against my bottom lip. I'd be surprised with anyone else if they suddenly pulled out a tube of makeup from mud-splattered clothes, but not with Evie.

I close my eyes and inhale a shaky breath, hold it, and then exhale slowly. Evie's hand falls away from my face.

"Layla." I blink open my eyes. Evelyn smiles gently at me. "It looks amazing. I know it's not what you planned, but—they're coming here for you, not the scones."

That doesn't make me feel any better. Anxiety winds tight in my chest. "They're sort of coming here for the scones," I contest. And the custards. And the tarts. And everything else on the special menu stenciled on chalk-board out front. All of that stuff only exists in my trash bins out back. A breath wheezes out of me.

Evie shakes me a little. "Layla, honey, everything is going to be—"

"Hey." Caleb's interruption is smooth as he suddenly appears at our side, dirt on both of his knees and in a swipe across his forehead—his t-shirt still twisted inside out. He reaches for me and the relief I feel is immediate. Something about his arm winding around me, holding tight and sure. It's a warm pressure expanding in the center of my chest—an unraveling of that twisted, tangled up knot. I'm reaching for him before I even realize it, my hand looping around his wrist. His shifts until our fingers twine together, his long fingers overlapping the back of my hand. He tips his head closer so I can hear him over the noise of the kitchen. Specifically the sound of Beatrice barking orders like a war general. "Can I borrow you for a second?"

I nod.

Evie pokes him hard in the chest as he tugs me towards the back door. "Don't mess up her makeup."

"Noted." His lips twitch and his gaze settles on the swell of my newly-stained bottom lip with interest. "I won't keep her long."

The backdoor swings shut behind us and he leads us down the same stone pathway we took last night. When he held me in his arms and we gazed at the front of the bakehouse like it was every dream I ever had come true. It feels more like a nightmare today. Like I'm wearing a pair of shoes that don't quite fit.

Like I'm an imposter.

"Caleb." I pull on his hand, sure now of his intention. "I don't want to."

He ignores me and picks up his pace instead. I huff and drag my feet behind him. I have half a mind to cling to my azalea bush and kick my feet. Maybe I'll disappear among the branches and just live there. They can interview me from between the leaves.

I keep my eyes firmly on my feet as we round the front of the building and Caleb lines me up in the same spot we were standing twelve hours ago. He drapes his arms over my shoulders and tugs me into his chest.

"Look."

I shake my head. I don't want to see my own disappointments, my unmet expectations. I don't want to see the result of all my painstaking effort reduced to some ... ramshackle attempt. Caleb huffs, his hand gentle beneath my chin. He brushes a kiss to my temple and guides my face up.

"Look, Layla."

I reluctantly look up at the front of my bakehouse. The hanging flowers that I could see from the windows last night are gone, the discarded petals swept up and the floor bare. The stems that were on every table are missing too, the mason jars back in their usual spot, stacked behind the counter. It looks like the bakehouse on any other day. Big windows and wooden tables. Thick pine trees crowding close.

Perfectly normal. Perfectly plain.

"I'm so proud of you," he tells me, his voice warm in my ear. The exact same way he said it last night, when this place looked like magic.

I let my head fall back against his chest and look up. I can only see the curve of his jaw, the lines by his left eye. I can't tell if he's being honest.

"Why?" I ask. "All of my work, everything I did—it was for nothing."

"It wasn't for nothing."

"It was, because right now all I see is the usual. Nothing special."

He makes a disbelieving sound under his breath. "Nothing special?" He swallows heavily, a click in the back of his throat. "You don't need all of that extra stuff. The flowers were nice, but they were just details. I tried to tell you that last night."

"Tell me, what?"

"It's you, Layla. Without the frills, maybe, but this place is you. Your heart. Your kindness. Your butter croissants and your coffee. There isn't a single person who walks up those steps that isn't charmed by you."

I exhale a shaky breath and turn in his arms. I try to believe the words he's saying, but it's hard.

"You really think so?"

His palm slides down the column of my spine. "I know so, and so do you. Where is the Layla that takes my compliments with a grin and a nod because she knows they're exactly what she deserves?"

"Hiding," I mumble. She's buried under layers of self-doubt and exhaustion. "Maybe try again."

I can feel his smile loosening his shoulders, relaxing his body. I tuck a small one right in the middle of his chest.

"You're amazing, Layla," he whispers. "If I could only eat one thing for the rest of my life, it would be your butter croissants."

I snicker. "Liar."

"It's true. I want a picture of one to keep in my wallet for when I'm feeling lonely."

A laugh bursts out of me. I rest my cheek against his chest again and squeeze tight.

"I'm going to get Nova to tattoo one on my body."

Now there's an interesting idea. I flush warm with the possibilities. Maybe on the span of his ribcage. On the jut of his hipbone. In that delicious line that runs down the middle of his abs. Someplace I can trace with my tongue. It's a lovely distraction.

I rub my nose into his chest, like one of Beckett's cats. I let out a deep, rattling sigh. All of my anxiety and frustration and disappointment tumbles right out of me into the summer air.

"Thank you," I whisper. "For being here."

He cups his hand around the back of my neck and squeezes. I feel his lips somewhere in my hair.

"I wouldn't be anywhere else."

THE PEOPLE from *Baltimore Magazine* arrive at ten o'clock on the dot to a clean, air conditioned bakery—blueberry scones and strawberry shortcake filling every inch of the display cases. The bakehouse is bustling with a line out the door. I think the entire town is here, waiting for something to eat. Not only the people who showed up at the crack of dawn to help me piece myself back together, but a bunch of new guests, too.

Sheriff Dane Jones stands near the front of the line, his hand looped around Matty's elbow, his hat tucked under his arm, a rare but bright smile hitching at the side of his mouth when Matty leans into him and whispers something in his ear. Jeremy and his mom are caught somewhere near the middle, Jeremy breaking away every now and then to bounce up and down while shooting me an energetic wave. And Charlie, somehow down from New York—wearing a crisp dark suit with his nose buried in his phone, leaning up against the coffee station with a blue-berry scone in his hand. He glances up briefly and does a double take when he sees Nova, Beckett's youngest sister and resident tattoo artist, examining the chalk drawings on my menu board.

But my eyes find Caleb. He's sitting in the corner with Beckett and Luka, all three of them looking like they just went ten rounds in a mud pit, sipping tea out of tiny china cups. Apparently they went scavenging through the fields for all the wildflowers they could get their hands on. The bakehouse is dotted with splashes of color—the smell of honeysuckle threading with warm butter and fresh blue-berries.

Caleb catches my eye with a wink, and my nerves settle a little more.

I finger a bouquet of daisies by the cash register and watch as they approach. There's only two of them, a casu-ally-dressed man with dark blonde hair and a small woman with a camera looped around her neck. I watch as the man's head tips back as he looks at the restored wooden beams slanted across the ceiling, the wicker baskets we turned into lampshades. A smile starts in his eyes and tugs at his cheeks until he's grinning, spinning on his heel to take it all in.

They make their way through the crowd of people—the crowd of my *friends*—and I stand a little taller. I find that quiet well of pride that burst to life my very first day here, a set of keys in my hand. I sink into it and my smile settles into something sure.

"Hey. I'm Layla." I introduce myself, the sounds of the bakehouse flowing around me like the tide. A tea cup settling into a saucer. The grind of coffee beans. A bright laugh, over by the chalkboard. "Welcome to my bakehouse."

"DID you see his face when he tried the scone?" I grab two fistfuls of Caleb's t-shirt and shake him back and forth. Well, I do my best, but he's about as solid as a small mountain, standing propped up against my counter. "He looked like he ascended."

Caleb scrubs the back of his head. "I saw his face when he was looking at you," he grumbles.

I wave that away. "They seemed really happy. They stayed longer than they said they would, and then took so many pictures!" Anita, the photographer, barely stopped to eat. Will, the reporter, ate six scones and two cups of shortcake. He asked for a box to go. I am high on the endorphins of adrenaline and exhaustion.

Caleb's face softens. "Of course they did."

"I think it'll be a good feature."

"Of course it will." He presses the back of his hand against his mouth to stifle a yawn, then shakes his head like he's trying to force away his own fatigue. He reaches for a hand towel and folds it into neat squares. "It was great, Layla. Even if Bill couldn't keep his hands off of you."

"Will," I correct with a small smile and a poke to his forearm. "And he shook my hand. That was it."

"It was a really friendly handshake," Caleb insists.

"Relax." I untie my apron from around my back and stretch out my neck. "You're still stuck with me for another week. I don't plan on ending our arrangement early."

A part of me is considering extending our arrangement. I've thought about it more than once over the past week. But I still don't know what parts of us work within the parameters we've created for ourselves, and which parts are truly, genuinely us. I still don't trust anything this good to be real.

I glance up and meet Caleb's eyes, his lips tilted down in a frown.

"What is it?"

He pushes himself off of the counter and wipes his palms against his jeans. He still hasn't fixed his shirt. "Has it been three weeks already?"

I nod. "Yep. Your final evaluation is going to be a real banger."

The joke lands flat between us. I shift uncomfortably on my feet and search for something to say to get rid of all this awkward tension. "What do you—" I watch as he traces an aimless line against my countertop with his pointer finger, face still set in sharp edges. "What do you have planned for your last date?"

He considers my question for far too long, a deep breath curling his shoulders forward. He collects himself slowly, a smile at half of its usual wattage nudging that dimple awake. He stops fussing with the stuff on my countertop and stands to his full height.

"You'll see when we get there, yeah? I'm not giving up my secrets now." He meets my eyes. Warm, golden brown. Flecks of amber. My favorite crinkles at the corners. "How about I start with giving you a lift home?"

Relieved, I drape my apron over the hook.

"Yeah. That sounds really nice."

TWENTY-ONE

CALEB

I DIDN'T REALIZE we only had a week left.

I think I stopped keeping track after the escape room incident. Maybe our picnic on the beach. It's easy enough to get swept away by Layla, so I don't exactly blame myself for not marking the days with a bright red "X" on the dog eared calendar taped to the side of my fridge.

I don't know how I feel about it. The deep swell of hesitation in the pit of my stomach feels a bit too dramatic, and the anxiety clawing at the back of my throat feels like too much, too. At the start of this we said that things would go back to normal between us. We agreed that there wouldn't be any bad blood, but ... will I be able to stand on the other side of her counter three days a week and pretend everything is normal? How do I stop ... wanting her so much? Will I be able to watch her smile and laugh and spin around the bakehouse and not want to press my lips to the edge of her smile? Feel the joy thrumming through her?

Fan my fingers out between her shoulder blades and tuck her closer to me?

Layla had joked about it earlier—our last date together. Maybe I need to take a step back. Get some perspective. Isn't that what I am trying to get better at doing?

An end to our arrangement doesn't have to be a bad thing. In fact, it could be a very good thing. Maybe—maybe this could be the start of a new thing. A more serious, intentional thing.

I'd love to stop thinking about the word *thing*.

I fall back on Layla's couch with a huff, my palms digging into my eyes until I see spots.

I just have to convince her that I'm worth the chance.

"What're you thinking about?" she yells from her kitchen.

"My croissant tattoo," I yell back. But really I'm sitting on her couch with my feet propped up on her coffee table trying to figure out what sort of date might tip the balance on the Layla scale in my favor. What sort of thing might leave her wanting to reconsider the terms of our arrangement.

I'm also trying not to fall asleep. And wondering why no one told me my t-shirt is on backwards and inside out. My heavy eyes slip further shut and I reach for one of her throw pillows, cradling it close to my chest.

This couch is soft. Comfortable. Warm.

It's possible the day is catching up with me.

I'm exhausted and nestled into a couch that smells like

whipped cream and sugar, hints of fresh baked bread and warm pie crust. It's like being in a cloud or a ... dream. It might be a dream, actually. It might be my favorite sort of dream.

Especially when Layla pads in from the kitchen with a plate in each hand. I perk up a bit and glance at the slices of pie she's holding. Questions slip through my mind like wisps of smoke or bubbles in a champagne glass. As soon as I catch the edge of one, another replaces it. When does she make all of this stuff? Where is she hiding it? Is she tired at all?

Luckily, I'm able to voice the most important one.

"Is that blueberry?"

I practically slur the words. I sound drunk. Sixteen bottles deep.

"It is." She sets the plates down on the table out of reach. If I had even an ounce of energy, I'd be reaching for that pie. As it is, I sprinted the length of the farm twice over gathering wildflowers for the bakehouse and my legs feel like they have decided to call it a day ahead of the rest of my body. Layla collapses on the couch next to me and all I can manage is a subtle tilt of my body. My eyes slip shut and I rest my chin on top of her head. She curls into me.

"You look like you need a nap more than you need some pie."

"I always need pie," I mumble.

She sifts her fingers through my hair, nails scratching

at my scalp. I make an embarrassing noise that's part whimper, part growl. She huffs a laugh.

"Take a nap. The pie will be here when you wake up."

"Will you stay with me for a little bit?" I like the way she feels with her body next to mine, her fingertips working down my neck in smooth, easy glides.

"Yeah." She presses a kiss against the hollow of my throat and I slip both arms around her waist. "The pie will keep."

I WAKE up face-down on the couch, one of my legs hanging off the edge and a chunky cable knit blanket thrown over half of my body. I can hear Layla in the kitchen humming along to a song on the radio, a mumbled string of lyrics every now and again that are definitely wrong. Socked feet shuffle across the floor, an uneven step that tells me she's dancing. Or trying to, I think, as she thunks her knee on a cabinet with a muffled curse. I smile into a throw pillow.

My dreams come back to me in flashes of color and sensation. There's a heaviness in my chest, a warm curl of wanting that coils tighter the longer I listen to Layla in the kitchen. A lick of comfort, too, in all the sounds and smells that fill her home—in the place she's carved out for me in it. The simple joy of listening to another person inhabit the space around me.

Layla hums a little louder—just slightly off key—and

some of the loneliness that feels like a constant companion eases. A knot unravels around my heart.

I lean up onto my elbows and drag my hand over my face. The shuffling in the kitchen stops.

"Hey," she says, a smile in her voice as she pops her head into my line of sight. "You're awake."

"Am I?"

My voice sounds like sandpaper. It doesn't feel like I'm awake. It feels like I'm still caught in a dream. I sit up and yawn so wide my jaw cracks.

Layla's laugh is warm and easy as she moves around the tall counter that separates her kitchen from the living room. She must have changed while I was asleep. Tiny, soft-looking shorts and an oversized t-shirt that falls off of one shoulder. Some flour on her elbow and something that looks like strawberry jam on her jaw. My heart hits double-time.

"You are, in fact, awake," she tells me. She stops right in front of my slightly parted legs, one of her bare feet tapping at my shin. "Do you want your pie now?"

It's the temptation of all her bare skin—maybe the mention of pie. I don't know. I don't want the pie at all. I only want Layla and her laugh and her smile and her hazel eyes shining bright with happiness in this cozy little house. I want the flour on her hands streaking through my hair, maybe that strawberry jam on my tongue.

She sways further into me and my hands find the warm skin behind her knees, fingertips tracing twin figure eights. One of her legs buckles and she grips my shoulders.

"Caleb."

"Hm?"

"What are you doing?"

I'm trying to hold myself together, but I'm fraying in the middle. Every moment I spend in her space, I only want her more. I only *like* her more. I run my hands up and down the back of her legs, a little higher with every pass. How haven't I been touching her every moment of every day? My restraint deserves an award. My name in lights above the back counter at the bakehouse. Maybe one of those little golden plaques they sell down at the pawn shop.

I drop my head against her chest and she cards her fingers through my hair in that way I love so much.

"Were you baking?" I ask, my voice muffled by the material of her shirt. She smells like clean detergent and brown sugar. I want to live in this exact spot for the rest of my life.

She hedges. "Maybe."

"Do you get tired of baking things?" I rub the hem of her shorts between my thumb and forefinger. Gray. Some sort of sweatshirt material. I want to sink my teeth into the waistband and tug.

"Not really." She pauses and considers. "Well, sometimes. If it's just for myself, I can't muster the motivation." She makes a small, interested sound in the back of her throat as I curl my hand around her thigh, my knuckles edging under the hem of her shorts. I squeeze possessively. "But you're here," she breathes on an exhale.

I nod. I still haven't moved my face from her chest. I nuzzle at the curve of her breast through her shirt and she shifts on her feet. I can't figure out if she's wearing a bra.

"What were you making?"

"What?"

"Just now, what were you working on?" I drag my chin down her sternum, teeth barely grazing the soft swell of her.

Nope. She's not wearing a bra.

"Oh." Her back arches towards my mouth. "Jelly thumbprint cookies."

I groan. I can't help it. Something about Layla and cookies. Her laugh is husky and knowing.

She tips her head down until her mouth is right at my ear. "Marmalade," she whispers. Goosebumps erupt along my arms. I shiver. "Shortbread," she says, slower.

She makes a high-pitched squeaking sound as I stand from the couch, my hands just below the curve of her ass and her legs high around my hips. I consider the wall by her window, then the countertop still covered with flour and a little jar of orange marmalade. Neither option will work for what I want with her, but there's an interesting idea on the tip of my tongue for the spoon resting across the half-open lid. I want more space than the countertop will give me. I want to take my time.

"Can I make you come again?" The question slips out of me, more blunt than I like to be. But need has me frantic, hands shaking and mouth working at her neck in between every gasped word. Layla drops her head back with a pant and I give into temptation, pressing her up against the wall at the start of her short hallway. One of her frames rattles, and she grabs my jaw with her hand to guide my mouth to hers. Our kiss is messy. Hot and wet and desperate. There's nothing else I want more than to sink to my knees on this colorful, plush rug and hook her thigh over my shoulder. I want to know what she tastes like, what she sounds like, what she looks like completely bare in the glow of the late afternoon sun.

Layla still has so many secrets that I haven't uncovered.

I nose at her oversized t-shirt and bracket her hips with my hands. She keeps wiggling against me and I can't—I can't think. I can only remember the last time I had her this close to me. The sounds she made with my body between her legs. The color in her cheeks as she got closer and closer to what she needed.

We only have one week left together, and I intend to make the most of it.

I cup her breasts through her t-shirt and rub my thumbs over her nipples. Her head drops back against the wall and she drapes her arms over my shoulders, watching me with lazy eyes.

"What kind of dreams were you having on my couch?" she sighs out.

I smile and slip my hands underneath her shirt, the fabric bunching at my wrists. I don't move them, I just feel the warmth of her skin against my palms. I try to memorize this moment, when she's looking at me like I'm someone she could want.

"Good ones," I answer.

"Hm, feel free to elaborate."

"Well." I pull us away from the wall and move in the direction of what I assume is her bedroom. "There were thumbprint cookies."

She laughs as I open the first door on the left side of the hall and almost dump her into a collection of winter coats. She drags her teeth across my collarbone and I can feel her smile against my skin. "That's oddly specific. Anything else happening in that dream of yours?"

"Marmalade," I tell her. She laughs again, husky and rich. "Shortbread."

I try another door and I'm greeted by a pale pink shower curtain—a tidy row of plants on a low shelf below a frosted window. My gaze snags on an interesting piece of lace dangling from the curtain rod. Something with straps and the smallest bow I've ever seen, right in the middle.

I stare at it for one second, two, as Layla sucks at my neck. Her clever hands sneak into the waistband of my jeans and my patience evaporates.

"Layla." I readjust her in my grip and cuff her wrists with one of my hands. I need her to stop touching me or this is going to end the exact same way it did last time. Horrifically quick and embarrassing, if not also wildly satisfying.

A heavy glint of interest shines in her eyes and I arch an eyebrow, squeezing her wrists just the slightest bit tighter. Her back arches with the angle and her cheeks flush crimson.

I brush a kiss over the curve of her jaw.

"I need you to tell me where your bedroom is."

"Last door on the right," she pants.

I release Layla's hands and charge in that direction, both of her arms wrapped tight around my shoulders. We're kissing again, her hungry sounds caught on the tip of my tongue, pressed against my teeth. I slip one of my hands up the back of her shorts, nothing but smooth skin and the thinnest strap I've ever felt in my life greeting my touch.

Desire burns like a wildfire through me and I practically kick in the door to her bedroom. It bounces off the wall where she has another collection of mismatched frames. A picture of her and Stella and Beckett that I barely glance at. While her living room was a collection of color, her bedroom is simple and welcoming. A big bed with a fluffy comforter, a small mountain of pillows stacked neatly against the headboard. White and cream and taupe and oatmeal. We tumble into the bed together and it's like falling into a cloud. Like twisting around and around in one of those cotton candy spinners, sticky sweetness clinging to my skin.

I brace myself with my arms planted by her shoulders, her smile wide as she beams up at me. She is the most lovely thing I've ever seen. I finger a lock of her hair and tuck it behind her ear.

"What do you want, Layla?"

I tell myself that by asking her, I'm trying to hold on to the safety vest of our relationship. This is supposed to help her vocalize what she wants and needs in bed. But really I just want to watch desire paint colors over her skin. I want to watch her lips form the words and hear in detail all the things she wants me to do to her.

"Well." Her hands slip under my shirt, nails scratching lightly at my torso. "I liked what you asked me in the living room, to start."

When I asked if I could make her come. My whole body flushes hot and I give in to her pulling on my clothes and let her drag my shirt up and over my head. She throws it somewhere in the corner of her room, palms tracing up and down my torso. Her tongue licks at the corner of her mouth and her eyes shine like twin gemstones.

"How do you want to come?" I urge her chin up and press a kiss to her bottom lip. I suck it into my mouth and I drag my thumb down her throat and hook it into the top of her oversized t-shirt. "My hands?" I slip my whole hand inside the collar of her shirt and palm her bare breast. "My mouth?"

A deep breath rattles out of her and she shifts her legs wider beneath me until I'm cradled between her open thighs, my erection thick and heavy where she's soft and warm.

"Time for another confession," she gasps as I pinch at her nipple, legs shifting against my hips. "No one has ever —I've never had someone go down on me before."

I drop my forehead against her collarbone with a groan. The thought that I could be the first to know her like that—the only one to ever make her come with my head between her legs, I'm—

I'm breathless. Mindless. Overwhelmed with the need to touch and taste.

My hands flex. "Is that something you want?"

"I'm not sure," she whispers. "I think I do."

I push up until I'm on my knees in front of her, hands at her hips and my thumbs dipping below the waistband of her tiny, distracting shorts.

"We could try," I offer. "Just like before. We can figure out what you like together."

She gives me a nod and I pull her shorts down another incremental inch. Her shirt is rucked up around her belly button and all I can see is smooth, pale skin. The dip between her waist and her hip. The very edge of her lilac underwear and a peek of ink, right below her hip bone. My mouth goes dry and I pull her shorts down to get a better look.

A tattoo, no bigger than a half-dollar. A whisk and a kitchen knife crossed together and surrounded by a wreath of flowers. The small tattoo is placed right below her hip bone, on the gentle slope along the inside of her thigh. I trace over it with my thumb, the delicate lines raised beneath my touch, and her whole body relaxes beneath my touch.

"Nova did it," she explains. "I wanted to get something just for me."

I lean down between her open legs until I can press my mouth to it. I kiss it once. Twice. On my third kiss, I give in to temptation and lave my tongue against the ink. I seal my teeth around it and bite.

"No one else has seen it?"

She shrugs and tilts her head against the pillow. I rest my chin against the inside of her thigh. I want us to have every conversation exactly like this. Her fingers in my hair, the scratch of her nails soothing along my scalp. "No one else has commented on it. But I guess no one has ever looked at me the way you do."

"Good." I scrape my teeth along the edge of it again and she lifts her hips into me. "Then it's something just for you—and a little for me, too."

She makes a sound—pleased, I think—as I drag her shorts the rest of the way down her legs. I leave her pretty purple underwear right where it is, lace and satin and another impossibly small bow right on top. I can see the jut of her nipples through the thin material of her t-shirt, her chest heaving. It takes every ounce of my restraint not to rip everything off of her and follow her down into her pillows.

I inhale through my nose and try to slow myself down. Layla deserves patience, not me rutting her down into the mattress like a maniac. I want to know her. Learn her. Understand all the things that make her pant and shiver and shake.

"These are nice." I drag my thumb across the thin band at her hip and follow the line of her underwear across the top to the small bow in the middle. I stop there and twist my hand. I drag my thumb straight down the middle of her. I can already feel how wet she is through the thin material. How warm. I do it again and reach for my jeans with my free hand, undoing the top button.

"I like nice things," she says, staring hard at where my briefs peek out from beneath my waistband.

"You deserve nice things," I tell her with a laugh in my voice. If she wants that nice thing, she can have it, too. But I want to make her come first, just like she asked. I hold steady with my hand on her, gentle swipes of my thumb between her legs. I trace every inch of her until her arm is flung over her face and she's chasing my touch with smooth rolls of her hips.

Pretty. She's so fucking pretty.

"Caleb."

I brush a kiss against the inside of her knee. "Hm?"

"Are you going to—" She lets her question trail off into a soft moan.

"What?"

"You know."

"I don't know if you don't ask me." I move my kisses higher to the smooth stretch of her thigh. "Didn't you tell me you like to be teased?"

"Is that what you're doing?"

Sort of. Mainly I'm trying not to go too fast. I want this moment with Layla to last. I want to remember what she looks like exactly like this—long, lazy limbs and bare skin. Pink cheeks and her eyes on me. All of these new and secret pieces of herself that she's entrusting to me.

I press at her hip and she lifts her knee, tilting her legs

open wider. An invitation. "You're supposed to tell me what you want, remember?"

Her arm shifts and she peeks one hazel eye down at me. Her lips are curled at the edges. I reward her with a kiss right where her thigh meets her hip and she makes another soft, sweet sound.

"You can tell me what you need and I'll give it to you." I add another kiss higher, light and easy, right over her underwear. She tilts her hips up with a sigh. "I'll be happy to give it to you."

Her arm slips back over her head, twisting with her hair against the pillows. She stares down at me, face open.

"I want your mouth on me," she whispers.

I brush a kiss against her thigh, a reward for her honesty. "Where?"

My voice is all grit, a command from somewhere deep in my chest. I want to know exactly what she wants. I want her to *ask*. I want to hear the words.

"Caleb, please."

I slip my thumbs under the waistband of her underwear and snap it against her skin. She huffs a frustrated sound and I grin. I like teasing her this way, too. Hearing her beg just a little.

"Where, Layla?"

She leans up on her elbows and huffs a frustrated breath. "You know, if you're going to be difficult, I can just do it myself."

Heat licks down my spine and settles heavy between my legs. The thought of Layla touching herself while I watch—I swallow against the heady rush of wanting. Her ferocious scowl dims and a brush of pink lights up her cheeks.

"Maybe that's not the threat I thought it was," she says faintly.

"No," I manage through a throat that suddenly feels bone dry. "No, it's really not." A cascade of possibilities slip through my mind. But one—one has my breath coming short, her skin a temptation half-an-inch away from my lips. I tear myself away and crawl up her body until my hands are planted by her shoulders. I hover there with my nose against her cheek and my mouth against the corner of hers. I drag a kiss against the swell of her bottom lip and then catch it with my teeth. I tug until she moans and leverage myself up so I can see the length of her spread out against the sheets. Bare skin, legs tipped open. Eyes heavy and a strand of hair, stuck to her neck.

God, she's beautiful.

"Could you show me, Layla? Could you show me what you like?"

TWENTY-TWO

LAYLA

I STARE down my body at Caleb, shirtless and kneeling between my thighs. Waiting for my answer. He looks positively indecent like this. Tan, broad chest. The button of his jeans undone. The strong cut of his hip where it disappears below the hem. Dark eyes and swollen lips.

I had a dream like this four days ago. In my dream, he came up behind me while I was mixing cookie dough and slid his hand in the collar of my dress. He cupped my breast with his mouth at my neck, fingers pinching and plucking. He was wearing an apron and nothing else, I'm pretty sure. There was chocolate sauce involved.

This is better. His tongue licks at his bottom lip as his eyes blaze a path from my forehead to my exposed belly button and the twisted line of my underwear beneath. His eyes catch and spark like embers in a campfire.

This is so much better.

I squirm against him. "What?"

"You heard what I said." His firm tone makes my blood run a bit hotter. His hands glide over my thighs, fingers spread out wide like he's trying to cover as much skin as possible. I'm not even sure he realizes he's doing it. His gaze is fixed firmly on mine. "Can you show me how you touch yourself?"

I shift my bare legs against the blankets. It's one thing to whisper things in the heat of the moment, another to show him in the afternoon sun drifting through my curtains how I like to be touched. His eyes soften the longer he looks at me, heat and need replaced with gentle affection.

A smile tips the corner of his mouth as he ducks down and nudges my nose with his. "You're safe with me, remember? We can do anything you want or nothing at all. We can stop right now."

I nod, barely brushing his mouth with mine. I test him with my fingers against the skin of my belly and his gaze sticks there, watching. I clear my throat and he drags his gaze back to mine with significant reluctance. I like it, I realize. I like the way he's looking at me, like I'm everything he could possibly want. Like he would be happy with just this, sitting on the edge of my bed and learning what sort of touch I like the best.

It's enough for me to shake off the rest of my hesitation.

My hand drifts lower.

"We never have to do anything you don't want to do," he tells me. It's like that with Caleb, an ebb and flow between control and release. Demand and desire. The best sort of dance.

"I know."

"We can go back to the kitchen. Have some of that pie."

I bite my cheek against a smile. "Let's stay here."

I want this. I want to explore all the ways he makes me feel different—makes me feel *better*—than anyone else ever has before. I want to watch the way his jaw clenches as my hand moves against my body. I want to watch his eyes flash a shade darker and the muscles in his arms jump. I want to unravel him, bit by bit. Test that meticulous control of his.

I want him to be just as overwhelmed as I feel, a buzzing beneath my skin and an ache low in my belly. Like we're teetering on the precipice.

"Alright," he whispers. His thumb traces lightly against my thigh and then he pulls his hands away from me completely. He kneels on my bed and squeezes his hand around the back of his neck. A man wrestling with his control.

Oh, I like it so much.

I pull at the edge of my shirt and then drag it up again. I don't know if I should take it off, or keep it on. For all my enthusiasm, I actually have no idea where to start. "Should I just—"

Caleb is fixated on the three inches of skin between my belly button and the hem of my underwear, but he blinks back towards my face when he hears the hesitation in my voice. A smile starts in the lines by his eyes and he releases his neck.

"Close your eyes," he tells me. I arch an eyebrow and he gives me a half-smile, his dimple blinking to life in his cheek. He drags two knuckles over my knee and up my thigh. Back down again. "Close your eyes, Layla."

I huff, that damn firm tone making my insides flutter again. "You're bossier than you let on."

His laugh is a dark, wicked thing—warm air against my neck as he leans back over me. "You have no idea."

He doesn't give me time to think about that interesting little statement. He just leans forward and catches my mouth with his. He licks into me like I'm that blueberry pie I left on my coffee table. Deep. Devouring. Consuming. My eyes slip shut and I kiss him back just as hungrily.

It's easier to follow his directions like this. To turn off the part of my brain that is still riddled with anxiety from this morning. The part that is turning over the consequences of this thing I'm doing with Caleb, examining every angle, over and over again. He kisses me and I don't care about a single thing except his mouth on mine, his palm at the back of my neck and his warm, bare skin pressing me down into the bed.

"I thought—" Caleb moves his mouth to my neck and I arch beneath him, my fingers finding the belt loops at his hips. I tug on them and try to pull him closer. "I thought I was supposed to be touching myself."

"You're welcome to start whenever you'd like." Caleb laughs, soft and warm. It feels like the first blast of heat from the oven, when I'm too impatient and I crack open the door to get a peek at what's inside.

"You can, too," I breathe. "Touch me, I mean."

He nudges below my ear with his nose, his exhale long and slow. He sounds like he's gathering himself. Like he's barely holding the pieces of himself together, actually. "Noted. But you go ahead and start for me, yeah?"

I reach between us and drag the palm of my hand over my breast, just barely grazing my nipple through the soft material of my shirt. The almost innocent touch feels electric with Caleb's eyes on me, a pulse of slow-rolling heat that settles between my legs with a hollow ache.

I do it again, lingering with a gentle pinch, and Caleb grunts like I've punched him in the chest.

"More," he tells me.

"Greedy." I smile and keep my eyes closed. "I'll be going at my own pace, thank you very much."

He huffs. "I feel like I'm the one being teased now." His words are clipped, short.

"Mmhmm." My left hand leaves the loop at his waist and I slip it beneath my shirt, cupping my bare breast. I drag my thumb back and forth—forgetting, almost—about my very captive audience. This is how I touch myself when I'm alone at night. When the wanting and the waiting and the loneliness get to be too much and I pretend my hand belongs to someone else. My breath hitches and Caleb shifts above me, the sheets rustling with his movement. I feel his palm at my side, his fingertips glancing along my ribs as he inches my shirt up.

"Can I see?" I nod and he drags my shirt higher. "Can I watch what you do to yourself, Layla?"

"Yes."

I lie beneath Caleb with my eyes closed and listen to the pattern of his breathing as I touch myself. I grip my breasts just the way I like, teasing touches and light circles. I pinch at my nipple and my back arches, my knees spreading and pressing into Caleb, balanced above me. He catches my leg and holds it there, his thumb tracing a line down the back of my knee that feels like it's right against my clit. I blink my eyes open and—oh. *Oh.* Watching him watching me is so much better.

He looks absolutely wrecked. His jeans are tugged down low, lower than they were before, like impatient hands were nudging them down. His body is all lean lines, smooth muscle and warm, tan skin. His zipper is undone and I can see the edge of his black boxer briefs, the crisp white band around his hips. A dusting of dark hair just below his belly button. My gaze dips lower to where he is hard and straining and a fierce tug of need grips at me.

"Touch between your legs," he tells me, his voice low. "Show me there, too."

I slip my hand beneath my underwear and I last one stroke, two, before I'm reaching for Caleb with my other hand. I curl my hand in the hem of his jeans and pull.

"Your mouth," I pant. His eyes snap to mine and hold. "I want your mouth on me. Please."

"Ah, Layla." He practically collapses on top of me and drags his teeth over my tiny tattoo—brushes his lips from hip to hip and uses his shoulders to edge my legs further apart. My body burns liquid, velvet hot. "You never need to say please to me. But fuck. I love it when you do."

The first touch of his mouth over me has my legs scrambling against the sheets, heels digging into the mattress as I try to ground myself. His mouth feels *incredible.* Like nothing I've ever felt before. He catches my hips in his hands and holds me against my bed as he licks me through my underwear, slow and thorough and fucking divine.

He drops his forehead against my belly button and pants an uneven breath. "Layla," he says, and stops there. His hands on my hips squeeze, fingers tangling in satin. "Can I take these off?"

"Yes. Yes, I want that."

It's a flurry of limbs and motion as Caleb tugs my underwear down my legs and twists them through his fingers. I watch as he shoves them in his back pocket—like I won't notice later that he's pocketed some of my most expensive underwear. But I don't care. *I don't care, I don't care, I don't care* because he wraps his hand around my ankle and urges my legs wide, his big body sinking between them. I watch as his dark head bows over me, the blush along the tips of his ears. How his hands flex and retract against my skin.

He makes a low grunt of appreciation as his mouth finds me again and every particle in my body lights up. Pleasure—hot and wet and silky smooth. I clench my hands in his hair and grind myself against his greedy mouth, tiny little rocking movements that make everything feel more incredible.

My moan chokes out of me. "Oh my god, Caleb."

I've never felt anything like this. Not ever. Wet, sucking kisses against me, every stroke of his tongue deliberate and rough. Just the way I like it. Just the way I showed him.

"That's it," he mumbles against the inside of my thigh, hand palming at the swell of my ass, thumb reaching to the crease of my hip where my tattoo is. He traces it with his thumb right as he bites down against my leg with his teeth. "Show me like this, too. Take what you need."

I do. Caleb gives and I take and I take and I take until my whole body is shivering beneath his mouth, my thighs pressed tight to his ears. I roll my hips and chase that stardust feeling until I'm strung tight with it—vibrating, reaching, climbing closer and closer to that edge I so rarely get to find—

And then Caleb pulls away. Chest heaving, he drops his forehead against my hip and reaches between his legs. His hand dips in the open material of his jeans and I watch as he strokes himself once and groans.

"Wh—what?" My voice sounds seven octaves higher than usual, breathy and thin. "Caleb, what are you—"

"Shh." He pulls his hand out of his jeans and smooths his thumb over my ribs, rising higher and brushing over my breast. "I'm going to get you there, sweetheart. I promise."

"Why did you stop?"

He crawls up my body, dropping kisses like secrets along the way. The ticklish spot on my left hip, the smattering of freckles that cluster between my breasts, the curve of my shoulder, and the dip in my chin. Each one feels like touching the edge of an exposed wire, a lick of electric heat from my fingertips to my elbow. My pleasure sharpens.

"Caleb."

"It's better this way, sometimes." His mouth is hot on my neck. "When you're brought to the edge and kept waiting."

"I don't wanna wait," I whine. I'm trying to pull the most stubborn man alive down on top of me. "I've waited enough."

He chuckles somewhere against my collarbone. "Alright." He brushes his lips to the corner of my mouth and I moan when I taste myself on him. He makes a sound, too. Something low and deep and warm. I'm going to be hearing that sound every time he orders a croissant on the opposite side of my counter for the rest of forever. "You're right. I'm being rude."

He slips his hand back between my thighs and my back arches up off the mattress again, heat rushing through my chest and tugging me under. His thumb strokes my clit as his mouth hovers over mine, one finger and then two slipping inside.

"I can't believe—" He bites at my bottom lip and sucks it into his mouth. I grab frantically at his shoulders. "I can't believe I get to be here with you," he breathes, a touch of wonder in his voice. "I can't believe I get to touch you like this."

I can't believe we've been doing anything other than this. It's so good between us—better than I ever could have imagined. Better than I have imagined every night for the past two weeks, alone in the dark of my bedroom—his laugh and his smile and that damned Hawaiian shirt flickering through my mind.

The edge rises faster this time, my body shuddering beneath every deliberate stroke. I breathe his name, our bodies rocking together.

And then he stops. Again.

My nails sink into his shoulder and I make a garbled sound. My eyes clench shut as the throbbing between my legs intensifies. Caleb tries to pull away but I cling to him tighter, trying to roll my hips against his hand.

"Caleb." My voice is a broken whisper. "I don't want to be teased anymore."

"That wasn't for you," he tells me quietly, a bashful smile in his voice. I can picture the look on his face, a little bemused and a little shy. A twist to his lips and pink on his cheeks. "That was for me. I—I need a second."

I push my hips up. "Make it a quick second."

A laugh rumbles out of him and his thumb swipes against me once. Groans catch in both of our throats. "You sure you don't want to be teased anymore?"

I shake my head.

"What do you want, then?" His thumb rolls over me and my legs tip open. He huffs a satisfied sound, right in the shell of my ear, and then catches it between his teeth. His hand moves slower, harder, and I feel myself start to climb again.

"I want to come," I whisper into the hot skin of his neck. I drag my teeth over the column of his throat and cling to him.

He sighs, satisfied, and begins to work me harder. He drives me right back up to where I was before he stopped and then higher still. Somewhere with the sun and the clouds and all of the stars. A million wishes dancing like comets in the sky.

"So good, Layla." He pinches my nipple in the exact way I showed him and I begin to crumble. Deep, heaving breaths like I can't quite get enough air into my lungs. "You're doing so, so good. Such a good girl for me, sweetheart."

Two words—*good girl*—and my orgasm rushes up and over me. I tumble beneath the wave of it, my nails digging into the small of Caleb's back, my entire body drenched in warm, golden light. I can feel every place Caleb is touching me as my orgasm steals my breath. His mouth, just above mine. His hips tucked against my thigh and his fingers between my legs, still moving slowly, pulling every last bit of pleasure out of me. I move with him as the heat and the tender pulse of it echoes and spreads.

"Caleb," I gasp. I curl my hand around his jaw and guide his mouth to mine. He kisses me with a warm laugh, the edges of his smile biting against mine.

"Yeah?"

I hum, sated and a little limp. "That was nice."

His hips nudge against my thigh as he settles at my side. He curls his arm under a pillow and he's so beautiful I can hardly stand it. Rosy cheeks. Hair all over the place. An impression of my teeth against his collarbone I don't remember leaving.

"I certainly hope it was better than nice."

"It was very nice," I amend. "Cream-cheese-frosting nice. Brownie-in-the-middle-of-the-pan nice."

He nuzzles his nose in my shoulder and slips his hand over my belly. "Butter-croissant nice?"

Butter croissants. The not-so-special thing I make every single day that Caleb orders without fail three days a week. The thing he's always wanted. A scale tips in my chest and something plucks tight. I blink twice at the scratchy feeling behind my eyes.

"Butter-croissant nice," I agree, my voice a little bit rough. He moves against me again, getting comfortable in all of my pillows and blankets. His hips twitch forward and I feel him, still heavy and hard against my leg. My hand slips down his side and toys with the band of his underwear. He sucks in a sharp breath. "Caleb?"

His eyes are closed, a little furrow between his brows. "Hm?"

"What can I do?"

His eyes open—a brilliant, shimmering gold. Pupils blown wide with want. "About what?"

I roll onto my side and trace a single finger down the

thick line of his erection through his jeans, my mouth at his neck. "About this."

He groans, hips flexing into my touch. He places his hand over mine and squeezes, guiding my touch. Rough and slow, my palm grazes the hair below his belly button on every upward stroke.

"How about this time," I whisper against his skin. I tug at the waist of his jeans, pulling them lower. "How about this time you show me what you like."

It's exactly what I've been thinking about since he pushed me down into my sofa and held my hands above my head. Since he made me come with all my clothes still on. I push at his shoulder and we roll together, my knees on either side of his hips. He gazes up at me from my tangled bedsheets.

"Layla." He swallows around the sound of my name, his throat bobbing. His hands squeeze at my hips as I fight with the zipper of his jeans. "We don't need to do anything else. I can—I'll probably come in three seconds, if you keep doing exactly what you're doing."

I guess he means my knuckles dragging against his erection in stilted, uneven movements as I urge his jeans lower. I reach my hand into his boxers and wrap my fingers around him—hot and hard and deliciously big. He groans and drops his head back against my pillow, eyes squeezed shut.

"I don't want you to come in three seconds," I whisper. I stroke up, the movement frustratingly restricted by his damned jeans still around his damned hips. "I want more with you. Didn't you say you liked to hear what I want?"

His eyes open to twin narrow slits. "I did."

"Then trust me." I finally wrench his pants down to his thighs and he kicks them the rest of the way off. I'm pretty sure they land on the lamp by my closet. I do not care. "This is what I want."

Jaw clenched, hands clenched, every muscle in his body clenched—Caleb stares at me with dark eyes. "Is it the arrangement?"

I roll my hips against his and we both groan. "What?"

"If I'm going to fuck you, Layla," the words grind out of him, rough and tight. "It won't be because of any lessons or arrangements. It'll be because you want me, and I want you."

I breathe out, fingers inching below the elastic of his briefs. That's an easy enough solution. "Well, I want you. Do you want me?"

He flips me before I even realize his intention, his body heavy over mine and his hand cupped gently against my face. He traces his thumb from the corner of my eye down to my jaw. He presses one gentle kiss against my lips and leans back. Both of us, balanced on the edge of more.

My favorite half-smile hitches at the corner of his mouth. His dimples appear on both sides. "Don't ask questions you already know the answer to."

I DON'T THINK I've ever had sex like this before.

Honest and unencumbered and beautifully earnest.

Caleb climbs off the bed and shucks his underwear, delightfully bashful with his briefs around his ankles. I catalog all the lines and dips of his body with interest, my palm flat against my stomach. Tanned skin. Stacked muscle. The cut of his hips and a scar, right where his ribs curve in. He ducks his head the longer I look, hand on the back of his neck.

"Come here," I murmur.

He climbs back onto the bed one knee at a time, his big body eclipsing mine until all I can see is brown and gold and midnight black. He thumbs at my bottom lip as he kisses me, my thighs spread wide to welcome him, my ankle hooking behind his knee. Everything lines up exactly where it's supposed to and we make twin sounds of pleasured anguish. A gasp exchanged for a groan, mouths open against sweat slicked skin.

"Condom?" he asks.

I fling my arm towards my nightstand and the box of condoms I stocked the morning after he made me come on my couch, hoping we might—hoping something like this might happen. I drove four towns over to a 24-hour pharmacy in the dead of night, desperately worried I'd be the subject of the next phone tree message. I don't know what I'd do if Sheriff Jones got a voicemail about my condom purchases.

Caleb tears the wrapper with his teeth and slips his hand back between my thighs, thumb nudging. He groans when he feels how wet I still am, everything we've already done together not nearly enough to ease the ache.

"You feel so good, Layla." He licks a hot line up my neck and nips once at my jaw. "You're going to make me lose my fucking mind."

"Finally," I mumble. Maybe then I won't feel like the only one.

"Finally," he agrees, voice somber and serious. I watch as he rolls the condom down his length and settles between my thighs. He helps me guide my t-shirt over my head and then it's just us. Bare skin in the hazy light of a summer afternoon.

"Tell me you want me," he whispers.

It's the easiest thing I've ever told anyone. Truth in every syllable. "I want you so much."

He pushes inside of me with a decadent noise buried in my neck—a thick slide of heat that has me clutching the blanket on either side of my head. He slides his hands up my body and clutches at my wrists, then threads our fingers together and squeezes. I hold onto him and arch into the pillows, welcoming him against me—inside me—as he moves with tiny, careful thrusts. He feels incredible, even like this, as he searches for the right position. The right pace. The right angle that has me clenching and curling my body around his.

"Fuck," he slurs in my ear, his voice love drunk and low. His hips thrust against mine, a little bit harder, and I lose my breath. "Fuck, you feel—"

"—so good," I finish. I hitch my leg at his hip and he

moves faster, leveraging up on his knees, one hand planted on my headboard. Like this I can watch the way he moves between my spread legs. The clench and release of all those muscles. How the dips and divots of his abs strain and pull as he sinks into me over and over and over again. I kick out my foot and the lamp on my nightstand goes ... somewhere. I lean up and nip my teeth against his chest.

"You're gonna—" His eyes shut tight in concentration, face flushed. I stare at the fan of his eyelashes against the curve of his cheek as he chases his pleasure. "You're gonna make me come," he finally manages.

"That's okay," I smooth my hands through his hair and bite my way up his neck to the lobe of his ear. I suck it into my mouth and he makes a helpless sound. "That's good. I want to watch you, Caleb. I've thought about it so much, what you look like."

His eyes sweep open, hazy and hot. They lock on mine and he thrusts harder. The whole bed rattles. I drop my head back as he hits a spot that makes sparks dance behind my eyelids.

"You have?" he pants.

I nod. "I have." I tilt my head against the pillow that's moved halfway down the mattress and watch him, moving above me. His body is beautiful, his face twisted in a picture of delighted anguish. I smooth my hands down his chest and wrap my fingers around his hips. My nails sink in and he makes a ferocious sound.

"Will you show me?" I echo his words from earlier. "Can I watch?"

He comes with a gasp, his whole body bowing forward until his forehead is against my collarbone. His hips jump in uncoordinated, messy thrusts. It's almost enough to make me come again, the rough way he pushes me down in the bed and grinds into me. But I can't quite get there. Not as his movements slow just as my pleasure threatens to become something more. The tightness in my belly eases, my body teetering on the edge.

Caleb collapses his big body down against me and exhales, nose at my cheek.

I wrap my arms around his shoulders. He presses a kiss to my still hammering pulse point.

I wiggle beneath him. This is enough. My arms squeeze. This is more than enough.

"Did you come?" He mumbles the question somewhere in my neck. His voice sounds scratchy and raw and I like it very, very much. I shake my head and drag my palm down his back. His skin is warm, his chest still heaving against mine.

"No, but that's okay. I still—"

I don't finish my sentence before Caleb is pushing up and away from me. I frown at the loss of his weight and heat, my arm banded over my bare breasts. Is he—is he mad I didn't finish? A flush of embarrassment rushes up my cheeks and I tilt my face to the side, into my pillow.

"Hey, no," he whispers. "No, no. Don't do that."

He tilts my face back to his with his palm, a slow and lingering kiss to the pout on my lips. His nose bumps mine and I see the tilt of his smile. He brushes another kiss to the curve of my cheek, the edge of my bottom lip. His teeth nip and he props himself up on his arms, his body moving down, down, down mine.

I frown and try to snap my legs shut.

"What are you doing?"

He holds them open, a kiss pressed to my left knee and then my right. He looks up at me from beneath his lashes, framed by my open thighs and washed in warm, golden light. I can see the shine of sweat on his skin, his damp hair curling behind his ears. The strength in his arms and the cut of muscle down his abdomen. His dark eyes are locked on mine.

"This isn't going to work like that."

I swallow, my voice a whisper. "Like what?"

"I'm not going to leave you needing anything. So." He nips once at the inside of my knee, drags his mouth down my thigh. He grins at me, dark eyes shining. "Show me what you like, Layla."

And then he puts his mouth back on me, and I fall into my pillows.

TWENTY-THREE

CALEB

FOR SOME INEXPLICABLE REASON, **Charlie and Alex** are waiting in my classroom when I get back from bus duty. I look over my shoulder at the empty hallway, and then back to the two of them, sitting at desks that are far too small in the front row. Alex folds his hands neatly and looks at me from overtop his glasses. Charlie doesn't bother with a single glance as he works his way through what looks like half of my grandmother's Tupperware collection.

"She keeps giving you food?" I pull my door shut and walk over to my desk. I have no idea what this is about, but I might as well get comfortable. Alex isn't known for his brevity. I peer at Charlie's bounty on my way. My grandmother gave him tres leches ... again.

I reach for a swipe of cream off the top but Charlie smacks my hand away. "She made it for me."

I frown and collapse in my desk chair. "You do realize you're sitting in my classroom, right?"

"And that means I need to give you my dessert?" Charlie shakes his head with a menacing laugh. "I don't think so."

Alex ignores us both.

"We wouldn't be here," he says from his seat right next to Charlie. "If you hadn't been doing your best to avoid me for the last three days."

I haven't been avoiding him. I've just been ... busy. Summer school is wrapping up, Jeremy is almost done his love note project, and Layla is—

Layla is incredible. I've spent every free moment I've had sitting in her back kitchen, eating butter croissants and watching her work. Or propped up against the front counter, my chin in my hand and my heart in my throat.

Or at my house with her legs wrapped high around my hips, her back against the wall, my neatly arranged picture frames tipping sideways with our enthusiasm. Bent over the side of her bed with my hand at her neck, edging her to an orgasm that made her cry out my name in the sweetest sounding gasp I've ever heard in my life. Waking up with the sun to her alarm and slipping my hand over the curve of her waist to the place between her legs, listening to her whisper my name as the early gray light crawled through her curtains.

Falling asleep with her in my arms, one of her cold feet pressed between my calves, her nose in the middle of my chest.

I feel like we've completely abandoned the terms of our arrangement and it—it feels good.

It feels really good.

"I've had a lot of stuff going on," I mumble. I turn Fernando around on the corner of my desk. I don't need his judgment right now.

Charlie points a fork at me. "You've been wrapped up in Layla Dupree and ignoring the real world, my friend."

I snort. I do not need to hear this from him, of all people.

"Haven't you been doing the same thing with Nova Porter?" I fire back. He thinks he's being smooth about it, but I know that's the real reason why he's down here every other weekend from New York. I almost always see his car parked outside of the space Beckett's youngest sister has been eyeing for her new tattoo shop.

"Nova Porter won't give me the time of day, but that's alright." Charlie cheerfully folds a tortilla into a neat square and shoves the whole thing into his mouth. "It's about the long game, bruv," he tells me around a mouthful of food. "And don't change the subject."

"I'm worried about you," Alex says, face earnest and hands still clasped on top of the desk. He looks like my father, every single time he ever had to have a serious conversation with us as kids. Down to the glasses perched on the very edge of his nose and the twist of his mouth. "This thing with Layla—"

I scrub my hand across my forehead. "This again."

"Yes, this again." Alex leans back in his chair, knees

bumping the underside of the desk. "You need to hear it. When is your arrangement with Layla done?"

I've been trying not to think about it. "Sunday is the one month mark," I answer reluctantly.

"And what are you doing on Sunday?"

I busy myself with a pack of sticky notes on the edge of my desk, flipping them one way and then the other. "We're having a picnic," I mumble.

"That sounds nice," Charlie offers.

"It sounds like you're hoping she forgets it's the end of your arrangement and the two of you can continue whatever the hell you're doing without talking about it like adults," Alex explodes. The desk goes screeching two inches forward.

Charlie scoops another bite of food into his mouth. "It also sounds nice. Are you taking her to that little field of flowers on the farm?"

"We're going to the pond, actually."

"Cool."

"Caleb," Alex's voice softens and he takes off his glasses, two fingers against the bridge of his nose. "What are you doing?"

I know what it looks like. I know my track record isn't the best with these sorts of things. But Layla is different. What I have with her—what I feel for her—it's different. I'm not projecting anything. I think it's because of the arrangement that I'm being more realistic and honest than usual about my feelings. Layla and I—we've never tried to be anything except exactly ourselves.

"I don't know. If things are working between us, what's the point of ending it?"

It's my secret thought. The one I've been holding close to my chest these last couple of days. Why does anything have to change? Why can't we keep going out and getting ice cream? Why can't I sit in the back of the bakehouse and watch her sing the wrong lyrics to eighties ballads?

Alex looks at me like I'm an idiot. Charlie mirrors the look with a touch of pity. Even Fernando has judgment in his tiny little ceramic eyes.

I have no idea how the damn turtle got turned around again.

"You have to end the arrangement," Alex says.

Charlie nods. "Yeah, man. You can't build something on a shaky foundation."

But our foundation doesn't feel shaky. I think about her hand in mine, her mouth below my ear. The smile she gets when I walk through the front door of the bakehouse. I've shared more of myself with Layla than I've ever shared with another person. Thoughts and secrets and dreams.

I feel like our pieces fit together perfectly.

"I don't know," I mumble again, finding the laces of my shoes infinitely more interesting than the looks I'm getting from the front row of my classroom.

"Have you talked about it with her?" Alex slips his glasses back over his face. "What happens at the end of your month?"

Vaguely, I guess. Half-hearted jokes about not having to put up with each other any more. But we haven't discussed the specifics in a while. My face must answer the question because Alex lets out another disappointed sigh.

I try to defend myself. "I was going to bring it up."

"Yeah? When?"

Sunday. Probably. If she brought it up first.

Charlie shoots Alex a vaguely irritated look out of the corner of his eye. He's wearing a three piece suit today, a button-up vest overtop a dress shirt that looks more expensive than the combination of my entire wardrobe. His cuffs rolled and his jacket slung over the back of one of my classroom chairs. I hope it's not the one Tyler wrote PENIS on seventy-five times. It doesn't look like the type of suit that handles ink transfer well.

"What Alex is trying to say—" Charlie clears his throat meaningfully. "—is that it's obvious you have real feelings for Layla. And if you want something real with her, you need to have a conversation about your arrangement first. You can't just keep on doing what you're doing—this whole practice nonsense. You need to be honest with her that you want more. End the arrangement, and start something new. No qualifiers."

I don't know why that feels so difficult to me. Fear that she'll laugh in my face, maybe. Or that she'll say I'm not what she wants. It's easier to have the hope. "I can't just keep going with my mouth shut and hope for the best?"

Alex cracks a half-smile. "And how has that worked out for you in the past?" When I narrow my eyes at him, he throws up his hands and sighs. "No, Caleb. You can't do that. Tell her how you feel. How you really feel. Look at you. You've been floating around these past couple of weeks. You look like a—like a—"

"Like someone introduced you to masturbation for the first time," Charlie supplies around a mouthful of rice. "You've always been a happy guy, my dude. But you've reached new levels."

I roll my eyes and turn back to Alex. "What if—" I swallow and rearrange the pens in my cup. "What if she doesn't feel the same?"

I was hoping I could just ignore this finish line. If I never brought it up, maybe I wouldn't have to be disappointed.

Alex sighs. "Be honest with her. Tell her what you want, but manage your expectations a little bit, okay? Remember this whole thing was an arrangement for the both of you. It's normal if feelings are a little exaggerated. You both were looking for some sort of solution."

I frown, picking up on his subtext. "You don't think she feels the same?"

Charlie and Alex exchange another series of looks I can't interpret. Charlie mouths something and makes a complicated gesture with his hands. Alex widens his eyes and then they both dissolve into furious whispers. Not unlike the two girls from the softball team that sit in those very seats during my third period Spanish class.

It doesn't give me much hope.

"What the hell is going on with you two?"

They stop abruptly. Alex meets my gaze, but Charlie looks up at the ceiling, his lips in a thin line.

"Talk to Layla."

I ALMOST LOSE MY NERVE.

She comes skipping down her front steps Sunday afternoon in a cotton candy pink dress, sleeves slipping off her shoulders and sunlight dancing down her skin. Bright red ribbon in her hair. Picnic basket on her arm. She looks like one of those candy hearts you get in a box on Valentine's Day and sift through until you find your favorite message. SWEETER THAN PIE, hers would say. BE MINE.

A laugh trips out of her when she opens the front door of the Jeep and sees my failed attempt at a strawberry shortcake on the passenger seat. I wanted to sweeten her up, maybe, for this conversation. I thought baked goods might do that.

I just underestimated my ability to bake a cake.

"What the hell is this?"

I frown at it. "It's a strawberry shortcake."

"It's a strawberry something," she says with a sly smile I want to bite the edge of. Still, she's careful as she slips it from the seat and places it in the backseat next to her picnic basket, hopping in and planting a smacking kiss against my cheek. I told myself on the drive over here that I wasn't going to kiss her until we had our conversation. I wasn't going to touch her until I know where we stand. No use in making things more difficult for myself.

But my candy heart probably reads CRAZY 4 YOU. I tilt my face down to hers and catch her lips with mine, my hand sifting under her hair to toy with the edge of her cherry red bow. I curl it around my palm and tug, smiling when I hear the catch in her breath.

We're ending the arrangement today. We don't have to end anything else. Charlie and Alex were right, even if their approach was less than subtle. If I want a real shot of something lasting with Layla, we need to have an honest conversation.

But it's hard for me to voice those thoughts when it feels like everything is going exactly right between us. The closer we get to Lovelight, the higher my anxiety spins. By the time we make it to the fields and she's towing me across to the pond at the very edge of the property, my lungs are tight and my heart is doing double-time. I watch her pink skirt flutter around her thighs, the bounce in her step as she hops around the neat rows of produce Beckett planted earlier in the season. I squeeze the handle of the basket and try to remember myself.

She knows who I am. She likes who I am, I repeat like a mantra. *Our pieces belong together. This isn't going to be like every other time.*

"Layla," I start, and let the wind carry away the rest of my thought. She looks at me over her shoulder and I almost lose my breath. Slowly sinking sunlight and gold catching in the necklace looped around her neck. An easy breeze that meanders through the tall grass and lifts the edges of her hair. Fireflies that blink to life in the field around us, rising from the willows like tiny, fallen stars.

"What is it?" she asks.

I shake my head and swallow the words. I just need a couple more minutes. "Nothing." I clear my throat. "You want to set up here?"

"Here is good." She spins in a circle, skirt flaring, head tilted back to look at the sky. She's so beautiful my heart gives a single painful thud right in the center of my chest.

I look down at the ground and toss out the blanket. "You gonna make fun of my cake some more?"

"Depends on what it tastes like." She drops right next to where I'm kneeling, her elbow balanced on my shoulder and her mouth at my ear. She smells like summer nights and warm pastries. A smile quirks the edges of her lips. "Sometimes the best tasting things aren't the prettiest."

I'm pretty sure she's full of it, but I appreciate the concession nonetheless. I gather her arm from my shoulder and press a quick, unthinking kiss to the inside of her wrist. My lips linger and then I flinch away like she's burned me.

She stares at me, her face collapsed in confusion. She cradles her arm close to her chest, fingertips rubbing over the place my mouth brushed.

I'm doing all of this wrong. I can't figure out what I want to say or how I want to say it. Maybe I should have made notecards and slipped them into the back of the basket.

"Hey." Layla's fingers are hesitant as she reaches for me and traces an aimless design against my forearm. "What's going on with you? You're being weird."

"I know I am," I mumble. I drag my palm down my face

and keep it cupped over my jaw, eyes tired as I gaze over at her. She holds steady, her hazel eyes searching. I drop my hand and reach for honesty. "I need to talk to you."

"Okay." I watch her brace herself, settling back on the blanket with a neat pocket of space between us. She curls her hands around her elbows, body folding in. "What is it?"

"I—"

I don't want it to be an arrangement anymore. I want to be everything to you, my mind supplies. *Just like you're everything to me.*

"I want to end our arrangement."

She nods, a single curl slipping free from the scarf in her hair to flutter across her face. She pushes it back with her hand. "Okay. That was our plan, right? We're almost at the one month mark, I think."

"Today is the one month mark," I blurt. She blinks quickly, eyelashes fluttering. I need to get control of myself and not just yell things like a lunatic. I take in a deep breath through my nose and let it out slowly. I try again. "Today is the one month mark and I want to end our arrangement."

"Oh," she says. If I weren't watching her so closely, I'd miss the minute way her expression changes. The twist in her bottom lip and the quick flare of pain behind her eyes. She rolls her shoulders back, bracing herself. "Oh," she says again.

"I was thinking maybe we could—"

"Of course," she cuts me off quickly, hands against the

skirt of her dress. She curls them into fists and then flattens them again. For the first time I notice the tiny strawberries painted on her nails. Pale, pale pink. "Of course, you're right. We should end our arrangement."

She doesn't quite look at me, her eyes somewhere around my knees.

It's the exact same thing I just said, but her voice is all wrong. Her smile, too, something brittle and broken. "Alright. I—"

"I didn't realize it had been a month already. I thought we were close, but—" She shakes her head, teeth clamping against her bottom lip briefly. "I'm sorry. Were you waiting long to have this conversation with me? I didn't mean to drag this out for you."

"What?"

"You're probably eager to get back out there."

I glance over my shoulder. All I see is rolling fields of gold, a big red barn off in the distance by the road. "Get back out ... where?"

Finally, she meets my eyes. She watches me carefully, her gaze distant. I don't think Layla has ever looked at me like this before.

"Dating," she says with a slight flinch. "For real this time."

Something sharp and ugly wedges in my gut and I have to swallow three times in a row before I manage to get a single word out. "For real," I say faintly. Every single thing I've ever felt with Layla has been the truest sense of real I've ever known. "This time."

She nods and toys with the edge of her scarf against the curve of her collarbone. Restless, absent movements. "I'm sorry you had to bring it up with me. It looks like it's been weighing on you."

It has been weighing on me. Every time I close my eyes, I see Layla. Every time I roll over in my bed, I feel her bare skin against my fingertips. Every time I saw this damned date on my calendar, my chest seized and my breath came short. It has been weighing on me, but only because I want more. I want all of the pieces she's given me and the rest, too. I want every smile, every croissant, every brush of her hand against mine. I want roller skating and ice cream melting over my knuckles. Nachos in a field.

Layla in the middle of my kitchen, big smile and flour on the palms of her hands.

"Yeah," I manage. "It has."

"Oh," she says again, softer this time. "That's, um—" Her eyes slip away from me to the neat stack of Tupperware at our side. Her shoulders curl back and she starts to collect the items she's just pulled out of her basket—cups and plates and what looks like the same bottle of champagne she bought all those weeks ago at the liquor store. Orange with a gold foil top. When she reaches for the pastry box at the edge, I wrap my fingers around her wrist to pause her movement.

"Layla. Listen to me for a second. I'm nervous and I'm not—I'm not doing a very good job of explaining this."

She pulls her hand from my grip and gathers the

pastry box close. She holds it against her chest like a piece of armor. Like she wants to disappear inside of it.

"You don't need to explain anything."

"Layla—"

"Please, Caleb. Don't explain anything."

"Why?"

"Because it's okay. I get it. You don't have to—you don't have to tell me I'm not the right fit for you." She twists her arm in my grip, pulling away from me and pushing off the blanket. I watch her skirt for a moment as it catches the breeze, my brain stuck on the phrase *right fit for you*. It's scratching like a record, over and over until the words lose meaning.

"I don't think I was ready for this," she finishes on a whisper. I have no idea if that was meant for me to hear or not.

"I'm not—hold on." I reach for her and my fingertips glance against the very edge of her dress. I curl my hand into a fist. "I'm not breaking up with you."

"Okay. Ending our arrangement."

"Yes, I want to end the arrangement, but—" I blow out a frustrated breath. This conversation is going in circles. Maybe Charlie was on to something when he said I should practice in front of the mirror. "I was hoping maybe we could start something new."

Her hands freeze for half a second, hovering over the containers. I can't see her face, curtained by her hair. But I can feel every single silent second like a thumbtack against my skin. Anticipation. The worst sort of it.

"I don't know," she says slowly. "We said we'd give it a month. And it's been a month."

"Can't we add another month?" I drag my knuckles down her arm. I hate the note of pleading in my voice. I swallow around it. "I want to try this with you."

She looks up at me with wide, hazel eyes. Her bottom lip trembles, and I almost rip the blanket clean in two. I don't want to see her cry. I don't want to see her cry because of *me*. "I don't know if I can," she finally says.

"Why not?"

"Because—" She looks away, over my shoulder, her hands curling over her elbows and tugging her arms close. "Because this is turning into something we didn't agree to. I'm not even evaluating you anymore, Caleb. It was supposed to be fun and easy and now it's—"

She stops mid-sentence and clenches her jaw. The hands on her arms have a white-knuckled grip.

"What?" I ask. "Now it's ... what?"

I hover there on the edge of uncertainty, holding my breath. I feel like we're back in that Escape Room and her elbow has made direct contact with my eye, my throat— the soft, squishy place inside my chest that feels like it's being ripped apart. I can't manage to say anything else, my throat clogged around a sinking feeling of unease.

I know I have a habit of projecting my feelings—imagining things that aren't there. But this doesn't feel like that. This feels like something else entirely.

Layla was upset when she thought I was calling off the arrangement. I thought it meant she might share some of my feelings. But maybe it was because she wanted to be the one to end things first? I don't understand.

"I don't understand," I repeat, out loud this time.

She takes a deep breath. Releases it on a shaky sigh. Her eyes flit up to meet mine and then back down again to her fingers twisting in her lap. I have never seen Layla Dupree shrink herself down to size. It doesn't suit her.

"Everything with you has felt too easy. I think I'm always going to be waiting for the other shoe to drop. I've wanted something like this forever and I'm not—I'm not sure I can trust myself," she finishes on a whisper. "I'm just —" She looks up and blinks rapidly. "I don't know how to do this."

"Layla." Her name gusts out of me. "Of course you do. You're already doing it."

"I'm not so sure." She runs a shaky hand under her nose and blows out a shuddering breath. "It's easier for us to end it now, before we get any further. Before I—before I —" She stops with a high-pitched sound that is far too fucking close to a sob for me to handle. Something terribly dark and deeply possessive curls right in the center of my chest. My hands ache with the effort not to reach out to her.

"Before you what? Talk to me."

It feels monumentally important that she finishes that sentence.

But she doesn't answer. She just shakes her head and tucks her hands under her knees, bottom lip caught between her teeth.

"What are you afraid of?" I ask. It tumbles out of me, guided by frantic frustration.

Layla doesn't hesitate. She finally angles her chin up, meets my gaze and whispers, "Myself."

"Help me understand."

She lifts herself onto her knees, back to collecting all the pieces of our picnic. A single tear glances down her cheek and my chest seizes.

"I've always had the worst taste in men. I know I joke about it, but my track record really is the worst. I—" She shakes her head, lips pinched like she's trying to keep herself from crying. "I can't trust myself when it comes to this kind of decision. And I won't hurt you in the process, Caleb."

I am hanging on to this blanket for dear life, trying not to touch her. She drops the neatly wrapped plastic silverware bundles back into the basket, the napkins tied with a red string. Another tear lands on top.

You're hurting me right now, I want to say.

"Nothing has to change," I say faintly. "Not really. Just what we call it. Everything we've been doing together—Layla. You can trust me."

"I know I can." She wipes under her eyes with the back of her hand and stands on unsteady legs. "It's me that's the problem. There are parts of me that are broken and I don't—I don't know how to fix them for you, Caleb."

"You don't have to fix anything for me," I tell her. I'll take all of her, exactly how she is. We'll fit our pieces together until we're something whole, together, our broken edges smoothed into something beautiful.

She smiles sadly at me, head tilted to the side, eyes soft. "I just don't think we should go any further if I'm—if I'm figuring things out. You deserve someone who can give you everything, Caleb."

"I want you."

She makes a small sound under her breath. "I know you feel that way now, I just—" She shakes her head. "I think we need to take a few steps backwards from this. See how we really feel."

How we really feel. I know how I feel. Now more than ever, I know how she feels, too. I see it every time she looks at me. Every time she reaches for my hand with hers. I *know* it. "Layla."

"Please," she whispers. "Please stop saying my name like that."

"What can I do?"

I want her to tell me how to fix this. I want to know how we can go back to the place where she was rushing to meet me, smile beaming out of her. I want to take all of her fears and crumple them in a ball. Launch it into space. Set it on fire. I want to punch every piece of shit who ever treated her like garbage to begin with. Launch them into space, too.

"I want you to—" She sucks in a sharp breath. "I want you to come into the bakehouse every Monday, Wednesday, and Friday. I want you to stand across the counter and order one coffee, just cream. I want you to get a butter croissant and not take your first bite until you're halfway down the front steps. I want you and I to still be okay."

I stand up until I'm curved around her, shoulders hunched. My hand cups her face, my thumb at her chin. Another two tears drop from her eyelashes and land against the back of my hand. "I don't know if I can do that, Layla. I don't know if I can do that and not want you."

The look on her face cleaves my heart in two. "It'll fade with time. I promise. It always does."

I don't think it will. I'm going to be on the other side of that counter thinking about the patch of freckles on the inside of her elbow. The way her laugh sounds when it's muffled by a kiss. The tiny tattoo on her hip and roller skates with miniature skulls and crossbones. Vanilla custard on the beach. A pack of frozen produce over my eye and her fingertips gentle against my skin.

Falling in love.

Slowly and carefully and then all at once.

I feel it like a nudge, right between my shoulder blades. Something that twists and pulls until it settles in the center of my chest. Layla is too used to people letting her down. She's conditioned to brace herself against disappointment.

Has anyone ever fought for her the way she deserves?

Layla clasps her fingers around my wrist and I drop my forehead to hers. Our noses brush together and she lets out a shuddering sigh. I don't know if she's holding me against her or pushing me away. It feels a bit like both.

"I'll still see you?" Her bottom lip brushes mine and my whole body jolts. "Monday, Wednesday, and Friday?"

If that's what she needs. If this is all she's ready for, if this is how I prove to her that I'm exactly what she deserves to have, then I'll be the best damn customer the bakehouse has ever had.

"Yeah, sweetheart. Every Monday, Wednesday, and Friday."

We stand there under the shade of a tree and sway back and forth, clinging to each other. Birds call to each other from the branches. The grasses twist at our ankles. Her lips stay a millimeter away from mine, her hands clutching my wrists.

"Can I ask for something?" I barely manage to get the words out, rocky and rough. "Before we go?"

She tries to smile, but it wobbles at the edges. A pained sound catches in the back of my throat.

"Just the one," she says.

I clear my throat. "I guess if I only get one, I should pick something good."

She stares up at me—remembering. Our very first night together. "I guess you should."

I drag my thumb over the swell of her cheek. The last time she said that, she had been smiling. Now she lets her eyes slip shut, a ragged exhale chasing her words.

"Can I kiss you?" I ask.

She keeps her eyes closed as she nods.

I hold myself still in front of her and wonder how I should kiss Layla Dupree for the very last time. What's the best way to get someone to remember you? To want you back?

I press my mouth to hers and cup my palm around the back of her neck. We linger there in the space between breaths, standing perfectly, painfully still. I'm afraid to move. I'm afraid of letting this moment end. But it only takes her shuffling another half an inch closer to break me of my careful restraint. I can't help it with Layla. I've never been able to.

I tilt my head and she makes a sound—something low and uneven that hooks in my heart and tugs. Sad, I think. Unsure. I exhale sharply through my nose and kiss her slower. Begging.

Don't go, I try to tell her. *Stay with me.*

Trust me.

She tears her mouth from mine with a gasp and presses the back of her hand to her lips. She takes one step back and then two, stumbling over a tree root. I reach for her, but she shakes her head. She picks up the pile of containers at her feet.

"I'm—" She hitches her thumb over her shoulder. "I'm going to go to the bakehouse. There's a—I should check on some things."

I shove my hands deep in my pockets. "That's alright." I tip my chin up at the blanket and try not to rub my fingertips over my lips. I want to brand the feel of her into my bones. Ink it onto my skin. "I'll clean everything up."

She blinks quickly and her lower lip trembles. She feels so very far away when she says, "I really am sorry. I wish I didn't feel like this."

I shake my head. "You have nothing to apologize for."

Not really. I'm the idiot that broke my own heart on this one. We entered this arrangement to help cure me of this problem and look. The same exact thing happened.

I look at my boots in the dirt. The edge of the blanket.

"Okay," I hear her say. "I'll see you tomorrow, right?"

She'll see me tomorrow. She'll keep seeing me. The last time I kiss Layla won't be in the middle of a field with tears on her cheeks.

I nod and glance back up at her, my palm against the back of my neck. I squeeze so I don't reach for her hand instead. She stares at me with her bottom lip caught between her teeth, like she's got something else she wants to say.

But she doesn't say it. She just gives me another small, sad smile and turns. She walks away from me, her pretty pink dress a deep red in the melting light.

I stand there and watch her go.

I watch her go until it's just me and the trees.

TWENTY-FOUR

LAYLA

"I'D LIKE A BUTTER CROISSANT."

I don't bother looking up from my notepad, listing out the ingredients I need to stock up on during my next trip to Annapolis. We're going to need more sugar on this run. Probably the wholesale oranges, too.

A new soul, maybe, for the bakeshop owner who crushes the hearts of sweet, adoring men in her free time.

"We don't have any butter croissants."

Gus makes a grunting noise. He's never been much of a morning person. "Then why am I looking at an entire case full of butter croissants?"

"Those aren't for you."

I came in earlier than usual and made three trays of butter croissants. I kept my hands busy to ignore the rolling in my chest, the tightening in my throat every time I thought of his face in the dwindling sunlight, hands reaching for me. The hurt in his eyes when I flinched away.

And it worked, for a little bit. The croissants. It was enough of a distraction to keep me from overanalyzing all the things I said last night—all the things *he* said last night. I finished one batch and slid them in the oven. I watched them through the little window and immediately felt the press of the pre-dawn silence. Too damn quiet.

I stood there and felt all of my aches. My shoulder. My neck. My heart. Everything felt sore. I think the worst sort of thing you can do after making a questionably poor decision is to give yourself space to think.

So I started another batch.

And then another.

I tried to time the last one perfectly with his scheduled arrival so they might still be warm. A poor consolation, probably, for the way I handled things yesterday, but an apology all the same.

I got scared last night with Caleb. I know I did. When he sat down on the blanket and said he had something to tell me, I immediately thought the worst. He said he wanted to end the arrangement and it felt like every bad break-up I've ever had and then some. After a month. I didn't realize how deep I had fallen into Caleb until exactly that moment. It wasn't joy that accompanied that particular revelation, but bone-deep panic.

I just—I panicked.

I don't think I'm ready to give Caleb everything he

deserves. I meant it when I said I think something might be broken.

"Then who are they for?"

"Not you, Gus."

"I don't understand."

A zing of awareness zips up my spine. Caleb's voice, the pained *I don't understand*. I flinch and shake my head. I sat on my couch last night and ate Caleb's ugly strawberry shortcake straight out of the container while I stared unseeingly at the television screen.

I don't understand.

Talk to me.

Layla—

There's a sliver of it still sitting on my countertop, next to a crumpled up paper bag that used to have a bagel sandwich in it and a half-dried bundle of lavender.

"You can have a blueberry muffin."

Gus frowns at me. "I don't want a blueberry muffin."

He's about to get the damn blueberry muffin whether he wants it or not via creative method of entry when the bells above the door announce someone's arrival. I check the clock. 7:43am on the dot. Just enough time to grab his usual and then make it over to the school.

I have to work up the nerve to look up from the counter. His footsteps seem to echo in the small space. Casual. Controlled as usual. My gaze cements somewhere around his waist as he strolls to a stop. Brown leather belt. Pale blue button down shirt. His favorite sunglasses tucked against the collar. I swallow hard and drag my eyes to his.

"Hi."

He braces his hand against the counter. His brown eyes burn umber, streaks of gold.

"Hey."

We stand there, staring at each other. It feels like the whole world has crawled to a stop. I drink him in like I haven't seen him in twelve years, not twelve hours. His shirt is wrinkled at the bottom, like he pulled it from the depths of his dresser drawer. Probably the second one down, where he keeps his nice shirts for work on one side, and old, faded comfy t-shirts on the other. I watched him open that drawer three days ago while I was naked in his bed, the sheets up to my chin. He only had his jeans on, slung low around his hips. He had pulled out an old band shirt and tossed it in my direction with a wicked gleam in his eyes. A suggestion in the lift of his brow. I don't think I even tugged the sheets all the way off before he was urging me back into them.

I yank myself out of that memory and watch as this version of Caleb drags his fingers through his hair. His hand trembles, the only indication that maybe he's just as nervous as I am.

I reach for something to say. "What can I get you?"

He opens his mouth and then closes it. Averts his eyes and squints at the menu above my head. Something in my chest fractures and I try not to look at the glass case full of butter croissants.

It doesn't matter, I tell myself. *He doesn't need to eat a butter croissant.*

"I think I'll have some avocado toast." His usually deep voice is hoarse. He clears his throat and drags his thumb over his left eyebrow, still squinting. "And a green tea to go."

I don't move an inch to get any of the things he just asked for. For some inexplicable reason, I want to cry. "That's not your order."

He drops his hand. "What?"

"That's not—You get a butter croissant. A coffee with cream."

Caleb searches my eyes, looking for something. His lips twist down in a look that's far too serious for his handsome face, dimples nowhere in sight. Solemn doesn't suit him.

He looked solemn last night, too. Solemn and sad.

My chest squeezes.

He doesn't blink away from me when he says, "I'm going to try something different this time."

"Why?"

The question slips through my lips without permission. His hand flexes on the countertop.

"Because different is good sometimes," he says with one stern brow slightly arched, the faintest brush of pink lighting on his cheeks. This man. Always a contradiction.

I give him another lingering look and fish a takeout cup out from beneath the counter. I make him his toast, fetch his tea, and place both neatly in front of him. I even straighten the edge of the toast so they're completely parallel, just the way he likes. But he doesn't glance down at his order. He keeps staring at me. I don't think he's looked away from me once since he walked in here.

I don't think I've taken a full breath, either.

He reaches for his food on the counter, but his hand finds mine instead. My whole body jolts in surprise. His big hand circles my wrist and he brushes his thumb across my pulse point, slow and deliberate. His touch drifts and he traces each of my knuckles, the valleys in between. Goosebumps erupt all the way up to my shoulders, even though it's close to twelve hundred degrees outside and I've had my body halfway in an oven all morning.

"Do you remember what I told you?" he asks me, his voice low. His thumb presses into the middle of my hand. "That day you were making all of those baked goods?"

I shake my head. To be fair, he's told me a lot of things, most of them while I'm making some form of baked good. Smile lines appear by his eyes like he knows just what I'm thinking, even though that smile doesn't quite reach his mouth.

I'll take it—a step in the right direction.

"I told you that you deserve good things," he says quietly. "And I think I could be one of those good things for you. I'm pretty sure of it, actually. You deserve to have someone try and you deserve to have someone care. I—" He sighs, slow and deep, the look in his eyes so tender I have to curl my hand around the ratty old washcloth looped through my apron strings. I want to press my face into the hollow of his throat and breathe him in. I want his fingers tangled through my hair. I miss him *so much*—and isn't that terrifying, in all of its breathtaking agony? To miss the person standing right in front of you.

"I know I can be too much, but I think I'm just enough for you. I have no interest in forcing you into anything," he continues. "But I want you to know that this past month with you has been the very best I've ever had. I should have told you that last night, but I was overwhelmed and nervous and everything came out wrong. Arrangement or no, everything I've felt with you, everything I've said to you —" He shakes his head slightly, that smile finally tripping from his eyes to the curve of his cheeks. I get the barest hint of a dimple before it's gone again. "It's been the most honest—the most real thing I've ever felt." He glances over his shoulder at the half-full bakehouse and then back to me, tipping his head forward and lowering his voice. Probably because Cindy Croswell is standing immobile at the condiments counter with her devious little ears pointed right in our direction.

I lean into him, his nose grazing my ear. I trade in my goosebumps for a full body shiver. If he notices, he has the decency to not comment on it.

"I know you're not ready right now, and that's okay. I'll be—I'll keep coming here. Every Monday, Wednesday, and Friday. You let me know when."

He releases my hand without another word and snatches up his bag. He turns and strides across the small dining space and straight out the front door without a single glance back. My wreath of peonies swings lightly back and forth with his exit. I stare at it for a long time, the flutter of the petals and the scratch of the ribbon against the window. I stare and I stare and I stare, my throat tight.

Gus coughs. I guess he didn't move that entire time.

"Can I have a butter croissant now?"

I blink away from the door and turn back to my list. "The answer is still no."

STELLA FINDS me in the back storage closet, sitting cross legged on top of a sack of flour. If I had a smoking habit, I'd probably have a cigarette hanging out of my mouth right now. As it is, I could only find a pack of stale licorice and I'm hoovering them into the mouth like the hot mess express that I am.

Stella stands in the doorway, a halo of light behind all her curly hair. She looks like the patron saint of judgment. "Oh, wow. This is—Layla. This is something."

I can only assume she is talking about the baking tray littered with crumbs at my feet. The one that was definitely lined with shortbread cookies when I came in here. I've decided the best way forward is to eat my feelings, and I started with whatever was in sight.

Cookies. Candy. Who knows what's next.

The world is my oyster.

"Caleb visited," I offer without any context whatsoever. Stella closes the door carefully behind her, cloaking us in darkness and the glow of the string lights I wrapped around the edges of the shelves about six months ago. It's my favorite place for a mid-afternoon nap.

Or emotional breakdown.

Take your pick.

"He ... often visits the bakehouse."

I nod.

Stella waits with her shoulder propped up against a shelf full of flour sacks. The girl pined after the same man for close to a decade. No one does patience like Stella Bloom.

"Our arrangement ended yesterday."

"So soon?"

I shrug. "It's been a month. That's what we agreed to."

Stella shuffles forward and makes herself cozy on the shelf at my side. She tries to fluff a bag of sugar like a pillow and all she gets is a slow leak of it onto the floor. It feels very symbolic of the current state of things. She huffs and tries to fix the hole, but only makes it worse. I drag a bowl over with my foot and drop it under the leak. I'll fix it later.

"Is that why you're in here eating contraband cookies and candy?"

"They're not contraband," I mutter. "They're mine. Fairly obtained within legal measures."

"Okay. Good to know. But ... Caleb?"

I sigh and pick at some crumbs left on the sleeve of my shirt. "Am I a hypocrite?"

Stella, bless her, doesn't so much as trip on the abrupt shift in conversation. "Layla, you are one of the rare few that leads with an open heart. No, you are not a hypocrite."

Except it doesn't feel like my heart is very open. As

soon as I got a hint of something real with Caleb, my open heart felt more like a locked safe at the bottom of the ocean.

Surrounded by landmines.

And man-eating sharks.

"I feel like I've been waiting forever for love to find me. I've put myself out there—over and over and over. I went out with a guy once that guessed my weight the entire way to the restaurant. I even said yes to a second date with him." I yank another piece of licorice out of the bag. "I'm used to watching the hands of the clock move and I didn't even realize my month with Caleb was up. I think—I think I forgot it was an arrangement."

Stella fishes around in my bag for a piece of licorice for herself. "And Caleb wanted to keep it within the predetermined limits?"

I shake my head.

It's been the most honest—the most real thing—I've ever felt.

"No, he didn't. That's the hypocrite part. I feel so stupid," I say. Stella hands me a small throw pillow she digs out of ... somewhere. I clutch it close to my chest. "All I've ever wanted is a good relationship, and the second I find one, I sabotage it."

"Awareness is half the battle," Stella murmurs, fingers pushing some of my hair behind my ear.

"Why did I sabotage it?"

"Because you are afraid," she says quietly, blue eyes warm. In the warm glow of the twinkle lights strung over metal beams, she looks like a snow angel. Something you'd find in a snow globe. "And because you've dated a string of terrible men that have left you battered and bruised. It's okay to be afraid when your heart gets involved."

"I think I like him too much," I whisper.

Stella hums.

"How can I trust my heart on this? Every time I think I'm making a good choice, it ends in flames. Flames doused in gasoline. My heart has never once pointed me in the right direction. All of these relationships that have failed, all of these false starts, I feel like they've been chipping away at me. I've only got slivers left, Stella. And I'm afraid if I give them to Caleb—" My voice snaps off at the thought of it. I don't think there'd be anything left of me.

Better just to be disappointed now than later. It's safer this way. Easier.

Stella keeps quiet, munching thoughtfully on a short-bread cookie I must have missed.

"How many slivers do you have left?"

"What?"

"Your slivers." She gestures at my chest, right where my heart is. "How many do you think you have left?"

I blink at her. "I don't know if I can quantify how many are left."

"Think about it."

"I am."

"Well, think harder."

I want to grab my best friend by her arms and shake.

"Stella."

"If you think you only have a couple left, I understand. I really do. You know I do. It can be hard to be brave when you feel like the next disappointment will break you to pieces."

When Luka confessed his love, Stella quite literally ran for the hills. She didn't believe she could be loved by the same person she had been loving. She thought her feelings went exactly one way and was terrified to face the consequences of something going wrong and—

Realization slams into me.

"Oh."

She nods. Takes another aggressive bite of cookie. "There it is."

"Why does it sound like you have a second part to that statement?"

"Because there is a second part to my statement." She slips off the shelf and stands in front of me, palms brushing against the seat of her denim shorts. Her lips curve in a gentle smile and she snags another piece of candy out of my bag. "I was going to say, if you have some slivers you're protecting, that's fine. But I think you need to consider how many slivers actually belong to you, and how many you've already given to Caleb. And trust that maybe your heart has finally found the right person to bet on."

TWENTY-FIVE

LAYLA

"YOUR TARTS LOOK LIKE SHIT."

I sigh and resist the urge to slam my forehead into the metal table right next to my tarts that look like shit. It's shiny and would probably leave a very satisfying dent. But Stella paid extra for the glossy shine and I'd hate for her to waste her money because of damage from my forehead.

"Beatrice." I lean up from my crouched over position and stretch my neck. It's a miracle I can even stand straight at all with how many hours I've been putting in at the bakehouse. "To what do I owe the pleasure?"

She gives me a look from just inside the doorway, a stack of shortbread cookies tucked under her arm. "It's Wednesday."

"Correct." I rub my palm over the ache. "But not the third Wednesday of the month. Unless I slipped into a medically-induced coma and somehow woke up without the knowledge."

Wouldn't that be nice. I'd love to sleep my way through the next three to six months. Bury my head in the sand until this pressure on my chest disappears.

Caleb has returned every Monday, Wednesday, and Friday at exactly the same time, just like he said he would. Just like I asked. He stands on the other side of my counter and squints at the menu like he doesn't know the damned thing by heart. And when he reaches for whatever nonsense I've stress-baked the night before, he shifts his hand just slightly and traces his fingers over the inside of my wrist. The back of my hand. The pad of my thumb. An innocent touch, by any measure, but combined with his heavy looks and his endless patience, I'm just—

I'm balancing on the very edge of losing all of my marbles. Every time he comes in, I don't know whether to breathe a sigh of relief or burst into tears. I'm caught between desperately wanting to move on from our experiments in dating and asking him to start all over again. I'm confused. And upset. And not sleeping very well without my nose pressed into the strong column of his spine, my arm around his waist. All of it is manifesting into a very short temper, and my—my tarts look like shit.

Beatrice snickers and closes the door behind her with a flick of her wrist. She tosses her boxes on the counter in an undignified heap, the corners pressing in on the sides. I flinch. I swear she does it on purpose, knowing how meticulous I am with twine and cardboard.

And how much I value a shortbread cookie.

"Don't do that," I snap.

"Do what?" She blinks her eyes innocently and opens my fridge, bending to inspect my bottom shelf. She makes a face and swings it shut again.

"You know what."

She props her hands on her hips. "I don't appreciate the tone you're taking." She levels a look at me that would have anyone else shaking in their boots. As it is, I know she has a secret knitting habit and she's been the one making tiny sweaters for Beckett's cats. She couldn't be less terrifying if she tried. "What's gotten into you?"

Stupidity. Fear. A complete and total inability to figure my shit out. A pinch of frustration and a significant amount of wallowing.

"Nothing, I'm—" I drag the palm of my hand across my forehead and feel the swipe of something cool. Great. I'm fairly confident I just swiped lime custard across my forehead.

Maybe I should dip my whole face in it. Then I'll look like the clown I am.

"I'm fine," I finish.

Beatrice circles the big island in my tiny kitchen and stands right in front of me. She's a little bit shorter than I am, but what she lacks in inches she makes up for in presence. She tilts her chin up, a wisp of gray hair brushing against her cheek. She looks like an oil painting of an ancient warrior. I feel like she should be holding a flag and a sword.

"I think you like dating idiots," she says with a bark.

She snatches the piping bag out of my hands and nudges me out of her way.

My spine snaps straight. I can feel both of my eyebrows climbing up my forehead. Another lick of irritation adds to the inferno building in my chest. I haven't slept soundly in days and Beatrice thinks it's a good idea to come into my kitchen and insult me? "Pardon me?"

Her eyes narrow and she tilts her head to the side, fixing the horrible icing job I was doing at the border of the tart. I was trying to line them with hearts, but they all look like sad little ghosts instead. It feels appropriate.

Beatrice doesn't look up. "You heard me."

"I did."

"Then what's the question?"

"Uh, my first question is: what the hell are you talking about?" I bump her out of the way with my hip, but she just circles around to the other side and yanks my tray over with her. "Second question is: why the hell are you talking about it?"

"The whole phone tree is talking about it," she mumbles. "And you shouldn't try to do any skill work when you're in shambles," she adds, louder.

"The phone tree?" No point in addressing the shambles piece. She's right about that.

Beatrice looks up with a sigh. "Yes. The phone tree. You've heard of it?"

"I'm familiar. But I haven't gotten any messages since—"

I think back. The last message I got was something

about a new chicken pesto pizza at Matty's. Luka called Jesse at the bar who called Dane—who, I'm sure, was shocked at the news considering he sleeps in the same bed as Matty every single night—who then called Susie who then called me. That must have been—

I freeze as realization strikes, quick and sharp. I haven't received a single message since Caleb and I started our arrangement. Caleb mentioned a couple of weeks ago that he wasn't getting anything either, and I know how Darlene likes to inundate him with mundane things. Beatrice snickers again, low and amused. "Did you figure it out?"

"Does the entire town really have nothing better to do than to pass along gossip about people who may or may not be dating?"

"I can't believe you even need to ask yourself that question," Beatrice says. "And you were the only two who insisted that you weren't dating. It looked a lot like regular dating to the rest of us."

"Alright, I'm—" Still trying to come to terms with everything, but my brain skips back to the rocky start of this uneven conversation. "Hold on a second. Let's go backwards."

"Thought you might."

"I don't like dating idiots."

"Sure you do."

"No, I don't. It's why I agreed to the dating thing with Caleb to begin with. I wanted to try something different. I wanted to feel good, for once."

Beatrice sets down the piping bag on the counter and

moves the finished tart to the tray I've been lining them up on. She grabs another, but doesn't move to fix the wobbly lines. She just looks at it for a long time, twists it to the left, and then to the right. Then she gently picks it up and puts it right next to the perfect one.

"And are you still dating Caleb?"

My heartbeat thunders in my chest. It feels like I'm out in that field all over again, watching his face crumple in confusion, then transform into stark, disappointed understanding. Like he could see this coming from a mile away. Like the terms of our arrangement were all we'd ever get.

"No." My voice cracks at the start and at the end of that very simple word.

"Then my point remains." Beatrice nudges the tray back in my direction and reaches for one of her discarded boxes. She opens it and pulls out one pristine, perfect shortbread square. Sets it down in front of her and reaches for another piping bag that I never bothered to fill. "You like to date these silly, stupid boys because it's easier. It's easier to have a stupid man disappoint you, then a good man break your heart. One of those things is significantly kinder to recover from than the other."

I blink once, and then twice. I curl my fingers around the edge of the baking tray. "You think I'm afraid?"

"Yes."

Something in my chest rattles and then falls silent. An acknowledgement, I think. Silence weaves between us as I stand stock still at the counter and Beatrice continues to work diligently on the cookies she brought with her. I think she came to give me some company—in her own stubborn, aggressive, curmudgeon way.

I watch her work and the words slip out.

"I want to stop being afraid," I whisper. "When will I stop being afraid?"

Beatrice smiles and hands me the cookie she's been working on. A gladiolus in bloom, purple petals reaching up, up, up to an unseen sky. Beckett has lectured me enough about flowers that I know this one blooms with the summer months. A stubborn flower than can blossom again and again if it survives the cold winter months.

"That's the trouble with falling in love. It's a messy, ungraceful stumble into a whirlwind of chaos. It doesn't always feel good. It's a fall." She pulls out another shortbread cookie, a smile hooking at the side of her mouth. Her eyes are far away, glassy with remembering. I wonder who she's thinking about with that look on her face.

Who she fell with. Who she fell for.

"You just have to trust that the person you're falling with is smart enough to catch you before you hurt anything important."

HE'S LATE ON MONDAY.

By thirteen minutes.

I try not to spend the entire time staring at the clock, but I'm a bundle of nervous energy. I keep fisting my hands in the material of my apron, tying and retying the scarf in my hair.

The third time I slip it out and run it through my fingers, Gus makes a *tsking* sound from the booth in the far corner. He's taken to sitting there every morning like some grumpy gargoyle, eating all the butter croissants Caleb has abandoned and providing a running commentary that I'm sure he thinks is amusing but really just adds to my agitation.

"He won't care what you're wearing," Gus sing-songs. My cheeks burn hot and I toss a glare in his direction. He shrugs and holds up his hands. "Just sharing my thoughts."

"Yeah, you're always sharing your thoughts. No one wants your thoughts."

"Plenty of people want my thoughts."

"Keep telling yourself that."

Caleb appears seven minutes and two hair scarves later. I see the top of his head as he moves through the thick cluster of trees that surrounds every side of the bakehouse. Messy hair like he's been running his fingers through it again. My heart automatically speeds to double-time in my chest and I dig the heel of my hand against my sternum. It's probably not healthy to feel this way every time I see his face.

But here we are.

He rounds the corner where a beautiful Blue Spruce spreads her branches out like open arms—the one Luka has named Spruce Springsteen—while I pretend to restock the red striped paper straws right by the register. He adjusts his bag against his chest and tips his head down, smiling at something—some*one*, I realize—and that's when I notice her.

Emma Waterson. The eighth grade English teacher at Inglewild High. Caleb's co-worker. Caleb's very pretty, probably very well-adjusted, and emotionally superior co-worker.

They walk through the trees side by side and stroll to a stop at the bottom of the steps. Like the glutton for punishment I am, I keep looking, a handful of straws frozen halfway in mid-air. I watch as Emma steps forward into his space, as she angles her head back and gestures at something with her hands. I watch Caleb's face twist in amusement, the slight tilt of his head to the right that tells me he's really listening. Eager and earnest and all the lovely things that make Caleb who he is.

Meanwhile, my stomach feels like it's filled with glass marbles. A headache threatens at the base of my neck. I'm torn between wanting to hide beneath my countertop and catapulting myself down the front steps. I guess this is what I need to get used to—this iron-hot spike of feeling right in the center of my chest. Jealousy, probably. A touch of regret.

I barely manage to put the straws down before a laugh bursts out of Caleb. I can hear the sound of it through the thick glass of my windows. Warm and low. Smooth, rolling amusement. I can count the times I've heard Caleb laugh on a single hand, and all of them were with me. I keep each of those memories tucked close in the secret, sacred place close to my heart—for me and me alone.

And now he's laughing. With someone else.

All of my fiery resolve to *move on* tumbles headfirst into heartbreak.

I look down at the counter as the bell above the door jingles. Heavy footsteps and the bang of his elbow against one of my clear glass jars that's holding biscotti. He always hits it, no matter how many times I move it just slightly out of his way.

"Hey, Layla."

His voice is warm. Friendly.

I keep my eyes firmly on the countertop and poke at some of the straws I let tumble out of the glass.

"Hi," I say back, a storm cloud of feelings. "What can I get you two?"

There's no reason to be upset by this. I told Caleb our arrangement was over. He's free to do exactly as he pleases. Emma is beautiful, kind, and an excellent choice for everything Caleb has to offer. She is exactly what he deserves. Probably exactly what he's looking for.

I bet her croissants taste like garbage though.

"Two?" Caleb sounds confused.

I manage to look up about as high as his chin. I hold my eyes firmly there, unwilling to look anywhere else. "Yes. What can I get you two?"

"Oh, ah—" I watch his hand creep over his shoulder to the back of his neck, his big palm massaging the muscles there. A nervous tic, when he's not sure what to say. "It's just me. But I could order two of something, if you wanted?"

My eyes snap up to his. "Where's Emma?"

Caleb looks at me like I've just asked what his horoscope of the day is. "What?"

"Emma," I explain slowly. I don't think I imagined her with him, but I haven't been sleeping very well lately. "The woman you were laughing with just outside."

"Oh." He looks over his shoulder. "Oh, yeah. I ran into her on the way in."

"Hm."

He turns back to me and takes in the look on my face. I don't have a mirror, but it's probably a cross of *I just ate an oatmeal raisin cookie and I thought it had chocolate chips in it* with *there are no cookies left in the jar.*

His eyes narrow. "What's that sound about?"

"What sound?"

"The *hm.*"

I shrug and try to push against the ache that swells the longer I look at him. "Nothing. It was just a sound I made." I grab a paper cup from beneath the counter with too much force. When I set it down, it's crushed on one side. I toss it into the trashcan and grab another. "Do you want tea or coffee?"

"I want to talk about why you're so upset."

"I'm not upset." My voice shakes at the end like the traitor it is.

"Layla."

"Great, I'll get you a coffee."

"Layla," he says again, softer this time. He reaches for my wrist before I can spin my way to the espresso machine. His hand squeezes and I angle my chin up, intent on a mask of absolute indifference. But the hot, embarrassed, ugly feeling in my chest spreads the longer I look at him, and I feel my bottom lip tremble. His eyes glance down and hold. His entire body collapses inward, curling towards me.

"Layla," he repeats, with a note of pleading this time.

"No." I pull my hand out of his grasp. I don't know what I'm saying no to. This day, maybe. This entire situation. This jealousy and sadness and the inescapable feeling that I'm constantly turning in the wrong direction. I want to stop being afraid, but I don't know *how*. I want to believe Beatrice about trust, but *I don't know how*. I want to accept that maybe I've finally made the right choice in a man, but *I don't know how*.

I clear my throat. "There's coffee cake in the back," I say under my breath. "I'll be right back."

I disappear through the door before he can say anything else. It's easier, back here, to press my palms against my forehead and try to collect the scattered bits of myself. I breathe in deep through my nose and try to count to twelve. I attempt to channel some of those old yoga videos I sent to Stella a lifetime ago.

This will fade, right? This feeling? It has to.

"Layla, wait a second. I want to—"

Caleb crashes through my back door and stumbles right into me, the both of us collapsing against my island. The last time we were back here together, he had me hitched up against the wall by the fridge, his arm banded under my ass and his mouth at my neck. Wet, sucking kisses that I wore the mark of for days.

I think he's remembering too, because I feel his shaky breath against the back of my neck as he holds me steady, his hands squeezing gently at my upper arms. We're pressed together shoulders to hips, his chest against my back.

We stand there together and breathe. It's been almost a week since he's touched me in any way and I can't believe how much I've already forgotten. The way it feels when he drops his head against my neck. How warm and solid and good he feels.

"Layla." He breathes my name against the hollow behind my ear, nose nudging. Both of his arms wrap around my middle and he squeezes. "Why are you upset?"

"I'm not," I say immediately, voice thick, hands trembling. I should pull myself out of his arms. I should act like I'm fine. But I can't. I *can't*.

"You are. Why?"

Because I saw you with someone else and I didn't like it, I think. *Because I don't know how to stop being afraid.*

"I don't know," I say instead. A lie. "I'm not." Another lie.

He pulls back with a sigh but keeps his hands firmly on my arms. He turns me until I have no choice but to look at him. The stern set of his brows and the lines bracketing his mouth.

I want to rub my thumb against them until they disappear.

I want him to leave my kitchen and pretend like this morning never happened.

I don't know what I want.

"Why can't you be honest with me?"

"I am being honest with you."

I flinch at the end of my sentence. I am absolutely not being honest with him. I'm taking the coward's way out, over and over again.

Caleb's hands squeeze and then release. "Are you upset that you saw me with Emma?"

"No." *Yes.* "I wish you the very best of luck with her. I hope you employ the dating tips and tricks you learned during our time together."

I feel sick even saying it. It's rude, and mean, and not how I feel at all. But I'm all jumbled up. I feel like I'm on tumble dry, spinning around and around. Caleb takes a half-step back and looks at me like I just punched him in the face.

"Is that what you think?" His palm scrubs at his jaw. "You think it's that easy for me to just find someone else? That all I wanted from you was *tips* and *tricks*?"

"Wasn't it?" I move around the countertop until there's a mixing bowl and three feet of solid kitchen island between us. "You said you wanted to be better at dating. Have at it. Get out there and—" I do something weird with my hand. "Do your thing."

His jaw clenches tight, eyes blazing. He doesn't say anything for a long time before he finally tells me, voice low and barely contained, "That's not all I wanted from you."

"What?"

He walks around the countertop—chin up, shoulders back. Breathtaking in his calm, quiet confidence. "That's not all I wanted from you," he repeats quietly, moving forward until I have to tip my head back to stare at him. "I didn't ask you to start this whole thing because I wanted tips, Layla. I liked *you*. From the very start."

"I—"

"Emma has a crush on another teacher at school—Gabe," Caleb interrupts. "She's been trying for weeks to work up the courage to say something to him. His classroom is two doors down from mine. She would stop in my room when she got nervous and find something to talk to me about. She happened to be outside when I was coming into the bakehouse this morning and thought she should apologize for all her visits. She finally talked to Gabe on Friday. They're going out to dinner this week."

Relief makes my knees weak. I find something over his shoulder to look at as embarrassment climbs over my cheeks. Caleb reaches up, cups my face with his hand, and guides my eyes back to his.

"Stop treating me like I'm the guy with the lint roller or the guy at the tiki bar. Stop acting like you're someone I can move on from. I don't want to be anywhere but right here with you." His thumb drags across my blush and his eyes soften. "Don't underestimate how long I'll wait for you."

"I don't—"

"Please don't lie to me either."

My mouth snaps shut.

His hand slips to the back of my head. He watches me carefully—quietly—eyes tracing every inch of my face. He sighs and tugs me forward, a firm kiss in the middle of my forehead. My arms hang at my sides. My heart sits somewhere in my throat.

"I miss you." He tucks the words against my skin in a rough whisper, almost like they were never meant for me to hear. A sigh loosens from his chest and he drops his hand. He takes two steps back and looks towards the door.

"This part is up to you, Layla. What happens next." He drags his knuckles against the center of his chest and then pats once over his heart. Like he's trying to rub something away. He looks back to me and gives me a sad, half-smile. "It's up to you," he says again.

And then I get exactly what I was hoping for when I first saw him on that path with someone else. The thing I thought I wanted, but I don't really want at all.

Caleb walks away, and I'm alone.

TWENTY-SIX

CALEB

I WAKE up to the sound of pots and pans clanking in my kitchen.

For a single, heartbreaking moment, I think it's Layla, using the key I keep under the edge of my front mat. The one I showed her two days before everything went to hell in a hand-basket, telling her in stumbling, stuttered words that she could use it whenever she liked.

I roll over in bed and let myself run away with the fantasy. I picture myself coming down the steps, finding her at the stove in the soft, oversized t-shirt she liked to steal from my drawer. Nothing underneath. My chin at her shoulder and my arm around her waist. Something low on the radio. Coffee warm on the counter. Sunlight beaming in through the windows and her smile a brand against my skin.

But then I hear the muted sounds of a telenovela—a string of curses in faint Spanish and the squeak of my grandmother's house slippers against freshly scrubbed floors—and I bury my face in my pillow.

"Abuela," I greet as soon as I gather the motivation to leave my room, eyeballing the four pots she already has steaming on the stove top. I kiss her on both cheeks and then head directly for the coffee machine. "What are you doing here so early?" I ask in Spanish.

"No es temprano," she responds. *It's not early.* She turns halfway and arches an eyebrow. "Where is your shirt?"

I huff a laugh and nod towards the sweatshirt slung over the back of one of my kitchen chairs. I'm surprised it's still here and she hasn't tried to wash every textile in sight. I slip it over my bare shoulders and zip it up halfway. "Better?"

"Sí." She hands me a heaping plate of eggs and chorizo, tetelas on the side still warm from the pan. I slip into a chair and try to settle into the comfort of a warm meal cooked by my grandmother, an old episode of her favorite show playing in the background, the odd notes of a song she used to sing to us when we were kids hummed every so often, preoccupied as she stirs.

"Have I told you the story of how your grandfather and I met?"

I pause with my fork halfway to my mouth, eyebrows raised. "Yes."

About seven thousand times. It's one of my favorites. I used to make her repeat it to me again and again when she'd put me to bed. The blankets tucked high to my chin and her hand gentle in my hair.

"It was at the market," she says, like I didn't just answer her question. "He—"

"Bought all of the shoes you were selling," I answer, knowing the story by heart. "He walked you home and came back the day after. He kept coming back."

My grandmother taps her wooden spoon on the edge of the pot and sets it down to the side. "No," she says. "That is not how it happened."

I frown. "Yes, it is."

"Oh?" She turns to face me, arms crossed over her chest. "And you were there, were you?"

I fork a mouthful of eggs into my mouth, properly chastised. I swear my grandmother created the stern look when she had children, and honed it to perfection with her grandchildren. "No, abuela. Lo siento. Please continue."

She makes a clicking sound with her tongue. "He did not buy all of my shoes in an attempt to woo me. He stumbled into my stand because he was not paying attention. He knocked an entire side down, and he had to buy all my shoes because he ruined them. Your abuelo did not look at me in adoration when he first met me. It was fear."

I set my fork down on the table and stare at her. "What?"

She shrugs and goes back to stirring her pot. "I thought he was a *peinabombillas*."

Someone who combs lightbulbs. It's my grandmother's favorite insult and it doesn't make a lick of sense.

378

"Why—" I try to swallow around thirty years of lies. "Why did you tell the story differently?"

"Because your grandfather was a romantic man." My grandmother smiles. It's a soft and sad one, the kind you feel deep in the echoes of your heart when you're remembering someone you've loved and lost. A bittersweet ache that ripples out. "Because he liked to be the hero of the story. That tale he told you about the shark was a lie, too."

"He didn't punch a shark in the nose while saving a boat full of children?"

A cackle bursts out of her. "No. You saw that man, osezno." She rolls her eyes. "He had almost no upper body strength. He was a lover, not a fighter."

"Huh."

"I can't believe you believed it as long as you did."

"Neither can I, I guess."

Good to know my whole life has been a lie. I cross my arms over my chest and lean back in my chair. My grandmother looks over her shoulder and makes another *tsking* sound, turning off the burners and joining me at the table. She sets a bowl down in front of me, and one in front of herself.

"I tell you this because—" She scoops her spoon around the outer edge, eyes far away. "I tell you this because you are so like your grandfather."

"I see things that aren't really there?" My stomach swoops low. "I embellish?"

"No," she says with a steely thread of determination.

"Because you love with your whole, entire heart. And that is a beautiful thing."

I pick up my fork again with a frown and poke at some of my eggs. "It doesn't feel like such a good thing."

It feels like the worst thing. It feels like the thing that keeps hurting me, over and over again. I have no idea if Layla will change her mind or not. If she'll ever want me the same way I want her. Right now my big heart feels like a big curse.

My grandmother's hand reaches out and curls over mine. She squeezes. "It is the best thing," she says fiercely. "I know our family worries about you, about your unguarded heart. But it makes you kind and generous." She sucks in a deep, wavering breath. "Your grandfather would be so proud of the man you are. You must promise me that you will never stop trusting your heart."

I think of Layla's face behind the counter when I walked in earlier. The tears she was desperately trying to hide, the tremor in her hands. I think of my lips against her forehead, my body tucked tight against hers. How it felt to have to walk away from her.

"What if it's wrong this time?"

"It's not," she says, quick and sharp. "Don't you think that girl deserves someone who offers their full heart? Don't you think, after all of these men she has wasted her time with, that she deserves someone who will return her affection without thinking twice?"

Something in my chest eases. "Yeah. Yeah, that's exactly what she deserves." I blow out a deep breath and look at the table top. Layla's worth waiting for. I know that. It's just hard to see her and feel all the distance between us. Phantom pains, almost. Right in the center of my chest. I glance up at my grandmother. "I'll keep trusting my heart."

My grandmother nods. "Bueno." She scoops a spoonful of food out of her bowl and pops it into her mouth. I can feel her considering me, her warm eyes narrowed in concentration.

"What is it?"

"Perhaps this is the reason you've had such trouble with women in the past."

"What is?"

She smiles, the lines by her eyes deepening. "Because it has never been the right woman."

I'M HALFWAY through my morning run through the park when my phone rings. I glance at the caller ID, see Charlie's name, and promptly ignore it.

I need time to decompress, not discuss something ridiculous. The last time he called, he tried explaining the benefits of finger guns as a pick-up tool. Another time it was a video call from the inside of a J.Crew dressing room and he wanted to know which cable knit sweater matched his eyes better.

I shove my phone back in the waistband of my shorts, turning around the bend without losing my stride. With every slap of my shoes against the pavement, I think of

Layla. Her laugh. Her smile. Her god damned butter croissants that I'm craving like my next fix. I don't know why I
thought it was a good idea to abstain from them while
we're apart. I think some part of me wanted to show her
that I can try different things. I don't know. It felt like a
good idea at the time.

But fuck, I miss those croissants.

My phone rings again, vibrating against the small of
my back. I ignore it.

It vibrates again. And again.

I resist the urge to fling it into the woods, but it's a close
thing. I answer on a frustrated panting breath, my sweat-
soaked hair falling into my eyes. I push it back.

"What?"

"Inglewild phone tree calling," Charlie sing-songs.
"Here to pass along a message."

"Since when?"

"Since when, what?"

"You don't usually call me. Darlene does."

"Ah." There's a muffled sound on the other end of
the phone. Like he's just fallen down a flight of stairs or
he's single-handedly putting up a last stand against a
family of raccoons. "Well. There's been some
restructuring."

"Restructuring?"

"You heard me, bear cub. Don't ask questions. Do you
want the message or not?"

I pinch the bridge of my nose. I swear I have a constant
headache these days. "What's the message, Charlie?"

"Word on the street is Layla locked herself in the freezer at the bakery."

My stomach plummets. Panic pulls every inch of my body tight. I imagine the absolute worst, her small body huddled up in the corner of her industrial freezer.

"What?" I breathe.

There's more commotion on the other end of the line, and then I hear the very clear voice of Stella whisper-yelling, "Charlie, what in the actual hell?"

"What?" he whispers back, phone angled slightly away from his mouth. His voice sounds tinny and far away. "She said get him to the bakehouse."

"She didn't say give him a heart attack."

"Fine." His exhale is loud in my ear. "Hey, Caleb? Sorry about that, man. You need to get to the bakehouse. There's a fire."

"Charlie!"

There's a scuffle on the other end of the phone. I hear muffled cursing, a sound like someone's just dunked their head underwater and a thud. Then Stella's voice is on the line, apologetic and soft.

"Caleb?"

I have no idea what's going on.

"Is Layla okay?"

"She's fine. Don't—don't listen to Charlie." She sighs and mumbles something on the other end of the phone that I don't quite catch. "Do you think you could swing by the bakehouse? Layla wants to see you."

My heart pounds in my chest. It's a combination of

strain from my run, adrenaline from Charlie scaring the shit out of me, and apprehension that Layla actually wants to see me. A thought occurs.

"Are you guys meddling?"

Stella hums. "This is probably about twenty-five percent meddling, but it's well-intentioned." She pauses and lowers her voice. "She just needs a nudge. I promise she wants to see you, Caleb."

"You're sure?"

"I'm sure."

IT'S the longest half-hour of my life.

I abandon all traces of apprehension on the second half of my run. I set a new personal best on my way back home and practically fall up my porch steps, knocking over a vase and an umbrella as soon as I'm in the entryway of my house. I take a quick shower and pull a random t-shirt over my head and trip out to my Jeep like the bakehouse really is on fire. Like my house is on fire, too.

By the time I pull into the little gravel parking lot behind the bakehouse, my heart is thundering in my chest. I try to manage my expectations, hands flexing on the steering wheel. It's possible this isn't anything at all. Maybe I left something here earlier in the week. Maybe she needs me to try a new recipe.

Or maybe she wants to tell me she made a mistake, asking me to come three days a week. Maybe she wants to tell me to stay away.

I blow out a deep breath.

Best just to get it over with.

I pass my hands over the branches as I walk along the path. It's one of my favorite parts of this place, the massive flat stones laid carefully among the trees. It feels like you're the best sort of lost, wandering a path that's familiar and treasured. Footprints dot either side of the path from those who have already come and gone this morning. Sunlight is muted, hidden by thick branches. It's like being somewhere else entirely. Inside a snow globe, maybe. Or a postcard.

I turn the last corner and it's my second favorite part of walking up to Layla's. I can see right through the big windows in the front to Layla, standing behind the counter, a scarf in her hair and her head ducked down in concentration. Even all the way back here, I can see the way she's got her tongue caught between her teeth. Her body angled slightly to the left as she works.

She's the most beautiful thing I've ever seen. The most beautiful thing I ever will see.

She glances up from the counter and spots me, standing just outside the edge of the trees. A smile starts slowly as she places her icing bag to the side, spreading wider the longer she looks at me. I move towards her.

I feel like I've always been moving towards her.

She comes out from behind the counter and pokes her head out the front door.

"Hey," she says, that smile still on her face like she's

glad to see me. Hope beats a wild war drum in my chest. "What are you doing here?"

"You were trapped in a freezer," I offer. Her face crumples in confusion. "Nevermind. Charlie was being ... Charlie." I scratch at the back of my head and try to shake off all my nervous energy. It's just Layla. "Did you want to see me?"

She bites at her bottom lip. My hope deflates like a sad little balloon.

"Oh, ah." I glance over my shoulder. Maybe I'll wander back through the trees and keep going. Past my Jeep and into the fields. Let Mother Nature do as she will. "I'll just—"

"No. Caleb. Wait a second." I watch as Layla fusses with the strings of her apron in the propped open doorway. "Stay right there. I have something for you."

She disappears before I can say anything else. The door swings shut behind her, the bells above the door a muted sound through the thick glass. I stand there and try not to stare at the place she was, but my eyes drift through the windows without my consent. I watch her slip behind the counter and search behind the register. She lifts up a coffee pot and peers beneath it. Rearranges the oversized mason jars by the display case until her face lights up with a grin.

"Here we go." She appears again in a flurry, skipping down the steps to land with a light jump in the gravel of the walkway. She strides over to me and hands me a folded-up piece of thick, white paper. Her hand trembles as she waits.

I stare at it. "What is this?"

She thrusts it forward. "Open it."

"What is it?"

She snatches her hand back. "You have no imagination. I'll read it to you." Her eyes blink up to mine before they dart away and focus back on the paper. "It's a grading sheet," she mumbles.

"For what?"

A blush warms her cheeks. "For our experiment."

"Oh." That is not what I was expecting. "For me?"

She nods and brings her thumb to her mouth, biting down on the edge of it. It is somehow enticingly sexy and adorably endearing in the exact same breath. "This might have been a terrible idea," she says, so low I have to strain to hear her.

"No, no." I try to stand a little straighter. Muster all of the courage I possess. I did want her to tell me how to be better at dating. That's how all of this began. Might as well finish it out. "I want to hear."

"Okay, well." She glances at the paper again, her blush burning darker. I watch with interest as it spreads to the top of her collarbones. "It's sort of stupid, but—"

"Layla. It's not stupid. Tell me."

"I broke it into categories," she confesses in a rush. "Your final grade. Enthusiasm. Originality. Kindness. And a—a random bonus category." Her hands fumble with the edge of the paper.

I cock my head to the side. "Are those the Miss America categories?"

"No." She rubs her palm against her forehead. "Maybe. I don't know. Just—go with it, for a minute? I'm trying—I'm trying to do something. I'm trying to apologize."

I frown at that. "I already told you. You have nothing to apologize for."

"I know. You also said what happens next is up to me." Her nerves ease and her smile comes easier. When she flicks her eyes up to me again, she's able to hold my gaze for a little longer. Gemstone green, clear and sure. "Alright. Here we go. In the enthusiasm category, you get a 10 out of 10. Exceeds expectations. The comments say—well, the comments say that you always displayed an enjoyment and enthusiasm to be present. That you seemed genuinely interested in every aspect of the dating process."

That's good news. But the way she said it—*comments say*—she's removing herself from the equation. I take a half-step forward. "And what about you, Layla? What do you say?"

"I say—" She blows out a slow breath, her eyes still on the paper. She crumples the edge and then tries to fold it straight. "I say that I've never felt so special to anyone in my entire life," she whispers. "I say that the way you smiled in the front seat of your car that very first night made me think I could love you, just a little bit."

All the air eases out of my lungs in a slow, choppy breath. "Just a little bit, huh?"

"Hawaiian shirt notwithstanding."

"Of course."

A smile kicks at the corner of her mouth. She keeps looking at the card stock in her hands. "Okay. Originality. Another 10 out of 10. The comments say dates never felt orchestrated or overly planned. Dates' interests were thoroughly considered and applied."

"And you?"

"And me." Layla's eyes finally flick up and hold mine. "I don't think I've ever laughed so much. I thought maybe I could love you some more, with frozen corn over your eye."

My heart pounds out a staccato in my chest, quick and thundering. "What's next?"

"Kindness," she breathes. "8 out of 10, and the comments say that's only because you're kind to a fault. And you should do more to protect yourself against things that might hurt you."

"Hm." I take another step closer and reach for her left hand. I gently guide her fist open and trace the tip of my fingertip over her knuckles.

I don't have to ask this time. She just tells me.

"I say that your kindness, your open heart, your capacity to care and love—those are all the best things about you. I've been—I've been having such a tough time, Caleb, trying to find the courage to trust myself. To trust us. I want this to be real so bad."

I thread my fingers through hers. "It is, sweetheart. It's real, I promise."

She squeezes my hand. "Which brings me to my last

point. The random bonus category." She swallows and drops the paper to her side, letting it go. I watch it drift on the edges of a wind before my gaze is swallowed up by Layla beneath the afternoon sun, painted in golds and pinks and bright, summer blues. A tentative smile and love shining like a beacon in her pretty eyes. My heart feels like it's going to fall out of my damned chest.

"This whole time—I think I've been falling in love with you," she tells me. "I didn't recognize it because I've never felt it before. And when I did, when I realized, I kind of freaked out. I'm still kind of freaking out about it. It turns out the thing I wanted most is pretty scary when it comes down to it. You're going to have to be patient with me."

"I can do that," I grit out, voice thick. "I think I've been falling in love with you for a while, Layla. One butter croissant at a time."

One smile, one secret, one soft touch at a time.

Her smile is a soft, tremulous thing. I want to trace it with my thumb. I want to paint it in the sky. I want it iced on top of a cake.

"Good," she says. "Because I'd like to discuss terms for a new arrangement."

I move closer and reach for a strand of her caramel hair. I rub it carefully between my thumb and forefinger then twirl it around twice and tug. She smiles at me and something cascades through my chest, warm and lovely.

"A new arrangement, huh?"

She nods and grabs two fistfuls of my t-shirt, tugging me even closer. "Yeah."

My nose bumps hers. "I thought you didn't want any more arrangements between us."

"This one is different."

"Tell me."

"Well, to start—" She nudges me with her nose until I tip my chin up, her mouth at the space just above my heart. She curls her arms around my waist and presses a soft kiss just there.

"Dates," she says into my t-shirt. "I want lots of them."

I hum and rock us back and forth lightly. "I think we can do that." I pause. "As long as it's not the escape room again."

"No promises on that. Minus the black eye, I think that went very well."

"Oh yes, besides that."

She grins, and her eyes soften. "No more grading. No more pretense. It's just going to be me and you from here on out. Honest with ourselves and with each other."

I press my nose against her temple. I slip my palm to the small of her back and tuck her even closer. We stand together in the middle of the trees. "I like how that sounds."

One of her hands releases my shirt to curl around the back of my neck. Her palm is cool in the sticky summer heat, fingers drumming. "Vanilla ice cream on the beach," she adds. "Kisses in the rain. The sound you make, right here ..." She trails one finger down the line of my neck and taps at the hollow of my throat. "When I make you feel good."

I make a smaller version of that sound right now, something deep and wanting. I tug her tighter against me. "Butter croissants," I say, my voice low. "Strawberry shortcake. You tell me what you need, when you need it. I'll be right here next to you."

She nods. She tips her head back until her eyes can search mine, wide and open beneath the endless summer sky. My heart lurches, and everything I am belongs to her.

"One more thing," she says.

I nod and tuck her hair carefully behind her ears. "What is it?"

"Falling in love," she says. "Falling together."

I slip my hand down her neck to the center of her chest. My pinky catches in the collar of her dress. I spread my fingers out wide until I can feel the gentle pulse of her heart beneath her skin. "I agree to your terms."

"Good," she says. She lets her mouth brush mine, back and forth once. She tastes like strawberries and champagne. Buttercream icing. My favorite kind of forever. "Because these terms are non-negotiable."

"Finally. We're in agreement."

She smiles into our kiss just as a tear slips down her cheek.

Relief. Pure, perfect happiness.

The best arrangement I've ever agreed to.

I grin and pull her face to mine.

"Finally."

EPILOGUE

LAYLA

TWO YEARS LATER

"WHAT IS HAPPENING?"

I'm frozen in the entry of the kitchen, Caleb's shirt skimming my thighs and a lukewarm cup of coffee in my left hand. He woke up before me this morning and delivered it to my nightstand like he always does, the crossword left waiting and a gentle kiss just below my ear. It's my favorite way to wake up.

Well. Second-favorite way to wake up. My favorite way involves Caleb and his mouth tracing a meandering path down the soft skin of my belly, his hands pushing my thighs wide and his teeth grazing my tattoo.

Caleb turns halfway and glances at me over his shoulder. "What?"

Standing like that, I can see the picture that hangs over

the stove. A cutout from *Baltimore Magazine* with one of the pictures they featured.

My favorite picture.

In it, Caleb is sitting at that little table in the corner with a flowery tea cup in his hand, legs splattered with mud and dirt, face exhausted. But he's looking at me with such tender affection I feel it like a kiss against the back of my neck. A knuckle under my chin. In the picture I'm behind the counter and he's at the table. He's looking at me like I've hung the damn moon.

I think I have forty-seven copies of that magazine.

I take two shuffling steps forward and slide onto a stool. When we decided to move in together, we didn't choose his place and we didn't choose mine. We chose a new house altogether, right behind the bakehouse in the middle of Lovelight Farms. Construction took a while, but the kitchen is huge and I get to sleep in a little bit later in the mornings.

And Caleb gets to walk me to work every single day.

I drop my chin in my hands and roll my lips against a smile. "Are you wearing a harness?"

He turns fully and I finally get a good look at the black straps over his shoulders. It is a harness and right in the middle of his bare chest is Poppy—the tiny little gal Beckett rescued and coerced Caleb into adopting. He told him she was supposed to be a police dog, but I can't picture it.

First of all, I think she weighs ten pounds soaking wet. And second, I don't think I've heard her bark once.

She is the sweetest little thing. I went with Caleb the day he met her. He got down on his knees and held out his hand for her, palm up. She took one look at him, curled up in his lap, and fell right asleep. They've been inseparable ever since.

Including, apparently, during breakfast preparation.

Caleb turns back and forth, Poppy safely strapped to his chest with a series of buckles. She tilts her head up and stares at him adoringly.

"What?" he asks. "Is it too much?"

I shake my head and huff a laugh. "Just enough."

He grins at me. My favorite half-grin that makes his dimples blink awake. "Good, because breakfast is ready."

He slides a greasy bacon, egg and cheese bagel across the counter to me and my stomach makes an appreciative grumble. Apparently Caleb made all those bagel sandwiches he brought me when we first started dating. He makes them for me on weekends, now. And on special occasions.

Today is neither of those things.

He removes Poppy from the harness on his chest and presses a quick kiss to her nose, dropping her in the fluffy bed shaped like a muffin in the corner of the kitchen. It's perfectly situated in a patch of sunlight, her small ears perked up as she makes three tiny circles and collapses in a heap. Her eyes follow Caleb as he moves around the kitchen, wiping things down and putting away ingredients.

Mine do, too.

I watch the flex of his bare shoulders as he reaches in the

fridge. The strong line of his biceps as he pours himself another mug of coffee. We've been together almost two years now, and I still can't quite get over him. Loving Caleb feels like stardust and cupcakes and really good wine. A warmth that starts somewhere in my chest and rolls out until I feel it like sunshine on my skin. Constant. Effusive. Lovely.

I still get unsure. I still have doubts about myself and how we fit together. But he helps me through it. His lips at the back of my neck and his strong arms around my waist, he helps me.

I spent a long time looking for the right kind of love, only for it to walk right through the front door of my bakehouse every Monday, Wednesday, and Friday. We talk about it a lot. I like to whine how long it took me to see him on the other side of that counter. Caleb likes to smile, rub his thumb under my ear and tell me, *It all worked out in the end.*

He catches me staring and raises one dark eyebrow, a blush rising in response. I love that he still blushes with me. That I can still make that pink flare to life on his cheeks with a single look.

I take a monstrous bite of my bagel.

"W'ha s'ocas jon?"

Caleb's smile widens. "What was that?" He reaches for the newspaper folded up on the edge of the counter and flips through it until he finds the recipe section. He hands it to me without a word, tucking it neatly under the edge of my plate.

I swallow around perfectly crisp bacon and cheesy egg. "What is the occasion?"

"I can't just make you a bagel whenever I want?"

Suspicion blooms. I narrow my eyes. "You're always more than welcome to. It's just—you also have your shirt off."

He glances down at his bare chest, eyebrows raised. His palm smoothes at the skin between his pecs, drifting down the line of his abs to his belly button. I am mesmerized. I'm pretty sure a piece of bagel falls out of my mouth and lands on the edge of the countertop.

"I do have my shirt off."

I place my sandwich down and reach for Caleb's glass of orange juice. My gaze is still stuck somewhere between his arms and the hem of his sleep pants. "It makes me think you have a request."

Bagel sandwiches and a shirtless Caleb are a pretty much guaranteed way to get me to agree to anything. It's how he got me to trim back my hours at the bakeshop last summer when I kept falling asleep standing up at the back mixer. It's also how he got me to agree to a couple's fishing trip with Beckett and Evelyn.

Never again.

"Ah. Yeah. About that." He braces both arms against the countertop, face serious. My heart flip-flops in my chest. A little bit of apprehension, but mostly a lot of joy. Happiness, too. It's easier to trust myself when I wake up next to this man. When his face is the first thing I see when

I wake up and the last thing I see before I go to bed. "I wanted to ask you something."

"If you want to go on another couple's trip with Beckett, I'm going to—"

"No, no." His grin tugs further until the lines by his eyes deepen. "It's not that."

"Oh. What is it then?"

Caleb pushes off the countertop and reaches in the pocket of his faded flannel pajama bottoms. I'm busy making eyes at my bagel sandwich so I almost miss it when he drops whatever it is on the counter and slides it across. It bumps up against my knuckles, and I almost fumble the glass of orange juice when I realize what it is.

A small black box, no bigger than my favorite tiny spatula. Velvet. A hinge on one side.

I stare at it and then stare at it some more. My heart thunders in my chest. Caleb clears his throat.

I look up at him. Pink cheeks. Messy hair. My favorite two dimples. He's smiling at me with his heart in his eyes —that big, beautiful heart that waited and waited for me. The one that changed my life. He has to clear his throat two more times before he can manage the thing he wants to say.

"Layla." His voice is hushed in the quiet of our kitchen, a smile tucked at the edges. "I think we should revisit the details of our arrangement."

THE END

OTHER BOOKS BY B.K. BORISON

Lovelight Farms
Luka & Stella's Story

In The Weeds
Beckett & Evelyn's Story

COMING SOON

Charlie's story will arrive in Fall 2023.

Sign up for book alerts to receive the latest news.

THANK YOU

Thank you from the bottom of my heart for letting Lovelight into yours. I hope you know it means the very world to me.

E, I know it's hard to lose me to other worlds during the months I spend writing these books, but please know the love stories I write are only possible because of the love we have and the love we grow together. Our little family is my favorite love story, and my favorite to read again and again. I promise I'll take a break now.

Annie, sharing this with you is the best sort of gift. I am especially grateful for it this year and how selfless you continue to be despite your own universe being shaken up. Your capacity for love and generosity and kindness are the things that shine brightest around you. I hope you always know how much I treasure you and our friendship. I hold it very close to my heart. There's a corner of Lovelight with a garden waiting and the flowers are always in bloom.

Sam, your talent is only outshined by your kindness. I treasure every single cover you create for me and hold them close to my heart.

Britt, what a delight it was to work with you on this project. I loved every second of it, and I'm so grateful for your work, your big heart, and your enthusiasm to do things very quickly. Thank you for being flexible with a wildly chaotic timeline and always giving me the best parts of yourself.

Sarah, thank you for holding my hand and listening to my rambling messages and sitting with me in city bars as we talk about fictional characters. My very favorite place to be is in the seat next to you, talking about people, places, and things that only exist in our hearts and heads.

Adri, there will always be pizza crusts waiting for Poppy at Matty's. Thanks for lending me your baby and giving her to Caleb.

And last but not least, an extra special thank you to Kelsey and Marisol for jumping in and helping make this story better. Kelsey, in my mind you are Canada's finest export. You have been such a lovely presence in my life and I'm grateful. Marisol, your eyes on this book are extra special to me and I can't thank you enough for taking the time. I never thought I'd find such lovely people on Instagram and I am so, so grateful.

I couldn't do any of this without all of you. Thank you for letting me tell stories.

ABOUT THE AUTHOR

B.K. Borison lives in Baltimore with her sweet husband, vivacious toddler, and giant dog. She started writing in the margins of books when she was in middle school and hasn't stopped.

instagram.com/authorbkborison

Made in the USA
Monee, IL
30 August 2022

12929669R00233